JOURNEY INTO THE UNKNOWN

Dessa was going home to Kansas City. But on the train taking her there from Montana was Ben Poole, who was everything that her high society suitor in Kansas City was not.

They stood alone on the rear platform in the cool of the night. The sky was ablaze with stars, but Dessa saw none of them. For Ben held her by the shoulders. He had her pulled up so close, she could feel his warm breath on her cheek. She could smell him, too. This man. Oh, this wonderful man. She swayed against him.

"Oh, God, Dessa." He gave her a demanding kiss, and the flavor of him encompassed her. She was on fire when he touched her breast. And she held him there, waiting for the shards of pleasure to tingle every nerve ending.

Dessa was on a different kind of journey now—to a destination yet unknown but one she longed to reach. . . .

TOPAZ

Journeys of Passion and Desire

☐ **YESTERDAY'S ROSES by Heather Cullman.** Dr. Hallie Gardiner knows something is terribly wrong with the handsome, haunted-looking man in the great San Francisco mansion. The Civil War had wounded Jake "Young Midas" Parrish, just as it had left Serena, his once-beautiful bride, hopelessly lost in her private universe. But when Serena is found mysteriously dead, Hallie finds herself falling in love with Jake who is now a murder suspect.   (405749—$4.99)

☐ **LOVE ME TONIGHT by Nan Ryan.** The war had robbed Helen Burke Courtney of her money and her husband. All she had left was her coastal Alabama farm. Captain Kurt Northway of the Union Army might be the answer to her prayers, or a way to get to hell a little faster. She needed a man's help to plant her crops; she didn't know if she could stand to have a damned handsome Yankee do it.   (404831—$4.99)

☐ **FIRES OF HEAVEN by Chelley Kitzmiller.** Independence Taylor had not been raised to survive the rigors of the West, but she was determined to mend her relationship with her father—even if it meant journeying across dangerous frontier to the Arizona Territory. But nothing prepared her for the terrifying moment when her wagon train was attacked, and she was carried away from certain death by the mysterious Apache known only as Shatto.   (404548—$4.99)

☐ **GOLDSPUN PROMISES by Elizabeth Gregg.** The beautiful and young Tressie Majors is left alone after her mother's death. She must now find her father, who is searching for gold in the west, and her only hope is the handsome Reed Bannon, who is seeking a future free from the prejudice against his Indian heritage. Together they embark on a quest that will take them to the depths of danger and heights of passion.   (405633—$4.99)

*Prices slightly higher in Canada

Buy them at your local bookstore or use this convenient coupon for ordering.

PENGUIN USA
P.O. Box 999 — Dept. #17109
Bergenfield, New Jersey 07621

Please send me the books I have checked above.
I am enclosing $_____ (please add $2.00 to cover postage and handling). Send check or money order (no cash or C.O.D.'s) or charge by Mastercard or VISA (with a $15.00 minimum). Prices and numbers are subject to change without notice.

Card #_____ Exp. Date _____
Signature_____
Name_____
Address_____
City _____ State _____ Zip Code _____

For faster service when ordering by credit card call 1-800-253-6476

Allow a minimum of 4-6 weeks for delivery. This offer is subject to change without notice.

Moonspun Dreams

by

Elizabeth Gregg

A TOPAZ BOOK

TOPAZ
Published by the Penguin Group
Penguin Books USA Inc., 375 Hudson Street,
New York, New York 10014, U.S.A.
Penguin Books Ltd, 27 Wrights Lane,
London W8 5TZ, England
Penguin Books Australia Ltd, Ringwood,
Victoria, Australia
Penguin Books Canada Ltd, 10 Alcorn Avenue,
Toronto, Ontario, Canada M4V 3B2
Penguin Books (N.Z.) Ltd, 182–190 Wairau Road,
Auckland 10, New Zealand

Penguin Books Ltd, Registered Offices:
Harmondsworth, Middlesex, England

First published by Topaz, an imprint of Dutton Signet,
a division of Penguin Books USA Inc.

First Printing, August, 1995
10 9 8 7 6 5 4 3 2 1

🅃 REGISTERED TRADEMARK—MARCA REGISTRADA

Printed in the United States of America

To my daughter Jeri,
who always knew I could write
and nurtured my need to do so.

Thanks, sweetheart.

Chapter One

Dessa leaned back against the hard seat of the lurching stagecoach and closed her eyes. Strands of long dark hair escaped from under her stylish blue hat and stuck to her sweat-dampened brow. Kansas City had been hot, but this . . . this incessant and dust-filled wind left her gasping for air. With a tired sigh she unpinned her hat and placed it in her lap, touched a fingertip to the bedraggled quail feathers. By the time they arrived in Virginia City, the hat would be ruined and so would she. What a dreadful trip. Who in their right mind would want to live out here in Montana Territory, anyway? Montana indeed. What was her father thinking of?

The howling August wind puffed clouds of dust around the window shades so that she nearly choked with every breath. Perspiration ran between her breasts, soaked the stiff corset and camisole. She made a childish face and hooked a thumb under the fabric to scratch.

What she had seen of this horrendous wilderness during the brief stops since leaving the train station at Devil's Gate had not been encouraging. No matter what Mother and Daddy said, she would not stay one minute more than was absolutely necessary.

From a limp reticule she removed a fragile fan and

waved it in front of her face. The effort only made her hotter and she dropped both hands into her lap. Despite the dust, she leaned over and rolled up the curtain on the far side of the coach to let in some air. Some choice! Choke to death or fry.

She was fastening the shade when a horse galloped into her line of sight, the rider stretched high in the stirrups. He wore a red bandanna pulled over his nose and a sweaty black hat crammed so low she couldn't make out his eyes. He held the reins in one hand, while the other waved a long-barreled pistol.

His shouted command was buffeted along in the turmoil of wind and dust and heat so that the words arrived disjointed and easy to disbelieve. "Rein up, rein up there before I shoot."

From up top came a mangled reply, the fierceness of a battle yell, and the sharp crack of a whip. The stage lunged forward, and Dessa grappled frantically for something to hang on to. She bounced around in the empty coach, thunking up and down painfully. The wild and terrifying ride was punctuated by a couple of shots, a scream of agony, and shouted curses that set her heart thundering.

"Whoa down, you ornery cusses. Whoa down!"

The stage rocked to a halt. Frozen with fear, she knelt on the floor, peering as best she could through a crack along the bottom of the window covering. Thank the Lord she hadn't opened both sides, or they'd see her for sure.

In the next breath she realized how foolish was such a thought. No one would rob a stage and not look inside. The realization gave her such a chill that her teeth rattled. Surely they would hear!

From outside came the windblown snorts of horses; in her chest, the rumble of her own heartbeat. Her temples throbbed and she saw intermittent flashes like stars flaring out at dawn. This was a holdup, an honest-to-goodness holdup, and here she was right in the middle of it! She caught her breath and remained hunkered where she was. Maybe she could wish herself invisible and they'd just ride away. But then what? Suppose the outlaw had shot the driver and the man riding up top, the disgruntled one who was supposed to protect the stage with that fearsome-looking gun he carried.

She closed her eyes tightly, clenching her fingers together until they hurt. Nothing would happen to her. Surely. Surely, it wouldn't.

The door jerked open. She had pressed up against it so tightly that she almost tumbled out onto the ground. Teetering there, she sucked in a breath, afraid to look, afraid not to.

The bandit grabbed her arm. "Get down out of there, little lady. Come on, now, don't be shy."

He dragged her out by one arm and tossed her on the ground. She landed on her rear end, legs spraddled in a very undignified sprawl with the skirt of her blue dress hiked to show lacy, beribboned pantaloons.

To her horror both the driver and guard lay sprawled nearby, neither of them moving or making a sound.

"You . . . you killed them," she said.

The horrid man stood over her. "And you'll be next if you don't behave." His voice was raspy, his eyes cold and hard. Nothing like the romantic figures portrayed in the dime novels she read on the sly. This man's nasty manner was realistically threatening, and he stank like a sweating animal.

"Well, ain't you a fancy little thing?" a younger voice said from out of her range of vision.

Two of them! She was too frightened to look around, so she continued to stare at the scuffed, worn boot toes of her captor. Her daddy was right, she should have traveled with him and Mother. If he was here right now, he'd soon put these scoundrels down. As for that no-account buffoon they'd hired to accompany her, she hoped he rotted in that saloon in Devil's Gate where he was no doubt still drinking and gambling. Some reliable protector he was.

Now she would be killed out here in the middle of nowhere and no one would ever even find her bones. The thought made her more angry than fearful. Hadn't her parents been through enough, losing Mitchell in the war? Tears welled in her eyes and she sniffed.

Red Bandanna said, "Aw, look at this. You've gone and made her cry. Ain't you ashamed of yourself?" He grabbed her wrist, hauled her to her feet, and tugged at the ring she wore.

She jerked her hand away. "No, you leave that alone, you uncivilized animal."

He laughed harshly and tucked the long-barreled pistol into his waist. "What's this? Little fancy wants to fight. Well, come on, honey. I'll tussle with you awhile. Got nothin' better to do anyways. I want me that gold ring. Lookee there. What does that *F* stand for? Fancy? And look at these purty jewels. See 'em shine. Bet this is worth a lot."

Dessa thought her heart would leap from her mouth, and it probably would have except that her tongue and lips were so dry it just got hung in her throat. She couldn't even swallow or speak except to croak. The rank smell of the outlaw washed over her as he locked both arms around her shoulders and lifted her easily off the ground. This was worse than anything she could have imagined while lying on her bed back home reading *Hurricane Nell* or *Bess the Trapper*. This was too real, too dangerous.

"Coody, dammit, quit horsing around. I can't find the blasted money box. Leave that little gal be and get up here."

"I aim to tie her first. I'm taking this one with me."

"Yank'll have a fit."

"It's that or kill her, you lamebrain. You done called me by name and she heard you. How'd you like it if I just come right out and told her what you're called, too? Then she could go right to the sheriff with it. Like that, would you?"

"Holy cripes. Here's the blamed box, jostled tight up agin the rail with this bag over it."

He opened the offending leather satchel—her satchel—and dumped it. A stiff mountain wind grabbed at Dessa's clothing, sailing dresses and undergarments off into the stark wilderness in billowing clouds of color.

Tossing down the heavy metal box, the younger one jumped nimbly from the top of the stage. He let out a grunt when he landed, his worn boots sending up puffs of dust. "Do what you're gonna with that gal and let's get out of here 'fore someone comes along."

Coody hooted. "Yeah, like who? Give that railroad a little more time and won't no one be riding this trail. Won't no towns at all be in this godforsaken country. Won't even be no stages to rob."

While he talked, Coody unceremoniously bundled Dessa up under one arm and draped her facedown across the rump of his horse. He lashed her wrists together behind her, hitching up the leather thong so tightly it cut into her flesh. She bit her lip, refused to cry out.

The other one guffawed. "She ain't gonna stay on that way, you lophead. Start trotting that horse and she'll bounce right off into the dust. Apt to kill her. Here, let me show you."

The younger outlaw dragged Dessa off the horse and plucked at the knots of rawhide his partner had tied.

"Well, hell," Coody shouted, and jumped the smaller man. "You leave her be 'fore I swat you up the side a your head."

Dessa felt as if she were living in a nightmare. Yes, that was it. A dream. Only a hideous dream from which she would awaken and be safe and sound in her bedroom in Kansas City.

Her knees grew weak and she sank abruptly to the ground nearly under the nervous horse's belly. Long legs danced one way, then another, the large hooves barely missing her. She thought of the riding stable in Kansas City and the shiny, groomed gelding she rode every Sunday afternoon. A far cry from this disgusting, unwashed thing that suddenly let go a big smelly green splat almost on the hem of her dress and then gave a whinny that sounded like a laugh aimed directly at her.

Enough. Dream or real, she'd had enough. The men tussled with each other like overgrown boys. Without another thought for her safety, she scrambled to her feet and lit out running, shaking free of the loosened thongs to hold her long dress up out of the way of her ankle-high shoes. Gasping for every breath and afraid to look back for fear that big ugly man was looming right over her, Dessa sprinted through knee-high grasses and dodged scatterings of rock. But she was no match for the long-legged Coody. She heard his harsh breathing just before he latched one arm around her waist, lifting her so that her legs continued to pump air.

She jabbed at him with an elbow and felt a satisfying thud.

"Danged little hellion. You're just what I've been looking for," he panted, and tossed her without ceremony into a clump of bushes.

Up until the moment he covered her body with his, his tobacco-stained mouth sucking at her clenched lips, she had truly thought deep down inside that this wasn't really happening to her. It was, indeed, some kind of dream that she would awaken from before real harm could come to her. But then she looked into that dirty, pockmarked face and felt his stinking body mashing her breasts and stomach and thighs, and she knew it was real. Sick fear squeezed at her insides, and she tumbled mercifully into a black abyss of unconsciousness.

When she came to, she was riding behind the man, wrists bound together around his waist. The thongs had cut into her flesh until both hands were numb. Between her legs, the hot hairy hide of the horse chafed through the thin fabric of her pantaloons. He hadn't had his way with her. Not yet, anyway. She would know for sure if he had.

Her cheek lay against his back and she looked directly into the flaming ball of a setting sun. She closed her eyes, trying not to move and let the man know she was awake. Blessedly, the sun finally sank behind the ragged mountain peaks to the west. Then the horses turned and they were headed in the direction of the flaring orange and purple sky. She must have done something to alert her captor that she was conscious, for a chuckle rumbled in her ear and vibrated her body where it pressed against his.

"Little one's back with us. What we'll do, kid, is stop for the night up ahead in that wash. No sense in trying to get back in the dark."

Her heart tumbled all over itself.

"You just wanta roll around on the ground with that little gal, and you figger Yank'll take her away from you, we go on back to camp."

"Let him try," Coody said. The menacing tone was oddly tinged with fright, like the snarl of a wild thing threatened by a more powerful enemy.

"You say that now."

"Well, I'm stopping anyway. I ain't gonna get my mount's leg broke going over that mountain in the dark. Or my own blamed neck, either, for that matter. You do what you please."

The other man fell back to ride where he could study Dessa. She got a good look at him for the first time. He was little more than a boy, with fuzzy cheeks and a large hat that folded out the tops of his ears. She was reminded of a child playing dress-up. Everything he wore seemed to be too big. Briefly she wondered why he gave orders to the one he called Coody with such alacrity. Maybe they were brothers, or more likely he was just the smarter of the two.

The thought came to her that they were going to use her completely up and then kill her. It was almost a revelation; all of a sudden, the light dawned and everything was crystal clear. No one would come to save her. She had to do it herself or she would die, slowly and harshly. An uncontrolled whimper bubbled from deep inside, but she swallowed it down. If she was going to die anyway, she'd make a quick job of it, and they'd be sorry when it was all over.

At that moment the mountains devoured all traces of sunlight and glowed with a pearly pink halo. The ground became shadowy and indistinct.

"Here. Right here'll do," Coody said, and drew up his horse.

She heard water running somewhere nearby. Oh, God, for a drink. For just a few sweet drops to moisten her tongue, to trickle coolly down the back of her throat. She almost cried out with the need.

Coody sawed the thong off her wrists, unleashing an excruciating pain. She held her silence and bit at her lip to keep from crying out.

"Pull her off here, kid, so I can get down. I'll swear, I'm so thirsty I could drink cactus juice with the spines left in."

The young one held her a bit too long when she staggered around on her feet. "Please," she said, her voice sounding like dry husks of corn rubbed together. "I need a drink."

Fingers of one hand biting into her upper arm, he guided her beyond a darkening thicket toward the sound of water. At the stream's edge he unceremoniously shoved her forward. She landed on both knees. Gravel bit through layers of clothing to puncture her skin, but she paid no attention. Like a dog she leaned forward on both hands and lapped at the water, sucking in the icy cold snowmelt and gulping down great mouthfuls.

It hit the bottom of her stomach like heavy stones, rolled around there for a while, and started back up. She groaned and sat down right there in the creek, hugging her belly and rocking. In the rushing water shreds of the lovely blue dress boiled up around her.

Once the queasiness was under control, she

cupped her hands and sipped delicately, stopping to wash her face and neck, then drinking again.

Coody finished his own noisy slurping and claimed his prize, dragging her out of the water and up the bank. She couldn't keep her feet under her, but he didn't seem to mind. The younger one he called kid had begun to pile up brush and wood for a campfire. Coody tossed her to the ground, and started flailing the boy around the head with his sopping hat. Curses of rage poured from him, and the boy threw both arms up to protect himself.

"How many damn times I got to tell you take care of the horses first? Look at 'em. Carried us all day, sweating and hungry, and there they stand. Unsaddle 'em and stake 'em to that grass yonder. Let 'em drink some first. I have to run with such a idjit."

Coody wound down at last and the kid surprisingly did as he was told. Frightened by the outburst, Dessa moved backward into a thick growth of brush with dry, crackly leaves. It was dark there in the wash, but she could still see the shadowy outline of objects back the way they had come. Trees and outcroppings of rock humped blackly into the silver glow of the night.

She didn't really think about what she was going to do, or even consider her chances. If she stayed, this animal would have his way with her, and she would die before she let that happen. She had to try. As quietly as she could, she crept along in the darkness cast by the huge trees that grew on the creek bank. And all the while, all she could think of was the heartbreak of learning of Mitchell's death in the war, of the way Mother looked when she found out, as if her very reason for living had just flown out of her. The anguished gaze in both her parents' eyes when they learned of his death would remain with Dessa always. If she died here, what would it do to them? They lavished all their love on her—so much sometimes that she felt smothered.

At last her eyes grew accustomed to the darkness and she was able to make out an enormous pile of boulders at the foot of a rise. If she could reach the deepening shadows, Coody would have no idea where to look for her.

Every nerve in her body urged her to bolt for safety like a stampeding animal. She forced herself to measure the distance, judge her chances, and gauge the right time to go. Hair on the back of her neck prickled, chills tightened the muscles of her stomach, and her wet dress weighted her to the ground. Coody was still cursing the boy at the top of his lungs, his back turned to her. She had to do it now or not at all. It was time to move. She slunk away, hunkering low so she wouldn't cast even the vaguest of shadows when she left the shelter of the trees and headed for the rocks.

Crouched far back in the refuge offered by the immense boulders, she knew when he discovered her gone. The curses that had been aimed at the boy were turned on her. Vile, evil names he called her, shouting them into the night in a high, screeching voice. She made herself as small and insignificant as she could in the darkness of her hiding place. Though every ounce of her wanted to run as fast as the wind, she scarcely even breathed.

He couldn't possibly know which direction she'd chosen if she didn't make any noise. And luck might take him away from her; that's all she could count on. Luck. Her own, not his.

Coody stomped up and down the creek, his voice

growing hoarse with shouting, before he finally quieted down. That was scarier than hearing him rage, for he might be sneaking right up on her where she hid among the rocks. She had to get farther away as quickly as possible, but she dared not move until he stopped looking. He would find her or he wouldn't; she could do nothing more but wait.

Despite being cold and uncomfortable in her wet clothing, Dessa finally dozed from pure exhaustion. She didn't know what woke her or how late it was, but a small fire flickered in the camp where the two outlaws now appeared to be sleeping, and their prey not five hundred yards away shivering with fear and chills.

For what seemed like an eternity, she stared at the two dark mounds that had to be Coody and the kid. Nothing moved or made a sound. Even the horses slept. How she wished she could sneak back into camp and mount up, ride like the mountain wind, far and fast and free. But that would be much too dangerous. Instead she decided to make her way around the point and head back in the direction from which they had all ridden earlier. Somewhere back there they had left the road, and once she reached it, surely she could find a town or a house or meet up with a traveler. If not, dying in the middle of nowhere in the brutal sun of the next day would be better than having that hairy man putting his hands all over her, defiling her body. She knew one thing for sure, the light of day would have to see her far from here. Come morning, if Coody decided to track her on horseback, he could ride her down in no time. She could only hope that the outlaw's need to return to camp with the stolen strongbox would be more pressing than his desire for her. His fear of the mysterious Yank was a palpable thing, and perhaps that would save her in the long run.

By the time the sky to the east silvered, Dessa's feet were burning with blisters, and the calves of her legs, unused to prolonged walking, were knotted. Arid throat locked closed, she watched with dread the rising sun, for it signaled another long, hot day. For a while she prayed for rain; then, seeing the uselessness of that in this parched land, she began to pray for the strength to survive. On she trudged, once in a while stumbling to her knees. After a moment she would rise again, but each time, she knew, might be her last. How much farther she could go, she had no idea. If she had reached the road in the night, she had missed its tracks, and so she could do nothing but head into the rising sun.

About noon, as she could calculate by the position of that ghastly burning ball crossing the white-hot sky, all energy seeped from her tortured body and she collapsed in the rocks and dirt and scraggly grass.

Just let me lie here a little while. Just a minute or two and I'll have my breath back, and then I'll go on. Please God, then I'll go on. And I'll get out of this awful nowhere place. There'll be a house with white sheets flapping on a clothesline and a stone well in the yard with a wooden bucket overflowing with cool, clear water.

The vision came to her so intensely that she imagined the smell of wet green grass and lye soap.

There will be kids playing out back, laughing and chasing each other, and their mother will come to the door and call out, "Mitchell. Dessa. Come in to supper now."

And the boy will stand straight and tall and look at

me when I come up the lane to the house. The wind will blow his dark beautiful hair and his eyes, green like mine, will widen with recognition.

Tears overflowed and trailed down her cheeks. She forced herself to rise, first to her knees, then to her feet.

"Oh, Mitchell," she sobbed.

The young boy beckoned, reached out, and faded into wavering ripples of heat.

She would follow, she would find him. She would not lie here and die. And so on she trod, marveling that after all these years, the youthful ghost of her dead brother had returned to save her life. The thought didn't seem at all odd. Mitchell's spirit had been with her since the day he left, and despite everything, she felt in the deepest part of her heart that he was alive out there somewhere.

When she told Daddy, he said, of course, Mitchell lived in her heart and always would. But that wasn't what she meant, and he wouldn't listen.

On and on she staggered, fists clenched around wads of her clothing in an effort to hang on to something. Stumble, fall, get up, and move on. Mitchell would have it no other way.

Afternoon came and went, the angle of the sun ever changing until at long last she felt the coolness of its absence and realized it had disappeared once again behind the mountains. And still she had found no road and nothing else, either. But blessed darkness, in the end, saved her, for no sooner had dusk melted into night than she spotted a dim glow off to her right. Someone had lit a lamp or built a fire.

She sobbed and veered toward the yellow pinpoint of light, stumbled, and fell. Counting how many times she fell and climbed back to her feet became a deadly game. Her time was nearly up, every ounce of strength almost gone. Soon she would fall and not be able to rise again. She tried to cry out, hail the house, but no sound save a croak could she force from her swollen throat. Surely she wouldn't come this far only to die within sight of salvation.

All she remembered after that final silent plea was crying out feebly, stumbling one last time as the door swung open and spilled out a long shaft of golden light. And her shouting and shouting and shouting. Then falling, only instead of hitting the punishing ground, she was swept into strong arms and carried, head snuggled against a muscled chest that smelled vaguely of coal oil and woodsmoke and leather.

The whiskery face she looked into when she regained her senses did not belong to the man who had carried her. This one was small and stringy and hairy, and he smelled of horses and tobacco. No, this was not her rescuer. But it didn't matter. She was alive, and oh, how wonderful it was.

The hairy man offered her a tin cup and she took it, wanting to gulp at the soothing water. His gnarly old hand stayed the impulse.

"Take 'er easy, now. A little more, and then wait. Don't want you sick on us."

She nodded mutely, accepted the sips as he offered them, and looked around the small room. Rough-hewn bunks, a long table and four chairs, a cookstove with a huge pot of something bubbling off steam, some shelves along one wall, and the window through which still shined the light that had saved her life. It came from a plain kerosene lamp. There were no delicate roses painted on the glass shade that had grown a bit smoky from an improperly trimmed wick, but that flickering glow was the most beautiful sight she had ever seen.

Men lived here. No woman's touch anywhere.

After yet another small sip of water, she mumbled, "Where—" at the same time that the grizzled old man asked, "Now what in the thunder is a pretty little thing like you doing wandering around in the night?"

Before she could answer, the door swung open. She cringed back into the corner of the bunk, desperately looking for a place to hide. Surely that horrible Coody hadn't found her already!

The old man gentled her. "Now, now. It's jest ole Ben Poole. He found you and brung you in. Now, little lady, it's jest ole Ben, who wouldn't hurt a flea, despite his size." The old man patted ineffectually at her arm, but she wasn't ready to calm down just yet. Not until the huge shadowy hulk came into the lamplight, not until she saw a head of shaggy blond hair, remarkably fine features, and the kindest blue eyes that must exist in the whole wide world. He had black lashes that made him look like he was wearing eye paint. How startling. How fascinating.

Embarrassed that she had stared, Dessa dropped her glance to the broad chest covered by a faded shirt open at the throat. The very place where she had rested her head while his strong arms carried her to safety.

Hot tears spilled down her cheeks. The man said nothing, just settled his gaze in first one place, then another, looking not at her but around the cramped room as if he'd never seen it before.

"Here, now, young'un," the old man soothed. "You just lay yourself down and get some sleep. Everything will be fine come sunup. Ain't nobody going to hurt you here. Ain't that right, Ben? Oh, by the way," he continued as he covered her right up to her chin with a threadbare quilt as if she were a child, "I'm Wiley. Wiley Moss, and this here's Ben Poole, but I done told you that, I reckon."

He must have had more to say, for she fell asleep to the murmur of the old man's voice, her gaze fixed on the broad back of the blond giant as he slipped from the cabin without ever speaking a word to her.

Chapter Two

Ben pulled the door shut at his back and stood there a few moments, eyes turned up toward the star-scattered ebony sky. A fingernail moon had set soon after dusk. Lucky for the girl. If someone was looking for her, moonlight would have been her mortal enemy. He sucked air down into his lungs and let it out slowly. Damn anyone who would hurt such a helpless little thing. He could hardly stand to look at her and think about it.

He shook his head and grinned at his own foolishness. This was the first time he'd ever gone plumb dizzy-headed over a woman. And at first sight, too. Never had known what to say to females anyway, but that just caused him to avoid most of them. Once his mouth opened, he felt utterly foolish, whatever came out. Maggie said it came from being raised up knocking around on his own without a mother. She always added that learning to kill when he was fourteen hadn't helped much, either.

He'd killed his first man at Gettysburg. Two years later, barely sixteen, he followed Lee out of Richmond in the last days, no longer knowing how many he had slain, and he didn't weep when Lee surrendered, he simply sank to the ground in exhaustion, too hungry and too weary to go on. He tried not to think of the war anymore; it was a long time ago and that kind of killing didn't really count. To his great regret he had killed one last time, and he was still paying for that mistake.

Inside was one of the prettiest women he'd ever laid eyes on, even with the scratches and torn clothes and sunburned skin. Her being pretty wasn't all of it, though. It was the way she felt in his arms when he'd carried her those last hundred yards to safety. Thinking about what she'd been through left him speechless and nearly sick to his stomach. He was afraid of what he'd do to any man who would commit such an act.

Just now in there, something behind her eyes told him that whatever had happened to her—and it must have been horrible—she was above it all. Better than anyone; proud, tough. She'd slug it out and get up again, ready to fight, in spite of her fear. He sensed, though, that she was also someone he should definitely steer clear of, for while he admired such courage, he could tell she came from a high-toned family. He sure didn't measure up to be worthy of her attention.

He had no bed to call his own but that one he made beneath the freight wagon wherever he and Wiley happened to be. He found his women at the Golden Sun Saloon, in their own perfumy beds, and then he went back to sleep on a blanket on the hard ground. That's all the kind of man he would ever be, and that little gal in there would set her sights on better. Way better. Probably already had. Sure didn't hurt to admire, but he'd best do it at a distance—a far, far distance.

The way she looked at him, he figured his best bet was to steer clear. She might want to come out and play once she got over whatever had happened, and he wasn't up to such antics. He had a hunch that with a woman like her, playing was all it would be. He'd never gone in for such nonsense and he didn't intend to start now.

It was a long time before he fell asleep. The ground felt hard and lumpy as mountain boulders, his thoughts more disturbing than usual, his desires riding close to the surface so that they prickled his skin and made him ache. When Wiley Moss came out at dawn to relieve himself around back of the station, Ben rose stiffly and unwillingly.

He went to stand a few feet from the old driver and couldn't help but ask, "She okay?"

"Durn right. Tough little critter. Ain't up to walking no more for a while. Feet's all blistered up. I told her we'd take her to Virginia City, seeing as how that's where we're going, and her, too. Soon as you fix that blamed wheel, that is."

Ben gritted his teeth as he buttoned up the front of his pants. "Why'd you tell her that?"

Wiley jerked a quick look at him. "Well, boy, she cain't walk it. What's the matter with you?"

"Yeah, but she could stay here, get all rested up, and we could send someone out to get her. A woman, maybe, who could be of some . . . some use to her." He bit off the words, blurted, "She'd be okay here. Only be another day."

"I'm plumb amazed at you, Ben Poole. Something has surely addled your brain. Leave that young'un out here alone to the mercy of whomsoever might come along? After what she's been through? Suppose the men that did this to her was to be following, and they found her here all alone? You ought to be ashamed for even having such thoughts."

"Aw, hell," Ben muttered. "I didn't mean ... It's just— Shoot, I think I'll get on that wagon wheel. We need to be getting out of here. Costing Bannon money, his freight wagon being laid up this way."

"Well, that's better. I'll go in and git breakfast for all three of us. I'll shout when it's ready."

"Don't bother, I'll work right through. I can eat when we get to Virginia City." Ben purely hated to make that concession; he did enjoy his food.

Wiley stomped away, shaking his head and muttering under his breath. Ben paid him no mind. He would stay away from the girl, no matter what Wiley Moss thought. She made him nervous as an old Tom throwed down in a pen full of cute little pussy-cats. He had this urge to cuddle her up in his arms, and he had a feeling she'd scratch and spit something awful if he did. What he'd do if she started purring he had no idea.

She came out the door while he was sitting spraddle-legged behind the wagon wheel tending to its woes, and he couldn't help but watch her a moment. She was barefooted and limped slowly. The morning sunlight made a halo around her hair that needed combing real bad, but was as dark and shiny as a slab of polished walnut lumber.

She made her way carefully around the side of the station, and he blushed hotly, aware that she was headed for the privy.

"Think about the wheel, fool," he said, and went back to work self-consciously. Still, he couldn't help but watch her when she returned.

He could tell right away that while she might be bent, she wasn't broken. She held that head high and her shoulders struggled to square off even as she favored one leg. Whoever had done that to her ought to burn in hell for an eternity. He despised bullies who picked on the small and helpless. And men hurting women or children was his particular worst peeve.

He tapped at the metal, tapped again. The rim waddled, loose as a goose.

"I wanted to thank you," she said right behind him, and he squawked with surprise. "And tell you that breakfast is ready. I'm so hungry I could eat a whole bear if you'd go get me one. I have to say you look as if you could, too. But I can't feel right about sitting down to eat with you out here working. So won't you please come in and join us before I starve to death?"

He knew all along she'd talk like that. Light and airy and sure of herself, babbling on and on like all he had to do was pay attention. That cultured high-bred tone she'd had to learn in some fancy back-East school. He cleared his throat. It wasn't polite to just plain not answer her question, and he guessed he could sit here forever and she'd just stand there looking down at him, waiting for a reply. It made the top of his head burn.

"No time. Besides, I'm not hungry. And even if I was, I don't like Wiley's cooking." It was more than he'd meant to say.

Dessa studied the shoulder blades, drawn up as if to ward off a blow. "Come on, Mr. Ben Poole. You wouldn't want to be responsible for me falling down starved, would you?"

Her lips and tongue around his name, said like that, did all sorts of strange things to him. One was to make him thump his finger with the mallet.

Well, hell, if she put it that way.

He sucked on the mashed finger and scrabbled to

his feet, not daring to spare her a look as he strode to the house. He forgot to hold the door for her and she swung it back open and stood there glaring.

"I suppose you're mad at me about something I don't remember doing," she said in a voice still hoarse from her ordeal. "But that's no call for you to be rude, Ben Poole. You act just like you were brought up in a barn."

He was fixing to seat himself in one of the chairs, but her words caught him and he looked right at her. Her eyes were flashing as bright as her hair did out in the sunlight, and he could see his own reflection in the pupils. Instead of saying anything, he just looked and looked, right down into them, seeing her in there. The real her, not the one she was putting on to cover her feelings about what had happened.

"I apologize," he said softly, and pulled out a chair for her. "I'm sorry you were hurt, and I'm sorry I've acted like a fool. Sometimes I just plain don't know any better. Wiley says I ain't had proper raising."

He grinned crookedly, catching Dessa totally by surprise. Struck mute, she dragged her gaze away from him and gentled herself into the chair, babying the sore spots all over her battered body.

Wiley broke the long silence. "Might be you could tell us what happened out there. Who did that to you." He pointed at her with the tines of a fork.

She shuddered at the memory. She hurt all over, from the bottoms of her blistered feet to the top of her sunburned head. It could have been a lot worse and so she put off crying about it. For an instant she let her eyes drop to the plate and picked with trembling fingers at the edges of a tough biscuit. Ben was right about Wiley's cooking.

"Two men . . . well, one was just a boy. The other . . . he . . . he was horrid."

Remembering, she temporarily lost her voice and took a careful sip of the steaming black coffee. Putting the tin cup back on the table, she struggled to continue with her story.

Ben interrupted. "Ma'am, you don't have to do this now if you don't feel up to it. Plenty of time to tell the sheriff."

"No," she blurted. "I have to tell it. There's two dead men out there. They killed the stage driver and his . . . the man who rode with him on top."

Wiley brought a fist down on the slab table. "Aw, hell. Reckon who it was, Ben?"

The large blond man shook his head, furrows wrinkling the sun-gold skin across his forehead.

"Anyone else, ma'am?" Wiley asked.

"No, I was alone in the stage and they . . . they took me with them."

"Filthy skunks!" Wiley said.

Ben studied her a moment, the blue of his eyes frosty around the edges. "Did they . . . did they . . . hurt you?"

"Hurt me? Yes, Mr. Poole, they hurt me. But if you mean did they violate me, no, sir, they did not. They would have had to kill me to do so." She drew herself up and those green eyes shot sparks halfway across the room.

The change in her demeanor amazed Ben. The words were all brittle, angry, and defensive, as if he had accused her of something vile. He wondered how she had gotten out of the men's clutches, but decided not to ask. Not with the mood she was suddenly in. She'd probably throw her coffee at him.

For a while all three concentrated on the food on their plates without speaking further.

Wiley broke the silence. "Who you going to Virginia City to visit, ma'am?"

"What? Oh, my parents bought a mercantile store there, from a Mr. Yoes. Trevor and Mae Fallon. Do you know them?"

Ben stuffed a wad of biscuit in his mouth and shook his head. as if she had asked him, when all along she'd been addressing Wiley.

The old man sopped the hard biscuit in a pool of redeye gravy before replying. "No, but we ain't been back through long enough to meet anyone here lately. Ever one in that town finally gets their family belongings hauled in, we might get to rest a spell. Reed and Tressie Bannon's making a killing on this freight line."

Ben stopped chewing and appraised her with a blue-eyed gaze. "You gonna live in Virginia City?"

"No. Oh no. We live in Kansas City. We were planning on getting the store going, hiring a manager, and then we're going to Denver for a few weeks. We'll return home before winter."

Ben looked back down at his plate, at the strip of overcooked fatback. Wiley always did turn meat into leather before he considered it done.

Quickly Ben forgot the overdone meat and went back to considering the woman. She was rich and she wasn't going to be in town long. He considered that a good omen. Her presence disturbed the hell out of him, and he couldn't have explained it if he'd had to. Not even to Maggie or Rose, the only two women he'd ever been around, and both of whom he loved like the mother and sister he'd lost so long ago.

He couldn't even explain it to his friend Wiley Moss, and most especially not to himself.

He considered that the way he was feeling was probably what folks called smitten, and he wanted no part of it. It was god-awful uncomfortable. Fisting up the rest of his biscuit and the blackened strip of fatback, he kicked away from the table, making a terrible clatter.

"Got to get back on that wheel if we're ever going to be on our way. Nice to see you're okay this morning, ma'am, and I'm sure sorry about your ordeal. I expect Sheriff Moohn'll get up a posse first thing and put them boys on the end of a rope. And they'll want to send someone after the bodies before—" He broke off self-consciously. No sense talking about what a pack of wolves could do to dead men.

"My name is Dessa," she said, and favored him with the tiniest of smiles. Her lips were dry and cracked and the delicate skin on her face was scratched and burned; still, that was the most beautiful thing Ben Poole thought he'd ever seen in his life. That smile. Those eyes. That lovely name. Dessa.

He nearly fell over himself getting the hell out of there.

Wiley chuckled. "Like I say ever' chance I get, that boy ain't had much raising. You'll have to forgive him. Strange, though. I've known Ben a lot of years and that's the first time I've ever seen him act so bumfoozled. Must be something in the air." He rolled light brown eyes up under wrinkled lids and chuckled again, then finished sopping the greasy gravy.

She eyed the unappetizing mess on her plate. She hadn't had a bite of decent food in a long while. Railroad fare was only a touch better than the poor meals the stage line furnished. Hunger pangs knotted her stomach. Hunger for civilized food like a light and fluffy omelette sprinkled with cheese, hemmed on the plate with thin slices of hickory-cured ham. She dearly hoped the town of Virginia City had a decent restaurant. More than that, she prayed for a hot bath and clean sheets and a soft featherbed mattress.

She sensed the older man watching her and glanced up. He dropped his gaze back to his plate, which was empty now. "Do you suppose I could clean up a bit before we leave?" she asked him.

"Oh, yes, ma'am. I'm purely sorry for not thinking. I'll draw you some water. There's a kettle on the stove. That'll take the chill off, and I'll clear out. You'll be alone here. They stopped having an agent at this stop when the stages quit running but now and then. This place just kinda looks after itself when ain't no one stopping over."

Moving like a cricket, the small man fetched a sweat-stained hat from a nail on the wall and crammed it on his head. "I'll just bring you that water, then leave you be. Sorry we ain't got nothing for you to put on."

She looked down at the filthy, tattered blue dress and shrugged. "I've got clothes in town. Mother and Father brought a trunk ahead for me so I could travel light. Those men, they dumped my satchel out all over the place, and stole my . . . stole my ring." She felt tears welling in her eyes and turned away to stare out the window. No sense being a baby. It was all over now, and she didn't want this kind man to think her weak.

Mitchell always said that inner strength was the

only thing no one could take away from you. She wondered for the millionth time how someone had managed to kill him, with all that strength he had possessed.

Wiley opened the door, stopped, and turned back to her. "Don't you worry none. They'll get those varmints and string 'em up."

In a few moments he returned with a wooden bucket slopping over with water and set it on the table. "There's a washpan over there on the stand. Sorry there's such mean supplies, but that rag'll have to do you."

She nodded and, as soon as he closed the door, began to undo the buttons of her dress. She was struck suddenly with a memory of wearing the teal-blue dress for the first time after picking it up from the dressmaker. Andrew had taken her to the park and they walked along the riverbank. A brisk wind had caught at her hair, and he pushed a strand back away from her eyes and looked down at her. He loved her and she knew it, wondered why she couldn't return that love. It was as if she were looking for something in him that just wasn't there. A spark, an excitement of expectation, not knowing what tomorrow would bring. But he and Daddy had the future all worked out and in it was no room for the unexpected, the exciting. Andrew would continue to work for the Fallons and eventually, when Daddy retired, take over the business. With the only Fallon male heir dead, it would work out just fine, keep the business in the family.

Despite those plans, she spent the summer of this, her eighteenth year, searching through an assortment of men who satisfied her need for excitement, leaving Andrew dangling in the wings. Where he still dangled. This was the first time she'd thought of him since leaving Kansas City. What did love have to do with it?

She pulled the shredded dress gently down off one shoulder, then the other, wincing from her bruises. When she returned, she must tell Andrew that she wouldn't marry him, that she couldn't be the one he carried over the threshold into that exclusive house on the hill above the river. It would be hard. And hard on her parents, too. They already envisioned the grandchildren who would play beneath the large old oaks in their own backyard. The small dark-haired boy who would fill the cold corners left in their hearts by Mitchell's death.

The ripped bodice and sleeves fell down around her waist, and she dipped the rag in the washpan of cold water warmed with a splash from the black iron kettle on the stove. She had progressed to her legs, standing beside the chair with one foot propped up on it, when she glanced out the window to see Ben Poole driving the freight wagon around to the front of the station. Fascinated by his lithe movements as he wrapped the reins around the brake handle and hopped to the ground, she didn't realize that he was headed for the door until it was too late to do anything but gape at the sight of him.

As the door swung open, he looked right at her, dress hiked up above her thighs and one leg showing bare skin all the way to the swell of her buttocks.

Almost too late she remembered to cross her arms over her chest, but not before he glimpsed the rosy nipples and the sheen of creamy skin still moist from her bath. He expected her to turn away, but she didn't move an inch in any direction. Ben stood right where he was and got an eyeful. It was as if both had been temporarily but instantly frozen by a blizzard wind from high off the Montana mountains. They would simply remain that way, staring at each other, until sunlight could thaw them.

She licked her lips, and hugged herself tighter. Something strange was going on all over her body, and it wasn't the aches and pains from her ordeal, either. It was a wet and warm sensation that turned cold, then hot as it rushed through her vitals.

He wanted to make a clever remark and set them both at ease. But he never had been good at that, and so he settled for saying nothing at all and enjoying the sights. Her legs were long and shapely, the skin creamy except where great long scratches and ugly bruises marred their beauty. The inside of one thigh sported a brutish purple mark almost the size of his fist, and he was filled with a need to bash in somebody's head for hurting her like that. Fool that he was, he didn't look at the exposed breasts as she crossed her arms protectively across her chest. Maggie would have thought nothing of such a thing. This one would. She continued to watch him like a stricken animal in the woods.

He had a sudden all-over feeling of what love would be like with her. The prospect both thrilled and frightened him. What would be expected of a man who loved such a gorgeous woman? More, he'd allow, than he could give. He had to move from the spot to which he was staked; somehow he had to simply back out the door and close it. He tried to shift his feet, but nothing happened. God, she was lovely.

"Ben Poole, what the thunderation you think you're doing?" Wiley Moss shouted, and, coming up behind him, whopped at his backside with his hat.

"Quit peering in at the young'un. You got no manners at all, boy? Get your tail outta there 'fore I thrash you."

The spell broken, Dessa laughed at the sight of the wiry little man flailing away at the much larger Ben Poole, who had turned a vivid red and was making tracks as fast as he could, impeded as he was by Wiley's hat swatting around on him.

On thinking about the incident, she wondered what in the world had come over her, letting Ben see her like that and enjoying his reaction as well as her own. This might call for a little looking into. Getting better acquainted with Ben Poole could liven up the two or three weeks she would be forced to spend in the godforsaken town of Virginia City out here at the ends of the earth. Again, she wondered why in the world her father had chosen to open a mercantile in a town mined out and bypassed by the railroad.

Soon her mind was occupied with seeing her parents and she put memories of the brief but explosive encounter with Ben in the back of her mind. Sore and achy as her body was, it took all her concentration to endure the rough ride aboard the freight wagon.

The three arrived in Virginia City around midafternoon. Dessa was weak with exhaustion and hunger. She could hardly wait to find her way to her parents' quarters above the mercantile, get out of the torn and soiled clothes, and luxuriate in a hot bath. She thought of the food she would order afterward when they went out to dinner. Perhaps a thick steak and baked potato, some vegetables if they had any out here in the wilderness.

Ben had scarcely spoken during the trip, but Wiley had kept up a running commentary on subjects all the way from wondering who had been killed in the stage robbery to how good it would be to get off that blamed wagon for an hour or two.

He drove directly to the freight depot and pulled up. "Big Ben here can see you safely to your hearth's door, child," he told Dessa, then aimed a hard stare at his friend. "And you keep your eyes and hands where they belong, young sir. This is a lady."

Ben flushed. "You don't have to tell me that, I know. You take her. I'll deal with Bannon."

"And have some yahoo make light of her? With you along, they'll think twice. Now do as I say. Take this little girl home so she can rest. I'll get this done and go talk to Sheriff Moohn about the killing."

With that, Wiley leaped from the wagon and headed for the depot door.

"He takes no lip from anyone," Ben said.

"If you want away from me so badly, I'll just get down and walk," she said, and started to rise from the seat.

Her tone surprised him. What had he done? "I'll take you." He took up the reins and clucked at the horses, the movement throwing her back onto the seat.

On the verge of collapse, she hung on dearly and snapped, "Don't put yourself out. You know, Mr. Moss is right about you. You're plain rude. Not having any upbringing is no excuse. Or maybe everyone here in the territories is shy of any manners."

Ben colored. "I've got plenty of manners. You ought'n to act so uppity about being from the States. It ain't no big deal, little Miss Fancy Pants."

Dessa blew a strand of hair from her face. "Well, Kansas City is certainly a bigger deal than this . . . this rat hole. It's unsanitary and the people look like bums. I can see now why you act like you do, living in such squalor."

In his anger Ben smacked the rumps of the horses with the fat reins. "You act that way around folks in town, and you won't have any friends. They'll stay away from you like the plague."

She swung around and glared. "Well, maybe I don't want any friends here. Anyway, we won't be—" She broke off when Ben reined in the horses and rose to his feet, a look of dismay on his handsome face.

"Lord God almighty," he breathed.

What was left of Yoes Mercantile smoldered thin tendrils of smoke that blew away in the wind.

"What? What is it?"

"Did you say Yoes Mercantile? Your folks bought Yoes Mercantile?"

She nodded dumbly and stared at the blackened heap of rubbish. "Was that . . ."

Ben badly wanted to turn right around and head the other way, but it was too late. He had driven her right up to the blackened ruins that had once been a fine two-story structure. He wanted to gather her in his arms when she cried out forlornly, but he didn't get a chance.

She scrambled down from the seat, swayed on her feet, moaned. "Mother, Daddy. Where are they? What happened? Oh, look. What am I going to do? We've got to find them."

The sad desperation in her voice tore at his heart, and he did what he had wanted to do a moment earlier. He hopped from the wagon and simply folded her up in both arms. He held her trembling body, shielded her against his chest, and did his best to protect her from the onslaught of emotions.

She leaned limply into the embrace, and soon her tears moistened the front of his shirt. He put his lips in the tangle of her dark hair and closed his eyes.

Poor little thing. What would happen to her next?

Chapter Three

For a long while Dessa remained in Ben's arms. She tried not to think of what was yet to come. If she never asked, would she have to find out what had happened to her parents? If she remained hidden within his strength, then she wouldn't have to face the truth. He was hard and soft at the same time, and power emanated from him like warmth from a fire. A gentle power that didn't frighten her. For the moment it was enough to ease the dread of what was yet to come.

Filled with hopeful denial, she sniffed into his chest, sniffed again, and stopped crying.

He took her by the upper arms and pushed her away to look into her face. "You okay?"

She nodded woodenly.

"Okay, then. We'll find out what happened. The sheriff will know. And then we'll . . . well, we'll do what has to be done."

"Yes, fine. That's what we'll do," she said in a voice as flat as a wooden plank.

He studied the glazed look that had clouded the shine of her green eyes. "You're sure you're okay. You're not going to faint or anything."

"I don't faint. Let's find the sheriff."

Without his help she scrambled up onto the

wagon seat. After climbing aboard, Ben smacked the horse's rumps with the heavy leather reins and turned the wagon in the street, heading back toward the sheriff's office. Dessa clung to the edges of the seat, feeling as if her world had spiraled completely out of control. How could so much go wrong in so short a time? It was like a nightmare that had begun with the stage robbery and hadn't yet ended. She felt as if she had fallen into a void that had no bottom or anything to cling to.

She glanced at her companion. He sat tall, head and shoulders held stiffly, facing straight ahead with a somber expression tightening the finely sculpted features. Sweat gleamed along the line of his jaw and a small muscle danced just beneath his ear. She felt desolate, but at the same time sheltered by this stoic giant.

"Ben Poole," she said softly.

He glanced at her.

"I'm glad you're with me. Thank you."

"Yes, well . . . fine." He didn't know what to say, and so just left it at that. His heart ached for her. He understood what she was going through, for he had never forgotten the day bushwhackers had murdered his entire family, left them strewn like butchered animals for him to find when he returned to the ransacked cabin. A boy only just thirteen. Oh, God, yes, he knew, and he felt her loss keenly.

At the sheriff's office Ben helped Dessa off the wagon seat. She stumbled and he clasped her arm, guiding her through the open door. He feared she would fall, but some inner strength held her upright. Ben hoped it didn't desert her, for he had a very bad feeling about this.

Sheriff Walter Moohn reclined in his chair, boots

propped on the bottom drawer of a mammoth oak desk. He picked at his teeth with a broomstraw and made no comment until the two young people were inside with the door shut.

Then he said, "Seen you come into town, wondered where you got your passenger. Old Wiley ain't been by yet, expect him soon for our usual game of checkers. This little gal looks tuckered. Set her down, Ben. What's up?"

Dessa wobbled but didn't take the empty chair. "The store that burned—where are my folks? Are they okay?"

Moohn sat up, boot soles hitting the floor with a thud. "Mr. and Mrs. Fallon, wasn't it? Bought the Yoes Mercantile. It burnt last night, still smoldering, I reckon. Nothing we could do. I'm sorry, girl, plumb sorry. You got kin you can wire, someone who can come help you take care of . . . uh, the arrangements?"

"Arrangements?" Dessa swayed, reached out, and Ben took her hand. "No. No, not my parents. But they just got here. How could this happen, Ben?" She cast a pleading glance up into his concerned face. *Make it go away,* she pleaded silently. *Tell the sheriff he's wrong, that he's talking about someone else, not Mother and Daddy.* But no one said anything.

Ben's eyes gleamed and he blinked several times, quickly. He wanted to say something, anything that would ease her sorrow, but no words came.

She swallowed hard, asked in a whisper what she already knew. "Are they dead?" This was crazy. It couldn't be happening. She wanted to wail and pound her chest like women of old. Instead she just stood there, vision all but blank to anything but memories.

In the narrow tunnel of sight she watched the sheriff nod sadly, felt her knees buckle, and sank into a vast, deep cavern.

Ben caught her before she hit the floor, lifting her in his arms like he'd done only the night before when she'd come stumbling toward the stage station like someone half dead.

"Damn it, Moohn, couldn't you have been easier on her?" His voice caught over the words.

The gruff sheriff shrugged. "Sorry, boy. I don't know no way to tell someone their folks is dead but to say it right out. It's a sad and sorry thing, but it happens. And I have to deal with it best I can.

"Whyn't you get her a place to stay. The bodies'll keep till she comes out of it. Now go on."

Ben moved through the door and stood on the boardwalk outside the sheriff's office, momentarily at a loss. People stepped around him while they eyed the unconscious girl in his arms. He thought about the stagecoach holdup. He should have told the sheriff. Then he looked down into the pale face of the girl. A bruise highlighted one cheek and several scratches ran down the side of her neck. Anger rose once again from deep in his throat. He'd see those bastards strung up before this was over. Meanwhile, Wiley would have to take care of telling Moohn about the robbery. He had himself a big enough problem right here, and he wasn't sure what to do with her. No money meant no hotel room.

That left only one place for Ben to take Dessa, and that was the Golden Sun Saloon and Rose Langue, whose penchant for caring for the lost and orphaned had once saved Ben himself. Rose and Maggie would know what to do with his sorely wounded girl. He stepped down into the dusty street and strode through meandering horses, wagons, and people, carrying Dessa as easily as he would have a stack of down pillows. He nodded grimly at those who watched, but offered no explanation.

Dessa awoke to a still and mellow darkness. Across the strange room in which she lay, a candle sputtered, sending out a frail beacon but doing little to illuminate her surroundings. She lay up to her ears in a feather mattress, and no longer wore her ragged clothes. Instead she was wrapped in a soft gown, its fabric soothing and fragrant. As she grew more aware, she heard distant music and the peal of occasional feminine laughter broken by rougher guffaws, obviously male in origin.

She turned her head and moaned. The back of her neck ached and there was a throbbing at her temples. She licked at lips so dry her tongue stuck to them. In the gloom she made out a pitcher on the side table and near it a glass. She raised herself on one elbow, feeling every muscle in her body cry out, and filled the glass with water. For a few blessed moments she remembered nothing, as if her head were full of cotton wool and nothing else, as if all memory hung beyond some darkened curtain waiting for her to pull it open. All she knew was the cool sweetness of the water and the softness of the bed and the soreness of her body. A stranger's body cradling a stranger's mind.

When memory of what had happened came back to her, it came suddenly and brutally, all in a rush, making her cry out. The robbery, the escape from the two awful outlaws, Ben Poole and Wiley Moss taking care of her, the sheriff's dreadful words.

How could this be? How could she go on? It

wasn't fair. She'd struggled so hard to stay alive and return to her parents, and now they had died. How could they do that? Her heart and soul ached; her brain felt numb. No answers came.

She finished the glass of water and lay back in the bed. A welcome darkness enveloped her once again.

Seated at a table with Rose, Ben finished his sorry tale of Dessa Fallon's troubles and the cold-blooded killing of the stage driver and the man riding shotgun. He sensed her gaze waver and glanced up to see shrewd eyes studying him intently.

"What is it?"

Rose blinked and looked down at the table, then quickly back up into his face. "My darling Ben, you're worse than this old gal when it comes to being a pushover for a sad story."

"Yeah," he said, and grinned a bit. "And where do you suppose I got it from, dear Rose?"

Rose shook her head, loosening a curl from the blond mass of piled-high tresses. "Don't lay that at my feet. I just nourished me a starving pup, and look what I got. A great big galoot a touch too soft for his own good. You can't even put two bits together, Ben. And why is that?"

"Aw, hell, Rose. You know. Maggie always needs something, and then there's Sarah and her twins. Their daddy getting killed like he did, and leaving them and their ma with nothing."

Rose laid her hand over his fingers, which nervously picked at the rough wooden surface. "Wasn't your fault, Ben. When are you going to realize a wild bullet is just that? You were doing what needed done and he got in the way."

He shook his head. "I should have taken more

care, Rose. A man has to be responsible for his actions, and that's all there is to that. Killing a man, Rose, that's just about the worst thing that can happen. I was sick of it when I got here, so sick I wanted to die."

Rose got up from her chair. "I'll go up and look in on your poor little orphan, Ben. You have yourself another brew and turn in. Go crawl under that blamed wagon and sleep on the hard ground one more night. Maybe one day you'll get tired of punishing yourself for all the ills of the world."

Ben grinned up at her. "Aw, hell, Rose. I'm doing just fine. Between you and Maggie babying and mothering me, I reckon I'll make out. I think I'll pass on the beer and get me some sleep. I'll check back on Dessa in the morning before me and Wiley leave out."

Rose watched Ben saunter through the batwing doors and out into the night.

If it hadn't been for Ben, she would have gone crazy in those years after Jarrad Lincolnshire fetched his wife and put her out there on the hill in that castle he'd built. And turned his back on Rose like their love had never been. She would never love another man, but being occupied with Ben Poole when he rode in, scarred and half dead from the war, had saved her sanity. He had become like a son to her. And now she could walk right out in the middle of the street and stare up at that pretentious stone monster clinging to the side of the mountain and feel nothing. Well, almost nothing. The Englishman had died last year, his wife and children returned to England, and the castle stood empty, as did the ugly, washed-out mine above the town.

Rose shrugged and tossed off the memories. Best

let the past remain just that. Dead and gone and buried. She lifted the skirts of her shiny gold dress and went up the stairs to see about her newest charge.

The next time Dessa awoke, it was to brilliant sunshine. The red brocade drapes had been drawn aside to let in the morning, and before memory claimed her once again, she actually felt a lift in spirits. What a lovely room, with its bright reds and shades of rich cream. She lay nestled within thick layers of silk and satin. Who lived in such glorious splendor? And how had she gotten here?

The flood of bitter memories came then and she began to cry. So intense was her grief over the death of her parents that she didn't immediately recall the ride into town with Ben Poole or the visit to the sheriff's office. When she finally did, she wiped her eyes and crawled from the bed, wincing with the pain in her sore feet.

On the other side of the room stood something she had never thought to see out here on the frontier. It was a bathtub! In all its glorious splendor. What a marvelous place. Where was she? Had Ben Poole brought her here, undressed her?

She crept to the door, opened it a crack, and listened. Deathly silence greeted her and she stuck her head out to look around. Other doors besides this one opened off one side of a wide balcony. Quietly she eased over to the rail. Down below she saw a great mahogany bar backed by oval mirrors and paintings. A glorious Cremona rested against one wall. She had heard piano music! How many nights she had danced the hours away in the arms of one beau or another, a player piano such as that tinkling gaily in the background. She'd not thought to see one out here on the frontier.

She wiped tears from her eyes at memories of that life when Mother and Daddy were alive.

From below came a sound and she looked to see a bearded gentleman wearing a striped shirt, black pants, and an apron. He hummed softly and mopped at the plank floor among tables with chairs turned upside down on their tops. No one else was in sight and no sounds came from behind the row of closed doors along the veranda. Hadn't she heard music, laughter? Or had that been in the night? She shook her head, confused.

Dessa went back in the room where she had awakened. She didn't know what to do. There was no sign of her clothing and she considered it rude to open any one of the armoires in the large room. She was stuck there in a nightgown, and beginning to need to relieve herself.

A male voice boomed out below and floated upward. After a moment someone tapped on the door. She crossed both arms over her breasts, stood there at a loss for a couple of seconds, then bounded back into the bed and under the covers as the door swung open, accompanied by a greeting.

"You awake, ma'am? It's me. Ben Poole. You okay?" All this he said before he caught sight of her, bedclothes wadded up under her chin and eyes wide with dismay.

"Where am I?" she asked, then thought what a foolish greeting for this man who had obviously taken such care of her.

He stopped in the center of the room. "I didn't mean to bother you. I just wanted to see if you were . . ." He glanced around and flushed. "Wiley . . .

Wiley and me . . . we're just leaving out. Wanted to see if you need anything."

"Clothes," Dessa said in a small voice. "I don't have any clothes." Her eyes filled with tears that she couldn't control, tears that had nothing to do with an absence of clothing.

"Aw, honey, don't cry," Ben said, and came to her like a great bear, kneeling on the floor beside the bed and gathering her in his arms. He patted awkwardly at her head, then said softly against her cheek, "Go ahead and cry. That's a girl. Cry and get it over with. It's okay. I'm sorry about your ma, and pa, I wish it could have been some other way, but it'll be all right, I promise. It'll finally be all right."

She fisted up wads of his rough homespun shirt and clung tightly while she grieved. This had to stop. She had to get hold of herself. So much had happened so fast that her normally tough exterior had been badly damaged.

"I don't usually do this," she snuffled into his chest.

And I don't usually do this, Ben thought, but didn't say. Holding her in his arms produced a rush of all kinds of feelings he just wasn't up to dealing with. An occasional romp with one of Rose's girls never produced such enormous compassion, such heart-rending, head-pounding need. Not of a physical nature, but simply the desire to take away Dessa's pain, to make her laugh again. To have her smile at him and care about him and . . .

Holding her got to be too much. He grasped both her wrists and put her away from him, firmly but gently. She had stopped the harsh sobbing, but tears still leaked from the corners of her eyes when he released her. He dared not touch her again, not the way he was reacting to being near her.

He rose. "You gonna be okay now?"

"Yes, thank you."

"Well, then, I'd better . . . go on. Maggie'll be here in a while and she'll get you something to wear. Your dress and all, well, it was just ruined."

Dessa darted a quick look up into his face. Had he helped undress her? Seen her naked? A fire burst into flame between her breasts and spread up her throat.

But when she started to challenge him, she found he had left, the sound of his boots silenced by the rug. Crawling from the bed, she hurried across the room and out onto the balcony in time to see him fetch a disreputable hat off a hook on the wall beside the door below, cram it down on his head, and burst outside like he was pursued by the devil himself.

From down the hallway a small brunette came out of one of the rooms. She was dressed only in a scandalous red corset and filmy black robe. Mesmerized, Dessa remained at the railing, clutching it with the fingers of one hand and watching the woman approach.

She smiled at Dessa and the tired eyes lit up. "Hi. You must be Ben's friend. I'm Maggie, Ben's friend also. How are you this morning?"

Her voice was low, and when she spoke, she unconsciously moved her exquisite hands as if using them to accent the meaning of her words.

"I don't have any clothes," Dessa said again, as if that would explain her standing out in the open in her blistered bare feet and clad only in a nightgown.

Maggie eyed Dessa's lean, athletic frame and shook her head. Tapping scarlet-nailed fingers to her lips, she considered the problem in silence. At last she reached a decision. "Virgie's built some like you. We'll get you something to do you for now."

Maggie trotted off, leaving Dessa to stare after her. She considered her surroundings for a moment or two, leaned over the railing, and looked down once more.

All of a sudden she put everything together and realized what kind of a place this was. Ben Poole had brought her to a brothel! That big grinning heathen had dumped her in with a bunch of . . . a bunch of fancy women. The little trollop called Maggie was no doubt much more than just a friend of Ben's. And what did Ben Poole think, bringing her to a place like this?

She stormed back into the room, stood in the middle, and glared around. Now it was easy to see what this room, that luxuriously appointed bed, was used for.

The door burst open and she whirled to face whomever might enter. "I have to get out of here. Now. I can't stay here in this . . . this disgusting place. Get my clothes. I'll wear my own clothes, not some whore's."

"Whoa, now, child," the regal woman with a head full of blond curls said. "Calm down. You've had a tough time, but don't you go getting snippy with me. This 'disgusting' place, as you call it, sheltered you when you had nowhere else to go. And I'll not have you looking down your pretty little nose at me or my girls.

"Now, if you want to cry over your troubles or throw things, that's fine, but you just settle yourself down when it comes to insulting me."

Under the tirade Dessa staggered backward a step

or two. She was used to getting her own way. This didn't bode well, this beautiful blond woman who was obviously the head madam of this whorehouse, talking to her like she was one of her soiled girls.

She drew herself up, ready to fight, fists clenched at her sides and mouth set firmly.

"That's better. Look me right in the eye, child. Stand up to me. But don't you dare act better than me, because you're not. And you're not better than my girls. One more step in the way you're going and you might not have many choices, either. It can happen that fast. If it weren't for Ben Poole and a few others, you'd have slept on the street last night, and who knows what would have happened to you there."

Dessa nodded. The woman was right, and she felt chagrined. Her daddy would have been ashamed of her behavior. She raised her chin and refused to let the tears begin again. There was too much to do for any more crying.

The older woman crossed the room and put an arm around her. She smelled of sweet talcum and lavender, and wore a sun-yellow dress with a massive skirt and a hat tilted perkily on her carefully coiffed curls. She carried a folded parasol over one arm and her reticule over the other. These she placed on a padded chaise near the bathtub.

"Now, child, if you can see fit to speak, perhaps we can visit a spell, get acquainted while Maggie fetches you some decent clothing." She grinned wryly. "My name is Rose Langue, and this is my place of business."

Dessa nodded and sank to the edge of the bed. Her feet still bothered her and the muscles in the backs of her legs ached from the long trek. But nothing hurt quite so badly as her heart, and it was breaking. "I'm sorry," she said, lower lip trembling.

"And I, too, dear. About your parents, that is. What a terrible loss. But we mustn't dwell on it overmuch. You've got to look forward. Do you have any people?"

"No. Just my parents ... and me. My brother Mitchell died in the war, and there is no one else. I don't know what to do." She nearly cried the words, but controlled her emotions so that she didn't act like a baby.

"There, there. Take a deep breath. What about money? Your parents owned the mercantile that burned. Did they have anything else? Any other property, any funds?"

"Oh, yes. My father owns—I mean owned—general stores all over the country. Besides several in Kansas City, he had two in St. Louis and three in Denver. And since the Union Pacific laid out their route to Promontory, he'd had a few more built. I'm not sure how many. Everyone wondered why in the world he bought one here, and I guess we'll never know now."

"Well, then, there shouldn't be a problem. You'll need to send a wire to whoever helped your father run his business. There are surely accountants, attorneys, and the like who will need to be notified, if the sheriff hasn't done so already. They will no doubt send you some money and you can go back home."

Dessa stared down at her hands lying limply in her lap. Go home? Ride that dreadful stage and that noisy, gritty train all the way back to Kansas City, when she had just suffered such a horrific time getting here? Well, she simply couldn't think of that.

"I can't go home. Not yet. Not after what's happened. I don't think I could bring myself to climb back on board that dreadful stage."

Rose chuckled. "I can't say as I blame you for that. Riding very far in one of those contraptions will shake your guts right out."

Dessa gasped. She wasn't used to ladies talking in such a bold manner. But then she supposed women who could live on this frontier had to learn to give up some niceties in order to survive. Delicate speech probably was the first to go, right along with modesty, if her own experience was any example.

Rose studied her a moment, then sat beside her on the bed and took her hand. "Ben told me what happened. You were very brave and very lucky. Traveling alone, a girl like you can get in all kinds of trouble. It seems strange that your parents would allow such a thing. But you're here now, and safe. And you'll get through this, strong child that you are. We'll help you, and so will Ben."

Dessa clenched her fingers together in her lap. She wanted to defend her parents, tell Rose all about the gentleman escort, employee of her father's company, entrusted with her safekeeping. And how he'd been lured away by a weakness for gambling and loose women. Lured to a place much like this. She'd been better off alone. But her stomach rumbled loudly and interrupted her thoughts.

Rose made a clucking sound. "Oh, dear, I expect you could use some breakfast. I'll go hurry up those silly girls. They're probably having one of their girl talks, and we'll go out to breakfast."

"Oh, I couldn't let you do that."

"Nonsense. You can do the same for me someday soon. Oh, by the way, there's a chamber pot under the bed and I'll have a boy bring some hot water so you can wash. I'll wait downstairs. But don't you tarry. I don't think that empty stomach of yours can wait much longer."

Chapter Four

While Dessa and Rose ate breakfast at the Continental House, a large band of men rode out of town accompanied by a ballyhoo of shouts and shrill whistles.

"Walter and his posse," Rose remarked, and nibbled at a puffy biscuit.

"After the men who—" Dessa broke off. The china teacup rattled from her fingers into its saucer.

"Yes. Too much of that going on around here lately. Right after the war there was a spurt of outlawry, but things were cooling down with the failure of the mines. Got to where there wasn't much to steal. And old Sheriff Plummer getting himself hanged as the head of a pack of road agents put a damper on thievery for a while. But that was a few years back, and now, I don't know. I just don't know.

"They say there's a passel of road agents hiding out in these mountains. Some even claim that devil Yank to be leading them. Say he come out of the Union Army crazy in the head and out to avenge ever' shot fired at him. I don't know about that. You'd think they'd move on down South and start robbing the trains, what with all that excitement down in Promontory last year. Imagine riding coast to coast by rail.

"I suppose, though, it's a little harder to rob a train

than it is a stagecoach or bank. Won't be long before they'll figure it out, I expect."

In Dessa's mind the only questions she could really consider were those regarding the death of her parents, so she added nothing to the conversation. Even the brief hours spent with that awful man Coody and his partner had blurred with the reality of her tragic loss.

Rose glanced up and patted her perfectly painted red lips with a linen napkin. "What is it, child? You've scarcely touched your food. Eat, keep up your strength. You'll need it."

Rose's no-nonsense approach lent Dessa a bit of courage. Whorehouse madam or no, she acted like she really cared—and her not even knowing Dessa or her troubles till yesterday. It was hard to keep from crying if she let herself dwell on what had happened, so she bravely lifted the fork and delicately deposited a minuscule bit of potato on her tongue.

Rose shook her head. She saw the tears pooling in the child's eyes and didn't want to chastise her, but just the same, if she'd eat more, she'd feel better.

"I don't know what to do, Rose," Dessa said, and lay down the fork. It was no use; she couldn't swallow another bite. She might as well have been trying to eat a chunk out of the boardwalk out front.

"Oh, I know you don't. But one thing at a time, without thinking ahead, is the best course for now. I spoke to Walter, and he knew nothing about who to notify, so I suppose you should start there."

Dessa nodded. "There's just our attorney, the accountant, people who helped run the business. I suppose I should send a wire."

"Then we'll go to the telegraph office from here."

Being completely alone was a terrible feeling, and

all she wanted was to coil up in a dark corner until everything righted itself. An orphan at eighteen. What an awful thing.

"There's no one else," she told Rose. "No one. If my parents had any relations, I don't know about them. They married back in Pennsylvania and moved to Kansas City. I understand that my grandfather was in the same business as my father and set him up on his first venture. But he died when I was small. There were no other children. My grandmother died before I was born.

"My mother never spoke of her family. I always had the feeling they didn't approve of the marriage and so wanted nothing to do with us. I think they lived in Virginia somewhere, but I'm not sure. My father said once that Mother left home with only the clothes on her back, running away to marry him. I don't even know the family name."

Dessa picked up the linen napkin and wiped at her fingertips, then looked across the table at Rose. "So you see, I'm quite alone, and I'll just have to manage on my own. What I don't know is whether I should have them buried here or take them back to . . . back to Kansas City."

Rose studied the charcoal circles under the girl's green eyes. She couldn't imagine her turning around and making that dreadful trip by coach and train, and worse, taking along with her two charred lumps of human flesh that once were her beloved parents.

"Oh, child. What do you think of this? We'll have two lovely wooden caskets constructed. Mason Yell is a fine craftsman, and can do just what you want. Then we'll find a peaceful spot out at Boot Hill—I'll go with you, if you like—and just let the Reverend Blair speak a nice service. Everyone in town will come, give your parents a proper send-off. They would approve, I'm sure.

"No parent would want to see their child suffer any more than she must over this. I can assure you of that. Your mother would want what is the simplest for you to manage."

The pooling tears spilled over and ran down Dessa's cheeks, but she made no sound at all. This was all too much, and if it weren't for the kindness of this brothel madam, she had no idea what she would do. What her friends back in Kansas City would think of that, she had absolutely no idea. Imagine that, imagine that indeed.

She patted at the tears and nodded her head.

"Fine, then that's settled. You can stay with me awhile until you decide what you want to do. And do me a favor, will you?"

Dessa nodded again.

"Be nice to Ben Poole. He's walking on his own tongue dogging your every step." Rose smiled brightly, and though it looked somewhat forced, it made Dessa feel a bit better.

"I haven't been anything but nice to him. He's just so . . . well, so different from any man I've ever met."

Rose chuckled. "Well, I wouldn't have used the word *different*—it's too bland. Ben has his own row to hoe, and so far he's doing a damn fine job of it, seeing how he started. A half-starved young pup, dodging every time a gun went off, haunts of the war in those startling eyes of his. We all thought for a while he was a raving lunatic, but it turned out he was just a frightened boy. When he came here, he couldn't even read. My Maggie taught him. Maggie was abandoned by her parents, who were traveling to Utah with the Mormon train. Both being orphans, in a way, they just took up with each other, formed a sort of family. She's a smart little thing and doing her best, too.

"You know, child. You'd do well to consider what folks have had to put up with before you go judging what they've done with their lives."

Dessa hung her head. While she was happy that the subject had veered away from the funeral and her parents' death, she wasn't sure she liked this tack, either.

"I haven't judged anyone." Even as she said it, Dessa knew the words weren't exactly true.

"It's all right. Don't get upset, it was just a reminder that we can't be too harsh till we know all the rocks scattered in other folks' paths.'"

After wiring Kansas City, Rose send Dessa back to rest in her room at the Golden Sun and went to arrange for the caskets. Seeing no reason for delay, Dessa decided to schedule the funeral for the next day. Rose had Ed at the *Post* print a simple announcement about the services and hired Dickey Slater to tack them up around town. She assured Dessa that everyone who could possibly get away would be at Boot Hill the next day for the funeral.

Dessa thought how odd it was that total strangers would be seeing her parents off on their final journey.

All afternoon she dealt with wires of sympathy from the Fallons' many friends in Kansas City. A steady stream was delivered to the Golden Sun, carried by barefoot boys proud of being charged with the duty. Dessa noticed that Rose always pressed a shiny coin in each boy's palm before shooing him on his way.

Late that day a wire came from the Cluney &

Brown law firm with a transfer note for the bank in Virginia City. Dessa was no longer broke. She might be homeless, but she now had a bank account.

The only thing she could think of buying was a black dress for the funeral. At the dressmaker's she posed rigidly while the plump woman took her measurements and then fitted a cloth pattern to her body.

The woman had a strange way of conversing past a mouthful of pins. Dessa supposed that after a time one might grow to understand the mumbled words, but she simply nodded politely and occasionally murmured a noncommittal reply.

Once freed of the pieces of fabric, she donned the dress loaned to her by the girl they called Virgie. She felt extremely conspicuous. Its low-cut lace bodice revealed much too much of her bosom. She had borrowed a little jacket from Rose that helped some, and slipped into it as Mrs. Fabrini emptied her mouth of pins.

"I'll put this together tonight. Come for a fitting first thing in the morning and don't worry. It will be ready for the funeral. I am very fast. Ask anyone, they will tell you. Mrs. Fabrini is very fast." She stuck out her right hand, palm up to reveal the pads of her fingers. "See, see how hard they are. That comes from pushing the needle. Pushing and pushing it, day and night. Why I ever got into this, I don't know. But everyone needs dresses, yes? Cooking was my only other choice, and the Lord knows that would be my downfall."

Mrs. Fabrini pounded at her ample stomach with both hands. "This is what I get for cooking for Mr. Fabrini. Imagine if I cooked for everyone in this town all day, every day. No, it's better I sew the dresses." She lifted her shoulders in a shrug. "Still, I never get the new dress myself. There is never time, what with everyone else needing one for a funeral or a wedding or whatever. You come here from where, child?"

The conversation that had flowed from the woman once she unpinned her lips amazed Dessa. She managed to answer the question. It set the woman off and running once again.

"Ah, yes, that place. We were through there, Mr. Fabrini and I. Coming out West to make our fortune in the gold mines." A great booming laugh shook the homely woman. "It is a great and nasty town, is it not? But not nearly so stinking as New York. When we got off the ship, I told Mr. Fabrini that if we had to remain in that place, I would probably just kill both of us and put us out of our misery. And so, him not wanting me to do that, we started west. What a trip, what a trip. I am telling no one just how horrible it really was, because they would not be believing me."

Mrs. Fabrini patted at Dessa's arm and shoved her toward the door. "You must leave now, child, or I will not get a thing done but talking your leg off."

Out on the walk, Dessa leaned back against the building and laughed. She couldn't help it, the conversation had been so wonderfully distracting. Enthralled by Mrs. Fabrini's tale, she had been able to forget for a brief interlude that she had gone to the dressmaker for something to wear to her parents' funeral.

Wiley and Ben rode back into Virginia City at dusk, and Ben gladly left Wiley to his beloved paperwork and nightly checker game with Walter

Moohn. He told himself he was going to the Golden Sun for his usual glass of brew before hunting up some supper, but the moment he stepped inside and glanced around, he felt disappointed. It had nothing to do with wetting his whistle, either. He didn't see Dessa Fallon anywhere, but why should he? A girl like her would not hang around in a hurdy-gurdy house. Rose had her hidden away upstairs, no doubt.

Maggie and two or three of the regular girls were dancing with their partners, but he didn't see Rose. He ordered the beer and glanced toward the stairway. Maggie snuck up behind him and touched his arm, making him slosh foam over the rim of his glass.

"Want to dance?" she asked with a hint of the devil flashing in her hazel eyes. She knew Ben refused to dance in public and liked to get at him about it.

"Buy you a beer instead?" he offered, but kept his eyes on the upstairs balcony.

"Okay. Who you looking for?" Maggie leaned an elbow on the bar and the motion revealed the fullness of her breasts spilling from the low-cut neckline.

Ben pulled his gaze up to her heart-shaped face. He loved her as if she were the sister he missed so much, but sometimes she could be annoying with her teasing. Just like that sister would be had she lived, he supposed. He grinned at her.

"Rose. I'm looking for Rose."

"Sure, you big liar." Maggie sipped at the beer. "She's pretty, but kind of snobbish, don't you think?"

"Who, Rose?"

"Who, Rose? Oh, Ben, who do you think? That poor little thing you come striding in here with yesterday. Carrying her like she was some prize you'd won."

Ben remembered the soft touch of Dessa's breast against his arm, the suppleness of hip and thigh as he'd carried her across the street and into the Golden Sun. He thought of the silkiness of her hair tickling at his throat and her head tucked in against his shoulder, the bruise on the inside of her pale thigh when he'd shoved open the door and caught her bathing earlier that morning out at the stage stop. Quickly he gulped down the rest of the beer.

"Just wanted to make sure she's doing okay," he grumbled at Maggie, and stomped across the wooden floor, his worn boots thunking loud to show his annoyance.

"Where you going, Ben?" Maggie asked.

"Going to find me some supper, then off to bed."

"You coming back here for bed? Might get your mind and something else off that little thing who's much too fancy for the likes of you. If you'd like, I'll tell Virgie."

Ben glowered and Maggie ran back to the dance floor giggling.

A fellow in dusty pants and faded shirt handed her his token and hugged her frail body up close. Ben didn't see how she could put up with that all the time, but he tried to understand Maggie's life and why she had to live it the way she did. She might dance with anyone for a token, but Rose never made the girls take a man they didn't like to one of the cribs. That was strictly up to them. And Maggie was fussy that way. Very fussy indeed.

He hadn't been there with her since he was sixteen and Rose sent him over to be "broke in." That was five years ago, and Maggie had done many things for him since, but never in the bed. It just wouldn't be proper, considering how they felt about each other.

Dessa stepped quietly onto the balcony and peered down into the noisy room below. Before coming here, she never knew the difference between one saloon and another. But Rose had quickly set her straight.

Down at the Busted Mule a man could gamble and drink, but he came to the hurdy-gurdy house to dance with a pretty girl. Here he could still drink, in fact was encouraged to do so as well as buy his partner something. But he couldn't play a hand of poker. This was a dance hall, pure and simple. The cribs out back were something that Rose gilded over quickly. Dessa was pretty sure she knew what went on there, too, and the thought made her flush. At the same time, she wondered what it might be like to be with someone like Ben Poole. In one of the cribs. Without her clothes. Him naked, too.

She clapped a hand over her mouth. Of all things to think about. What had gotten into her, anyway?

Just as she leaned out over the balcony rail, Ben Poole, who had been ready to shove his way out of the batwing doors, turned to look upstairs and saw her there. He stopped cold right in the door and stared at her so long she wondered if something was wrong.

A whiskered man pushed his way past Ben, slapping up against him solidly. Ben stepped backward out of the way but didn't take his eyes off her. Then he smiled, tipped his hat, and moved through the doors and out into the darkening night.

Dessa pressed her lips together. Who did he think

he was? She hadn't given him cause to acknowledge her in any way, that ignorant heathen. And him looking right up there at her, so everyone could see, and acting like they had a formal acquaintance. Rose might think highly of Ben Poole, but Dessa thought he was nothing but a no-account waster, a lazy frontier oaf. That story about him coming into town starving was sad, but it didn't change things. All a person had to do was pull himself up by his own bootstraps and work hard to be a success in this world. Hadn't her own daddy said so? And just because Ben Poole looked like one of those figures painted on the wall of a church didn't give him call to get familiar with her. Tip his hat at her so everyone in the place could see. She wasn't about to let her feminine emotions get the better of her where this man was concerned.

But he'd held her. Oh, how gently he'd held her, and she'd shed her tears on his flesh. That wasn't so easy to forget.

It was difficult getting through the night. Nightmares kept waking her just as she would drift off. More than once she fell, fell into the blankness of sleep and along would come the face of that horrible Coody; flames roared through her dreams, curling them at the edges, heating her so that she awoke drenched in perspiration, tears flowing. By morning she looked and felt utterly exhausted, and wondered how she would get through the funeral.

After a hurried wash in cold water from the pitcher beside her bed, Dessa dressed and slipped downstairs. Out in the street she found the town struggling awake. A few horsemen moved along, the shod hooves kicking up dust and echoing eerily in the quiet. The air was mountain clear and tinged with the sweetness of wildflowers. She breathed deeply and stared with awe at the high peaks cutting into the silver sky. Just to the right of one snow-capped tip, a star winked and went out. Tears lurking near the surface welled in her eyes, brought about not by grief but by a sight so achingly beautiful it transcended all earthly cares.

"Wonderful sight, isn't it?" a voice at her back said.

Startled, she turned to see Ben Poole lounging against the front of a building. "What are you doing here?"

"Same as you, I reckon. Claiming my piece of the walk, enjoying my piece of the heavens." He straightened and touched the brim of his hat but didn't remove it. "I trust you're doing fine, ma'am."

She swallowed hard. He made her feel twisted inside, like something wanted to happen but couldn't. She could only nod mutely, and he kept those bright blue eyes aimed right at her, one corner of his mouth turning up ever so slightly.

"Well, you take care of yourself, Miss Dessa Fallon," he said, and crossed the street, brushing so close to her she could smell leather and soap. Her heart pounded.

Mother once said you'd know. When you met the man you would love, you would know, and nothing would keep you from him. Nothing. But this couldn't be that knowing, could it? No, this was just grief and the feeling of loss, of desolation.

Yet, for some reason she wanted to run after him, pound at his back with her fists, and scream. *Leave me be,* she would shout. *Don't do this to me,* she would beg. But she didn't, because she knew that she really didn't want him to leave her alone, no matter what she might claim.

She would get through this day. She was strong and stubborn. Hadn't Mother always said so? *Just like your father*, she'd said.

"Oh, dear Lord, I hope so," Dessa murmured, then turned her back on the vanishing figure of Ben Poole and lifted her skirts to make her way to the dressmaker's, where a light glowed in the front window. Mrs. Fabrini, true to her word, was at work on putting final touches to the black dress. It fit perfectly.

When Dessa returned to the Golden Sun and stepped into her room carrying the brown paper parcel, she saw that steam rose from the half-filled bathtub. Bless dear Rose's heart. She knew just what Dessa needed. How would she ever repay the woman for all she had done for her? Somehow she would think of a way.

Bathed and dressed in Mrs. Fabrini's creation, she sat in front of the mirror struggling with her hair. It had suffered dreadfully from the experiences of the past few days. Normally she spent hours on her own ablutions, and shampooed and styled the long umber tresses frequently. Since her coming out last spring, she had taken to wearing her hair up in the fashion of a grown woman, not hanging loose and free like a child. But this morning she simply brushed the fly-away strands till they gleamed and put on the small black hat Mrs. Fabrini had taken upon herself to order from the milliner.

With the filmy veil pulled down over her face, she felt sufficiently hidden from the curious stares that were sure to come her way.

After knocking softly, Rose entered the room. Dessa could see her in the mirror regarding her solemnly. Rose, too, wore black, and she was stunning. The blond hair and wide-brimmed lace hat set off her clear complexion and exquisite features. Dessa decided that no one could possibly tell by looking at her that Rose was the owner of a brothel.

"Walter is here to escort you, child," Rose said.

"Walter?"

"Sheriff Moohn. He insisted."

Dessa recalled the terse way in which the sheriff had informed her of her parents' death and wasn't sure she wanted to be on his arm during the funeral. She saw no way out of it, though, and so went with Rose downstairs. Their leather ankle-high shoes made dull echoes on the wooden floors still shiny and smelling of lye soap from their daily mopping.

Outside, a black carriage waited. Sheriff Moohn stood beside it, ready to help her into the seat. He climbed in then himself and snapped the reins smartly onto the rump of a splendid black horse. A wagon waited on the street, two closed wooden coffins sitting side by side in the bed.

The sheriff and Dessa rode all the way to Boot Hill behind the wagon, not speaking. She didn't notice until they arrived that a great long procession followed them. Men, women, and children rode in wagons and carriages, others sat astride horses and a few mules, still others walked. It seemed to take forever for the crowd to make its somber way to the grave site on the slope of the hill.

Dessa had decided on holding the services out here in the open as the early sun splashed the valley with golden light. God's own cathedral, and it couldn't have been more beautiful. Reverend Blair, minister to the congregation of the raw-board church hastily finished for his arrival, had acquiesced to her wishes.

Moohn put his arm around Dessa's waist as the

preacher began to speak, and she was suddenly very glad the gruff sheriff was there. Rose stepped in on the opposite side, and the two held her upright as well as together, for she feared she'd shatter in a hundred pieces.

Dessa stared at the coffins as long as she could, while the words of the preacher reached out to the crowd. Abruptly she felt as if someone were watching her, and raised her eyes. Through the riffling of the dark veil she saw, across the way near a grove of trees, a man moving into the open. A brief recognition caused her heart to flutter up into her throat. Something about his stance was oddly familiar. She squinted, trying to see his face, but he was too far away. He clutched a black hat in both hands in front of himself. A breeze tossed his thick crop of dark hair and the sun struck a startling white streak there.

For the slightest instant she thought the man was someone she knew, but that was ridiculous. It couldn't be. He reminded her of . . . She lost the thought, and lifted the veil to stare so hard at him that her vision blurred.

The stranger must have noticed, for he melted back into the shadows until she couldn't tell if he was even there. She shook away the uncomfortable feeling that she'd seen him somewhere before. Perhaps he would come to her after the services, when everyone would be expected to offer their condolences. She dragged her attention back to the preacher and, in the throes of her grief, forgot about the odd figure.

Moohn remained by her side as the entire procession of townspeople filed past. Each in turn clasped her hand briefly and murmured sympathies. At times

Dessa thought her legs would just give way, that she wouldn't be able to stand there another minute. Then Rose would squeeze her hand reassuringly, and a new bit of strength would arise from down inside.

At last the end of the line drew near. And there, bringing up the rear, was Ben Poole. He had wet and combed his unruly long hair and was freshly shaved. He wore a cravat at the neck of his homespun shirt. The worn boots showed signs of having been polished at, even though the effort didn't seem to have done much good.

He looked down into her upturned face, his black-lashed blue eyes appearing to gaze right through the veil. Then he lifted her hand and kissed it gently. Before she could react in any way, he was gone. The feel of his hand holding hers, the warm spot where he had placed his lips, remained. She felt more comforted by his brief action than any words he could have spoken.

She asked to remain behind to be alone with her parents for a while, and Moohn and Rose Langue strolled discreetly a few paces away to stand beside the carriage and wait while she whispered her final good-byes.

Kneeling beside the caskets that would soon be lowered into the earth, Dessa thought of all her life spent with these two wonderful people. She refused to let her mind stray to what it would be like without them, but rather replayed over and over the happy times they'd had together. The years of laughter and tears, of joy and sorrow, of sharing and caring. She could not mourn those, for they must sustain her for the rest of her life.

Dry-eyed she rose, patted her fingers gently on the rough pine boards, and, holding her head high, managed to walk without collapsing back to where Moohn and Rose waited.

Chapter Five

After the funeral, Rose put Dessa to bed for the remainder of the day. The task proved easy. Dessa was totally exhausted by her ordeal and grief. Maggie peered in around noon carrying a tray, and found Dessa staring dry-eyed toward the draped windows.

"I brought you something to eat. Rose says I'm to stay and make absolutely sure you eat every bite."

Dessa rolled over on the silken sheet and faced her visitor. The petite woman had draped a gossamer satin robe over the scandalous red corset that pushed her small breasts up so they threatened to burst from the confines of the garment. Her tiny feet were bare, and the brunette tresses tousled, as if she hadn't brushed her hair yet. Surely Maggie had attended the funeral, but try as she might, Dessa couldn't recall a single face. No, that wasn't entirely true. She remembered Ben holding her hand up to his warm, velvety lips and gazing at her for a long moment, sadness darkening his intense blue eyes.

And the man in the woods with the streak in his hair. His image returned quite suddenly and vividly. Who was he and what did he want?

"Are you feeling okay? You've gone all white as a sheet," Maggie said, and placed the tray on the bedside table. Without waiting for a reply, she began to fluff pillows and stuff them behind Dessa. "Sit up. Eat. Or you'll face the wrath of Rose, and she's tough to cross."

Dessa did as she was told, smoothing the quilted comforter over her lap so Maggie could place the tray there. When Maggie lifted a towel off the food, a billow of aromatic steam fairly made Dessa's mouth water. She was surprised that she actually wanted to eat, and tackled the savory meat smothered in a thick brown sauce with chunks of potatoes and carrots. A hunk of bread lay on a separate plate. There was butter in a bowl, salt in its crystal cellar, and a fragrant cup of sweet tea. All were served on blue and white Bristow china.

Business must be good in bawdy houses, Dessa thought wryly.

Silently Maggie watched her devour the meal.

As Dessa swallowed the last bite, Maggie said, "There's apple pie, too, but I couldn't get it on the tray. It wouldn't do me to wait tables over at the Continental; I'd dump it all down someone's shirt front."

Dessa managed a weak smile at a vision of the red-corseted Maggie serving up meals at the chic eating establishment, her luscious breasts spilling out every time she bent to a table. The smile turned into a moan at the idea of eating anything else, even if it was her favorite dessert being offered.

"I couldn't eat another bite. I'm already stuffed. But apple pie? Maybe you could sneak me a piece for a snack tonight? That is, if I ever get over stuffing myself so. I can't think what got into me."

Maggie smiled with delight. "Plenty of good food,

I'd say. I'll bring you a big slab of pie with a glass of milk later . . . uh, before we get too busy."

Spreading a hand over her bosom, Dessa tried not to think of what getting busy later that evening would mean to Maggie. Perhaps the girl only danced with those scruffy men who came into the Golden Sun, but somehow Dessa doubted it. In an effort to change the subject, she asked, "What was that wonderful stew?"

"Venison. It's the specialty of the house. Sometimes it's the only dish of the house." Maggie laughed at the look that crossed Dessa's face.

"Venison?"

"Deer, you know."

"Oh, dear, I think I do." Both giggled at her unintentional pun, before she continued. "I never thought I'd actually eat one of those lovely little creatures, though."

"Well, you didn't exactly eat the entire thing. Just a chunk or two." Maggie giggled again and took the tray, placing it back on the table. She plumped herself down on the edge of the bed, obviously eager to chat awhile. "What do you eat? Back in Kansas City?"

"Beef. We eat a lot of beef and some pork. Goose and duck, pheasant sometimes. Chickens, too, and fish."

"Beef is a cow. What's the difference between that and deer?"

Dessa looked rueful. "Not as much as I thought."

Maggie chuckled, apparently quite enjoying their visit. "We eat fish here, too, when we can get one of the men to catch a mess. Tell me, what's it truly like back in the Americas?"

"Have you never been there?"

Maggie shook her head. "I barely remember. We came out with Brigham Young when I was little. I . . . I've been kicking around out here in the territories ever since."

"Well, I've lived all my life in Kansas City. The streets are lit with illuminating gas lamps. We can stroll in the park at night, down by the river. People drive around in marvelous carriages, landaus and runabouts and phaetons, some black with gold stripes. Very elegant and not at all like these chunky old wooden wagons out here. Last year Daddy had water piped into the house and installed a water closet. Not like here, where you either use the chamber pot or run out to the privy.

"We have servants who cook and clean and sew. Some of my friends have personal maids, but my daddy isn't quite that rich. He says we should take care of ourselves anyway, and now that I'm here, I see that he was right."

Dessa hadn't realized until she paused for breath that she spoke of that life, of her parents, as if she had only temporarily left it behind and could return whenever she wished. Harshly, hurtfully, she realized that she had not only lost her parents, she had lost that life. Perhaps not forever, for surely she could return home one day soon. But it would never be the same without them. She would have to carve out a new existence for herself. And everyone would expect her to marry right away. Oh, dear, what a terrible catastrophe.

Entranced, eyes shining with pleasure, Maggie encouraged her to continue her tale. "And what about dances? They have fancy balls, don't they?"

"Oh, yes, the ladies' gowns are beautiful, with yards and yards of tulle or taffeta. Some even wear the newest bustles and no crinolines. And the men dress in tight trousers, and shirts so white they dazzle the eye, and single-breasted waistcoats that plunge in the front. And the music is exquisite. The latest in polyphons with disk after disk of all the most popular songs.

"Just before I came out here to the frontier, we attended the summer cotillion at the Riverside Ball Room. I will never forget it—it was glorious. We danced the night away."

Maggie nodded. "And there must be plays. We have some plays here, too, at the opera house, and sometimes Rose takes one of us with her. Now that *he* isn't around anymore."

Though caught up in her own memories, Dessa couldn't help but notice the accent Maggie put on that mysterious *he* in Rose's past. She had to admit to being somewhat curious about who the man Maggie spoke of could be and what had happened to him. The subject wasn't something she cared to discuss with Maggie, so she would remember to ask Rose when she knew her better.

A terrible clatter arose outside, bringing a halt to their chatter. Maggie jumped from the bed, drew back the heavy draperies, heaved open the window, and leaned out. The girl appeared to have no shame at all in exposing herself while half nude.

Her head still poked out the window, Maggie said to Dessa, "It's the posse, coming back empty-handed. I guess no one told you, they brought the bodies in yesterday. The men who were killed when the stage was robbed? Everyone is in a fair uproar. J.T. and Artie were both well liked. The vigilantes won't rest till they stretch the necks of those owlhoots, but sometimes I have my doubts about our good sheriff.

He prefers checkers and Rose to carrying out the law."

Maggie turned from the window, hand over her mouth and eyes wide. "Oh, my goodness, I forgot. You saw them, didn't you? I mean, the men who did it. Rose said they dragged you off and would have done dreadful things to you and probably even killed you if you hadn't run off and found Ben.

"He's smitten with you, you know," Maggie finished with a giggle.

Dessa frowned. She was beginning to like Maggie despite her chosen occupation, but she didn't care to discuss Ben Poole with her or anyone else. Everyone in this place doted on him. She couldn't help wondering what they saw in him. She squeezed her eyes shut and felt again his strong but gentle arms enfolding her, his satin-smooth lips touching the back of her hand ever so tenderly.

Angry at her own weakness, she mentally scolded herself. He was nothing but a useless and lazy frontiersman who would never amount to anything. One of those men who likes to play helpless so women will cater to him. Ben Poole was certainly not the kind of man a woman with her breeding should think twice about. And he never had anything worthwhile to say, if he chose to speak at all.

Maggie interrupted her ruminations. "Well, you could be nice to him. He really is a good person.

"I'm going down and find out what's going on. Rose says you're to stay in bed and get some rest, get your strength back. She'll be glad to see you ate your dinner."

Maggie grabbed up the tray and was gone before Dessa could say a word in her own defense about her feelings on the subject of Ben Poole.

Those feelings were reinforced later that afternoon when someone banged on the door a couple of times, then barged into her room. Half asleep, she lurched to a sitting position to see Ben Poole standing in the center of the room, big hands hanging loosely at his sides. His pants and shirt were powdered with dust and there was a sweaty ring around his golden hair where a hat had rested.

"Oh, I'm sorry, ma'am, I thought—"

"Get out!" she shouted, and tugged the covers up over the bodice of the gown she wore. Too skimpy, too lacy for her taste.

Ben backed up a step or two and grinned, looking like a kid caught at a pie set to cool on the windowsill. He hurriedly found his voice. "Seeing as how I'm here, I'll ask how you are before I go."

Enraged, she pointed past his shoulder. "Go, now! Get out of my room."

"By the sound of things, I guess you're better, or at least got your second wind. Glad to see your spirits haven't been dampened any."

Before Dessa could vent her rage at Ben's brash familiarity, Rose appeared in the open doorway behind him. "What in the thunder is all the shouting about? What are you doing to this girl, Ben?"

Turning to face Rose, Ben spread his palms and shrugged. "Not a thing, Rose. I just came in to—"

"He broke in on me while I was asleep, that's what. Scared me half to death. I'll thank him to leave my room this instant. He had no business—"

Ben smacked his chest with the flat of his hand, making a sudden hollow sound. "Tell me, don't tell her. I'm not deaf."

Dessa rose up onto her knees, forgetting to hold

the covers over her bosom. "I did, and you just stood there like a—"

"Whoa, now. Both of you." Rose slipped past Ben, who looked as if he couldn't decide between getting an eyeful of Dessa in the thin gown or running for his life.

Rose solved the problem. "Stay right where you are, Ben. And you, child, will kindly not speak in that tone of voice. This is not your room; it belongs to me."

"But he—" Dessa sputtered, and realized that the silken gown was clinging to her nipples, which were rigid with the excitement of the moment. She scrabbled around to cover herself once again.

Ben managed to come to his own defense, but he couldn't tear his gaze from the flustered and angrily beautiful girl on the bed. "I thought Virgie was in this room, Rose. Tell her to stop yelling. I'm sorry I—"

"Both of you shut up, this instant. I never heard so much caterwauling in my life."

"He's looking for a fancy woman?" Dessa cried.

"Ben," Rose scolded.

"I didn't do anything."

"You came in my room without knocking, you . . . you lunkhead."

"I did not. I knocked. Hard. I did, Rose, I swear. You know I don't bust in on the girls."

"I'm not the girls," Dessa shouted.

"Hush, now, this instant, the both of you," Rose said, and shut the door on a crowd of curious onlookers behind her.

As far as Dessa could see, the group was made up of half-clothed men and women. Instantly understanding what they were all doing just prior to her fracas with Ben, she wanted to crawl under something and hide.

Rose crossed both arms beneath her ample bosom. "Now settle down and we'll straighten this out." She indicated a straight-backed wooden chair. "Ben, sit. Dessa, behave yourself. You're acting like a spoiled child. I realize you've had a tough couple of days, but it's not Ben's fault. In fact, he's been more help than anyone, where you're concerned, and you need to recognize that."

"But I—"

Rose leveled a long finger at Dessa. "No! When I've finished."

Dessa clamped her lips shut. She only wanted to tell Rose that a decent woman did not have a man in her room while she was in bed, but obviously that didn't hold true in a brothel. She began to look around for an avenue of escape. It was entirely possible that Rose was setting her up for this clodhopper she was so fond of, and Dessa would have no part of it. Somehow she had to get out of here.

"Dessa, we offered you our hospitality, and we expect you to act like the lady you say you are. And Ben, you will apologize to Dessa for inadvertently barging into her room. She will be staying here for a few more days and I'd appreciate your remembering that and giving her the privacy she needs. Do you understand?"

Ben nodded, and then had the audacity to wink openly at Rose. The gesture infuriated Dessa. How dare the two of them talk around her as if she were deaf? They were the ones who didn't know how to behave properly.

"You go on to your fancy woman, sir," she said as sternly as her emotional state would allow. "And I will be out of this place just as soon as I can manage. I'm sorry if I have offended either of you with my manners." Her stern tone belied any penitence, but then to her horror she burst out crying and lost the advantage she imagined she had gained.

"Now look what you've done." Rose rushed to her side while chastising a befuddled Ben.

He gave them both a look that plainly said he would never understand women, and what's more, he wasn't sure he cared to, and then he slunk out of the room. The two of them had made him feel at fault for the entire episode, when all he'd wanted was for Virgie to give him a hot bath and rub his aching back with liniment.

Damn, that was the all-fired prettiest woman he'd ever seen, even when she'd slept and cried all day and didn't have any clothes on and her hair looked like a fly-away horse's mane. But he'd be blasted if he knew how to handle her. She had a mouth on her. That only made him admire her the more. There was no place in the territories for weakness. It was plain he was doomed to keep running into her in the most unexpected ways. And it was also plain that she'd as soon see him in hell as look at him.

Grumbling, Ben went in search of Virgie and his hot bath and massage, and maybe even something else, and to hell with them all.

Back in Dessa's room, Rose tried to comfort the crying girl. "It's all my fault, dear. Mine entirely. You've just been through so much and then I jump all over you some more. But please don't blame Ben."

Dessa dragged in a deep breath. Her eyes ached, her head pounded, and her throat felt raw. She had to stop this crying, and soon. And if people didn't

quit defending Ben Poole to her, she was going to
. . . well, she didn't know what she was going to do.

"He's like the old hound everybody in town feels
sorry for and pets and feeds," she blurted to Rose.
"And now he comes licking at my heels and I get in
all kinds of trouble because I don't want to pet him,
too."

Rose's mouth dropped open and she regarded
Dessa for a moment before bursting out laughing.
She whooped awhile, then slapped her thighs and
whooped some more.

The hilarity, even though Dessa didn't think what
she'd said was at all funny, proved catching, and after
a while she laughed away her own tears.

When both women had calmed down, Rose gave
her a big hug. "Now, you don't worry about how long
you stay. Ben won't bust in here again, and neither
will anyone else. When you feel ready, then you can
decide what you want to do, but until then, you're
welcome here. But honey, Ben is about as far from
being an old hound as you'll ever find, and I think
you'll learn that if you're around very long."

Dessa kept her silence, but she had no intention
of getting any better acquainted with Ben, no matter
how long she remained in Virginia City. The way he
made her feel wasn't natural, and it frightened her.
She'd been around men, been squired by the best,
and had never experienced such a range of emotions
as she did simply by being in the same room with
him. It was terrifying. It must be that he awoke the
animal in her. The one Mother always said was hidden in the best of females, the one that brought
about feelings that must be held in check at all cost.
Daddy had been a bit of a scalawag, had not always
succeeded in taming his wilder side, but he was a

man and that was to be expected. Women must control their baser desires, Mother would remind her often after she began to keep company with young men.

She had to be very careful indeed, for she might be just like her daddy, who on occasion had satisfied what she'd heard Mother refer to as his evil lust outside the marriage bed. A family secret mother shared with a few of her closest friends when she thought her daughter couldn't hear.

Dessa shuddered and snuggled deep under the luxurious covers. If she slept the rest of the day and night away, maybe things would look better come morning. Anyway, no one would think the worse of her for doing so after all she had been through.

Ben and Rose settled comfortably at a table where she could keep her eye on the entire dance floor so that no man might accidentally take advantage of one of her girls.

"Have any trouble on the trail today?" she asked over the foam-topped glass.

Ben glanced around, unable to keep his eyes from straying to the empty second-floor balcony and the closed door beyond. "Nope. Things have been pretty quiet since the killings. Must have scared them plumb to death. Walter have any idea who done it yet?"

"Hasn't said. Who do you reckon they were?"

Ben shrugged and downed half the glass of dark brew. "Yank's men, I'd say. But probably not the man himself. Being the kind of war hero some have made of him, I can't see him grabbing Dessa and trying to do her harm. The man may be wild as they come and willing to shoot a man who faces him off with a gun, but roughing up a woman? Not his style.

"In fact, I'd judge that he found out about those rascals' deed and did some punishing of his own. That may be the last we'll see of them around these parts."

Rose studied Ben intently. "You talk about him like you admire what he's doing."

"Nope. I just understand what the war did to men. No matter what side they were on."

"And you? What about you, Ben? What did the war do to you?"

He grinned in that lopsided way she so admired. "Hell, Rosie, you see me, what do you think?"

"I think men like Yank've got no excuse, not even the war, for robbing and killing, that's what I think. And you're proof of that."

His blue eyes clouded, flat as tarnished silver. "Since when am I so lily-white, Rose?"

"That wasn't your fault, Ben, and you dang well know it. When you going to quit flailing yourself about it?"

Ben finished the beer and stood. "I quit doing that a long time ago, but I don't aim to forget my responsibilities, either."

Rose sighed and got rather stiffly to her feet. It had been a long day. "You're a dear, sweet, stubborn boy, Ben Poole."

"And if I don't take myself off to bed, I'll be unemployed, too."

Ben reached the door and was putting his bedraggled hat on his head when a pale feminine face appeared in the darkness peering over the batwing doors. It so startled him that he jerked backward a few paces.

"Is Miss Rose there?" the woman asked in a wobbly voice.

Dumbstruck, Ben nodded. He recognized her, and wondered what the wife of Preacher Blair was doing out on the street this late at night. More important, what was she doing coming around the Golden Sun Saloon and requesting a meeting with its proprietor? Ben wasn't sure he wanted to stick around to find out, but his curiosity was such that he could no more leave than walk naked down the street at high noon.

"Please fetch her for me," Molly Blair ordered, her words crisper now as she gained courage.

"Yes, ma'am," Ben murmured, and backed up a few paces, bumping against a table. He righted a teetering chair and looked around for Rose. Seeing her behind the bar, he motioned.

Rose pointed at her own midsection and gave him one of those *Who, me?* looks. Ben nodded, darted a glance back toward the batwings to make sure he hadn't been seeing a mirage, then beckoned impatiently. The pale, moon-shaped face was still there, looking strangely as if it hung suspended all on its own.

Rose finally strolled over. She gave Ben a second look that told him she thought he had taken leave of all his good sense.

"Mrs. Blair is out yonder. Wants to talk to you."

"Who?"

"Mrs. Blair, Preacher Blair's wife. You know, Rose. The Virginia City Congregational Church."

Rose self-consciously touched her hair and straightened her low-cut dress. "What do you suppose she wants?"

"I don't know, but if you don't go see, I'm just going to go right up to her and plain ask. One thing's for sure. She don't want to dance."

Ben followed right on Rose's heels as she made her way toward the waiting woman. He overheard almost all of Mrs. Blair's curt request.

". . . outside here a moment, I would like a word with you."

"Well," Rose said quite loudly, and pushed open one of the double doors, "Why don't you come right on in and join me in a drink?"

Ben flinched. That wasn't what Rose should have said.

Molly Blair drew herself up stiffly. "I should say not."

She was a plain little thing, as one expected a preacher's wife to be; her sandy hair was pulled so tightly into a bun toward the top of her head that the corners of her small eyes slanted upward. Nothing about her, thought Ben, was remarkable except perhaps the primness of her lips and a flaring of her rather wide nostrils. Even if it were allowed, she wouldn't have been pretty.

"Well, then, Mrs. Blair," Rose boomed, "I'd say that if you refuse to come into my place of business, then we haven't anything to say to each other."

The nostrils made ready to spout flames. "Then I'll say my piece from this very spot, madam. I . . . we *ladies* of the church intend to see that Virginia City is cleared of establishments like yours and the riffraff it attracts. We want to make this town a safe place for decent folk to live in. A place where we don't have to cover our children's eyes and ears when we walk with them down the street. It's time you and your fancy women were run out."

Molly Blair delivered the entire speech looking

past Rose's shoulder, her hazel eyes hard with disgust. Ben felt like dodging the glare, standing as he was a little to the right of her aim and at Rose's back.

When the altercation had started, everyone in the hurdy-gurdy house stopped what they were doing. Even the tinkle of music from the Cremona had faltered and died. No one appeared willing to wind it back up. Dancers gathered in a scraggly line at the edge of the sawdusted floor, their partners gaping openly at the unusual conflict. A showdown between Rose and Preacher Blair's mousy wife might get more interesting than shuffling around in circles hoping for a fleeting touch of feminine flesh.

Even the Golden Sun's unflappable bartender, Grisham, was stricken dumb at the site of Miss Rose standing still for a tongue-lashing from Molly Blair.

The latter, evidently drained of the last of her courage, lowered her head, twirled, and clumped away before Rose could cut loose on her. The solid *chunk-chunk* of her shoes on the boardwalk echoed back out of the darkness and faded. Everyone, including Rose, remained silent for several seconds, then someone laughed nervously, and someone else joined him.

The piano was rewound, the bartender went back to drawing beer from the wooden kegs under the bar, and Rose planted her hands on her hips and whirled on Ben, her cheeks flushed redder than the paint on them.

"What in the thunder was that all about?"

He fiddled with his hat a moment, then finally screwed it back on his head. "I'd say you got yourself a battle to fight. But I wouldn't worry too much about it. She's pretty frail. Up beside you, she won't stand a chance."

"Get out of here, Ben Poole. Go crawl underneath your wagon and tuck that smart-aleck face down under the covers before I yank one of your ears off. Go on, git!"

Ben laughed heartily as he crossed the street and headed for the freight yard and his bed. He predicted that Rose would make short shrift of Molly Blair and her bunch of do-gooders. It might be a battle worth watching.

Chapter Six

The steady chime of a church bell awoke Dessa the next morning. She'd forgotten what day it was, perhaps even where she was, until that very moment when she lifted her head and gazed out the window toward the distant mountain peaks. No one had closed the drapes the night before and she was glad, for the blue sky and clean bright sunshine began her day quite nicely.

She was filled with a vague sense of relief that the funeral was over and done with. Maybe that was the reason society insisted on such an arduous death ceremony. It cleansed the heart and soul, finalized the most senseless loss in a civilized way. She wanted suddenly to attend church and complete the ritual circle.

After a quick wash, she fingered the black funeral dress hanging over the back of the chaise. It would do. But the underthings were another matter. After due consideration, she managed to don the shameful silken underwear, but absolutely couldn't bring herself to consider the black, lacy, totally disreputable corset. Not in church. Not even if no one could see it.

She dangled it in one hand and remembered how she'd looked yesterday when Rose bound her up in the thing. Why, it had shoved her breasts almost up under her chin. There'd been no strength to object when she was being dressed for the funeral, and certainly not to that bull-headed Rose. But Rose wasn't here today.

Dessa shook her head and made up her mind. She simply couldn't make herself put the skimpy thing on. She dropped it on the bed and wondered fleetingly if the wicked garment might belong to Virgie, the girl Ben Poole was looking for when he had burst into her room. Did he like his women to wear things like that?

"Oh, pooh." She slipped the dress down over her head and buttoned the bodice.

Settled in front of the mirror, she brushed at the long curly tangles of hair and thought how wickedly good it felt not to have the bindings of a corset inhibiting her every movement and breath. She hadn't imagined the freedom of such a thing until she actually tried it. And even better, no crinolines to make her dress stand out all around like an enormous balloon. It seemed not to be the style out here in the territories, where practicality had to come first. Nor had she seen even one of the newfangled bustles that were all the rage in Kansas City. Secretly she thought the bustle a sensible replacement for the ungainly crinoline with its laced ribs.

Perhaps on the frontier women weren't so starchy about what they wore. She must ask. The thought made her blush, however, since the only women she knew worked at the Golden Sun. Perhaps their opinion wouldn't be the best to judge by.

Leaving her dark, fly-away tresses hanging loose, she found the slippers she'd borrowed and the black hat she'd worn the day before, and rushed from the room. If she didn't hurry, she'd miss the services.

What a rowdy and improper girl Mother and Father would think her, running off late for church without even a pin in her hair and improperly attired. Thinking of her parents threatened to bring tears, but she batted her eyelids and swallowed down the thick burning sensation. Not today. Today would begin the life she must salvage, and it absolutely could not start with crying.

At the top of the staircase, intent on keeping the hat on her head and hitching up the long dress, she took a step down and bumped right into Ben Poole.

He grasped her arms to steady her. "Oops, I beg your pardon, ma'am."

She impaled him with an icy gaze. "Can't wait to get to your fancy woman, Mr. Poole?" Immediately, she wished she could take back the words. The very idea. Letting him see that she even cared what he was up to.

He swept his hat off and bowed from the waist. "You are about the fanciest woman I know." Then he tripped on up the stairs, chuckling maddeningly.

She vowed she wouldn't look, but she did. Stopped right there, squeezing the banister until her knuckles were white, and turned to watch him stride the length of the balcony. Muscles rippled, tightening the threadbare shirt across his back. She wanted to reach out to him, but didn't.

Ben had a hard time walking away from her and that's why he almost ran. What had come over him anyway? Touching her like that, tipping his hat and actually exchanging such flippant words. They had just spilled from his mouth like he had no control at all over himself.

Tapping at the door of Rose's room, he balanced on the balls of his feet as if readying for a race. The girl made him jumpy as hell. Made him feel like he was filled up with something hot and fuzzy that needed to escape and the only way it could was for him to leap and shout and roll about.

Ben laughed. Complete nonsense.

Rose called for him to enter and he slipped inside, still thinking about Dessa and how lovely she looked with her hair hanging down around her shoulders, a dark frame for her delicate features. And that one hand up trying to hold her hat on so that her breasts poked at the black fabric of her dress.

"Where's she going so early?" he asked.

"Well, good morning to you, too, Ben." Rose smiled sweetly.

"Oh, sorry. Good morning."

Rose nodded and motioned him to the small table in front of a sunlit window. "Join me for breakfast?"

Ben eyed the plate of thin pastries and the china teapot painted with pink roses. "You call this breakfast? She going to church, you reckon?" He slipped into the dainty chair and ate three of the little pastries in one big bite.

"Of all the things I've tried to teach you, instilling some manners would seem to be my biggest failure."

"These are pretty good, but there's not enough here for both of us. I'd better git on over to the Continental and order me up some hash browns and eggs and biscuits and ham and—"

"The day you eat at the Continental will be the day pigs fly, and that'll be quite enough of your foolishness, Ben."

He grinned lopsidedly. "Yes, ma'am." He sucked at a tooth. "She okay today?"

Rose laughed. "Why, Ben. If I didn't know better, I'd think you were smitten. I thought you wanted absolutely nothing to do with Dessa Fallon, and here you are. Can't even stay off the subject for one full minute, not even to talk about food. Just what's going on?"

"Aw, hell, Rosie, I don't know. What is going on? My best intentions are to cross the street when I see her coming, yet I bull right up in her face every chance I get. That's the all-fired prettiest woman I've ever seen."

"You've seen plenty of pretty women around here. There's more to it than that, and don't think I don't know it."

"Well, there may be, but I don't know what it is, I swear I don't. She isn't going to give me the time of day, and why should she? Look at me, Rosie. And look at her. Even with not a stitch to call her own, all red-eyed and swole up from grieving her parents, she's pretty as a field of daisies nodding their shiny white heads in the sunlight. That girl's had a hold on me since I carried her in out of the dark of night all bruised and battered.

"I wish you'd tell me how to get out of this. I've thought of just riding off and not coming back, but there's ties here I can't break and I just won't do that. I keep hoping she'll up and leave, and things will get back to normal, but she's not showing any signs of that.

"What do you think, Rosie, what do you think?"

"I think you're smitten, just like I've already said. And the best cure for that is to just walk right up to the girl and tell her so."

Ben's eyes bugged. "Aw, no. I couldn't. She'd probably knock me a windin'."

Rose chuckled. "Well, of course not in so many words. Make your move, see where you stand. If she keeps pushing you away, then you'll just have to get over her. But you know something, I'm not so sure she will.

"She's a spoiled little thing and a lot younger than her age. That's from being overly protected and pampered by her rich folks. She can overcome that, given the right inspiration."

"Well, hell, Rose, I've never been anybody's inspiration, now, have I?"

Rose sobered and gazed at Ben, remembering the first time she'd seen him, standing at her door, hat in hand, the package in his fist that Ramey had sent over from the Busted Mule.

She shook her head, steered her thoughts back to Ben. He'd grown a lot since that day five years ago, put on weight from the good food, and lost his haggard appearance. The haunted eyes that had seen so much death at such an early age had cleared since he'd come to Virginia City, his own death nipping at his heels. And she'd grown to love him like a son. But she did wish she could teach him not to take life so seriously, not to take himself so seriously. That episode with Sarah's husband had been tragic, and no way out of it. But he did so need to get past it. Until he did, she feared he'd have no life to call his own. This unexpected interest in Dessa Fallon might just turn the trick.

Things came, they went. You had to reach out and grab a taste, lest you missed everything life had to offer. And so what if that taste was all you got? Something else would come along.

"Ben, you just don't know what inspiration you've been to this old lady."

Ben leaped from the chair, unable to sit still another minute. "You, an old lady? Why, shame on you, Rosie." He leaned down and kissed her powdery dry cheek. "Love you, old lady," he whispered, and bounded from the room, slamming the door so that it made Rose's eyes blink and release the tears standing there.

Dessa walked backward after she got downstairs, wondering what Ben was doing up there and who he was doing it with. Virgie, she supposed. The idea made her cringe. And why on earth did she care anyway? He was an uneducated man with no promise of a future. He'd probably get killed some dark night out in the mountains riding on top of that freight wagon, and no one would even know it for days. How awful, how absolutely awful to have no family. If she didn't watch out, she'd get to feeling sorry for him, and then where would she be? It occurred to her, as if she'd been hit broadside, that she was now in the same position as Ben Poole. Neither had kith or kin.

Oh, Dessa, she scolded, *get yourself on to church before you miss everything but the closing hymn. And stop thinking of that unschooled heathen who wears his hat in the house and probably burps at the table.*

She imagined the domestic scene of she and Ben sharing a meal. He would lean back so his britches stretched tightly across his stomach and burp softly behind one of those big capable hands, and look across at her with vivid blue eyes outlined in black lashes.

Stop that, Dessa, right this instant!

She bounded through the door. Out on the boardwalk, she glanced up and down the street. The church was back up the way Ben and Wiley had brought her into town, and she headed in that direction. Only a few people were on the street. She passed an alley in which there sprawled an old, white-whiskered man. Sleeping off a drunk, she supposed. She met a bearded, rotund gentleman who tipped his hat and walked on.

Lifting her skirts, she descended a few steps off the walk into the street and cut across toward the rather innocuous wooden building with its small bell tower. The double doors were open, and from inside came the sounds of the congregation singing mightily. Obviously folks around here made up for their plain appearance by being robust in their worship. She slipped inside and into a back pew just as they finished singing the opening hymn and rustled and clattered into their seats.

She settled in and gazed at her surroundings. A wide plank floor, so new it smelled of freshly cut wood, hanging kerosene lamps, rugs leading to the altar. The wooden pews were plain and handcrafted. There was an organ up front and on the wall above the altar was written, "Glory to God in the highest and on earth peace."

Peace. How wonderful.

She took a deep breath and felt a certain peace, sitting there waiting for the preacher to begin.

He approached the lectern and she leaned forward in anticipation.

At that moment someone whispered in her ear, "Excuse me. Is this seat taken?" The speaker's breath feathered warmly over her cheek, and she turned to look right into the earnest face of Ben Poole. Their noses almost brushed. For a split second neither moved or blinked. Then she caught her lower lip in her teeth and leaned backward to escape the warmth exuding from his shiny, scrubbed countenance. Idly she wondered why he wore no facial hair, as was the style of most men. At first she had thought him perhaps no older than her, but now she could see tiny wrinkles at the corners of his eyes and minute tracks from the finely sculpted nostrils down to the corners of his generous lips. Noticing her attention, he lifted those lips into a tentative smile.

"Well?" he asked.

The woman seated in front of Dessa tossed a quick, obviously irritated glance over her shoulder.

"Sit and be still," Dessa said, and bundled the black skirt up against one hip.

He slid in beside her, crossed one leg over the other, and placed his hat on his knee. The next thing she knew, he had leaned his lips up right against her ear and said, "Yes, ma'am, I'll do that. And I thank you for reminding me of my manners."

She suppressed a smile.

Ben wondered what in the world he was thinking of. All along he had been sure that the best thing for him to do was to stay far away from Dessa Fallon, and here he was just plain daring her to be nice to him. Begging her to pay attention, when he knew what he should do was run the other direction as if his tail were on fire and her with more matches.

Still, maybe it wouldn't hurt to try out Rose's suggestions. She was right some of the time, especially when it had to do with men and women.

All he knew for sure was that ever since he'd barged into Dessa's room at the Golden Sun and got an eyeful of her in her nightgown in bed, he'd been acting crazy, at least in his head. And now here he was picking at her like they were in the first stages of courting. Him who had never courted a woman, least of all an upstanding one like her. Well, he wouldn't let it get too serious, that was all. He'd just have a little fun, then back off before she could smack him one across the head. He enjoyed the way her eyes sparked fire from their green depths when he annoyed her. Like coals burned down there. She was the first female he'd ever enjoyed actually being around in a man/woman kind of way. It felt good, and definitely not the same as being with Rose or Maggie. He decided to take advantage of it, short run that it might prove to be. Dessa would never let it go on very long anyway, and why should she?

She had never been so conscious of the presence of anyone as she was of Ben sitting so close to her. He smelled of shaving soap and saddle leather, all mixed up with an earthy aroma she couldn't quite identify. His large frame seemed to fill in all the spaces around her, and he emanated a sensual heat that was very pleasant and disconcerting.

She didn't hear a word of the sermon, and after the closing hymn was sung, Ben stepped past her into the aisle and let her move out in front of him. He then cupped her elbow with one hand just as if they were a couple and walked her outside, where they stood in the brilliant late morning sunlight studying each other intently. The spell was finally broken when a few of the young married women dragged their husbands over to introduce themselves to Dessa and again voice their condolences over the death of her parents. They were all very friendly with Ben, and he with them. It was easy to see that everyone liked him.

The glorious day, kissed by a cooling breeze off the distant mountains, overpowered any inclination

Dessa might have had to become depressed. It was much too lovely a day.

And as if reading her mind, Ben, who stood quietly at her side, leaned down and said softly, "It's a beautiful day. Do you ride?"

"Yes, of course, but I—"

"Rose has a pair of blacks that need exercise. I usually take them out on Sundays and give them a good run. Come with me."

She gazed at a glint of sunlight off a distant snow-capped peak that jutted into the crystal-blue sky. Imagined riding beside him across a meadow, wind blowing through her hair. Blowing through his.

"I don't have a riding dress."

"If you did, would you go?"

She looked up into his blue eyes, as brilliant as the sky, and nodded. Yes, she would. And probably rue the day, but yes, she would, and she told him so.

Less than an hour later they rode out of town up the rise toward Boot Hill, Dessa clothed in a borrowed riding outfit and sitting in Rose's gleaming leather sidesaddle. She glanced quickly toward the raw mounds of earth where her parents had been buried the day before, then looked away.

Ben didn't say anything until they turned their mounts and headed into the glorious afternoon. "You'll miss them, but they loved you."

She glanced quickly at him, saw that indeed the wind was tousling his shaggy hair, just as she'd imagined, blowing it back from the sun-bronzed forehead and jaw line to reveal well-formed ears with large lobes. A fine sheen of sweat glistened on the chiseled features.

Abruptly he returned her look and she turned away, embarrassed to have been caught studying him so closely. There were things about him that surprised her, and she wanted to figure them out. But doing so might lead to something she was afraid she couldn't handle. Like a physical attraction. At eighteen, she had just begun to taste of the sexual play between men and women. She knew flirting, enjoyed casual touching like lips brushing the back of a hand, a joining of palm to waist during a dance. No man had ever gone any further than a casual goodnight kiss, and that was only from Andrew. She could see that Ben might do more, and she might let him. But she had no notion why.

The black that Dessa rode—Baron was his name—was a spirited gelding with an arched neck and delicate legs and feet, not much like the sturdier mounts most horsemen preferred for the mountains. Ben rode its perfect match, a feisty mare called Beauty. She didn't seem to know her companion had been gelded and tossed her head to show off for him, prancing sideways and occasionally rubbing shoulders in a coquettish way. It embarrassed Dessa, but only because of where the flirtatious actions sent her own imagination. Ben Poole was paying court to her, whether he knew it or not.

"Here, you silly female," Ben scolded once when the mare actually moved so close that he and Dessa rubbed legs. "She thinks she can tempt him even though he—" Ben broke off, realizing that he shouldn't refer to animal sexuality in front of this girl. He saw why Rose despaired of ever teaching him good manners.

Dessa laughed. "She's just doing a little harmless flirting. He doesn't have to be equipped to enjoy that, surely."

"You are a bold little thing, aren't you?" Ben asked.

"Bold? Oh, you mean about the gelding. We had a lot of animals when I was growing up. Their behavior is a fact of nature, and nothing to be embarrassed about. Ben Poole, I do believe you're blushing."

He took off his hat and rubbed an arm across his forehead. "It's just the heat. I thought you were a city girl, brought up in Kansas City, you said."

"Well, in a way. Daddy built us a large house when he began to make money with the business, but it was out in the country. Later we had a place in town, too, where we'd live in the winter. I liked the farm, but Mother preferred living in the city. We had a little of both."

He nodded, reined the mare up. "Yonder, down through the trees, is a creek and some shade. Let's ride down and get a drink. It's getting mighty hot in this sun."

Dessa admitted to that, but questioned how wise it might be to ride off the main trail. "I thought you were supposed to exercise the horses."

Ben studied her tilted head a moment, then kicked at Beauty's ribs. "Across the meadow and back again. Come on, let's go." His shout vibrated through the hot afternoon, and Dessa kicked Baron into motion, maneuvering in the tricky sidesaddle when the gelding took off.

By the time they reached the edge of the meadow, they were neck-and-neck. Ben turned the surefooted mare, clods flew from under her hooves, and Dessa leaned into the turn and followed.

Wind dried the perspiration trickling from under her heavy hair; the gelding's shoulder and neck muscles gleamed. She smelled the animal's sweat and the freshly churned grasses and soil, and then the sweet, damp odor of water as they neared the end of their race, back where they'd started. Beauty won by half a head.

Laughing, Ben leaped from the horse before she came to a complete standstill, captured Baron's bridle, and let Dessa dismount on her own. She did so with agility.

"Not by much, you didn't win," she said, looking up into his openly joyful face. He almost became someone else when he loosened up and laughed. Another person, the one she'd only sensed earlier, came out from behind the frosty blue eyes.

"No, not by much. But a win is a win."

"And me on a sidesaddle, too. Too bad you didn't bet anything."

"Like what?" he asked, and began walking through the trees toward the sound of flowing water.

Dessa slipped off the pair of buttery riding gloves Rose had insisted she use to protect her hands, and walked along beside Ben, taking two steps to his one. They entered a shady glen and the temperature dropped a few degrees. She smelled mosses and wet earth and last year's leaf fall.

A gentle breeze tickled the thick foliage.

She lifted her hair off her neck. "Ah, that feels good."

He eyed the perky rise of her breasts and quickly looked away. It might have been a very bad idea, coming to this remote spot with a woman he felt so drawn to.

He cleared his throat and strolled on, keeping his eyes off his companion. At the edge of the creek he dropped the reins of both horses. Together the blacks stepped delicately into the water and began to drink. She watched them for a few moments. They were absolutely beautiful, long of leg, shanks rippling with muscle, taut bellies, and flowing manes and tails. There in the hidden glen surrounded by enormous trees and trailing brush and the splatter of sunlight, the perfectly matched pair made quite a picture indeed. How cruel the male couldn't fulfill his nature.

Ben watched Dessa. While he was conscious of the backdrop that she so much admired, what he looked at was her. The gold riding outfit that Rose had lent her accented her dark hair and pale skin. She looked much like a hothouse flower unexpectedly blooming in an untamed wilderness.

Then she turned and met his gaze. A patch of sunlight flickered in his hair. She licked her lips and took a step toward him, fascinated by the glowing halo around his head. Her heart kicked at her ribs when he moved toward her. In a moment, in just one more moment, they would touch. And she wanted that, reached out for it tentatively.

He took her fingers in his, leaned forward, and kissed the tip of each one. His lips were warm and moist, sending tingles all the way up her arm and straight to the sensitive tips of her breasts. She took a very deep breath, and instead of pulling away, moved a little closer.

He slanted a glance up through his astounding dark lashes, then lifted his head even with hers. She leaned forward ever so slightly and their mouths brushed as fleetingly as feathers in a breeze.

She batted her eyes and sucked in a lungful of air, and he turned loose of her fingers and put a little more space between them. She touched her own lips, still watching him but seeing that he stared at the ground somewhere between them.

"Ben?"

He began to shake his head vigorously back and forth, but he didn't say anything.

Her breasts pressed rigidly against the silken underwear that belonged, she thought, to Virgie, and between her legs a pulsating warmth grew. It felt so wonderful and so naughty she could hardly stand still.

He put the back of his hand against his mouth, then held it out to study the skin as if he could see remnants of the gentle kiss outlined there.

"Oh, Ben," she breathed.

"No," he said sharply. "I'm sorry. It's my fault. I didn't mean to do that. Rose always says I don't have any manners, and that's all that was. A lack of manners."

He felt ashamed of his pulsating desire, even more ashamed that he had let it show. She was young and innocent, probably not experienced at all in things like this. Now he had her all wide-eyed and confused, and he would have to hurt her to put a stop to it. Or maybe, like he'd thought before, she was only toying with him.

He turned his back on her, fetched the horses with a kissing sound. Looking back at the expression on her face, he saw that he already had hurt her with the explanation, the denial of his need.

Well, that was best.

He reclaimed the hanging reins. "Come on, you lunkheads, You'll bloat." His voice sounded angry, and he could see that hurt her more, but he couldn't help it.

"Want a drink before we go?" he asked, holding the gelding's reins out to her.

"Yes," she stammered, and fell down on her knees at the water's edge. She splashed the icy snowmelt up over her face and neck, gasping. After drinking from cupped hands, she arose and took the leather reins without looking at him.

They walked back to the trail single file, not talking at all. He went first, so that she had to stare at the haunches and swishing tail of his mare all the way out.

Chapter Seven

Rose had problems of her own the afternoon Ben and Dessa went riding, for Molly Blair accosted her right out on the boardwalk as she took her afternoon stroll. Still dressed in her Sunday best, Mrs. Blair epitomized a preacher's wife. She wore a plain brown frock, obviously inexpensive, with a matching bonnet properly tilted to shadow her face. The toes of her polished black shoes barely peeked from beneath the hem of her skirt. Her long, rather bony face wore an expression that warned she was armed for battle. So did the parasol she shook in the direction of Rose's midsection.

Rose's inclination was to yank the sunshine-yellow parasol from her own shoulder and use it as a defensive weapon. A picture of two women dueling with parasols on the streets of Virginia City on a sleepy Sunday afternoon tickled her fancy, and she couldn't help grinning.

Molly Blair was having none of it. Splotches reddened her angry features. "One of your girls was in our church this morning. Sitting right there in the front pew as bold as brass."

"I should think you would be pleased," Rose offered, not knowing what else to say. She couldn't think who the woman was talking about. Probably

Maggie. Occasionally she had an attack of religion. But to sit in the front pew? She'd best speak to her about that.

"Pleased? Pleased?" Molly Blair bawled.

Spittle sprayed Rose, but she held her ground. "Please control yourself."

"It isn't I who can't control myself. Do you think we want those dirty, filthy fancy women darkening the door of our . . . of our Lord's church?"

Rose didn't miss a beat. "I believe He welcomed them, didn't He?"

Molly Blair narrowed her eyes and took a deep breath. Rose thought for a moment she would swing the parasol at her, club her over the head for daring to know the Good Book. Instead the woman shuddered in a most unattractive way and continued in a soft hiss.

"You keep your mouth off our Lord. I warned you that this town has to be rid of such as you and your kind. I'll not give you another warning. We will see Virginia City a fit place to raise children."

Rose wondered who *we* was, since no one seemed to be accompanying the woman, but she didn't ask. What a pity such a young woman found it necessary to make life so terrible for herself and those around her. Seeing her this way, Rose understood why Preacher Blair always looked so dour, like he'd had his nose down in the vinegar jar.

Rose decided against battle, and said sweetly, "It's been so nice talking to you, Mrs. Blair. I hope we meet again. Perhaps you'd care to come to my place for a cup of tea. Do bring the reverend with you. I have some marvelous biscuits from London that I'm sure you and your husband would enjoy."

Rose twirled her frilled yellow parasol, angled it

over one shoulder, and strode off, bidding the woman good day in a bright, controlled voice. An explosion was about to occur and she wanted to be out of range.

Ben and Dessa rode past Rose a few seconds later, he and Beauty several paces in front of Dessa and Baron, and both riders staring forward as if alone.

Rose watched the couple dismount at the livery and turn the horses over to the stable boy. She wondered what in the world was wrong with those two. They walked stiffly away from each other as if they might catch some dread disease if they lingered. She supposed Ben had gone and put his foot in his mouth again. She'd have a talk with him. On the other hand, maybe it was Dessa who needed the talking to. The poor child hadn't much of a good-sense upbringing, thinking that everything happened either to cause her pleasure or pain. In that respect she was more like a child of ten or twelve than a grown woman.

Rose hurried to catch up with Dessa, but the girl was stomping along at such a frenetic pace she was inside the Golden Sun and halfway up the staircase before Rose could catch her.

"Dear child, where are you going in such a rush? What happened?"

Dessa just kept moving, stumbling on the top step and fairly running into the room Rose had so generously let her use. The door slammed in Rose's face, and she twisted the knob angrily, throwing it back open.

"The very idea, Dessa Fallon. Where are your manners?"

Dessa whirled, features furrowed and stern. "Don't

you start telling me what a fine man Ben Poole is or I swear I'll be sick!"

"Here, now, calm yourself down. No matter what has happened, you've no call to be so inconsiderate. Now sit down and tell me what Ben has done this time."

Dessa glared at Rose for a moment. Done? Done? What had he done? Nothing, and that was the problem. He'd brushed her off, just as smoothly as you please. But how could she tell Rose that?

"Well," Rose said, tugging off her yellow gloves and depositing them along with the parasol on the bed, "don't tell me he took advantage of you."

Dessa laughed harshly. "Not hardly. No, he didn't take advantage of me. Quite the opposite."

Rose stared at her a moment. Then the light dawned. "The opposite? You threw yourself at young Ben and he didn't want to play? Oh, child, how perfectly awful for you. And so now you're very angry and think you've been right all along about his unsuitability for such as you?"

Dessa threw herself down on the bed. "No . . . yes . . . I don't know. Oh, Rose, I'm not sure what's going on. I feel very strange when I'm around Ben. I know that he and I are worlds apart. We don't think alike, we don't want the same things, and we certainly have nothing in common. But he is so . . . so . . . oh, I don't know."

Rose sat beside the distraught girl and put an arm around her rigid shoulders. "Yes, indeed, Ben is so . . . and there's no word for it, is there? Well, there is a word for the way you're feeling, and you might just stop fighting it and let things happen naturally."

Dessa sighed. "Oh, yes, there is a word. It's whispered in drawing rooms when men think women aren't listening. It's lewd and disgusting, and I know I should be ashamed of myself for feeling this way.

"Men. I've been around a lot of men this summer, and none of them . . . I mean, my crowd, we would have a little fun, laugh and tease and run away and run back. And it was all so innocent. Then I come out here to this wilderness and the first thing that happens is I get caught up in the arms of that silent blond giant and I go all soft and gooey inside and I can't think straight and everything comes apart. And all he does is look at me with those big blue eyes. So serious but so distant, like he's not even seeing me." She put her hands over her face and dissolved in tears.

Rose pulled her close and smoothed strands of damp hair from the girl's face. "Lewd and disgusting indeed. Oh, sweet dear one, it's not so tragic to fall in love, it really isn't. Oh, sometimes it'll hurt like the very devil, but other times will make up for that, believe me. You'll know rapture such as you can't imagine."

"I'm . . . not . . . in . . . love," Dessa sobbed.

"Oh, that's what you think," Rose murmured. Then she added decisively, "Now stop this nonsense, wash your face and comb your hair, and let's go to supper. You'll feel better."

With the sweet-scented cloth from the washstand, Dessa scrubbed at her skin and dragged in a ragged breath. Suppose Rose was right. What would she do then? She really hadn't even decided what she would do about Andrew, the business, or returning to Kansas City; now she had to consider what she would do if she were falling in love with Ben Poole. Oh, what a mess. One thing piled right upon another, without a chance to take a breath. If this was what it was like to be an adult, then she wanted no part of it.

She had been so excited at her coming-out ball only last April. Prepared to take on the duties of a full-grown woman. To consider beaus and pick the one most suited to her family's lifestyle. Get engaged, marry, have children, run a household. Now look at her. Perhaps she should return to Kansas City and tell Andrew she would marry him. What other choices were there for a young woman without a family? If only Mitchell were alive. He always knew what was best for her.

An unbidden image caught her totally by surprise. A memory of the man who had lurked in the edge of the woods during her parents' funeral.

Thinking of him, she held the cloth over her face for another minute. Why did she feel so odd, as if something were about to happen that she'd been expecting all along? She shook her head and folded the cloth across the rim of the china bowl.

Turning to Rose, she asked, "Do you suppose there would be a home here I could rent for a while? I mean, if I decided to remain in Virginia City?"

Rose smiled with satisfaction. "I wouldn't be a bit surprised. Just what do you have in mind? Perhaps we could talk about it over our meal. I don't know about you, but riding out with a man always left me famished."

She cast a sly look toward Dessa and almost burst into laughter at the flush that spread over the younger woman's throat and face.

"We didn't . . . I wouldn't—"

"Well, of course not, child. Isn't that what you said? Well, maybe not quite. You said he wouldn't, but then it's almost the same thing, isn't it?" Rose might have treated the matter lightly, but she was quite concerned about this young woman, who, she would bet her bottom dollar, had never been with a man. She vowed to speak with Ben very soon.

Dessa trailed along behind Rose across the balcony and down the stairs and out the swinging doors. The beautiful dance hall owner was more outspoken than anyone Dessa knew. Nothing seemed to faze her in the least, and she would joke about anything she pleased. It was taking some getting used to, but it must be the way of people in the territories.

Daddy had said that only the very roughest and strongest made their way out here. Of course, he was speaking of businesspeople, but it must hold with everyone. Men and women alike. Dessa would like to think she was strong and tough enough to forge a life in this untamed place. Or was she only being romantic? Getting along on her own would be hard anywhere, but more so here. Women just naturally seemed to need a husband to survive in today's society. And she really knew no one here. Well, hardly anyone. Perhaps she should return to Kansas City, but the idea of facing that trip again so soon was appalling. In time she would go.

Seated at the table with Rose at the Continental House, considering the menu blocked out on a chalkboard, it suddenly occurred to her that there was one kind of woman who never seemed to need a husband. A woman like Rose.

Embarrassed at the thought, she said shyly, "Don't you ever wish you'd gotten married? Don't you ever need a man?"

Rose laughed. "I need a man every whipstitch, but a husband, no."

"It just seems so unfair that women have so little

chance of survival, here or in Kansas City, without a husband."

"Well, life didn't come with a guarantee that it would be fair, child. We all just do the best we can."

The words were spoken with such melancholy that Dessa decided not to press the issue. Had Rose lost her one and only love and been driven to a life of prostitution? How sad.

Later that night, she lay wide awake in bed, thinking over her decision to remain in Virginia City temporarily. And she thought of Ben and the way his crystal-blue gaze had regarded her so coolly after their lips had touched. As if he had not been affected at all. He had kissed the tips of her fingers. He had precipitated the incident. How dare he walk away afterward, as if it meant absolutely nothing? Was he only playing with her? And just before she fell asleep came the most important question. Was she only playing with him like she did those young *hellions* who pursued her in Kansas City's society? And if she was, she had a feeling Ben Poole, once aroused, would not be so easily deterred by a conquettish laugh and a door closed in his face.

The next morning Maggie brought in a breakfast tray and shook Dessa awake.

"Come on, honey, get up. It's almost ten o'clock. My goodness, everyone's asking about you. Are you feeling poorly this morning?"

Dessa rose to her elbows and peered across the dim room, blinking when Maggie swept wide the heavy drapes and let in brilliant sunshine. Did it never rain in this place?

"Who's . . ." she snuffled, not yet quite awake.

Maggie held out a steaming china cup. "Here, this'll get you humming. I hear you went riding with

Ben yesterday." Maggie drew up a chair, as if prepared to hear the whole story.

Dessa sipped at the aromatic coffee laced with thick cream. "My goodness, did he tell you that?"

"Well, no. He didn't. He's not talking at all, so I thought . . . I mean, Virgie saw you ride out and she said Ben looked like he'd been at the cream pitcher."

"Oh, she did?" Dessa squinted at Maggie through the steam of the coffee. "Does he still look that way this morning?"

Maggie grinned wickedly. "What'd he try? What'd you do?"

Dessa glared. She couldn't admit it was mostly the other way around, yet she didn't want Maggie to think the worst. "We didn't do anything but go riding. Oh, we had a race across the meadow and back. He won, but only by a nose."

"Oh, that sounds wonderful. Ben doesn't have much fun, you know. He's so serious all the time, like he never learned how to laugh. And I suppose he didn't, really." Maggie hesitated a moment and studied Dessa thoughtfully. "I'm glad you went with him."

Dessa was surprised. "I thought . . . I mean . . . do you love Ben?" She surprised herself more than Maggie with the question.

"Well, of course I do. But not like you mean. He . . . I . . . well, when I first met Ben, Rose sent him to me to, you know, to give him his first lesson in manhood, if you know what I mean."

Dessa had sat up and eased her feet off the side of the bed, and now she picked rapidly at the food on the tray so she wouldn't have to meet Maggie's honest gaze.

Maggie laughed. "Rose said later that she sent him

to me because he was so innocent and tongue-tied with her, and couldn't keep his eyes off her bosom. She thought she knew just what would cure his hankering. But more than that, he needed someone to care what happened to him. And so we never did it again. I just couldn't, you see. He needed . . . well, he needed more for someone to be his friend, to take the place of the sister he'd lost, the mother he'd lost, the soul he'd lost. Neither one of us thought doing it together was right after that."

Dessa slanted a quick look at Maggie's sincere countenance. How very intuitive of her to see such yearning in another person. She wondered what kind of compassion it took to realize when someone was so deep in despair. Briefly she also wondered if Maggie was being completely truthful about her feelings for Ben.

Maggie smiled shyly and shrugged her pretty creamy shoulders. Her propensity to go around half nude no longer bothered Dessa. It was the way of this place, she supposed. And wasn't it odd that she had grown used to it so quickly? It was time she moved out of here and to a place of her own, before she started acting as loose as the women here. Immediately she was ashamed of such a thought, and realized that if she'd spoken it aloud, she would have owed someone an apology. Would she never learn to rein in her judgments?

She nibbled at a fluffy biscuit. "Maggie, I don't think you should count on me to improve Ben's naturally sour disposition. We don't really get along too well."

"Oh, well, maybe not," was all Maggie said, but Dessa could tell the other woman didn't believe her for one minute. There was nothing she could do about that.

Someone rapped on the door. Thinking it might be Ben, Dessa dived back for the safety of her bedclothes, but when the door swung open, it was Rose.

"Dessa, Cal Reimer brought this a few minutes ago. It's from Cluney & Brown in Kansas City. I thought you might want it right away. Maggie, there's a fella downstairs asking for you. I told him it was kind of early to do business, but he said it wasn't business. I'd suggest you get dressed before you go down. From the look of him, seeing you like that might be his undoing."

Maggie flew from the room, her expression a study in confusion, and Rose backed out and closed the door, leaving Dessa alone with the telegraph wire.

She read it quickly, then took her time going over the words again. Someone had made a very generous offer for her daddy's business. Mr. Cluney thought she should take it. Would she return to Kansas City to take care of the matter? And by the way, he added, additional funds had been transferred to the Virginia City bank for her convenience.

She sank down on the edge of her bed, holding the paper open on her knees. Stop. No. Yes. The words darted through her mind. Why didn't they just handle this? What did she know about Daddy's business? It was too much. Why didn't Andrew handle it for her? He'd worked for Daddy for several years and was supposed to be her intended. Why did they bother her?

Once again, she felt hollow and bewildered at being totally alone in this strange wilderness. Here she sat with nothing to wear but a black funeral dress, no place to live but a brothel, no friends but a madam and her girls, with a young heathen who might or might not be courting her, and some stuffy lawyer wanted her to come home and face an unknown cigar-smoking businessman and discuss something about which she hadn't the slightest knowledge.

Well, she wouldn't go. That's all, she simply wouldn't go. Andrew and Cluney could take care of it for her. She had money in the bank, and what she wanted to do was go shopping for some clothes and a decent pair of shoes, and then find a place to live. And then she would search for the strange man whose image had haunted her since his fleeting appearance at her parents' funeral. Those were the things she wanted to do and so that's what she was going to do.

She crumpled the wire into a loose ball and tossed it on the bedside table.

During her afternoon shopping spree she must have walked every inch of Wallace Street. She marveled at the brick and native stone buildings with their Gothic windows set deep in massive walls. The office of the *Montana Post* newspaper sported such windows as did the territorial capitol building housing the headquarters hastily moved there from Bannack back in the gold rush days. She learned quickly that natives referred to the town as simply Virginia, and they were proud of their somewhat bloody past.

One storekeeper hurried to point out that in Boot Hill, along with ordinary citizenry, five of Plummer's road agents were buried. Plummer, he explained, was the sheriff who split his time between Virginia and Bannack wreaking havoc with his infamous road gang and enforcing law to favor his own thievery. Five of his road agents were hanged, the man said, on January 14, 1864. Plummer was to swing later, with his wife beating at her breast and begging the vigilantes to spare her man.

One of the worst of the outlaws was Helm, the man confided in low tones, who it was known was a cannibal. He once shared a human leg with a half-starved Indian.

She covered her mouth and gagged, horrified and slightly nauseated by the story. She couldn't tell whether the twinkle in the stout storekeeper's eye meant he was having her on or he just enjoyed the effect of his tale.

Laden with packages, she returned to the Golden Sun just at dusk. The dressmaker had promised her several frocks by the end of the week, and she had bought two ready-mades, one suitable for riding. She would ask Rose if she could take out the gelding she had so enjoyed riding the previous Sunday. She also bought undergarments and shoes, and was surprised to find a few of the styles she had left behind in Kansas City displayed in the shops of this territorial town.

Ben was leaning against the bar when Dessa struggled through the swinging doors with her armload of packages. One tottered atop the stack, fell off, and hit the floor. A hairy fellow shuffled to her assistance, but Ben beat him to it.

"I'll get that," he said, and grabbed the package right from under the man's outstretched grubby hand. "Here, ma'am, let me help you." He managed to dislodge some of the bundles from her grasp without causing the rest to fall, and followed her up the stairs and right into her room, bold as could be.

She let the parcels tumble to the chaise longue

and turned to him. "Thank you, Mr. Poole. Just drop them there, if you don't mind."

He blinked and instead of letting go his load just stared at her. Why was she being so proper, so formal? What had gotten into her? He figured at best to get hollered at for coming into her room, at worst to have something pitched at his head, and here she was sweet as honey.

"Well, have you lost your tongue?" she asked, and dropped down on the twin chaise. "Oh, Lordy, I'm tired. What a chore, and it's not done yet. I never thought to find so many up-to-date fashions. And what a pretty town. I hadn't really looked at it before. A shame there are so many empty buildings."

"It's the gold," Ben finally said, feeling as if his tongue had been permanently stuck to the top of his mouth.

"Gold?"

"It's gone, mostly."

She nodded, wondering if that really explained anything, and automatically reached up and unpinned the bun she'd managed to twist in her hair that morning. Long burnished locks tumbled down around her face.

He spoke her name under his breath and she looked up at him expectantly.

Under her soft gaze Ben forgot what he was going to say, and she sat there with her brows raised, waiting, making him feel totally foolish. He tried to imagine she was Maggie or even Rose, with whom he conversed easily, but it didn't work. She looked at him with rich green eyes sparkling away her recent sorrow, tilted her saucy chin and smiled, and he was lost. Speechless and lost. What a fool he was. The more he told himself to stay away from her, the more he couldn't seem to do so. And on top of that, now she insisted on being nice to him.

He cleared his throat and at last put down the packages. "Well, then . . . I'd better be going."

She waited until he was at the open doorway. "Ben?"

He stopped, shoulders hunched, but didn't turn.

"Thank you for the help."

It was all she said, and he found himself somewhat disappointed. He wanted to run away, but he wanted to stay and talk. He had hoped she'd say more, yet chastised himself for thinking as much. Who would want to talk to someone who couldn't or wouldn't talk back?

Dessa sat on the lounge listening to his boots *thunk-thunking* down the stairs. One way or another she would break that barrier of silence he so quickly constructed when he thought his privacy was being threatened. It had almost come down Sunday when he asked her to go riding, and downstairs just now he'd started in just fine and then clammed up. It was more than just shyness, she knew. Some of the things Maggie and Rose had told her explained his reticence. The more she thought about what he had endured during the war, the more she compared him to her brother Mitchell. Could they have met somewhere on a battlefield? Or, if not, surely they had both suffered incredibly during the dreadful battles in which thousands of men were butchered in only a matter of minutes.

She had never stopped trying to learn about the war, imagining Mitchell's involvement. Now she put Ben there, too. But he was only a child, not a grown man. No wonder he had problems dealing with ordinary day-to-day living. She grew more and more determined to break through the shell around Ben Poole. It might even help her deal with the loss of her brother when she herself was so young. This change of heart surprised her almost as much as her decision to remain in Virginia City for a while. Things were happening to her which she didn't understand. Maybe she was growing up.

All summer men had chased after her, pursued her with serious and not so serious intent. She was used to it and was frankly intrigued by one who turned tail when she slowed to be caught. Ben obviously didn't know any of the rules of the game, but that was okay. She could teach him.

Tomorrow she'd see about renting a small place to live. Perhaps for a month or so. Despite her desire to just forget all about Kansas City, she did realize that a decision must be made, and soon. She was responsible for Daddy's business and it wouldn't be long before the famed Montana winter snows began to fly. She'd never get out of the mountains and down to the railroad if she waited too long.

Chapter Eight

"You didn't touch that girl, did you?" Rose asked sternly of Ben. He had joined her for an early breakfast before pulling out on a two-day run for the Bannon Freight Company.

"Which one, Rosie?" he replied with a glint in his eye.

"You know which one, and don't pull that cute-little-fellow-in-short-pants act on me."

Ben chewed much longer than was necessary while he thought about the question. He knew Rose and Dessa were on friendly terms. What had Dessa told her about him, or had she bothered to mention him at all?

Rose pushed sternly. "Ben, I don't like the look of this."

"I kissed her hand a couple of times. She's a pretty girl."

"That's precisely what she is. A girl."

"Well, Rosie, if you think she can't take care of herself, you're mistaken."

Rose looked him over closely, the breadth and height, her eyes measuring with exaggeration the broad shoulders and long legs. "Don't be utterly ridiculous, Ben Poole. No woman her size would ever be a match for a man, even one smaller than you."

His eyes flared. "Well, dammit Rosie, I'm not going to attack her. You ought to know that."

"Maybe not, but you can be mighty persuasive and she's not experienced in the ways of men. If I hear you've taken advantage of her, Ben, I'll thrash you, see if I don't."

His anger cooled by a vision of Rose thrashing him, Ben laughed. "Now, there's a picture, sure enough, Rosie. Thrash me, indeed."

"I mean it." Rose set down her china cup and glared at the man she thought of as her son.

He shoved his empty plate away and stood. "I know you do, and so do I. I was just enjoying myself a little. She liked it and I didn't push. In fact, I sensed she was a bit put out when I didn't go any further. We were just having a little fun, Rosie. Hell, nothin' wrong with that."

She smiled up at him fondly. He was right, of course, and she was glad to see him enjoying something for a change, but she still couldn't help worrying about the impressionable Dessa, who took everything so to heart. She changed the subject. "By the way, the next time you get free, I wish you'd go over my books. They're all a mess again. Give them your magic touch."

"It's not magic, Rose, it's just pure horse sense. If you'd spend a few minutes every day writing down your figures, you wouldn't have so much trouble."

"Hogwash, Ben. You see things I don't even understand when you look at all that jumble of numbers. I'll swear I don't know where you got the knack, but I'm pleased you've got it."

"Just born in me, I reckon. Numbers make sense, even when nothing else does. There are rules and you can explain them." He wanted to add that unlike his own feelings, he could deal with the ink scratches in her books, but he didn't. "Wiley and me'll be back from Three Forks tomorrow afternoon. I'll come on by and fix you up."

"Thank you, Ben, and mind what I said about Dessa."

Ben grinned and crossed to the open door. "I tell you what, Rosie. You quit worrying so much about everyone else and think about yourself a little. I been hearing some rumblings about the fine upstanding women in this town and what they'd like to do to you and your girls. You might ought to talk to Walter Moohn. Those ladies are serious. They could cause you plenty of trouble.

"One thing's for dang sure, Ramey over at the Busted Mule is plenty worried about what they can do to his business."

"Well, he's always had him a yellow streak where women are concerned. I swear if one looks at him cross-eyed he crumbles into a little ball."

"Well, all the same, Rose, I'd be careful if I were you."

Right after lunch Rose and Dessa located a small empty dwelling near the end of Main Street that appeared quite suitable for a temporary home for the younger woman. Through the murky windowpanes they could see that there were two rooms but no furnishings.

"I can order a divan and some tables for the parlor," Dessa said. "Then I'll need a bed and washstand and armoire."

Rose marveled at the lilt in the girl's voice. Perhaps this was a good idea after all, for it seemed to perk her up just having something to do.

"I would think Arliss could fix you up with a bed

right away. He's a right handy carpenter. Then, if you wanted to go ahead and move in while you waited for the rest of your things, you could. I'd be glad to loan you a feather bed." She tilted her head and regarded the girl a moment.

"You know, out here a woman who owns two kettles, a cast-iron skillet, and a coffeepot considers herself well off."

Dessa grinned, not sure if Rose was teasing, then threw her arms around her friend and hugged her right there on the street. "Oh, a feather bed would be wonderful, and so will sleeping in my own home again. Oh, not that I don't appreciate your hospitality, Rose. But I feel like I'm putting someone out being there, even though you say not."

Rose frowned. "I worry, though, about a young girl like you living alone. Won't you be frightened? There are some mighty unsavory characters n Virginia, sad to say." She pursed her pretty red lips and thought about what Molly Blair had said concerning the Golden Sun and the girls there. It was all in how you looked at a thing, she supposed. But still she couldn't' see that she and her girls were doing harm to anyone. They didn't, after all, go out on the street and drag men in against their will. It wasn't quite the same.

"Don't be silly, Rose. Right here on this well-traveled street? The sheriff keeps a lookout and his deputies, too. If it will make you happy, I'll put that lock on at night." She indicated the cumbersome padlock fastened to a hasp on the outside of the entry door.

"Arliss can put one on the inside as well. I think that's a good idea. Well, if you're sure this is what you want, let's get over to the bank and find out how we go about renting this place for you," Rose said, and took Dessa's arm.

When Ben and Wiley Moss rode back into town the next afternoon, worn out and dusty from the round-trip freight run to Three Forks, they noticed bright curtains on the window of the old Kraft place at the edge of town. Kraft had been one of the first prospectors to hit gold out at Alder Gulch, and he had thrown up the two-room plank house for him and his partner, no doubt thinking it a mansion after camping on the banks of a creek so long. Others had soon followed suit until the dwellings and their privies out back looked like a scattering of giant play blocks tossed across the town by a careless child.

As the wagon drew abreast of the house, the door swung open and out stepped Dessa Fallon in a bright blue dress and bonnet looking as much at home as any young woman in town. She looked up at the rattling of their passage and spied Ben.

Her hand came up in greeting, and Ben silently raised the Winchester above his head.

Wiley eyed him out of the corner of his eye. "Wanta git off?"

"Nope," Ben answered, and lowered the rifle.

"What it was, I seen you two lookin' at each other and figgered you just might want to be saying more than howdy." Wiley popped the leather reins on the horses' rumps.

Ben didn't answer, but he couldn't help turning to watch Dessa walk up the street in the direction of the Continental. Going out to supper, no doubt. Well, she could afford such a highfalutin eating place. He had to settle for beans and cornbread at

Doolan's, or at best Sunday fried chicken at the Montana House.

What was she doing at the Kraft place? Surely she hadn't moved in there. With that one, he wouldn't be too surprised at anything she did. He found himself hoping that she would still be at the restaurant when he got cleaned up. He'd saunter in just like he belonged and sit with her awhile, order a glass of iced tea or cup of coffee, casual as hell, and hope he could afford to pay for it. Maybe he could even think of something clever to say to make her laugh. She'd look up at him, her eyes would shine with mirth, and her pink lips would widen so those pretty white teeth could peek out. He had a powerful need to be in her company, and just thinking about sitting across the table from her made him shiver.

For a moment after he stepped through the door of the Continental twenty minutes later, Ben thought Dessa had already eaten and gone. Then he saw her sitting off in one corner. Despite the lamp on the table and the hanging chandelier, pools of darkness shadowed her features. All the same, he didn't need to see her face to know it was her.

It was going to be difficult to casually detour clear to the back of the restaurant and appear to accidentally spot her, but as it turned out, he didn't have to. Dessa looked up, saw him, and lifted her hand ever so slightly. He nodded, smiled, and made a beeline for her.

With an attempt at cool composure, she watched Ben approach. His hair was wet; he'd tried to slick it down with little luck. A few curls hung along the collar of his shirt and over his ears. She wanted to trail her fingers through the thick mass and was shocked at the unexpected desire. With delight, she noted that he had left his hat on the rack at the door, so he didn't make a habit of wearing it to the table like she'd suspected.

Resting her chin on folded hands, she glanced up with a deliberate coquettish flutter of her long lashes. She couldn't help but giggle, and said, "Won't you please join me, Mr. Poole?"

He pulled out the chair next to her. "I'd be most proud, Miss Fallon."

"I was hoping you'd come."

"Me, too," Ben said.

They both laughed.

Dessa sighed and lifted her napkin, then refolded it. "Well," she finally said.

"Yes. Uh, I saw you earlier. Coming out of the Kraft place. I thought it was empty . . . I mean, who were you visiting?"

"I wasn't visiting anyone. I rented it. I live there. Isn't that wonderful?"

"Alone?" He thought her youthful excitement quite refreshing, but he wasn't sure how he felt about her living alone.

"Now, don't you start on me, too. I had to convince Rose."

"No easy feat."

Laurie Sue came to their table to ask if Dessa wanted dessert and if Ben wanted anything. That forestalled any further discussion of Dessa's living arrangements for the moment.

They ordered blackberry cobbler and Ben asked for a large glass of milk, hoping he had enough money on him to pay for it.

Dessa watched him devour the large serving of cobbler and offered most of her own to him.

"Take it, I'm so full," she said, and held up the

dish, her spoon still sunk deep in the sugary purple crust.

He took the offered dessert and had the spoon in his mouth before he realized she had licked it. He held it between his lips too long, staring across the table at her and thinking of her small pink tongue lapping at the silver. Her gaze went from his lips clamped around the spoon to his gleaming eyes, and then she caught on, too.

He pulled the spoon free very slowly before licking it front to back and placing it in the dish. Gazing directly at her, he took a big drink of milk.

Dessa patted at her lips with the napkin. He was deliberately sending her a message, and she knew if she picked up on it, he would do just what he'd done when they went riding. Back off like a scared rabbit. She wasn't sure what kind of game this was, or if it was just his way, but she was determined to thwart him, one way or another, before the evening was over.

When they finished, Dessa waited for Ben to pull her chair back from the table, until she realized that he was up and gone, already headed across the room. He could do with some civilizing, but then she'd known that all along, hadn't she? And wasn't that one of the things that attracted her to him?

He stopped to pay his bill, and was shocked when the man handed him the tab for Dessa's meal as well. Amazed, Ben studied the figures. Three dollars and forty-nine cents for supper? Another two bits for his cobbler and milk? Hell, he could buy a whole supper down at Doolan's and wash it down with a beer for what his alone cost. Worse, he didn't have that much on him.

Dessa stood against his arm, peered over at the

two slips he held in his hand, and took hers away from him.

"You didn't ask me to supper, Mr. Poole. I certainly don't expect you to pay for it," she said loudly enough for those nearby to hear.

She noticed that Ben's ears turned red, but he didn't protest. Probably didn't have any money, maybe not even enough to pay for his own.

"Give me yours, too," she whispered.

Ben pulled it away from her reach, mumbled low, "No, I can pay my own."

"No, it's okay. I'll pay it," she hissed.

"You will not," he said aloud.

Several of the diners turned their heads to stare, and the man waiting for them to pay glared hard at Ben.

"Stop being such a dolt," Dessa said.

"I am not a dolt." Ben tossed two coins on the tray the man held imperiously before him and slammed out of the restaurant.

His heels came down so hard on the boardwalk they could be heard all the way up the street to the Golden Sun. He jammed his hands down in the pockets of his britches to keep from flailing them around in the air above his head as he muttered to himself.

"I'll show her dolt. Blasted spoiled little imp. She needs a daddy to give her a good spanking, that's what she needs. Too bad she ain't got herself any folks to teach her how to behave."

He reached the Golden Sun and was almost past the doors when he remembered his promise to Rose about straightening out her usual financial mess.

"Ah, dang it all and hell's bells." He was in no mood to put up with another woman, even if it was

Rose. All he wanted to do was ride out of town and sit on a damn rock and stare off into the night, so he just kept right on going.

A half-moon hung high in the sky, and as the sun crept behind the mountains to the west, its silvery light played peekaboo with the darkness. The elongated shadows cast by the buildings across the way looked like outsized tombstones shaped to fit all the men he had seen die in the war. Men who lay in mass graves, their bodies unclaimed. And striding along, he imagined the thunder of cannons, felt the solid jar of the earth up through the soles of his feet, and heard the eternal cry of that child he'd been.

Off in the distance a coyote set up a forlorn howl that fit Ben's mood like a coat. He definitely needed the soothing of a child's small hand in his. The softness of an innocent babe's cheek against his stubbled jaw would drive away the long and lingering memories. He'd ride out to see Sarah and the children, and everything else could just be damned. Rose and her books could just wait another day. She couldn't get them in much more of a mess than they already were.

He went down to the stable and asked for Beauty. Rose had left standing orders that he could have her anytime he pleased, and so no questions were asked. He saddled quickly, more anxious than ever to hold the babies in his arms and listen to Sarah's soft voice forgiving him once more.

Dessa had rushed away from the Continental as quickly as she could after Ben's rowdy exit. She didn't know what she'd expected of the rough frontiersman. Yet something deep inside her flared with compassion. He had been embarrassed and so reacted in the only way he knew. However, the scene went a long way toward convincing her that she and Ben Poole had nothing whatsoever in common. She just wished she could forget the touch of his warm lips on her hand, the way his frosty eyes thawed when she gazed into them, his heart beating under her cheek when he carried her in his arms—twice now—with such tenderness.

It was dark under the eaves of her new home when she arrived, and she had to work awhile to fit the key into the padlock. Arliss had left the original padlock on the outside of her door since the bank had given her the key, and merely installed a second hasp on the inside so she could lock herself in at night.

"Was a time nobody had to lock up," he explained, "but this town's got so wild, young woman like you has to be extra careful. All the riffraff and all. Wouldn't do to leave the latchstring out."

Dessa had instantly liked Arliss Long, a windburned and skinny old prospector who had hung up his pan and settled down to do odd jobs around town when the gold findings played out.

She was affixing the inside padlock when there was a rap on the door. At first she thought Ben must have followed her, but she dismissed that instantly. He had been much too embarrassed and angry, and was nowhere in sight by the time she exited the restaurant.

"Who is it, please?" She left the key inserted in the lock, waiting for a reply.

"Sheriff Moohn, Miss Fallon. I've got something for you."

Dessa unlocked the door and opened it. "If you'll

wait just a moment, I'll light a lamp. It grew dark while I was gone."

"These little places are plumb gloomy inside all day long, what with those tiny little peepholes of windows. I expect folks who built them didn't want to pay for glass, or just couldn't be bothered, seeing as how they spent their whole entire days and much of their nights out on some rocky stream bed panning for gold."

While the laconic sheriff drifted inside and made conversation, Dessa found the lamp and matches just where she'd placed them on a wooden crate that served as a temporary table. She removed the globe and lit the wick. Once the flame was adjusted, she slipped the glass back on and turned to face Walter Moohn. He held a wrapped parcel in one hand, his hat in the other.

She gestured around the parlor. "I'm sorry I can't ask you to sit, but I have no furniture yet to speak of."

"Doesn't matter, ma'am. I'm plumb ashamed of myself for forgetting this, but in all the excitement and getting up the posse and everything, I forgot. This must have belonged to your folks, Miss Fallon. Like I said, I'm sorry I didn't get it to you before this time.

"I was rummaging around through the safe this evening and run across it. That's the first I've thought of it since the fire and the stage robbery and everything. I apologize, and hope it wasn't something you needed."

Dessa had gazed at the parcel through his entire explanation, scarcely hearing his words. She recognized the brown paper wrapper, could tell right away it was taken from a roll of paper like that commonly used to wrap purchases in mercantiles. It was tied with plain white twine.

"I'm not sure what it could be."

"Well, ma'am, I'm not, either. All I know is it was laying out a ways from the upstairs window of the mercantile, you know, like it had been tossed out there when they seen they couldn't . . ." He paused and licked his lips.

Dessa grew extremely conscious of the sound of his tongue on the parched flesh and the flutter of the flame in the lamp. She felt as if her heart had stopped beating. Outside, someone shouted and a horse galloped away, making her jump.

Everything in her mind said grab hold of the package, hold it to her breast, take in the feel of her mother's hands as she wrapped the thick paper, tied the wrinkled string. But she couldn't lift her hands, take the package, though Sheriff Moohn held it so that it was almost touching her.

Unable to reach out, she swayed and closed her eyes. Flames tried to swallow her up in their heat and fury, curling around her toes and licking upward. The heat, the pain! Oh, poor mother. Poor dear daddy. She couldn't bear thinking about it.

Gasping, she said, "I . . . I can't . . . I mean, thank you so much. Could you just . . . would you please just put it there on the table beside the lamp? I need . . . I want to . . ." To her astonishment, tears gushed from her eyes and sadness overpowered her so that she almost collapsed to the floor.

Moohn grabbed her by one elbow and got rid of the parcel so he could support her. "Well, now, there, there. I didn't mean to upset you so. Can I get you anything? Could I go get Miss Rose for you?"

Dessa shook her head vehemently. It was time she

stopped leaning on everyone else. She had to learn to handle this grief; she couldn't just continue to expect someone else to take care of her. The unexpected tears were maddening, but she couldn't make them stop.

"No, no, thank you," she managed. "I'll just retire for the night. Please, just go now."

"Are you sure?" The lanky sheriff gazed closely at her. "You're pale as a sheet. Just let me get Miss Rose."

"No," Dessa shouted. She held out her hands, as if to soothe the distressed sheriff. "I'm sorry, no. I'll be fine."

"Well, if you're sure. I'll just go, then. If you need anything, you just open this here door and holler, and one of my deputies will be right here, you hear me, now?"

She nodded, unable to utter another word past the raging sorrow boiling up in her throat. Why didn't he just go, leave her be? Let her throw herself on the bed and cry this away?

Finally he did, and she didn't bother to lock the door before stumbling into the next room and throwing herself facedown on the sweet-smelling feather bed Rose Langue had provided.

The half-moon hung on the lip of the mountains to the west when Ben rode back into Virginia City. The *clop-clop* of the mare's hooves sounded hollowly in the silent town. Down the way, lights glowed in the Golden Sun, and farther on, the Busted Mule showed signs of some activity. Otherwise the streets were as still as those of a ghost town.

A large bird soared overhead, flying so low Ben felt the air stir with its passing. An owl out on its nightly hunt. He reined in the mare to watch the black shadow swoop to the ground, then glide back into the sky. The bird's passage blotted out the light of the moon for a split second and Ben blinked. For no apparent reason he could think of, he felt the sting of tears. He never cried, yet here he was getting all wet-eyed. What nonsense.

Lord God, what a night. The air was as soft as down, yet he could sense, creeping in around the edges, the coming snows of winter in the mountains. Yet another winter that would find him with no home to speak of.

He realized that the mare had come to a halt right in the middle of the street, and he made a kissing sound to her. She started, as if he'd awakened her, and Ben chuckled despite himself.

"Your bedtime, too, honey?" he asked, and headed her toward the livery stable.

He didn't slow when he passed Dessa's, but took note of a pale light still burning in the main room. She probably fell asleep and left the lamp turned on. What a waste, but he supposed she could afford to burn up all that coal oil for useless light.

After he left the mare at the livery, Ben walked back down to the Kraft place. To Dessa Fallon's place. He could no more have stopped himself than he could have followed in flight the owl he'd seen night hunting.

The door was off the latch. Foolish of her. Anyone could walk in. He grinned and eased it open, wincing when the boards creaked underfoot. If he awoke her, she'd be frightened, might even throw a lamp at him. Maybe could kill him outright, for all he knew. He paused in the doorway to the small bedroom and listened. Her breathing was wispy, but if he held his own breath, he could hear her inhale and exhale.

His heart began to pound in his chest and he held the flat of one hand over it. Surely she'd hear. For a moment he closed his eyes and breathed deeply of her scent, thinking of an early morning, dew-frosted meadow. A taste filled his mouth, the golden sweet taste of her skin, and he crept through the soft glow of the lamp to the side of her bed.

In sleep she looked even younger than when she was awake. One hand lay palm open beside her cheek, and the thick dark hair spread all around her head. Long eyelashes touched the pale cheeks like a dense fringe.

He felt a painful urge to touch her, kiss her, hold her like he'd done when he carried her into his life. Not knowing then that such a simple, effortless act could so interrupt his existence. Sucking in a breath, he bent and left a faint kiss on her forehead.

"Sleep well, Dessa Fallon, sleep well. I'll try not to mess up your life too much. If I can help it." He tiptoed silently away. "If I can help it," he repeated as he pulled the door closed and stepped out onto the boardwalk.

He only hesitated a moment before he snapped the outside hasp shut and fastened the lock through it. It would keep her safe, and she could get someone to open it for her come morning. He had to smile a little when he thought of how mad she would be when she awoke and found herself locked in. Of how she might even come looking for who would do such a thing.

She shouldn't be so careless, though, alone like she was. She just shouldn't be so damned careless.

Chapter Nine

The next morning Arliss came pounding on the door, waking Dessa. She had to throw her key out the slot of a window so he could open the lock. There was little time to wonder how the thing got fastened on the outside. By the time she had quickly dressed, Arliss and a young boy he called Thad had carried a three-drawer chest into her house, saying someone had ordered it, then didn't pick it up and it was just in his way. She insisted on paying him a fair price for the piece of furniture, and asked the men to place it in the smaller room. The dresser went well with the frame and headboard Arliss had fashioned of pine. With the borrowed feather ticking and bright patchwork quilts, the room took on a homey appearance.

As soon as he turned loose of his side of the dresser, Thad received a curt nod from the older man and raced out the front door. Down the street she heard the shouting of young voices and supposed he had gone back to his play. Children here on the frontier did little enough of that and she listened to their laughter with pleasure.

When she turned her attention back to Arliss, she saw he stood in the center of the small parlor, measuring the wall space with a length of cord, squinting his small brown eyes thoughtfully. He wore a leather apron that hung to his knees. Under it were the homespuns most frontiersmen wore, faded so that not much color remained.

"Could use a few pieces in this here space," he drawled, indicating with both hands the length of one wall. "Yonder, you'll have to put a stove ere you freeze come winter. See the pipe hole covered over there in the ceiling."

Dessa smiled secretly at his salesmanship. He would end up making every piece of furniture save the stove and divan. She didn't mind at all; he was a fine craftsman who never left rough or sharp edges and finished his work with flair. His talk about a stove moved her thoughts to the summons from Cluney & Brown to return to Kansas City. Perhaps she wouldn't be here to need a stove. Shaking her head over that unanswered question, she said, "I could use a table and chairs. I've ordered an upholstered divan."

Arliss grinned and revealed a gap center front where he was missing a tooth. "Case a young gentleman comes to call, you mean?"

Folks out here sure put themselves right into your life. She wondered if she would ever get used to their casual familiarity.

Arliss rubbed the callused palms of both hands down the front of his leather apron, making a scraping sound. "Table and chairs it is. Got any preferences other than they be usable?"

Dessa smiled at him. "No, usable is just fine. Whatever works best." She didn't ask him how much they would cost.

"I reckon I could have them brought by in a week or ten days. Got some other pieces to put together.

Women moving in means more work for me. Man, he's satisfied with a chair or two, maybe a bed, and he can knock together a plank table hisself that'll suit him just fine. But you women get turned loose in a house, and you want her right fancy. Oh, I ain't griping, mind. Good for my business.

"Made all the benches and desktops for the school, made the church pews." He laughed. "Funny, ain't it, how they'll build a school first, then a church? Women is right down funny, when you get to it."

"I reckon," Dessa said absently, then looked up at the man in surprise. Reckon? She was beginning to sound like these frontierspeople.

Arliss backed toward the door, which he'd left standing open, as was the custom when a man entered a single woman's room. "Lock working okay for ya?"

Dessa nodded. "Oh, yes, just fine. Thank you."

"I noted it was locked on the outside and was wondering if something is wrong with this one in here." Arliss tugged at the hasp.

"Uh, no. I don't know ... I mean, I thought ... Never mind, it was just a mix-up. Both are working fine."

Arliss squinted at her a few seconds, then nodded and backed out, pulling the door closed with a firm thud.

Who had locked her in last night, and why? She pondered that a few moments, then shrugged. Probably someone came along whom she knew and simply decided to lock up. It wasn't, after all, a dastardly deed, though it might have been bothersome had she not been able to get someone's attention right away. Dismissing the minor mystery, she whirled around in the pleasant room. She could imagine a warm fire in a potbellied stove, a floral print divan, maybe a fine sideboard over on the other wall. She could get one of those stoves that she could use both for heating and cooking. There was room for the table and chairs over there by the window near where she would put the sideboard. It would hold dishes and she could order a mirror to hang above it to reflect the room, and sunny yellow curtains to make the window look larger.

What was she thinking of? She was going back to Kansas City before the snow flew, wasn't she? This was only temporary, wasn't it?

In the bedroom, she began to fold her few articles of clothing into the chest of drawers. With trepidation she picked up the package the sheriff had delivered the night before. The wrapper crinkled under her fingers. It was just a package. Something her mother or father had thought valuable, perhaps. Or maybe it belonged to someone else. Someone who dropped it earlier and it just wasn't found until the fire. Not likely, though, she realized. No, this belonged to Mother, she was sure of it. She hugged it close for a moment, then placed it in the bottom drawer of the new chest.

Some evening she would open it, but not today. The day was too beautiful to be ruined by a fresh round of grief. After a night's sleep she was no closer to a decision as to what she would do. Go or stay. Go or stay. And what about Ben Poole? She really wanted to explore her feelings where he was concerned. And that was not easy to do, with him backing off at every turn. Maybe she could think of some way to get to know him better. Get him talking about himself and his dreams. There must be feelings fit to burst buried in a man like him. It wasn't a thing Dessa Fallon had ever had to do, woo a man. They had always come to her the minute she raised an eyebrow or crooked a finger. Ben came, sure enough, but then he ran away again. It was frustrating to be so attracted to him, only to have him flee before she could put a finger on what the attraction was.

Dismissing her wandering thoughts, she fetched her reticule from the bedroom and stepped outside into yet another glorious morning. Living in Missouri and on the banks of a river, she had grown used to long, wet days in September, fogs rising up off the water of an early morning. This dry mountain air was sweeter than a rose garden, cleaner than the streams that flowed down from the snowcapped peaks, and the indigo blue sky just spread out forever, bigger than anything she had ever in her life imagined. Montana Territory was indeed a marvelous place.

Gazing up into the morning sunlight, she turned a circle on the boardwalk and breathed deeply.

"A good morning to you, ma'am," a voice called, and she heard the familiar rattle of the freight wagon rumbling down the street.

Perched on the seat, Wiley Moss held two handfuls of leather reins, so he couldn't wave, but she knew it was he who had called out. Ben sat on the other side of Wiley, and appeared not to even be looking her way.

She sang out, "A very good morning to you, Mr. Moss, and you, too, Mr. Ben Poole."

Ben actually lifted his hat and leaned out where he could see her, but he didn't say anything at all. Hands clasped in front of her, Dessa watched the wagon until it curved out of sight around a bend outside of town. Raising her shoulders in a silent question, she headed for the Continental House for breakfast. She figured Rose would be there and they could visit awhile.

Rose patted the chair beside her when Dessa approached her table. "You look very well this morning, child. I believe you're finally on the mend. This mountain air will do it every time. Healing, that's what it is."

Dessa slipped into the chair and removed her gloves. "I'm in the mood for something special this morning."

"Perhaps a mushroom omelet. Or champagne with fruit. Have you ever drank champagne for breakfast?" Rose asked with a sly smile.

"Why, yes, I have. Do you think Kansas City is uncivilized? But don't tell me they have such cuisine here?" Dessa looked around the room.

"Katrina serves only the best. Her chef is from Switzerland."

Dessa raised her brows, impressed. "Well, then, I do believe I'm in the mood for champagne and perhaps melon. If that's what you're having."

Rose guffawed. "Hate the stuff, myself. I'm having an omelet, so light and fluffy it may float off the plate when the waiter carries it in. But do have your champagne, dear."

Rose took a sip of coffee, eyed Dessa over the cup's rim. "By the way, I thought you might enjoy attending a concert at the Opera House Saturday."

"A concert?" Dessa's eyes widened. "Oh, yes, let's do."

"Fine. But I won't be going, I'm too busy on Saturday nights. I have arranged for Desmond Venable to accompany you. He's eligible and should be com-

patible. Not as rough around the edges as our Ben."
Rose slanted a crafty look at Dessa.

What was she up to now? First she encouraged
her to take up with Ben, now she was shoving her in
another direction. Dessa didn't know what to make
of the situation, but didn't want to miss the chance
to enjoy a concert, whomever the escort.

So she agreed, and the matter was settled. Even as
she popped the first bite-sized piece of golden melon
into her mouth, Dessa couldn't help thinking of Ben
Poole, riding out across the rough countryside in the
dust and hot sun. Had he ever drank champagne for
breakfast? For that matter, had he ever drank champagne at all, or attended a concert or a ball? Probably
didn't even dance. Much as she had noticed his
presence when she stayed at the Golden Sun, she'd
never seen him dancing with the girls.

She didn't see Ben again until the night of the
concert. She wore a new dress, crimson with tiny
pale pink flowers and a full skirt. Mrs. Fabrini had
done a marvelous job with the fit. The waist hugged
her slim figure and the puffed sleeves were just the
perfect length. Gloved hand tucked into the crooked
elbow of Desmond Venable, she strode languidly
along the boardwalk, feeling almost as if she were
carefree once again.

Desmond was a pleasant enough young man with
automatic manners that offered her no special defer-
ence. They were just something he had learned, just
as he had learned to dress properly, comb his hair,
and speak well, as befits the son of a banker. With
her high-heeled button shoes she was nearly as tall
as he, and his flesh felt soft under her hand. He was
endowed with neither the strength nor the gentle-

ness of Ben Poole, despite his good manners and perfect hygiene.

All the same, she was pleased to be stepping out with a young man. It made her feel as if life might perhaps continue despite the tragedy of her parents' death and all the confusion that had created.

Together the two threaded their way along the boardwalk. The streets were crowded, and concert-goers were easily discernible from men headed for a night at the Busted Mule or the Golden Sun.

Ben Poole was one of the latter, but he was fresh from the bathhouse and the new barbershop, a welcome addition to town. He spied Dessa immediately, for she stood out among the crowd like a gold nugget in a frothing creek bed. The berry color of her dress made her look good enough to eat, and he had a sudden appetite for just such an indulgence. She had piled her dark curls high atop her head and wore a feathered hat cocked to one side. Her green eyes flashed with excitement.

Ben stumbled over a riser on the walk while staring at her, then nearly tangled his feet together. She spotted him and said something to her companion, causing Ben to register the young man. So that kind of dandy was what she really preferred.

Then Dessa came toward him, holding out one hand. "Why, Ben Poole. How . . . how nice you look."

Ben shifted and gazed down at his boot tops. If she was trying to embarrass him, she was doing a good job.

"Ben, this is my . . . uh . . . my friend, Desmond Venable. Desmond, this is Ben Poole, the young man who saved my life."

Venable tipped his expensive gray bowler as if to call attention to the difference in it and Ben's sweat-stained hat. Ben noted the man had doused his short hair with macassar oil until it gleamed. Venable offered to shake hands. Ben ignored him to stare at Dessa, who stared right back.

She knew as soon as she looked up into Ben's face that she would rather be with him in the back of a wagon than walking down the street with her arm tucked inside Desmond's. She spotted the hurtful look that passed quickly over Ben's features. Maybe he did care about her. Just a little.

"You look beautiful, ma'am," he said, and, like he had done so many times before, lifted her gloved hand. Just as he bent to kiss it, he turned her arm ever so gently and placed his lips at the bare pulse point of her wrist. She felt the briefest flick of his warm tongue at the throbbing of her heart, a gesture that sent delightful shivers deep into her core.

She sucked in a quick breath and nibbled at her lower lip as he let go of her wrist. He might as well have kissed her on the mouth, the way the act affected her. When he raised his head, he kept her fingers in his own broad palm and cast a sensuous look at her from beneath a long sweep of black lashes. Tiny flecks of deep blue flashed in the ice of his eyes and he held her gaze so long she felt herself growing light-headed.

Then he smiled, released her hand, and placed his hat back on his head firmly. He appeared to be screwing it down to his head, as if in preparation for battle. "Pleasure to meet you, Venable," he said in a brief aside, and strode off, not once looking at the man he addressed.

"Ought to've knocked his cocked hat off his cocky head," Ben muttered as he swung through the crowd on the boardwalk and made his way to the batwing doors of the Golden Sun. "Like to see that sumbitch even pick her off her feet, let alone tote her across a room, should she need it."

"Well, hello, Ben," Rose said from behind the bar. "You look sour enough to clabber milk." She drew him a brew without asking and sloshed some out when she slid him the foamy glass.

"Who's that yahoo with Dessa out yonder?"

"Why, Ben. By your tone you'd think you really cared for the pretty little thing. Couldn't prove it by the way you've been acting toward her lately."

Ben studied Rose thoughtfully, eyes squinched almost shut. "Whose idea was it, hers or yours?"

Rose spread a scarlet-nailed hand across her bare bosom. "Me? Whatever are you talking about?"

"I'm plumb ashamed of you. Didn't I do your books? Didn't I help you straighten out that mess before you got it so scrambled it'd took a act of God? Didn't I? And now you go playing games with me, like I'm some stupid kid."

Rose laughed with obvious delight and changed the subject. "Have you talked to Maggie lately? Seems she's got herself a feller. An honest-to-goodness admirer. I think you should speak to her. He's trying to get her to marry him, go to California. The girl is all aflutter."

"Marry? Maggie? Don't be ridiculous, Rose." He tipped the glass and polished off more than half the cold beer, still thinking of the way Dessa laid her hand on that dandy's arm. "Well, Rose, I'm not falling for your tricks, nor Dessa's, either."

He gulped down the rest of the beer and wiped the foam off his mouth with the sleeve of his shirt. "Where's Virgie? I wanta see Virgie."

"Now, Ben," Rose warned. "Don't go doing nothing you'll regret."

Ben didn't say anything, just threw her a disgusted look.

A tall, long-legged redhead rose from a table near the dance floor and made her way toward him through the jostling Saturday night crowd. A tubby little man ran along behind, hollering, "Hey, I got the next dance. I done give you my token. Come on, gal."

Virgie ignored him and tucked herself up under Ben's arm. "Whatcha need, honey?"

Ben's resolve faded. What he needed wasn't Virgie. It wasn't even a massage under her expert hands. He gave her a quick hug. "Never mind, Virgie. I got somewhere to be. You go on and dance with the champ there. He needs you lots worse than I do."

Outside he glanced up and down the street. The concertgoers had all settled into the opera house for their night of entertainment. Strands of music wafted through the streets, a sweet lyrical sound that tugged at his lonely heart.

"I hope she has a real good time with that no-account," he grumbled. "Serve her right if he proves to be as dumb as he looks. Just serve her right."

He scuffed off down the street, headed for the Busted Mule, where he could get in a good, cheap poker game at the back table that Ramey reserved for men like him.

Desmond fumbled with Dessa's key, finally getting it into the lock on her front door. She didn't open the door, but backed up against it, effectively barring his way inside if he had such a thing in mind.

He took her hand and kissed it. Nothing. Just a dry, polite touch of mouth to glove.

"The concert was lovely, Desmond."

"Yes, wasn't it? Liszt is a marvelously talented composer."

"Yes, but I prefer Chopin," she replied, though this night she actually had welcomed the fiery Liszt production performed quite adequately by the traveling orchestra. Chopin could be much too serene and lovelorn, which would only serve to depress her even more. Why couldn't she get Ben Poole off her mind?

"Well, perhaps next week? I see there will be a three-act play by Victor Hugo. I hear he's making quite a splash on the East Coast."

"Mmm. Perhaps. I'm really very tired now. Thank you again, Desmond."

She backed into the room and eased the door shut on something he was trying to say.

She had unfastened the bodice of her dress and slipped her arms out of the sleeves when someone tapped softly on the door. Desmond, coming back for something? She didn't think so. Who, then? The door rattled, and too late she realized she hadn't remembered to fasten the inside padlock.

"Dessa? It's okay, it's just me," a soft and very familiar voice said.

Before she could take any action, Ben stepped into the open doorway between the parlor and her bedroom. And there she stood in her camisole shift, the bodice of her dress draped down around her hips.

"Ben Poole, have you no manners at all? Walking into my house like this. Get out of here! What do you want?" She gestured with both hands. "No, don't answer that, just take yourself on out of here."

"Girl, you got to learn to lock that door," he said before actually catching sight of her. "My God, Dessa, you're so beautiful." He just stood there, the door ajar behind him, unable to take his eyes off her.

"Ben," she scolded loudly. "Out. Out, or I'll call someone."

He took off his hat and held it in both hands in front of him. "No, don't do that, Dessa. Don't call anyone. I'm going."

But he didn't go; he just remained right where he was, rooted to the spot, and so, for a beat or two, did she.

"You know I won't hurt you," he said, just above a whisper.

Oh, yes, you will, Ben Poole, she thought. But it wasn't in the way he meant at all. She found herself trembling all over just watching him watching her. There was a longing in his features that she had never before seen on any man's countenance. It gave her goose bumps to realize he could want her with such fervor.

He broke the long silence. "I was just going home . . . and I was worried you forgot to lock your door again. . . . I mean, I thought . . . I thought we could maybe talk, since you were still up and everything."

She nodded dumbly. So it was him who had locked her door. And what if he had come in first, watched her sleep? Shaking her head, she took a step toward him and the dress slid down around her hips.

Dear Lord, was she mesmerized?

She bunched the fabric up in both fists. "Wait in the parlor, then, I'll be right in."

He nodded and smiled. "Yes, yes. I'll just wait in the . . . the other room. You'll be right in."

He felt like a perfect fool as he sat on one of the two straight-backed wooden chairs in the otherwise empty room. It was a wonder she hadn't thrown something at him, barging in like this. But he couldn't help it. He no more could have walked past her place when he saw her shadow through the window then he could have flown up to the moon. He toyed nervously with his hat for a minute, then tossed it on the floor beside the chair and clenched his big hands together in his lap.

He ought to just jump and run, but all he could think of were the few times he'd been with this woman and how good it made him feel just to be in her presence. Even when she was annoying the thunder out of him, he enjoyed it. He couldn't remember ever feeling that way, unless it was back in his dim past before Mama and his three sisters were killed, slaughtered in their own home by faceless bushwhackers, and him away so he could do nothing but want to die himself when he found their lifeless bodies. Before he himself took to killing in the war. He had enjoyed that killing because it allowed him to vent his hate for the men who had slaughtered his family. Now all he wanted was peace, and Dessa gave him a peaceful feeling. Even Sarah's forgiveness couldn't grant him such serenity. He didn't know why, couldn't put his finger exactly on what Dessa did that was so different. There was a nagging something, though, in the far reaches of his mind, that told him he never could possess this woman. Not wholly or completely, and he was a fool to think otherwise.

She came back through the door, the dress on and properly buttoned up. She had removed the hat and in doing so loosened some of the curls so that they lay over one shoulder.

He rose and met her halfway. He'd never had the nerve to touch her except to hold her hand or arm, but now he extended his fingers to the curve of her cheek, where tendrils of hair hovered. Lamplight turned the curls auburn.

She looked up at him and ran the tip of her tongue over her upper lip so that it gleamed wetly.

Hungrily, he lowered his head and tasted that lip, and it was as if a hand took hold of his heart and squeezed. A small growling sound erupted from deep in his being.

Dessa gasped and leaned into his open mouth.

They stood that way for a moment, hands reaching for but not touching each other, lips and tongues exploring slowly, exquisitely.

Warmth and light poured through Dessa. The velvet, sweet-tasting softness of his mouth offered her succor of a kind she'd never expected. It was like drinking at the well of life, and she wanted it never to end. She stepped closer, not disturbing the kiss, but making herself comfortable against his thighs, his hard flat stomach, his quivering chest muscles.

He circled her waist with both arms, then snaked one hand up to cup her head.

Flashes of light burst behind her closed lids, and she felt herself losing all control. Her muscles tingled, as if overused and ready to collapse. Her breasts ached, her thighs trembled, and both legs went out from under her.

He caught her, deftly swept her up into his arms, and carried her to the bed, lying her there and kneeling beside her.

"Dessa, oh, God, Dessa. I want you. You're so beautiful."

He gave her another long, lingering wet kiss, to which she submitted totally. "But if I did this, Rose would have my hide nailed to a barn door. My dear sweet Dessa, I'll never hurt you. Never." He pulled back, took his hands away.

Her eyes were smoky with desire, her lips swollen; red spots flared on her cheeks, and he turned away to keep from throwing himself on her right there, hitching up the dress, and doing what they both wanted so desperately.

He sat with his back to her, gathering his strength.

"Ben?"

"Yes." Gruffly spoken.

"I've never felt like this."

"Nor me."

"Then don't turn away. You always run away."

"I want you so bad it hurts. I never wanted anyone like I want you."

She didn't believe that entirely. There were the women at the Golden Sun anytime he asked. He was their darling, and would never have to want for anything, much less the loving arms of a woman. But right at this moment it didn't matter. He was a man, and men had their needs, separate from women. But Lord, if his desire was more than hers at this moment, she certainly sympathized. Wondered how he was keeping any control. He was right, of course. They couldn't do what they wanted to do. It might be fine for girls like Maggie and Virgie, but not for her. If she let him soil her, then he would no longer want her, nor would any other man.

"Ben?"

Another gruff reply. "Yes, oh God."

"Are you angry with me?"

"Lord, no. What about you?"

"Me?"

"Don't be mad at me, either, Dessa. I tried to stay away from you, I promise I did. I know what I am, what I've done. I know a woman like you can't possibly . . . I mean, you will want to marry someone like Desmond Venable, or his like. Or someone back in Kansas City. Not a man who sleeps on the ground under a damned old wagon, a man who owes more than he can ever pay.

"I can't build us a life, and I can't ask you for anything, Dessa. And I'll try not to let this happen again, I promise."

He rose quickly, angry now, but only at himself. "Why don't you just go on back to Kansas City, Dessa Fallon? Go on back and marry you some rich man who can give you what you deserve. You don't need some ragtag like me. You surely don't."

He was out of the room and gone before she could form a reply, or even cry out his name, which she did after he slammed the door. Over and over, lying there fully dressed in her bed, still warm in the place where he had sat, she called his name.

Chapter Ten

"The man who drinks the red, red wine will never be a beau of mine. The man who is a whiskey sop will never hear my corset pop," Maggie sang as she tripped down the stairs at the Golden Sun.

While the song didn't exactly reflect her sentiments—Maggie didn't mind a nip or two of whiskey herself—she thought it a catchy tune and was amused by the lyrics.

She wondered if Samuel would be in tonight, almost hoped he wouldn't. It was better if he didn't see her doing her "job." Then he'd just start in on her again to let him take her away from all this, and she was afraid to allow her life to be in the control of a man's whim. But Lord a'mighty, he had the most beautiful eyes and the sweetest touch. Rose was no help at all, being such a romantic. She believed a woman should grab what she could get whenever she could get it.

Rose was pleased to see the girl so happy, but she wasn't fond of Maggie's little song. It reminded her too much of that bunch of teetotalers running with Molly Blair.

Ever since the gold strikes in California in '49, a small contingency of women had been crusading against liquor. To think that their influence had finally erupted in Virginia City was upsetting. Such a movement could mean the end of Rose's business. The dour preacher's wife had managed to gather a retinue of followers who were, if nothing else, annoying to the owner of a dance hall that also supplied doves and plenty of hard liquor to the needy of the male population.

This particular Saturday, a week after Ben's unfortunate experience with Dessa that had thrown him into a most foul mood, but which he refused to talk much about, Rose shifted her attention from Maggie to Sheriff Moohn, who slouched at one of the tables near the front door. She wondered where he stood on the issue between her and Molly Blair.

The dying sun threw long bars of fading gold across the plank floor. Moohn lazily kept an eye on what he could see of a street that teemed with humanity, as it had every Saturday in his memory. Since the stagecoach robbery and double killing, Rose had noticed that the sheriff appeared to expect trouble at any moment. She understood his reluctance to ride into Alder Gulch.

This night trouble would find both him and her. Only a few minutes later the group of women Rose had taken to calling the unholy brigade approached the Golden Sun from the north. They had obviously gathered at the church, planned their strategy, and set out, for their shouts preceded them along the length of Walker Street, causing quite a stir among the evening strollers.

Molly Blair led the pack. On one side strode the uncommonly stout Mrs. Johannsen, the druggist's wife, on the other, Miss Lorraine Twigg, the spinster sister of hotel owner Morris Twigg. The formidable front line brought the sheriff to his feet and outside in order to get a better look. Sensing more trouble than just a lot of noise, Rose followed him.

There were at least a dozen ladies sweeping along behind the three leaders. All carried exceedingly stern expressions. Each possessed a weapon: among them several garden hoes, a manure shovel or two, and more than a few straw brooms.

The ladies' long skirts stirred up a cloud of dust that hovered around them on this windless, and up to that moment peaceful, evening. The brigade fetched up in a seething clot outside the swinging batwing doors of the Golden Sun Saloon. Rose Langue was not surprised to be their chosen target.

Down at the far end of the street Dessa lounged comfortably on her brand-new divan delivered by a Bannon freighter—thankfully not by Wiley and Ben, whom she hadn't set eyes on since Ben left her bedroom the week before. The uproar outside interrupted her intent concentration on a pillow cover she was cross-stitching. She lay it aside to go to the window. Spotting the rowdy gathering at the Golden Sun, she forgot all about her needlework. What in the world was going on?

Hurrying outside, she lifted her skirts and ran in that direction. Soon she could make out a babble of harsh voices, but the women hadn't really developed any timing in their chants, so it was hard to understand their message.

She joined a growing crowd of onlookers. No one wanted to miss this. It might be more exciting than the three-act play about to begin at the opera house, in which it was rumored that the word *breast* would actually be spoken aloud on the stage.

Up on the boardwalk in front of the saloon, Sheriff Moohn and Rose bodily barred the door to the Golden Sun. At their backs clustered several of the girls, among them Maggie and a tall redheaded woman who shouted horrendous obscenities over Rose's shoulder. Several men in the crowd guffawed loudly and egged on both sides.

"You tell 'em, Virgie," one shouted, and spat a long stream of tobacco juice. It barely missed the boot of a man next to him, who gave him a shove.

Dessa studied the redhead. So that was the mysterious Virgie. The one Ben went to for back rubs, or so he said.

She glanced around and spied a large man with gleaming blond hair running toward the gathering crowd. Ben Poole. Her heart lurched. She had succeeded in avoiding even the sight of him all week long, ever since he had kissed her and carried her into her bedroom, only to stalk out of her house. She told herself she didn't want to see him now, but what she really meant, and she knew it, was that she feared her own feelings around him.

She edged her way deeper into the mass of onlookers just as someone screamed. Craning her neck, Dessa saw that Molly Blair had thrown herself up against Sheriff Moohn and was shaking her fist at the scantily clad women in the doorway behind him.

"Babylon whores," Molly cried, and took a swing over his shoulder with her broom, barely missing her target and Moohn's jaw.

Maggie knocked Moohn aside and lit on Molly Blair with both fists swinging. She locked her fingers in Molly's tightly pinned bun of hair, and the two women toppled to the boardwalk, where they rolled around.

"Bite 'er, Maggie girl. You got good teeth. Ain't you

sunk 'em in me often enough? Bite 'er, I say." The bowlegged man doing the hollering jumped up and down and swung a dusty hat over his head. It caught the fellow next to him across the back of his neck.

"You danged idjit," the fellow shouted, and shoved his energetic neighbor, who stumbled backward into one of the unholy brigade, who in turn took a mighty swing at his backside with her manure shovel. It made a satisfying *thwunk*.

Meanwhile, Maggie and Molly had rolled off the boardwalk and into the dusty street, where they continued to do very little damage to each other while they tumbled and kicked, locked together making noises like two bear cubs.

Dessa shoved through the excited crowd to get a front-row spot. Just as she emerged from between the sawing elbows of the barrel-chested blacksmith and a potbellied man she'd never seen before, the redheaded woman called Virgie literally exploded from the saloon. She wore even less clothing than Maggie, having removed her long stockings and whatever she might have worn over a black corset that didn't even entirely cover her breasts. At least Maggie had on pantaloons and shoes and stockings, too. Dessa shuddered to think what Virgie had been doing before all this started.

More concerned with fighting than covering up, Virgie launched herself into the unholy brigade, half of whom were swinging their odd assortment of weapons, while the other half crawled around in the dirt.

Behind Dessa someone stumbled and shoved her forward so that Virgie lit astraddle her back. Dessa went down, taking with her the spinster lady, Miss Twigg, who immediately lost what dignity she had left when she landed spraddle-legged with her dress up around her hips. Long legs kicking air, Virgie scrambled over Dessa and pounded poor Miss Twigg's head into the dusty street. One of the unholy brigade started whopping Virgie and Dessa with her broom in a very unladylike fashion. Dessa scrambled from the fray and headed for the safety of the board-walk. Someone grabbed her by one leg and dragged her back into the tussle. She kicked out and caught solid bone, bringing forth a grunt.

From the sidelines large hands grabbed both her wrists and began to haul her in the other direction, so that she felt as if she were being pulled apart like a wishbone. The one holding her leg fell away, taking her shoe with him, and she and her would-be res-cuer thudded up against the front wall of the Golden Sun.

By this time Dessa's hair hung over her face, so she had no idea whose stomach it was buried in. Whoever it was had hold of her upper arms and was trying to right her. She sputtered and struggled.

Behind her she heard Walter Moohn bellow, "Hold on. Ever one of you, hold on or I'll shoot."

No one paid him the least attention.

"Well, dang it, then, we'll just see," he shouted, and fired two quick shots.

From somewhere on the other end of town came answering gunfire, and those who had temporarily frozen at the first blast erupted into action again.

Dessa rolled around until she was sitting, and shoved the thick veil of hair away in time to see men flow out of the Busted Mule down the street, firing their guns into the air like they were being attacked by buzzards or the like.

Moohn holstered his gun, threw his hands straight

up, and waded in among the brawling women, ignoring everyone else. He got a firm hold on Miss Twigg's arm and dragged her, along with Molly Blair, off down the street toward the jail.

Molly waved one hand high and shouted, "We'll clean up this sinful Babylon if it's the last thing we do. Whores. Whores. God will smite you down. We'll make this a decent place to raise our children, see if we don't," or words to that effect.

Rose, who had remained well back from the commotion, staggered outside laughing so hard she almost busted out of her corset. This was probably the best Saturday night she'd seen since the night the town received word that the war had ended. After the fracas was all over, she'd wager she would sell more whiskey and dance tokens than ever before. She didn't notice for quite some time the couple sprawled side by side on the boardwalk, propped up against the Golden Sun.

Dessa decided Rose had temporarily lost her mind and turned to her companion, whom she hadn't yet identified.

"You hurt?" he asked, eyes twinkling with mirth. She didn't look hurt, did she?

"Ben?"

He grinned sheepishly. "Dessa."

"Ben."

He laughed. "Dessa?"

"This is silly."

"Sure is. Did you ever see anything like it? I wonder if it'll be in the *Post* tomorrow."

"What were they doing? My goodness, wasn't that the preacher's wife?"

"Yeah, and the sister of our illustrious Morris Twigg, and Van Cleve's wife and daughter both. Fine upstanding ladies, one and all. Didn't see Dimsdale anywhere, did you?"

"The editor of the *Post*? I don't suppose I know him on sight. Look at that, my new dress is ripped." Dessa held out one arm where the sleeve was torn halfway up the inner seam.

Ben cupped her chin in his palm, licked his thumb, and wiped a smudge from her cheek. "You sure you're not hurt anywhere?" He ran his hands down over her shoulders and arms, then encircled her waist, rising to his knees.

She lifted her head to look up at him. That's when she saw a fine thread of blood trickling from the corner of his mouth and a darkening bruise there. "I'm not, but you are. You're bleeding, Ben." With trembling fingers she touched the bruise.

His eyes grew dark with longing, like pools of woodland water, and he lifted her so they were both on their feet and standing close together. Whatever decisions he'd made about this woman, he was a sucker for compassion, and when anyone fussed over him, the orphan in him embraced the gesture gratefully.

With very little effort on his part, she was in his arms, locked up against his sweat-stained and dusty shirt. Palm flat against her back, he felt perspiration dampening the fabric of her shirtwaist.

She took a deep, deep breath and held on to the breadth of this man who always seemed to present himself as a somewhat reluctant but solid fortress at her beck and call. What in the world was she going to do about the way she felt when he did that? It would be easier to figure out, if he wasn't forever running away. Perhaps that's what she should do, too.

Run away. Go back to Kansas City and marry Andrew.

"Hey," he whispered in her ear.

"Mmm?"

"Let me take you home."

She nodded against his chest, then let him take her hand and together they started to walk past the door of the Golden Sun. They didn't make it.

"Ben, Dessa. Come in, have a drink," Rose called out when she saw them strolling side by side, gazing at each other so intently they'd probably fall off the end of the boardwalk if someone didn't wake them up.

"Want to?" Ben whispered.

Dessa glanced inside, saw Rose sitting at a table. "I'm an awful mess."

"Aw, Rose don't care," Ben said. "Come on, a good fight deserves a cold brew."

She let Ben lead her inside. He surprised her by pulling out a chair like a perfect gentlemen and seating her in it.

"My land, you two look like you were caught up in the fray."

Ben threw one leg over the back of his chair and sat down with a rueful laugh. "Dessa here was right in the middle of it. All I did was try to rescue her."

She punched at him lightly. "Oh, sure, Ben Poole. Rescue me, indeed. You like to pulled me in two pieces out there. And I was pushed. You wouldn't know anything about that, would you?"

He spread one hand flat on his chest and widened his eyes. "Not me. I only rescue damsels in distress, I don't push them around. Isn't that right, Rosie?"

"If it isn't, it damn well better be," Rose teased.

At that moment Grisham brought over three brimming glasses of golden brew. While Dessa had been guilty of trying a nip or two of brandy on occasion, she had never tasted beer. With a throat as parched as sand, she decided now would be as good a time as any. She lifted the beaded mug to her mouth, tipped it gingerly, and took a sip. The froth tickled along her upper lip. She swallowed and shuddered, screwing up her face.

Ben and Rose both laughed.

"Don't waste it if you don't like it," Ben chided. He pulled a bandanna from his pocket and blotted at her mouth.

"Let the poor child alone," Rose said. "It's an acquired taste, dear," she told Dessa. "Maybe you'd like some root beer or sarsparilla instead."

Dessa took another swallow of the beer, eyes locked on Ben.

Worse.

Maybe it tasted better when one simply drank it right down, all at once and fast. It was like medicine. And everyone knew you had to gulp that right on down and get it over with. So that's what she did with her mug of beer.

Tears burst from her eyes and she gasped several times.

"How was it?" Ben asked.

"G-g-g . . . awful," she sputtered. "Just awful. Why do you drink it, anyway? Why would anyone even want to acquire a taste for something so foul?"

Ben laughed and Rose watched him like a proud mother.

When he touched the corner of his mouth and winced, Rose asked, "Does it hurt?"

"Nah, I was just surprised. I don't remember being hit."

"Maybe someone hit you with her broom," Dessa said, her tongue and lips feeling numb. For no apparent reason, she giggled, then burped. Hand over her mouth, she glared at Ben, then Rose.

"I think you'd better take Dessa home, Ben. She seems to be a bit tipsy."

Ben rose obediently.

"Do you always do whatever Rose tells you to?" Dessa asked, and gave him a coquettish glance from under her lashes. "I don't want to go home. I want to hear what happened to all those women. I am most certainly not pipsy."

Rose smothered a laugh. "Walter put them in jail."

At the same time, Ben said, "You may not be 'pipsy,' but I always mind my elders. Let's get you home."

Rose slapped the back of his hand, which was spread on the table.

Dessa ignored the play and tried to stick to the conversation. "Really? The preacher's wife in jail? Oh, my, isn't that diriculous?"

Rose and Ben burst out laughing.

"What? What did I say?"

Ben stood. "Diriculous? You're right, Rose. Dessa is drunk."

"Am not," Dessa said, and came to her feet. She swayed, put one hand to her forehead, and Ben reacted just in time to catch her before she slumped to the floor.

With her in his arms, he grinned down at Rose. "This is getting to be a habit."

"She's a sweet little thing, Ben. You behave yourself with her."

"Dammit, Rose. I told you before, I won't hurt her." He looked down at the peaceful, dirt-smeared face resting up against his chest. "I would never hurt her," he said softly.

After he left with his light burden, Rose sat at the table for a long while, thoughtfully sipping at her drink. Sometimes Ben had no notion what would hurt a woman, but she hoped he was right and he would never hurt Dessa Fallon, for Rose had grown extraordinarily fond of the courageous young woman. She wanted only the best for her. Loving Ben might be just that, but then again, it might not.

Meanwhile, Rose had her own problems. She saw the trouble tonight with the unholy brigade as only the beginning, for when something like this got started in a town, there was usually no way of shutting it down. Those churchgoing women would keep at her till they drove her out of Virginia City, of that she was sure. Then where would she go and what would she do?

Ben gently lay Dessa on her bed. He bent to remove her shoes, only to find she was missing one. He pulled the other off and massaged her feet, taking them both gently in his large hands.

She moaned softly and he let go, rose, and sat beside her. For a long while he simply gazed down upon her sleeping face. There lay the one thing he'd ever found that he wanted with all his heart and soul. It was a strange feeling for Ben, who had learned early not to attach himself to much of anything, especially if it was valuable. It just made the losing of it more painful.

At long last he bent forward and kissed her, first on the forehead, then on each cheek.

"Oh, you sweet one," he murmured, feeling a constriction around his heart. What he wouldn't give to hold her, to make love to her, to feel her respond in kind.

With the tips of his fingers, he brushed a lock of hair back from her face. This was exactly what he had been afraid would happen, the first time he ever laid eyes on her. And now look at him. It was already too late for caution. He would never recover from losing her, he was sure. And he was also just as sure that he could never hope to have her.

She was attracted to him, that he could see, but it was a game with her. A game she'd played all too often, he'd wager, leaving broken hearts lying about her like stones in a creek. How could he think she might choose him? A woman like her, used to the finest. At the moment, she was enjoying playing her cat-and-mouse game with him because she was temporarily cast adrift, but once she got her wits about her, recovered from her grief, and returned to her home, she'd forget Ben Poole ever existed. It was just as well, too, considering the things he'd done. He had no business with a good woman, seeing as how he'd already ruined the life of one.

With tenderness he pulled the quilt up and tucked it firmly under her chin.

Studying her features as if he could memorize them for all time, he faced the truth. Dessa Fallon had left her mark on him, and it would be there forever, like a brand or a scar. For as long as he lived he would see her face every time he closed his eyes, even if he never saw her again.

Soon after Ben and Dessa left, Moohn joined Rose, declaring that his jail was fit to burst at the seams. "One cell's overflowing with yahoos, the other with some fine women who are downright plagued with me at the moment," he told her.

"How'd you manage that?"

"Once I got the attention of some of my deputies, who were out there in the midst of things themselves, it wasn't too hard to round up the ladies. The men took a bit longer. A conk or two on some heads worked wonders."

"You going to keep 'em the night?"

Moohn chuckled and shook his head. "I roused as many husbands as could be found to come down and rescue their women. Miss Twigg's brother was fit to be tied. He'll keep her locked up a week. I'll let the rest go at dawn. Sleeping on a hard floor won't do any of them too much harm."

"Walter, those women will never forgive you for this. They see me as the lawbreaker."

Moohn gazed balefully at the table. "I know, Rose. I know. But they disturbed the peace. It'd been you, I'd a done the same. Sorry about Maggie and Virgie, but they was in it tooth and toenail, too."

Rose took his sun-wrinkled hand. "I know. They'll sleep it off and forgive you. You're a good and honest man, Walter Moohn. But sooner or later, you're going to have to come down on the other side in this issue, mark my words."

Walter sighed. "You read the *Post* the other day? That letter from the feller trying to stir up more trouble. Could be what set off this particular uprising."

"I didn't read it," Rose said absently. What harm could a letter in a newspaper do?

"He wrote that it was time we pitched into that infernal nuisance called by some a dance house. Reckon that's your place, Miss Rose. He suggested that the license fee you pay is what makes the law excuse your misdeeds. Said something about drunken prostitutes and their partners making so much noise he can't sleep."

Rose drew herself up. "My girls don't fornicate in the streets, nor do they stagger around drunk."

Walter patted at her arm. "I know, I know."

"So what else? Did Dimsdale remark on it?"

"Oh, he'd already had his say a few months back when he begged the good Lord to deliver him from bluestockings, bloomers, and strong-minded she-males generally. But this feller what wrote the letter said he and his neighbors would be more than proud to make up the difference to the city what they'd lose if the dance house was closed down."

"Four hundred dollars? He's willing to come up with that to shut me down?" Rose was aghast. "And every year thereafter? This is plumb foolish, Walter. I'm not hurting anyone."

"I wouldn't worry too much about it. You know they ain't no law agin this place, Rose. And till they is, well, they're all just blowing in the wind."

"But they elect you to office, and they'll soon out-weigh those who want to keep these saloons. The law can be changed. It'll be a fair town one of these days."

Moohn squeezed her fingers. "Yeah, folks want to come out here to find what they're looking for, a wildness and newness. And they bring their society plunder with 'em, so they're right back where they started 'fore they come here.

"Hell, Rose, let's you and me just up and move on. We could fine someplace that's like this place used to be."

Rose pulled her hand away gently. "You and me, Walter?"

He nodded and pinned her with a squinty stare. "You and me, Rose. Oh, I know you loved that Englishman . . . and I know what kind of life you've led, but dang it all, I wouldn't care about that. Not if you wouldn't. I ain't so all-fired purified myself."

Rose dragged in a long breath. "Oh, I know, Walter. And it isn't like I'm saying no, exactly. It's just that you've surprised me with your asking, and I'll have to think about it. Don't take that as a no."

He rose from the table. "Oh, I won't, Miss Rose. I won't take it as a no at all. I reckon I'd better make my rounds and see everything's locked up tight." He stopped, his face twisted in a grin. "Reckon what them folks coming out of the opry house thought when they saw the street filled with fighting, tussling upstanding citizens. Might have been a sight more interesting than that naughty play they'd been watching, you think?"

Rose laughed. "Indeed it might have been. A wonder how men can be so titillated by a play that parades around the same nonsense they're used to seeing in my place any Saturday night."

Walter chuckled and waved a good-bye.

With a sigh, she rose and locked up. No use in staying open. Everyone was in jail or home with their wives trying to stretch their earlier experiences into their own bedroom. She wondered briefly if Ben and Dessa were together, then shook her head at her own romantic notions.

She still missed Jarrad Lincolnshire, but Walter's proposal was something to think about. It might just be time for her to move on to another place, a whole new life, before she got too old to enjoy it. Walter was a kind man, and if she knew anything at all, she knew that a woman couldn't do any better than to snag a kind man.

Chapter Eleven

Early Sunday morning Dessa awoke in her own bed before dawn, a coverlet pulled over her fully clothed body, not knowing how she had gotten there. Her tongue was coated with the bitter taste of beer. For a moment she could recall nothing except that crazy fight in the street the night before. All those women, righteous and sinner alike, mixing it up in front of half the town. Despite the foul taste in her mouth, she grinned at the memory.

The rest came back in a flash as she sat up and reached for the water she kept on the nightstand. Ben touching her. Ben licking his thumb and wiping a smudge from her cheek, Ben lifting her to her feet and hugging her . . . holding her . . . and her holding him. Then nothing. A blank. What had happened? Had Ben . . .

Of course he hadn't. She'd feel differently, wouldn't she? And besides, he wouldn't do something like that.

She decided to put off breakfast and take an early morning ride, and that's how she ended up at the livery stable long before anyone was up and about in the quiet streets.

No sidesaddle hung in the tack room. Then she remembered that a few days ago Rose had said that the girth had broken. It was probably at the leather shop being repaired. She lifted one of the western saddles from a stanchion along the wall. Unlike the lightweight English saddle she had grown used to in Kansas City, this one weighed almost more than she could heft.

To top it off, the gelding Baron danced and snorted, refusing to let her come near him, and she ended up putting the saddle on Beauty instead. After studying the leather straps a moment, she threaded the cinch properly and pulled it tight around the animal's middle.

Dessa had never ridden astride a horse, but could see no earthly good reason why a woman shouldn't do so if she wished. Feeling a strong animal between her legs couldn't be such a sin, could it? After she mounted, she saw that the stirrups were too long, she could barely reach them with pointed toes, so she slid off and adjusted them. Finally comfortably astride the long-legged mare—what would Mother and Father think of their properly brought up daughter mounting an animal like a man?—Dessa rode from the dark barn into the deserted street.

Beauty set a gentle pace, giving Dessa a chance to think. So much had changed in her life in such a short time. Oddly, that no longer made her sad. It was more like the way she felt after experiencing an especially poignant moment. Melancholy but assured that life offered more hope than sorrow. She had made new friends, Ben Poole among them; and of course Rose and Maggie. If she stayed here, there would be more.

Trust was important to her, and surprisingly she trusted Ben completely. He would never take advantage of her, just like last night when he carried her home, put her to bed, and left without so much as removing an article of clothing. She had been foolish to even think for a moment that he had taken any liberties. Realization of that trust produced a warm feeling next to her heart. She had experienced it with no one save her parents, most certainly not with men like Andrew. Look away and his hand shifted into a wandering mood.

Strange, when she thought of Andrew at all she compared him to Ben Poole.

Beauty kept to the main road leaving town, and she let the reins lie loosely in her gloved hand. The silvery dawn purpled, then glowed pinkly. A breeze blew down out of the mountains carrying the scent and touch of snow, and she breathed deeply of the damp sweetness. Oh, God, how lovely it was here, and how she hated to think of leaving. She had found her own paradise, quite by accident and under some pretty horrible circumstances, but nevertheless, her soul yearned to remain.

She tried to imagine the long winter, virginal snow piled high against the eaves to shut out the outside world, leaving her to deal with only her inner most murmurings. Her breath coming like clouds when she ventured outdoors, the clean air filling her lungs and making her skin tingle. And then, of course, there was Ben. He was as much a part of this place as that stand of stalwart pines up ahead.

The deep shadows beneath the trees brought to mind the mysterious but familiar man who had attended her mother and father's funeral. She was beginning to lose hope that she would ever know who that man was. At first she had thought that if she remained in town, he would one day approach, introduce himself. Explain why he had disappeared without speaking to her. But when that hadn't happened, the incident had begun to fade until she only thought of it at rare moments.

She came back to herself, halting her roaming thoughts. She had no idea where she was and had no desire to get lost in this immense country. The mare had steadfastly followed a little used trail and was moving along quite briskly, just as if she knew where she was going.

From the crest of the rise, Dessa spotted a house. A simple structure with clapboard walls and a long porch, it nestled snugly into a gentle south slope. There were a few chickens in the yard and wood-slatted pens out back. Long rays of sunlight broke across the meadow as the sun cleared the peaks and flashed on windowpanes.

Her mount slowed, walked leisurely into the yard and stopped without being bidden. She sat there a moment, puzzled. The mare knew where she was, obviously came here often.

Without any warning, two toddlers who looked to be the same age burst out the front door shouting with laughter, bare bottoms gleaming. Right behind them came a woman.

"Nathan, Jason, you come right back here this instant," she shouted, and made a swooping capture of both children. When she raised with one tucked firmly under each arm, she spied Dessa. "Oh, my. Hello. I didn't see you. Excuse these young heathens. I can't keep clothes on them."

Dessa smiled down at the woman. She couldn't remember ever seeing her in town. "Hello. I'm Dessa Fallon, and I seem to have let my horse lead me astray. Woolgathering."

The woman studied the black mare, a furrow between her eyes, then she, too, smiled. "Get on down and come have some coffee. I promise I'll put clothes on these two young'uns. My name's Sarah Woodridge. This here is Nathan." She jostled one of the boys. "This other'n is Jason. twins, and double trouble if ever there was any."

Dessa laughed and dismounted. She would enjoy taking coffee with this young woman, who appeared to be not much older than she herself. Looping the reins around a fence post, she followed Sarah up the steps and inside the neat small house.

"Set yourself there," Sarah said, motioning toward a rough-sawn wooden table with four chairs. "Coffee's on the stove. I'll just be a minute with these two."

She disappeared through a faded curtain hanging over a doorway that led from the larger main room, which appeared to serve as kitchen and living quarters. She returned quickly, trailed by the two boys, now clad in patched britches and faded shirts and acting quite shy of their visitor. They hung behind their mother, peeking out from behind her calico skirt.

Dessa winked and made faces at them, setting them both giggling. She saw no sign of a man, but he could be out hunting or working the fields.

"I don't get to town much, but I don't remember seeing you there," Sarah offered, and poured their coffee into mismatched cups.

"No, I've only been in Virginia City a short while." Dessa wondered if she should tell Sarah about her parents, but decided not to. That could wait until they were better acquainted.

"Well . . . is it . . . I mean, are you married or anything? How do you like Virginia? It's pretty primitive compared to . . ."

When Dessa realized the young woman wasn't going to finish the sentence, she said, "Oh, no, I'm not married. But I do love it here. It's so beautiful, the air is so heady and the mountains are breathtaking, not like the plains, so monotonous. Of course, some of Missouri is hilly, the Ozarks are quite lovely, but Kansas City is . . . well, it's busy and noisy and smelly."

"I'm from Philadelphia . . . so was my husband, Clete." Sarah abruptly looked away, stared out the kitchen window. Dessa had the feeling she gazed not at the view but inward toward some sorrow. "He died," she said then, and brushed angrily at her eyes. "Would you like more coffee?"

Dessa lifted her half-full cup and sipped. "No, I'm fine." She waited a moment in reverence to Sarah's grief, then said, "The boys, they're darling. They must be good company for you, out here alone so far from town. I don't see how you can stay. I mean, I would think you'd go back to your people, or at least move to town."

Sarah's eyes grew dreamy. "Clete loved this place. We worked so hard proving it up. I'd feel like I was betraying him, walking away."

"But how can you do the work by yourself?"

Sarah shrugged. "The place is getting in pretty sorry shape, but I have some help."

Dessa nodded, not knowing what else to say. After all, she knew little of the woman's situation. There could be a man courting. She decided she had stayed long enough for her first visit, and rose.

Sarah popped out of her chair. "Oh, are you leaving so soon?"

"Yes, I'd like to get back and go to church. Perhaps I could some again at a better time?"

Sarah nodded her head and held out her hand. Dessa took it, noted the cracks and calluses in the skin. A tough life, this one. She admired Sarah's strength.

Before she could cross the room, the sound of horse's hooves pounded up in the yard, and a harried Ben Poole burst into the room without knocking.

"Ben," Sarah said, her face flushing with pleasure.

Dessa echoed her, but without the pleasure. "Ben?"

"Sarah? Dessa? I thought the mare . . . I mean you . . . had run away, then I saw her outside, but I couldn't . . . What are you doing out here, Dessa?"

Dessa was dumbstruck, for Sarah had gone to Ben and was standing beside him like he was her man, staring up into his face. Very pleased to see him, from the look of it. Ben continued to glare at Dessa, total confusion distorting his features.

"Ben?" Dessa said with a hint of demand in her query. She wanted to tell him to explain this situation, but felt speechless. It was really none of her business, she just wished it was, so she kept quiet.

"You know each other?" Sarah asked.

"And you know Dessa?" Ben asked her.

Both women replied at once. "We just met."

"Well, I . . . I guess . . ." Ben jerked off his hat, and at that moment Nathan and Jason raced in from the other room and locked themselves firmly around each of his legs, squealing and laughing.

Ben whooped and lifted them both in his arms. "Hey, there, you tadpoles."

Dessa watched the horseplay in total amazement. Ben tickled the boys and set them to giggling. He didn't look at Dessa again, but concentrated on playing with the twins.

"I think I'd better be getting back to town," Dessa stammered, and ran from the room before either of them could say a word.

She fumbled with the twisted reins, her fingers feeling thick and misbehaving. Finally she captured them and climbed on the dancing mare's back. It was no wonder the animal had known her way out here. Ben rode her here often, obviously. What in the world was going on anyway? Ben Poole and that woman who said her name was Sarah Woodridge, acting so cozy, and him playing with the twins like they were his very own. Was it possible they were?

That she had been totally fooled by the man disturbed her equilibrium. Surely Rose wouldn't have allowed such a deception. He could be their uncle or just a close friend of their dead father. Yet she sensed something was going on here beyond normal friendship, and she didn't like it one bit. Those two in there were just too lovey-dovey. Maybe Rose didn't know.

Dessa tapped at the horse's ribs with her heels and headed for town, anger and confusion gnarling her emotions in a tight ball.

She remained in her house all that day, seeing no one. She was so upset she didn't even attend church or meet Rose at the Continental House for breakfast, as had become her habit. Rose came by and banged hard on the door, but Dessa didn't answer.

Ben wanted to rush out after Dessa when she ran from Sarah's house, but with the twins in his arms and Sarah demanding to know what was going on, he could do nothing but listen to the sound of the black mare's hoofbeats fade into the distance.

"Who is she, Ben?"

"Dessa Fallon."

Sarah tugged on his arm. "Silly, I know her name. Who is she to you, and why was she so upset? We were just having coffee and a visit. Why did she run off like she'd seen a ghost? I never have visitors, Ben."

Ben sighed at the familiar lament, then immediately felt guilty. He did a lot of that around Sarah, and it really wasn't her fault.

"Why was she here anyway?" Ben asked, and set the boys down to pour himself a cup of coffee.

"Said she was out riding and got lost, just rode up on the place by accident. Why?"

Ben gazed out the window across the meadow for a moment. Was that really the truth, or had Dessa followed him here earlier and returned to check up on him? He didn't know what to think, except that the look on her face told him she was hurt. He'd have to try to explain to her about Sarah and the twins. But how? How in God's name do you tell someone you care for that you're a killer?

Ben wasn't sure yet that what he felt for Dessa was love, for he had little experience in that realm, but he did know that he wanted to be with her, to touch her, to make her happy, to keep her safe. And he wasn't sure he could ever do that. It might be better to just let her believe what she wanted. She'd soon get over her disappointment in him, especially when she decided to go back to the city and stop playing her little games with her bumbling frontiersman.

Ben sipped at the hot coffee, his mind far from

the small cabin. Then he noticed Sarah staring at him, and he smiled at her. "You feeling okay?"

She nodded, her slate-gray eyes morose. "What is she to you, Ben? She's so pretty and so smart. Did you hear the way she talks? All smooth and smart, like a lady. Not rough and dumb like me."

"You're not rough and dumb, Sarah. You know you're not."

"Well, Clete certainly didn't think so. He loved me and only me, even if I did live on the wrong side of town." Sarah sniffed and turned her gaze from Ben.

He tightened his lips and set down the empty cup. His heart ached when she spoke of her dead husband. He was responsible; it was his fault that Sarah had no one to care for her and the boys.

The horrible scene in town last spring played itself over and over in his mind, but he couldn't make it come out any way but the way it had truly happened.

Despite all of that, he couldn't force himself to love this woman. He couldn't take that final step and marry her because of his guilt. But he feared that one day he might have to.

"Oh, Ben, I'm sorry," Sarah said, and threw her arms around him. "I love you, Ben. I don't mean to act that way. I do love you."

"I know you do," he said, and patted awkwardly at her back. How could he tell her that he didn't love her, that he never would, that all he could think of was that sprite of a girl who had rushed out of here with her green eyes afire?

Ben didn't know what he was going to do, but he was tired of being miserable over one woman or another. Maybe he'd just light out and go west to California. Leave both women and all his troubles behind.

* * *

Monday morning Dessa received another wire from the Cluney & Brown law firm in Kansas City, urging her to return before winter. Her presence, they insisted, was necessary whether she sold the business or not. Matters required her immediate attention if the Fallon stores were to survive the transition.

Considering what had happened out at Sarah Woodridge's the day before, there need be no further delay. If she had remained in Virginia City at all, it would have ultimately been because of her attraction to Ben Poole. All the other reasons were just rationalizations, after all. She had friends in Kansas City, people she'd known all her life. What had she been thinking, anyway, to even consider settling in this backward frontier town in the edge of nowhere? And all because of a man. Nonsense, utter and complete. There were plenty of men back home, and that's where she belonged.

She tucked the wire into her reticule and set out to find Rose. It wouldn't be an easy thing, leaving Rose and Maggie. She would miss them. Though she hated to admit it, she would miss Ben Poole the most. She hated giving up her dreams of a life that might have been theirs had things been different, but he had made such a fool of her, him and his teasing and leading her on. Playing hard to get just so she would want him even more. And all the time he had that woman on the side and two young'uns that for all she knew belonged to him. She had no idea how long Sarah's man had been dead.

She wanted to bust him one, just double up her fist and knock him a winding for what he'd done to her.

Rose didn't take well to Dessa's announcement that she was returning immediately to Kansas City. Wisely, Dessa mentioned nothing about Ben's part in her decision.

"Oh, I don't think that's a good idea, child. Bad enough you traveled alone coming here. You saw what happened, and the same goes for returning. You may have been hardheaded and spoiled enough to convince your parents it would be safe, but I know better."

"I have to go, Rose. I have obligations. My daddy's business was important to him. He worked very hard to make it what it was. I can't simply sit by while it falls apart."

"Then let someone go with you."

The two women sat on the chaise in the room Rose had lent Dessa when she first came to Virginia City. It had turned out to be Rose's private quarters away from the small cottage a few miles outside town where she lived—the cottage with the rose gardens where Rose went to relax and think calm thoughts when she could get away from the Golden Sun.

Dessa eyed Rose, wondering just what she had up her sleeve with the suggestion that someone accompany her to Kansas City.

"Who? Everyone has his own life here. I can't expect someone to just drop everything and go traipsing around with me. No, I'm not helpless." Her eyes teared and she wiped the moisture away angrily. "I have to learn to do things on my own. There isn't any choice."

"That's what you thought when those horrible men dragged you off that stagecoach. They could have killed you. It could happen again."

"Oh, Rose. Terrible things could happen to any of us, anytime. We can't go hiding out from them, being afraid to live because of them. Like Ben does."

Rose shot Dessa a harsh look. "What do you really know about what Ben does or why he does it?"

Dessa shrugged, sorry she'd said anything. It was none of her business anyway, though for a while she'd thought everything about Ben might someday be her business.

"You don't know the first thing about Ben and what motivates him."

Dessa squirmed. It was all she could do to keep from railing at this woman for what Ben had done. Rose was the closest thing to a mother he had, and Dessa should have known better than to criticize him to Rose. "I'm sorry, Rose. I didn't mean that. It's just that I wish . . . well, I wish things were different, but they aren't. And I must go. I simply must."

Rose stood, walked purposefully to her side. "Then Ben will go with you."

"He most certainly will not," Dessa sputtered. "Why in the world would he do that? And how can you even say he will without asking? And what makes you think I want him to go with me?"

"Calm down, child. Think about it a moment. You need someone to accompany you. Who better than Ben? You know you're safe with him. If it bothers you, offer to pay him. Make it a job."

"Ben would never accept such a job," Dessa said, and too late realized that with the statement she had allowed Rose to think she had capitulated. It really didn't matter, though. Ben would never agree to such a thing. Not in a thousand years.

She wiped at tears that surprised her in their suddenness. Why had he done this to her? And Rose thinking him nearly a saint.

"He'll be your bodyguard. Lots of people have them. It's not at all unusual." Rose chattered on, but Dessa shut out her words.

She tried to visualize Ben Poole in a drawing room in one of her friends' homes. She couldn't picture it, no more than she could picture him in her life in any other way. Not after what she'd seen this morning. It was impossible, utterly impossible.

Rose's words dragged her away from the wandering. ". . . we'll see to your place till you can come back. It'll be just fine."

Dessa rose and walked to the window. She peered down into the street below, unable to face her friend. "I'm not coming back," she finally said softly. The words cut a slice from her heart.

Rose was instantly at her side. "But my dear child, whyever not? I thought you liked it here. You talked about making a life here, not going back to all that big city hubbub. Here a woman's free, chid. Why, we've even gotten the vote in Wyoming Territory. Up in South Pass City they've elected a female justice of the peace. Soon it will spread. Just think of it, Dessa.

"Think, child. Think. Think what it will be like to help build this country, to be a part of it. I wish I were young enough to see it happen, but you . . . you can do it. You and Ben."

"Ben? Ben doesn't want any part of me; he's just been playing with me. Oh, Rose, please stop it. Just don't talk to me about your precious Ben Poole anymore. He's ruined everything."

"Child, whatever's the matter? What has that young hellion done to you now? I warned him. I'll snatch him baldheaded if he's hurt you." Rose gathered Dessa against her bosom and patted her tenderly on the back. "Whatever it is, he just doesn't know any better. I'll straighten him out right now. Come, child, don't be so upset."

Dessa caught her breath and moved out of Rose's embrace. "I don't know what I'll eventually do, but for now, I have to return and I can't leave everything dangling here for someone else to handle. I fear I won't come back, once I leave; and I have to leave."

Rose took Dessa in her arms again, trying to comfort her but needing comfort herself, for she had pictured Ben and Dessa hand in hand, cutting a swath a mile wide across this virgin land. Doing something big and brave and wonderful that she was too old to accomplish herself. She had to convince Dessa to let Ben go with her to Kansas City, she simply had to. He would come back and he would bring Dessa with him. She wouldn't lose this child who had grown so dear to her heart.

"I'll wire Andrew, have him come out," Dessa said.

Rose pulled away, held the girl by her shoulders, and gazed deep into her eyes. "Andrew?" she asked dumbly. Who the hell was Andrew?

Dessa met her friend's gaze and nodded. "A friend, Rose. A good friend. Don't worry about me. Please don't fret so. I've enjoyed being here, but it's not real. It's a fantasy, and one I can't have. I'll arrange everything. Someone from back home can come out and accompany me. Ben needn't be bothered."

Noticing the destitute expression on Rose's face, Dessa put her arms around her. Unbidden, tears flowed down her cheeks while Rose hugged her so tightly she could hardly breathe.

* * *

Rose sent word to Walter Moohn that when Wiley Moss and Ben returned from their freighting run, he was to tell Ben she must see him immediately. It was nearly nine o'clock when he strode into the Golden Sun Saloon, his face a mask of fury.

She drew him a beer and he drank it without even saying hello first. Then he slammed the mug on the bar, wiped his mouth with a shirtsleeve, and said, "I quit."

"Quit? Quit what, Ben? Acting like a jackass?"

"I ain't acting like no jackass. I quit my job. I'm going to California."

"You're what?" Rose screeched so loud all the patrons shut up and gaped at her.

"I quit my damned job. You yourself said more than once I had no ambition, that I wasn't getting anywhere. Well, now I am. And I hope every blamed woman in the world is happy." He glared at her and shouted, "Give me another beer."

Rose blinked in surprise and filled his mug. "Ben Poole, don't you yell at me. Just settle yourself down, now, young man. What are you railing on about? It sure isn't a woman's fault you're in the fix you are."

"The hell it ain't. That young brat come sashaying into Virginia like her pretty little tail was on fire, wanting a little of this and a little of that from me. Playing like we were fated, or some such nonsense. And Sarah's worse, pulling at me all the time, and then you, Rose. All of you never leave me be.

"I'm sick of it all. So I quit my job and I'm leaving town."

He fired such a look of defiance at Rose she gasped. She'd never seen Ben act this way, and wasn't sure how to handle him.

Gathering her thoughts, she wiped at the spilled

beer on the counter in front of him. It was obvious to Rose that Ben and Dessa were in love. All that was needed were a few nudges in the right direction, and they'd see their way through the mess young'uns always made of such a situation.

"Well, then, you can accompany Dessa back to Kansas City, seeing as how you no longer have a job," Rose said, and aimed her own defiant stare toward Ben.

"What? Haven't you been listening to a word I've said? I wouldn't go across the street for that stuck-up fancy flirt, much less travel all the way to that rotten city with her. Let her go alone, and good riddance."

"You don't mean that, Ben. You care for Dessa, and you blamed well know it. I'd think you'd be the last one to want her setting out on such a journey. Look what happened the last time she did that. You saw it for yourself, and now you stand there acting like a perfect fool. Those yahoos are still out there. Who's to say they won't do the same thing again?"

"Well, for sure not me. If they took such a notion in their head, I wouldn't be able to stop them. Besides, the stage has been left alone since that very day. I'd say they scooted right out of the country, what with the posse riding out every day for two weeks looking for them. Not a sound or sign from 'em tells me they're gone."

"Oh, well, mister know-it-all. I'm sure you're right and this country is perfectly safe for any young woman who wants to traipse around unattended. Just set her on the trail, let the Indians or outlaws or any drunken bum who takes a notion do what they please with her. That what you want?"

Ben clasped his large hands together on the bar and sighed. He felt himself losing this argument.

"You know it's not, Rose. But dadgummit, I don't want to go to Kansas City, or any other blasted city, for that matter. Why can't she just stay here? What put this notion into her head anyway?"

"Well, I guess you'll have to ask her that question yourself, because I don't understand it. From what little she'd say, it's something to do with you. What'd you do to her?"

"Damn it all, Rose. Damn it all."

But that was all Ben would say. Dessa would have stayed in Virginia if she hadn't seen him and Sarah together, and now she was leaving. It was clear why. If he gave in to Rose and went with Dessa, he'd be doing something out of his own feelings of guilt once again. When would he ever be able to do something just because he wanted to do it?

Rose picked up his empty mug and raised her brows. He shook his head no.

"I don't know," she said. "I've done everything I can to dissuade her, Ben. Only thing I can say is if you go with her, maybe you can make her come back."

Ben studied on that, knotting his fists together on the bar top. "She belongs in Kansas City, not here in this place. And I reckon if me going with her is what it takes to get her out of my life once and for all, then that's what I'll do.

"But Rose, I ain't bringing her back with me. And the sooner I can see her off that train and get myself headed back west, the better I'll feel. Then I reckon there'll be time enough for me to head for California." Ben hesitated a moment, seeing the despair on Rose's features.

"You and Walter ought to come along with me out West, Rose. Them women ain't gonna let up on you, and sooner or later the sheriff and lots of others in town are gonna have to side with them. Better you just up and leave before that happens."

Rose grew thoughtful. Maybe Ben was right, but she hated like the very devil to say good-bye to everyone, and most especially Dessa Fallon. Maggie and the girls might go to California with her, but losing Dessa would break her heart.

"Then I can tell Dessa you'll accompany her?"

"I'll tell her myself," Ben said, "right now, this minute. And we can have this whole thing over with, for good and for all."

Chapter Twelve

Dessa packed everything, leaving the contents of the chest in the bedroom until last. For a long while she sat cross-legged on the floor and held the forgotten, unopened package the sheriff had brought her soon after the funeral. She touched the knotted string tentatively.

She trembled, suddenly afraid without knowing why. What would she find in there? Opening it now when she was on the verge of returning to her old life but without her parents didn't seem wise. She simply could not bring herself to do so. Rationally, this was no time to open it anyway. Perhaps when she was safely back in the home of her childhood, she would spread the contents out on her bed and finger through them, remember the times she wanted never to forget, before the horror of her parents' death. What few precious possessions had her mother chosen to save for her in those last terrible moments when she realized she was about to die? Or had she simply panicked and tossed out the first thing she laid her hands on?

Dessa shook away the horrid images that rapped at her consciousness. She would open the package at home in her own room cradled by the familiarity of her own bed, let the tears of grief flow surrounded by all that had become so soothing in her life.

For now, she refused to begin a long, hard trip emotionally distraught. It was bad enough the way she felt about Ben, without adding reminders of her earlier loss.

Someone banged loudly on the door. She leaped to her feet, dropped the package in her trunk, and hurried through the parlor. Whoever could that be this late at night?

Leaning her cheek against the wood, she called, "Who is it?"

"Me, Ben Poole."

Dessa smacked the flat of her hand on the door. "Go away."

"Open the door, Dessa. Rose sent me."

"Tell me what she wants. I'm not letting you in."

"Come on, Dessa. I won't yell our business out here on the street for everyone to hear. Just open the door. This won't take but a minute. What's wrong, are you afraid of me?"

Dessa grabbed the key from its nail, unlocked the door, and threw it open. "I'm not afraid of you, Ben Poole, I'd just rather not see you again. Tell me your business from right there. You don't need to come in."

And then she raised her eyes to his. Such a feeling of pending loss swept over her that she swayed with the enormity of it, fingers pinching at the frame to hold herself up.

Ben took a tentative step. "Are you sick or something?"

The lamplight behind her threw her features in shadow. He knew every inch of that lovely face, and he fought the urge to trace its angular smoothness with the tips of his fingers, feel the warmth of her flesh against his own. She was very angry with him, and with good reason, but he refused to admit that aloud. Instead he just asked again, "You okay?"

She tightened her lips and nodded. "I'm fine. What did you want?"

Ben noticed she left the door open wide and he took another step toward her as he spoke. "Not me. Rose."

"Okay, what did Rose want?"

"She asked me to tell you that I will be able to take the job of accompanying you to Kansas City." He grinned despite himself. "Accompanying, that's what she said. Not my word."

"Oh, I know it's not your word." She was ashamed that her voice dripped with sarcasm and tried again, softening the tone. "Why would you want to go with me anyway? I'm going to wire a friend to come out and make the return trip with me."

"That'll take a while. I could have you home in a few days, save you waiting on him." He stared down at his boots a moment. "Who is he, some back East dandy? You think he could protect you if those ya-hoos take it into their heads to hit the stage again?"

"Oh, and you could? Besides, Andrew's not a dandy. He's an amateur boxer, among other things."

"Well, good. He could jump out of that stage and challenge them to a boxing match. Get hisself shot, is what he'd get."

"Ben, please. What good is this going to do?"

"To tell you the truth, I don't know. Rose talks a good argument. I think if we just do what she wants and get it over with, we'll both be happier, and she durn tooting will be. It don't hurt to please Rose. She's a good woman, and she loves us both."

Taken aback by the declaration and his use of the word *us*, as if the two of them somehow belonged together, she took another step backward. He went on in but left the door ajar behind him.

His talk about love momentarily overpowered her ability to say anything. Then she remembered the way Sarah Woodridge hung on him. No woman did that without just cause.

She cocked her head at Ben smartly. "And just what will your little pretty do without you while you're gone?"

"My little pretty?" He was perplexed for a moment, then realized who she was talking about. "Sarah is not my little pretty. Aw, hell, I'm sick to death of all this. Just get your things together. I'll get us tickets on the stage in the morning and we can get this over with. You'll be back where you belong, and I can go on to California with a clear conscience."

"California? You're going to California?" Something inside her plunged into awful darkness. She wondered why she cared, wondered further why she asked.

"Yes'm, I am. Just as soon as I get you back where you belong."

"Why do you keep saying that? Where I belong. I belong where I want to be. I suppose Sarah's going with you?"

"That's not your business. I'd appreciate it if you would be ready. The stage usually pulls in before noon. It'll only be here an hour or so."

She gave up. All she wanted was out of this place in the quickest way possible, and Ben's offer, even though under pressure from Rose, seemed the most sensible.

With a sigh, she said, "I'll be ready. Will you send someone for my trunk? It's heavy."

"I'll come get it."

"Good night, then."

"To you, too." He turned and left, and she slammed the door so hard it shook the walls of the little house.

Sometime during the night a storm hit, wind and rain rattling at the roof over Dessa's head. But it didn't awaken her, for she hadn't been asleep. Visions of Ben Poole's angry face remained in her thoughts. The hard set to his mouth, the frosty glaze of those blue eyes had bespoken a fury she had never seen in him before. What had upset him so? If anyone should have been angry, it was her. But it was all over now, the ridiculous desire that he might love her, the dreams of making a life with him. All over, and probably to the good.

Better an uneventful life with Andrew or someone like him than a bare existence with Ben Poole, who was nothing more than a frontier savage. She was glad he was coming with her, but dreaded making the trip with him. It would be very difficult to look into his eyes every day and deny the way she felt. Cover up the shivers of excitement when he touched her, hide the desire that burned inside. She would have to feed her own anger and his to make the trip bearable.

She had lost her parents to this ferocious land, and now she was losing Ben Poole, and there seemed nothing she could do about it. She finally fell asleep to the sound of rain on the roof, and dreamed of a furtive stranger, always just out of reach of her probing search. She had almost forgotten the man in the cemetery, and now that she was leaving, he came back to haunt her, to make her wonder who he could be. It was too late, though, and she would probably never know who he was. She was going home.

Ben hadn't been so annoyed in years as when he left Dessa's. In a fit of temperament he had agreed to do something he truly didn't want to do. He felt trapped, encircled, with no way to escape, but he would honor his word and go with her back to Kansas City. When she stepped from the train onto the platform, he would waste no time buying himself a return ticket. He had no desire to see Dessa in the company of her city friends. And that would probably suit her just fine, too.

Without thought of what he was doing, Ben stomped down the street to the Busted Mule and got himself in a poker game with a couple of traveling gamblers who took every penny he had. When he returned there would be his final pay from Bannon Freight, and that was all that stood between him and abject poverty. He thought wryly that it was a good thing they refused markers at the poker table, or he'd have kept at it till he lost things he didn't have and got himself killed.

Broke and morose, he retreated to the Golden Sun, fetched Maggie literally from the arms of a man on the dance floor, and dragged her upstairs to one of the cribs. Inside, eyes flashing like cracked ice, Ben began to strip off his clothing.

Maggie sat on the edge of the bed, eyes wide. "Ben, don't. Please, don't. You don't want to do that. Please, Ben." She just kept repeating the litany until he stood there in nothing but his underwear.

He seemed to come to himself then, his great hands fisted tightly while he stared at the woman he thought of as his sister.

"Goddammit, Maggie. Goddammit, why did she have to come here? I was doing fine, I was making it. Goddammit!"

He went to the bed, dropped to his knees, and laid his head in her lap. She smoothed his rain-soaked hair with one hand and patted at his heaving shoulders with the other.

"Oh, Ben. I'm so sorry. So sorry." She didn't know anything else to say, and so she just kept repeating herself and touching him, gentling him, until the worst had passed.

For the moment she forget her own distress. Samuel had laid down the law at last. Marry him or he was leaving for good, and Maggie was frightened. Love led women to situations that could be very dangerous. Men as husbands or fathers terrified her, but she loved Samuel. She hadn't decided what to do.

Later she left Ben sleeping in the bed and told Rose to tell the girls the room was taken for the evening. Rose raised her brows and Maggie said, "Ben is in there asleep." She didn't say what she was thinking. That love does terrible things to both men and women.

She did tell Rose what had happened between Ben and Dessa, or as much of it as she knew. The news distressed Rose greatly, for something terrible must have gone on between the couple, and she had no notion how to fix it. Not yet, at any rate.

And she didn't get the chance to try, for the next morning Ben Poole and Dessa Fallon caught the stagecoach for the first leg of their trip. Rose had given Ben some money, figuring he would be too proud to let Dessa pay for personal things, even though he was technically in her employment. It would never occur to the child to pay him until they reached Kansas City. Moneyed folks didn't think about what it was like to have empty pockets.

The couple would ride down to Devil's Gate, where they would board the train headed east. Rose was terribly afraid she would never see Dessa again, and so held her an extra long time when they said their good-byes.

The storm had moved out of the mountains at daybreak and the crisp, fresh air held a tang of ice off the high peaks. In silence Ben helped Dessa aboard the stagecoach for the first leg of their long journey.

Dessa leaned from the window and looked back at Rose and Maggie, standing in the street holding their skirts up out of the mud with one hand and waving with the other until she could no longer see them. Then she settled back in the seat, not sparing even a glance for her companion, who sat across from her beside a black-frocked, bearded gentleman who had been on the stage when it pulled in to Virginia City.

The first day of October, a Saturday, found Dessa and Ben boarding the eastbound Union Pacific train, 1,014 miles from Omaha, Nebraska. Had they headed west from Omaha to Sacramento, California, the trip would take four to four and a half days, the black-frocked gentleman informed Dessa before they left the stage to board the train. She only cared how many days it was back East to Kansas City.

Their companion's name was Bugler—"like the horn," he would say each time he introduced himself. He never mentioned a given name.

He was filled with information about the infant Union Pacific Railroad, and soon his stories drove away Ben's dark scowl.

As the steam engine huffed and hooted and hissed out of the station, Bugler related a tale that did little to relax Dessa for the long trip ahead.

"Back in January, a passenger train left Omaha headed West. Pulled by the steam engine *America*. She was really flying along, pushing their limits, they were. Well, sir, they soon paid for that little mistake. Weren't five miles out of Aspen, Wyoming, when all that speed done 'em in. The outside rails gave way on a curve and a coach and all three Pullmans rolled down the bank and landed upside down."

Bugler stopped. Later she would learn that he always paused at precisely the most climactic part of any story. He tamped down the tobacco in the stinking bowl of his enormous pipe.

Dessa eyed the thing and wrinkled her nose. It looked too heavy to carry around. Why would anyone want to constantly fool with something so ugly that smelled so bad?

Bugler puffed and gurgled at the pipe stem until Ben asked, "And then what happened?"

It was just what the man was waiting for, and removing the pipe from between his lips, he cleared his throat dramatically and continued the tale. "Two men were killed and more than a hundred passengers were beat up and bruised and slashed by breaking glass. A gory scene indeed."

"That's terrible," Dessa said, and stared out the window and down into a gorge. It gave her the shudders thinking about the car turning loose and rolling all the way to the bottom.

"Ah, little lady, don't you fear. That same thing

would never happen again. They've already had their share of hard luck on this line. Why, it weren't two months later when the *America* had been back on the western run less than a week that it was derailed by a herd of cattle in western Wyoming."

Dessa was appalled. "I thought you were going to tell us it was attacked by Indians. Cattle? My goodness, one wouldn't think they could turn over a big old engine like the one pulling this car."

"Indians." Bugler snorted. "That's another tale in itself."

"Oh, don't tell me."

Obviously pleased with his attentive and easily impressed audience, Bugler launched into a long, drawn-out story of an Indian attack that had occurred on the Union Pacific run back in August of that year. "They haven't tried since, though, and folks are getting mighty complacent. Would be about right for them to hit again, when our guard is down."

Ben drew himself up and turned from the window. "Sir, you're scaring the wits out of Miss Fallon. It'd be a good idea if you could talk about something else."

Bugler snorted again and looked embarrassed. "Sorry, ma'am."

Dessa shot Ben a grateful look and he watched her for ever so long, a pensive expression on his face. She wished she knew what he was thinking. They had scarcely spoken except when it was absolutely necessary, and the trip was becoming terribly boring. Not that she wanted an Indian attack, but a little frivolity wouldn't be unwelcome. Even under the circumstances. She remembered that she had vowed to bicker with him at every turn, but could think of nothing to say.

The train ground to a halt some moments later, and Dessa's heart thumped right up in her throat. "What is it? What's happening?"

Bugler opened the side window and leaned out. "Must be thousand-mile tree. If the photographic car is here, we can get our pictures taken, though it's more popular with those who have ridden all the way from California. The tree is exactly a thousand miles from Omaha and it's become a popular place." He slid from the seat and made for the exit.

"Oh, Ben, let's get our picture made there. I'd like to take it back with me."

"If you want, it's fine with me. I've never had my picture made, and I don't reckon I ought to start now. That's for rich folks and road agents, the way I see it."

Dessa laughed. "Oh, Ben. Come one. What will it hurt? Come on."

With her tugging on his arm, Ben could put up little resistance without making a spectacle of himself in front of the other passengers, who were smiling indulgently at Dessa. Some had even gotten to their feet and were making their way to the front of the car.

About that time Bugler came back in and announced that J. B. Silvis was indeed present and would be taking stereographic photographs for anyone who wished to pose beside the thousand-mile tree. "He's from Andrew J. Russell's original group, don't you know. They photographed the Golden Spike ceremony in Promontory last year."

"Oh, Ben." She danced beside him in the aisle, tugging him along by the hand, glancing back occasionally, her eyes sparkling with excitement.

He could no longer resist, nor could he stop just the tiniest of smiles as he followed her.

"Here, let me get down first," he said when they reached the platform. "It's a big step."

She backed up against the car to let him slide past her and their bodies brushed. Electricity crackled between them and Ben paused for a moment, facing her, the tips of her breasts brushing at his chest. She wanted to reach out to him, smooth back a windblown lock of golden hair, but she resisted, and if he'd had anything in mind himself he let it go, too. He hopped down the steps and reached both arms up for her.

Before she took the first step, she glanced through the hazy glass of the car directly ahead of theirs. A young woman—a girl, really—glared harshly at her. When Dessa smiled and nodded, the girl swung her face angrily away. From what Dessa could see of the coach, conditions in there were deplorable. It was crowded with roughly dressed families and hoards of children, and men who looked as if they'd not had a bath in their entire lives.

She wondered how far the young woman was going, and felt sorry for her in those crowded circumstances. Then her mind turned back to Ben and she bounced down the three steps. She had no chance to contemplate the sloping incline before Ben spanned her waist with both hands and swung her to the ground beside him. She'd never expected to be in his arms again, and she closed her eyes to keep him from seeing how she was affected by the experience. Her cheeks flamed with heat. Perhaps he would take their flush for excitement or exertion.

For a long moment he held her against him. A pain knifed him in the heart. He would never have her, and holding her like this was just being foolish. Just the same, he couldn't let her go. He took a deep breath to quiet the rumblings of despair and finally was able to set her feet down on the ground. Her green eyes gazed up at him, deep and somber, and he was sure he saw that same despair reflected there. Then she brushed her hands over the front of her elegant green traveling dress as if wiping away his touch, and turned from him.

She headed for the cluster of people waiting to be photographed, chewed at her lip, and tried to will away the heavy ache inside. How could she want this man so after all that had happened? He was, despite everything, the one she wanted kissing her, touching her, being with her always. She flung away the foolish thoughts. She was going home.

When it was their turn, Ben led her to stand under the tree. He put his arm around her shoulders so whoever looked at the picture anytime in the future could see that Ben Poole had his arm around the lovely Dessa Fallon on that bright, sunny October day before she left the West and him behind to return to her life. A defiant gesture to deny the truth. They would never be together.

When the photograph had been taken, he let his arm fall from her shoulder. He felt hollow for a long time after they climbed back aboard the train. He would never get over losing her, letting her go this way.

Rose had suggested they travel first class, and Dessa, who had already traveled by rail once, readily agreed, buying her own one-way ticket and a round trip for Ben. Conditions for passengers were appalling, but greatly improved over traveling by stagecoach. Why anyone would want to travel for

pleasure, Dessa had no idea. It was a necessity best
gotten through with fortitude. Ben's surly disposition
certainly didn't help, but she reminded herself once
again that it would be best if they didn't get friendly.
She turned more and more to the companionship of
Mr. Bugler.

When her stomach began to rumble for lunch,
Dessa remembered what she had forgotten about
that maiden journey she'd made from Kansas City to
Devil's Gate on her way to Virginia City. How long
ago that seemed now, and how different from this
trip. She had been warned about the food accommodations, but had scarcely remembered the pandemo-
nium involved until the train pulled into a station
and the conductor announced they were to take a
meal at this stop.

Mr. Bugler produced one of his now familiar
snorts. "Food indeed. Little better than slop. But
then, one must adjust. Let's hurry off, shall we? Perhaps we can avoid some of the worst of it."

He managed to herd a puzzled Ben and a reluctant Dessa quickly from the passenger car and into
the railroad station. Elbows out to avoid crashing
into milling crowds of bearded miners, disreputable
individuals in ragged garments with revolvers stuck
down in their belts, society matrons with gloved
hands spread at their throats, and a conglomerate of
those who looked much like Dessa and Ben, Bugler
managed to drag them through the food line.

As Dessa followed Bugler away from the serving
counter, she was bumped hard from behind and almost dropped her coffee. Some sloshed from the cup
over the back of her hand, but it wasn't hot by any
means.

She turned and saw the girl who'd glared at her

from the coach earlier. Dark hair hung in lank strands around her shoulders and it was obvious from the smell that the girl had been on the train a good long while without benefit of a wash. Her dress was threadbare and of the cheapest cotton fabric. A thick acerbic man clutched at the girl's arm.

Dessa felt so sorry for her that when the girl spat an angry epithet at her, she simply turned away. It hurt her deeply that the young woman seemed to blame her for the circumstances in which she found herself.

Ben, who had been trailing along behind Bugler and Dessa, stopped when she did, following her gaze.

"What is it? What happened?" he asked.

"Oh, nothing," Dessa murmured. "Nothing."

Ben watched the girl walk away. When he spoke, his voice sounded forlorn. "Well, come on. Let's get out of this place. It's worse than standing in a herd of wild buffalo."

"Oh, I suppose you expect me to believe you've stood in a herd of wild buffalo," Dessa said, and hurried off, having lost sight of Bugler in the crowd.

The sandwiches were soggy and the lukewarm coffee tasted bitter. They went outside the station and leaned against the wall to eat. After a second bite into what looked suspiciously like green beef, Dessa dropped hers.

Just then the conductor leaned down from the train and shouted, "All 'board."

A small, raggedy child pounced upon Dessa's discarded sandwich and wolfed it down as his mother dragged him and carried a squalling baby back aboard. Dessa ran back to the train, Ben right on her heels. He hoisted her up from behind and said into her ear, "You sure this trip is necessary?"

Dessa tossed her head and moved through the car back to their seats. She slid in, leaving Ben the aisle seat so she'd have the scenery beyond the window to look at during the long silences.

By the next afternoon they'd left the mountains behind and the Great Plains rolled out ahead of them and on to the horizon. Gritty air blew through the open window. The mixture of dust and punishing wind soon became unbearable, and Dessa strained at the window to close it. Ben leaned over and helped slide it shut.

"Thank you," she murmured.

"You're welcome," he said, but instead of moving over, he stiffened. "My God, look at that."

Rising above the prairie, a great black cloud boiled into the sky. They watched it in awe.

"What is it? Something burning?"

"No, it's not smoke."

By that time a murmur had passed through the car as passengers gathered at the windows on that side of the train.

"It's birds, isn't it?" one woman asked.

"Maybe," someone replied.

The cloud grew, spreading wider and higher as it approached.

"My God, my God, it's locusts," Bugler shouted. "Get the windows closed, now. Hurry. Hurry."

He ran up and down the aisles assisting those who were having trouble sliding the panes shut. The conductor came through the car to help, and soon everyone settled back to watch the approaching cloud of insects. Without air, the car grew stifling, and several women, tightly encased in corsets and yards of heavy fabric, swooned into their seats, where concerned husbands fanned at them with white handkerchiefs.

Dessa hid a satisfied smile. She had learned from her few weeks out West that the tightly laced and hideous corset must be the first thing to go if a woman was to survive the harsh demands of such a life, and so she had dressed in a camisole, pantaloons, and a petticoat beneath the brown linen traveling frock.

The locusts struck the moving train, the enormous cloud swinging in a wide arc so that, one by one, the cars chugged right into them.

Insect bodies soon blackened the windows as they flew head-on into the iron horse, smashing themselves one upon the other until gore ran down the glass.

Dessa huddled back in the corner, hands over her ears, to shut out the screams of all the women and frightened children and the sound of the hurtling bodies crunching against the glass.

Ben took in the sight with amazement and the beginnings of a grin. Obviously he was quite entertained by the entire show, inside and outside the railroad car.

"If we're not careful, they'll just pick us up and fly off with us, won't they?" he asked Bugler, who appeared casual and unconcerned.

Soon the train ground slowly to a halt, and everyone in the car grew deathly silent. Maybe they were only taking a breath before breaking loose with total hysteria. Before that could happen, the conductor shouted, "We'll be here awhile. Please remain in the car. Don't open the doors or windows."

"What is it? What's happening?" Dessa asked along with a few others.

Bugler leaned toward her. "The tracks are so slick with their bodies we can't move."

The thought made her queasy and she fought down a rising bile.

Bugler nodded with a knowing look. Seasoned traveler that he was, he showed a great delight in latching on to a couple like Dessa and Ben and impressing them with his knowledge.

The conductor came through with another announcement. "It'll take a while to clear the tracks, and then we'll be on our way. As soon as the locusts clear out, we'll open the windows and get some air, but till then, just sit tight, ladies and gentlemen."

Dessa wished the window wasn't covered with the insects' bodies. She wanted to watch as the survivors drifted off in an undulating black swarm. "Let me out, Ben. Maybe we can see out the back door. I want to see." She rose and shoved at his knees.

"I've never seen anyone get excited about a bunch of damned grasshoppers before," he grumbled, but slid into the aisle to let her out. "Especially dead ones," he added at her retreating back.

"Look, Ben, look." She leaned against the door glass, twisting her head to see the shrinking black cloud. "They're gone," she cried, and shoved open the door to stand on the platform.

Fresh air washed over her, drying the perspiration that plastered her shirtwaist to her body. She lifted her skirts to let the wind underneath. "Oh, that feels good."

At that moment she twirled and saw Ben watching her with such an expression of longing that she wanted to throw her arms around him. Before she could, he glowered darkly, then turned and walked away, leaving her all alone.

Chapter Thirteen

Just after dark, Bugler went off to heed the call of a gambler who had wandered through the car hustling up a poker game. A bit earlier, passengers had taken a second meal, no different from the first except the meat was pink rather than green and the bread was stale, not soggy. Ben had moved to the window across from Dessa when they pulled out of the last stop, and she soon lay down in her seat to sleep. Luckily the first-class car was not overcrowded like the coaches she had glimpsed while standing on the platform earlier.

For a while she couldn't sleep, but lay staring out at the glittering stars in an ebony sky. The bone-jolting starts and stops of the train made it impossible to relax, and so she was surprised when she was startled awake some time later. Sleep had come, after all. She sat up and rubbed at her eyes, wondering what had awakened her.

"Oh, God, he's dead. He's dead. Please, no."

She squinted her eyes in the direction of the pitiful cries. It was Ben, lying in the seat opposite her, his long legs stuck out in the aisle, his chest shuddering. She leaned toward him, touched his arm. He was wringing wet.

"I'm sorry. God forgive me, I'm sorry," he moaned.

She lay her hand on his sweat-drenched forehead. "Ben, Ben. Wake up."

He lurched upward, knocking her aside. "What? Where?" His shoulders heaved and he buried his face in both hands.

She moved to sit beside him, to touch him, to soothe him. "What is it?" she asked. "Are you all right?"

"I'm fine." A great shudder passed through him, vibrating the seat. He wiped at his face. "Sorry, didn't mean to scare you. A bad dream, that's all. Just a bad dream. Go back to sleep."

"Ben?" She touched his arm lightly.

"Leave me alone. I'm fine."

She pulled away, sat there for a long time waiting for his breathing to settle down.

After what seemed like hours of staring off into the darkness, he said, "Dessa? I'm sorry."

"About what? What are you sorry about?"

"Everything, I guess. I didn't mean it to end up this way." Regret echoed behind the words. "I thought we were going to have some fun, you and I. You're so . . . so carefree, and I liked that. I thought . . . I mean . . . well, hell. I didn't think it would get serious. You let me know right from the start what a buffoon you thought I was. Just an ignorant frontiersman.

"Now you're all puffed up and mad at me about something I don't understand, and next thing you know, I'm the one who's apologizing." He sounded far, far away.

It took her a moment to reply. "I didn't ask you to. There's no need for you to be sorry. And I did not."

He waited, too, like maybe she'd explain that last

statement. When she didn't, he asked, "Did not what?"

"Did not call you an ignorant buffoon."

He sighed. "You thought it, and I am."

"I did not, and you are not." She wanted to grab him, shake him as if he were a misbehaving child. In a way, though, he was right about what she had thought at first, but no longer. "You are a sweet, gentle, and very handsome man."

"Ignorant buffoon would still fit with all that," he said in a lighter tone.

"Well, it doesn't. You're the one who ... well, I mean, I was perfectly willing to ... uh, what you said, have some fun, till I found you with another woman."

"I found you with that other woman, Dessa. Not the other way around."

She straightened stiffly beside him. "Well, you know exactly what I mean, Ben Poole. And her hanging on your arm all lovey-dovey and those kids treating you like their papa, or at least a long-lost and well-loved uncle. I'm not entirely innocent, you know. I understand ... uh, arrangements like that."

"Arrangements? With Sarah? Oh, Dessa, my God, you don't know how wrong you are."

"Well, tell me, then. How wrong am I?"

From over the back of the seat, a voice hissed, "Would you two kindly shut up so we can get some sleep? It's the middle of the night, for God's sake."

"I second that," piped up another voice.

Ben rose and pulled her to her feet. "Come on, let's go out on the platform. It'll be cooler and I'm sure not sleepy anymore."

"Well, praise be," came the voice from the other seat.

They stumbled around in the dark, making their way to the rear of the car and the platform. Once outside, he held on to her. The train rolled and rocked along, the wheels setting up a clacking rhythm that formed a steady backdrop for their conversation.

"You were about to tell me how wrong I am about you and Sarah," she said after growing accustomed to the train's movement. She was achingly aware of his proximity, the warmth of his body in the coolness of the night, his arm encircling her waist to hold her steady.

"Sarah is . . . Sarah was . . ."

"Are the twins yours?"

"Mine?" He laughed bitterly. "Lord, no, they're not mine. But they have no father, and I just—"

"Sarah's husband? What happened to him?"

Ben cleared his throat. This was very difficult. He'd never spoken the words aloud, the ones he needed to say to Dessa at this very moment. He couldn't understand why it was so terribly important to him that she know about what he had done. Perhaps he was trying to drive that final wedge between them, the one that would assure she wouldn't want to be around him. Would no longer question him and care about him and play her games with him. *Tell her!* he commanded himself. *Tell her, so she can forget forever this clumsy frontiersman she met out West.*

"He died. I killed him. There, are you satisfied now? Are you happy to learn that what you thought all along was right?"

He had her by the shoulders, had her pulled up so close she could feel the warmth of his breath on her cheek. Smell him, too. This man. Oh, this wonderful man. She swayed against him.

"Oh, God, Dessa." He kissed her, a demanding kiss that frightened her with its intensity. A moan escaped his throat, vibrating over her tongue as she opened her lips to him. He released the tight grip on her arms and encircled her in an embrace that was anything but fierce. He cradled her lovingly, head bent down to taste her mouth, her eyes, her throat.

She collapsed into that caress, the flavor and texture of him encompassing her entire world. Where he touched her she was on fire, she yearned for more as he tongued the hollow of her throat. A sound like crying spiraled from deep within her. He lowered his head, nibbled at her breast through the thickness of fabric.

"Oh, Ben." She grasped his head, holding him there, begging for more as shards of pleasure burst through her to tingle every nerve ending.

The little nuzzling sounds he made were of pure content, pure desire, animalistic and unreal. The heat of his breath flowed through the material and over her breast, and she wanted to bare herself to him. Rip the dress away and feel his warm, moist lips fastened around each nipple in turn. Feed him, nurture him, hold him always and forever, while he awoke in her the fiercest passion she had ever experienced. Would ever experience.

She panted with the exertion, backed into the corner against the rail and the rear of the car. He fell to his knees, buried his face in the heavy folds of her dress so that the pounding of his hot, ragged breath filtered through to the flesh between her legs. She clung to him, with him, around him, as if he were inside her. The swaying of the train set up a rhythm and they moved with it.

He groaned and grabbed her buttocks in both hands.

She threw her head back and cried out to a black universe that rotated until she grew dizzy. She crumpled, and he caught her up close, nibbling and licking at her neck, repeating her name over and over.

She lay her head on his shoulder, gasping, trying to recapture some feeling of equilibrium. What had he done to her? How could this have happened? She had never heard of such a thing. Mother never talked to her about this.

"Ben, what . . .?"

He touched her cheek with the back of his hand. "Are you all right?"

She nodded, struck mute by the enormity of what had happened.

"Are you sure?" he asked, and brushed hair away from her face. "Here, let me help you up."

She felt wobbly, strange, as if just recovering from a long illness. "Not yet. Just a minute."

"I'm sorry, Dessa."

"No," she gasped. "No, don't you dare tell me you're sorry for . . . for this." She brushed her bodice, then his chest. "For what we've done. Don't you be sorry. I will not allow you to be sorry anymore, not for anything."

Ben untangled himself and rose, left her kneeling there. God, what had he done? He had wanted her, suddenly and so fiercely that he couldn't help himself. But she hadn't tried to stop him, had she? If she had, would he have been able to stop? How could he feel such desire for a woman like her? It was as if she had bewitched him with her city ways, and no matter what he did, he couldn't fight her magnetism.

He might as well have torn her clothes from her

body and had his way with her, considering her response. Dear God, they had both experienced a release of their pent-up desires; their passion for each other had been spent without the act itself being completed. He had never known such a thing could happen.

He wanted to explain it to her, somehow make things the way they were. How would they ever bear to part, feeling this way about each other? Or perhaps this wasn't love, but simply an animal attraction that would go away once they weren't in each other's sight any longer.

She collected herself and used the railing to stand. Without speaking further, he guided her back inside and to her seat. A metallic gleam lightened the eastern sky, warning of impending sunrise and another long day of traveling. He settled down beside her and pulled her head onto his shoulder.

She turned and nestled comfortably into the curve of his arm. She didn't think of his earlier confession until much later, after she had recovered somewhat from the incident on the platform.

He said he had killed Sarah's husband. How could that be? How could this gentle, beautiful man ever have killed anyone? She pushed the memory to the back of her mind. She would not ask him any more about it. She didn't want to know.

Oddly, she dreamed of Mitchell, and even more strange, he stood just out of her sight, beckoning from a thick and dark grove of trees. In the dream she could not recognize the place where they were, but she knew her brother, and he looked just as he had the day he rode away to war, waving his white hat high in the air until that was all she and Mother and Father could see—that hat gleaming in the ferocious sunlight.

Then a monster came to chase Mitchell away, to turn on her, and she saw that it was the vicious outlaw Coody.

She awoke with tears on her cheeks and her brother's name on her lips, but before she could talk about the dream, it had flown from her memory just like the dust blew across this endless prairie.

The day dragged on interminably, broken only by infrequent stops along the way and the sawdust taste of the awful food and brackish water.

The train had just pulled out after lunch when the door to the car burst open with such force that the resulting crack of it hitting the seats against the wood-paneled wall brought exclamations from everyone in the car.

"Robbery! It's a robbery." The words echoed from one to the other of the passengers. A tremendous man entirely filled the doorway. Legs spraddled, he held one arm cocked just above the butt of a huge pistol tucked in his belt. He wore a high-crowned black hat, a strange kind of leather britches tied on over dusty black pants, a faded shirt, and a black-and-gray-striped vest. A limp bandanna was tied around his neck.

Immediately Dessa thought of Coody and the stage robbery, and grabbed Ben's arm so tightly he grunted.

"Lookee here at the swells," the man crowed. "Well, let's just see how you like this." He yanked the tremendous revolver out of his waistband and fired it off, aiming toward the ceiling of the car. The bullet punched a hole through the roof.

Ladies screamed and men shouted. The man

laughed uproariously, fired the pistol a couple more times, laughing all the harder at the reaction. Women cringed and hid behind their men, who in turn blustered but did nothing to stop the wild man's antics.

Ben, who carried no weapon, put himself between the man and Dessa, a stalwart barrier of protection.

The conductor entered through the other end of the car just as the desperado backed out, slammed the door, and was gone.

Instead of going after the man, the calm railway employee made his way slowly up the aisle, soothing the passengers' fears and making sure no one was injured.

One exclaimed so that Dessa and Ben could hear, "Hurt? I could have had apoplexy. What is the meaning of such a thing? An attempted robbery, sir, and you not doing a whit about it. I'll report this to the president of the Union Pacific as soon as we reach our destination."

The conductor said, "He was just blowing off steam, sir. I assure you, this train has never been robbed. The cowpunchers, well, sir, they just have to blow sometimes. Some of 'em are riding back after a long and harsh trail drive pushing cattle north. It gets crowded and hot in the coaches and they will bring whiskey along . . . well, you understand."

He addressed the speech to everyone. Their murmurs and exclamations were quieting down now that the danger, if there had ever been any, was past.

"Damned fool," Ben grumbled. "Suppose someone on the car had a gun. Could have shot him. Damned fool."

"Happens a lot," Bugler said. He'd returned bleary-eyed and morose from his long stint at the poker table, and these were the first words he'd spoken since lowering himself with a groan into the seat an hour or so earlier. "Got robbed myself and no one ever drew a gun. I tell you, every time one of those card-sharps plies their trade on me, I swear I'll never do it again. But along one comes, and despite everything, I trot right on his heels and give him all my money.

"Took 'em a mite longer to break me this time, though. I reckon I'm learning their ways some."

With that statement, Bugler dropped his cold pipe down in the pocket of his jacket, leaned his head back, and went to sleep.

As the afternoon wore on, dust grew thicker until the windows had to be closed to prevent everyone choking. Dessa fussed with long strands of her dark hair that had come loose from the pins. Her black hat, the one she'd worn to the funeral and which seemed the best suited to travel with the veil turned back, had long since been removed in the hopes she would be cooler without it. Nothing seemed to help. Opening the windows was unthinkable.

Ben unbuttoned his shirt halfway down. "Loosen your dress at the neck. It'll help," he said.

She nodded, but glanced around to see if anyone was watching.

"Don't worry about any of them. They've all got their own troubles," he said, and began to undo her buttons. His big fingers were clumsy and fumbled with the small loops.

Dessa smiled at the furrow of concentration between his eyes, the firm set of his mouth, and gently grazed her fingertips over his cheek. Dear Ben. How could she have ever thought him bumbling and igno-rant?

He stopped, his hands grazing her hot skin, and tilted his head so that his lips touched her fingers.

At that very moment, the train lurched and emitted a hideous squealing sound. It jolted to a stop, and on down the line behind them car after car thudded into the one ahead of it. With each hit the car they were in leaped forward again, then it would groan to a stop. On and on this went, until Dessa thought her insides would be bounced out.

Once the train stopped moving and making the hideous screeching noise, everyone gathered at their windows to peer out.

Below, Dessa saw no land, just the yawing space of a deep gorge. At the bottom a miniature stream flowed, rocks and trees jutted out of a bluff far off in the distance.

"It's a trestle. We're on a trestle," Ben said, looking out the window next to her.

"Fire, fire," came the shout down the line as doors were flung open. "The bridge is on fire. A brigade, we need a fire brigade."

Ben left his seat. Bugler, roused by all the commotion, joined him. Dessa remained by the window, peering first toward the front of the train, which she couldn't see because it curved away out of sight, then to the back, which she could see. Thick, black smoke billowed into the sky where the wind tossed it away.

She leaped from her seat and ran in the direction Ben had gone.

"Please, ladies, keep your seats," the conductor urged as he hurried through the car. He stopped until Dessa took a seat, then went on. She sprang up as soon as he left the car.

Ben, where was Ben? Gathered on the platform

were several men, sleeves rolled up. One by one they were stepping down off the train and disappearing from her view. She hurried through the door in time to see the last man swing out of sight.

"What's happened? What is it?" a young woman from the coach ahead cried. She poked her head out the door, eyes huge, her face pale with fright. Dessa saw that it was the girl who had sworn at her earlier.

Ignoring her, Dessa leaned over the rail to see better. The men were inching along a narrow walkway alongside the tracks. Once again she glanced down into the abyss and gasped with horror. Just looking down made her dizzy. She had never liked heights. As a child she couldn't even climb trees or look out a second-story window. If any one of those men fell, he would be dashed to pieces on the jagged rocks in the stream below.

She imagined the bodies spiraling ever downward, and leaned back, holding a hand over her mouth. The thick oily smell of smoke and the depth of the gorge turned her stomach.

The girl said right at her elbow, "The train set the bridge on fire. The engine set the bridge on fire. That's what me man said. Isn't that a crazy thing? Who ever heard of such a thing? And where will they get water to put it out? I ask. Perhaps they can just piss on it, all of those men, and it will go out. That's probably what they all think, isn't it, now? Men would." She chuckled harshly.

Dessa was shocked at such language from the mouth of a lady, but before she could voice her opinion, the girl was off on another tack.

"I told Keenan, I says, this place is a crazy place. Bad enough to come to America, but then on top of it to traipse all over these plains. What are we look-

ing for? is what I'm asking. Now, if he gets killed out
there, falls off and smashes himself on the rocks below, what will I do then? I ask you, what will I do?"

How odd that the young woman spoke as if she'd
never been angry with Dessa. She had a thick accent
that made her hard to understand, but she seemed
to speak English without much trouble.

Dessa tried to reassure her. "He won't, I'm sure.
The railroad certainly wouldn't let its passengers risk
their lives, would they?"

"Well, now, listen to you," the girl sneered. "And
ain't you miss prim and proper? Riding in the ritzy
car while us that has naught is hauled along like
herds of swine. You think them rich bastids care
about the likes of us . . . or even you, for that matter?"

Shocked into silence, Dessa ignored the girl and
leaned out very cautiously, trying to spot Ben. Toward the rear of the train she saw a platform protruding out from the bridge, and on it a huge barrel.
A bucket brigade had been formed from the barrel,
which obviously held water, and the men from the
train, who had lined up to the place from which the
black smoke boiled, were passing the buckets along.

Balanced precariously as they were on the narrow
walkway, passing water to the fire was a slow and te-
dious job. She wished she could pick out Ben in the
line, but with the smoke and her eyes already
blurred from so much dust and sweat, and being
afraid to lean out any farther, she couldn't.

The girl who had rattled on in her strangely accented voice lifted her skirts and climbed up to sit
on the hand rail.

Dessa reached toward her, cried out a warning,

and the train shuddered. The girl lost her hold, tee-tered, and tumbled backward.

She screamed but managed to grab the rail with one hand. There she hung, legs kicking about and one arm swinging out in space. Her slight body twisted and turned. Her legs weren't long enough to put her feet down on the narrow walkway. Nor could she turn loose and drop, for she would surely lose her balance and her footing and fall from the bridge into the chasm below. She screamed again, a terri-fied, high-pitched wail that rent the air, overpowering the shouts of the men fighting the fire.

Dessa leaned out and grabbed the girl's wrist, as slick with sweat as were her own hands.

Oh, God, she couldn't hold on!

The girl raised frantic eyes, her loose arm clawing toward Dessa. No sound came from her open mouth. Horror had stricken her dumb.

Swallowing a great lump that rose from deep in her gut, Dessa shouted, "Hang on, hang on. I'll get you."

She peered over the side, closed her eyes, and swayed. Oh, dear God, she couldn't do it. She would fall! They both would fall.

She stepped down off the platform to the wooden step. A great chasm yawned in front of her. Turning her back, she reached blindly with one foot for the next step, and then the next. Her stomach quivered, and for a moment she froze in place. While the girl dangled by one fragile arm, Dessa finally found her footing on the very narrow wooden walkway of the bridge.

"Don't look down, don't look up, just don't look," she muttered. Hanging on tightly with one hand, she stretched the other toward the girl. The sound of her shoe soles sliding along the walkway grated in her ears, and stars shot through her vision. She was going to pass out!

A strange hideous gurgle came from the girl. "I can't . . . I can't hold on."

Dessa took a deep breath, gritted her teeth, and peered through the burning perspiration. The girl's wide-eyed glance locked on her. Pleading, begging. *Don't let me fall. Don't!*

Her outstretched hand still wouldn't reach the girl. Hanging on to the narrow rail posts with first one hand, then another, she inched closer. She did not look anywhere but into the terrified face watching her progress. Under the balls of her feet, the walkway offered safety, the rails gave a hold, and she just kept moving. *Don't think of what's below. Don't . . . think.*

The girl dragged in a great gasp. "Me fingers is slipping offfff."

"No, no," Dessa cried. Grabbing at the rail with her right hand, she flung her left around the girl's waist just as the girl's fingers slipped away from their flimsy hold on the rail.

The girl kicked and screamed and fought.

"Stop, stop it," Dessa shouted at her. "We'll both fall. I've got you, I've got you."

Muscles across her shoulders strained as she held up the girl's weight and most of her own with the grip of that right hand. "Put your feet on the walk."

Instead, panicked, the girl threw a frail arm around Dessa's neck and kicked and pumped her legs, trying to climb up her body. Gasping, Dessa clawed for the rail, got a firm hold, and there they both hung. The arms clamped around her throat were cutting off her air. She gasped and tried to move back toward the steps, but she couldn't do it.

They were both going to fall! They would die.

Her vision blackened, but she hung on tightly, inhaling the sour smell of fear from the unwashed body clinging to her. She clamped her jaws and struggled to pull them both along to the steps, such a sparse few feet away. They weren't going to make it. She simply couldn't pull the weight of both of them, not with the girl hanging on her like that. Dangling out over the precipice.

The girl was crying uncontrollably, making huge wet sounds down in her throat.

The fingers of Dessa's right hand slipped ever so slightly on the rail and she gasped for air.

Abruptly an arm clamped around her, a voice said sternly, "I've got you, stop fighting."

Ben, oh, Ben.

"Turn loose, little one, we've got you," another male voice said, and the weight of the girl was released from around her neck.

Dessa dragged in deep lungfuls of air, still clinging to the rail, even though Ben had a good hold on her.

As she was pulled away, the girl pawed out at Dessa, as if afraid to let her go. Then the other man had her. With one hefty sweep, Ben swung Dessa onto the bottom step of the platform.

Trembling so hard she couldn't speak, she latched on to the rail on either side and hung there, dragging sweet air into her aching lungs. Ben spanned her body from behind, his own hands closing over hers, and let her rest against him until she could climb the steps back to safety.

"What in God's name were you thinking of?" he said when he had her safely in his arms.

"She fell . . . she fell, and I couldn't . . . I couldn't let her . . . oh, Ben. I was so frightened. I couldn't see or hear. My voice wouldn't work. I have never felt anything like that in my entire life. I'm afraid . . . I've always been afraid of being up high and falling."

"Well, you didn't fall. And let's hope you don't ever try anything like that again."

Abruptly her knees turned to rubber and he swept her up in his arms, his mouth crooking into that familiar grin she hadn't seen in a while.

"Guess this is just becoming a habit we can't break," he said, and carried her inside to their seat.

Chapter Fourteen

B ugler, revived after the excitement of the bridge fire, filled them in on the history of the span that had almost taken Dessa's life.

"It's called Dale Creek Bridge."

"Creek?" Dessa said. "That's more than a creek."

"Yes, well, these railroad folk are prone to massive understatement quite frequently. At any rate, it's an engineering marvel. A timber trestle 560 feet long and 130 feet above that tiny stream. Everyone said it would fall under the first freight."

"Oh, great. Good. Not only do we set it on fire, we could have made it collapse under us simply by being there." Dessa shuddered at the recollection of dangling out over that sheer drop and tried to forget the heart-rending terror of it. "What set it on fire, by the way?"

"Sparks from the engine. That's why they keep buckets of water on those platforms. You'll see them on all these wooden trestles."

"You mean we may have to do that again?"

Ben laughed and hugged her close. "Well, not the part where you try to take a dive off the train, let's hope. No, we don't have to do that again."

The two men chuckled, but Dessa's attempt died in her throat. It really wasn't very funny to her. In her mind's eye she could still see her fingers slipping off that rail, and her and that irascible and hysterical young woman tumbling into the chasm of Dale Creek. The memory was too raw, too frightening.

Ben sensed her trembling, held her closer, and put his lips in her hair. "That was a very brave thing to do."

"I didn't think about it being brave. I just did it because of her eyes, the terror there. And me doing nothing might have been the last thing she saw as she fell. I knew if I didn't do something, I'd be seeing that face filled with terror for the rest of my life."

Ben knew exactly what she meant. He would carry forever the haunting memory of Clete Woodridge lying in his own blood in the dusty street, death already masking his features as he looked up at Ben, begged, "Take care of Sarah. And the boys, take care of my boys."

Ben shook away the memory. Clete hadn't known that Ben's bullet had killed him, but Ben knew, and so he'd promised. Rose kept telling him he was foolish, that sooner or later he had to live his own life and Sarah had to live hers. But he couldn't let go, he just couldn't. Not without seeing Clete's accusing stare for the rest of his days.

Right at this moment, though, none of that mattered nearly as much as the girl he held in his arms, and he gave her an extra big hug. He might live with losing her, but he couldn't bear to think of her dying.

She grunted and giggled. "You'll choke me if you keep that up. I'm okay, thanks to you. You weren't exactly a coward yourself. If it weren't for you, she and I would both have been smashed in the bottom of that rocky ravine."

He inhaled deeply of her scent. When he'd heard

the screams and saw her dangling out in space, he'd realized that he loved her more than life itself. He would have plunged to his death to save her, and it was a knowing that planted itself firmly within his heart and soul. He might never have her for his own, they would certainly have to part at the end of this journey, but he would carry that love for the rest of his life. And he knew, too, how very rare and privileged such a thing was. To love, to be loved. Could one outweigh the other? He didn't think so. And one didn't hinge on the other, either.

"Oh, Dessa, Dessa, I love you," he said in her ear.

Swallowing over the lump in her throat, she leaned back into his embrace. What would they do? Her on her way to take over the reins of her daddy's business in a city Ben would hate on sight, and Ben set to return to Sarah and her boys, whatever reasons he had for that relationship.

Why couldn't this trip last forever, miserable as it was? Then she could remain in his arms and never face the parting that must surely come.

She turned so that her lips brushed his jaw. "I love you, too, Ben Poole. I love you, too."

The sweet declaration was a balm for his battered soul. He refused to think of their parting.

Sometime later that afternoon, when everyone in the car appeared to be dozing, Dessa was startled by a tug on her sleeve. She opened her eyes to see the dirty face of the young woman who'd almost pulled them both to their deaths.

Dessa rubbed her hands over her eyes, thinking for a moment she was dreaming. "What? What is it?"

"Me man says I should ask you."

Dessa nodded and waited. What could she say?

The girl picked at a patch on her soiled skirt. "I

said no, and he got mad at me. Hollered was I a heathen or what? And I 'spect that's what I am, for sure." She fingered the rich cloth of Dessa's dress.

"Surely to goodness will never have a dress as fine as that, and your skin. Lookit." Roughly she grabbed Dessa's hand and rubbed her callused thumb over its back. The pad was so coarse it scratched Dessa.

Dessa pulled away. "What do you want?" Deep down inside, she was frightened of this little waif with the angry eyes and bad breath.

"You saved me hide, and I thought as how you'd seen fit to do that, you might . . . well, you just might give me and me man something. We tried to homestead some land, but nothing worked out for us and we near starved. Finally just give up while we still had the fare to come back East. Well?" Her filmy eyes fixed on Dessa.

"You want money?" She couldn't believe what she had heard. "You want me to give you money because I saved your . . . your life? That doesn't make sense."

The girl dropped her gaze. "I told him it wouldn't work. Rich folks don't ever see fit to share nothing, that's how they stay rich."

"Your husb . . . your man put you up to this?"

The poor waif nodded. At least she had the good sense to look ashamed of her part in the scheme. "I'm sorry. Oh, God, I was so scared when I pitched over the side. I seen me flat as a pancake down on them rocks. I do truly thank you, and I'll tell me man you said no." She slanted a quick look up through her eyelashes. "I reckon he'll smash me about some, but that's okay. I ain't dead on the rocks, now, am I? Thanks to you."

She rose from her squatting position in the aisle and started to walk away. Dessa grabbed her arm.

"Wait, don't go. Here." She dug around in her reticule. Most of her trip money was secreted on her person, not easily retrieved in public, but she did carry a small roll of bills for emergency expenses. She slipped it into the girl's hand and held on to her for a minute.

The idea that this child/woman would get beaten if she didn't return to her man with money outraged Dessa. She wanted to follow her into the other car and tell her man so, but that would probably only cause more trouble.

The girl didn't look at the wad of money, but searched Dessa's eyes beseechingly. "I'd get away from him if there was another way. But me pap promised me to him, and the money he paid fed me brothers and sisters. 'Tisn't so bad, really."

She stumbled away, not looking back or uttering a word of thanks. For a long time after the door had closed behind the girl, Dessa stared through the glass. How poor was the girl's existence, how luxurious her own. It amazed her how her life could be so richly blessed without her ever realizing it. The incident stuck with her a long while as she sat in silence, watching Ben sleep and listening to the monotonous clacking of the train wheels carrying her home.

Exhausted and dirty, Ben and Dessa at last detrained at Kearney, Nebraska, to catch another train south to Kansas City. She was almost home.

Standing in the station, luggage around her feet, her trunk left on the platform for transfer for the last leg of the trip, she was filled with a mixture of pleasure and dread. By this time tomorrow, Ben would be on his way back west; out of her life forever. She would never see him again.

Eyes filling with unexpected tears, she turned to him. "Ben, let's stay over a day here. We can get hotel accommodations, take a bath, eat some decent food. I'm not sure I can go on in such a condition." She held her arms away from her body and made a face, as if a bath were her only real concern.

She wanted simply to ask him to stay with her. Forget everything and stay with her when they reached her destination. But she couldn't. He would be miserable, and in time so would she. And suppose he refused? Suppose he turned his back on her and left anyway? That would simply kill her. Better to part knowing they loved each other. That if things had been different, they could have been happy. A mutually agreed-upon parting would be bittersweet, and it would remain forever in her memory, untouched by time or aging or strife. In a dime novel, the whole thing would be so romantic. But in true life, the hopelessness of the situation caused a terrible ache around her heart.

Ben touched the tip of her chin and stared down into her brimming eyes. He almost asked her at that moment to come with him. Together, they could climb on that train headed west and just ride until there was no place else to ride. Nothing but the ocean stretching to the horizon. He'd never seen the ocean, couldn't even imagine what it might be like to behold that great expanse of water flowing to meet the sky. He pictured Dessa at his side, took in a great gasp of air.

His voice trembled when he asked, "Won't he be looking for you?"

"He?" she asked.

"Arthur or Andrew, or whatever his name is."

"I can telegraph, say I'll be delayed."

He took her hand, held it to his lips for an instant. "Are you sure this is what you want?" One more night with her, one more night. Would that make their parting easier? The answer, of course, was no, but nevertheless he wanted this time.

She nodded solemnly, wondering exactly what she was agreeing to. Would she let him make love to her? The very idea made her dizzy. If she did such a thing and then he went away, no man would ever have her. She would have only two choices then: become a spinster or a loose woman to be whispered about all over town. Was that what she wanted?

"I only want a bath and a decent bed. That's all I want," she said aloud.

"Yes, of course," he murmured against her skin, and turned her hand loose.

And so she wired Andrew a terse message, and they checked in to a hotel near the Union Station, requesting separate rooms and hot baths. Ben paid for his own from the money Rose had loaned him. No telling when he could pay her back, but he would. He had no intention of taking money from Dessa for traveling to Kansas City with her. Once he got to California and settled down, he would find work. He'd heard that out there jobs were plentiful and the pay was good.

Ben carried his own bag and hers, and she followed along upstairs to their rooms. They arranged to meet for supper after they had bathed.

Even in the small restaurant of the hotel, Ben felt uncomfortable. It wasn't at all like Virginia City. They were "back East." They were in the United States. Men and women both dressed differently and spoke differently. Hell, they even walked strange. Seated at the small table across from Dessa, he found himself not knowing where to put his elbows. First he planted them on both sides of his dinner service; then, because that took up too much of the sorry little table, he tucked them down against his sides stiffly, and that made it difficult to eat.

What exactly was that green stuff on his plate, anyway? He poked at it with his fork, decided it was some kind of weed blossom, and shoved it aside to tackle the rest of the meal.

The tiny chunk of beef did look safe to eat, but there weren't over two or three bites. It was covered with a strange puddinglike sauce that he dipped a tine of his fork in and tasted cautiously. Definitely not gravy, but spicy. It would do, especially since he was hungry enough to eat a horse. He felt much like the frontier buffoon Dessa had thought him, and he couldn't wait to get out of this place. He wouldn't stay in Kansas City, either, for it was bound to be even worse. Ben Poole faced the fact that the States were not for him. He was a frontiersman, no doubt about it.

Dessa enjoyed the first decent meal she had eaten since leaving Kansas City to go to the territories. Looking around her, she sighed, then glanced at Ben, who managed to look quite distressed, though he was eating his meal with gusto.

She sipped from her glass of water, cleared her throat, plucked her napkin from her lap and patted her mouth. His discomforting scowl made her uneasy.

"What is it, Ben?" she asked in a half whisper.

His hand jerked, spilling food from the fork on its

way to his mouth. "Hell if I know. Eat it anyway, it's probably good for you."

Dessa couldn't help chuckling. "I didn't mean that, silly. I meant, what's wrong? You look like you swallowed a thundercloud."

He put the fork carefully in his plate. "They're dressed funny and this stuff tastes awful," he said, leaning toward her so that he could keep his voice low. "It's worse than the Continental in Virginia, but at least there folks don't put on such a show. Look at 'em, Dessa."

She did. The women wore crinolines so that their skirts billowed out around them to fill the aisles between the tables. The men were in frock coats with cravats at the throats of their boiled white shirts. She herself had owned one of the new bustles before leaving for Virginia City, and thought them much more comfortable than the crinolines. But if she were to admit the truth, she would agree with Ben. Folks on the frontier knew much more about dressing for comfort than the people here.

"Well, Ben, how you dress doesn't mean anything."

Ben guffawed and heads turned. "Would if I had to wear that getup," he said, and gestured toward a man nearby who had a bow tie up under double chins, the turned-over collar of his shirt buttoned so tight he was red in the face.

"Well, Ben, what I meant was that you look just fine."

He touched the rough fabric of his sack coat. "Wasn't talking about me," he grumbled.

If Ben thought these people were turned out fancy, wait until he . . . But then it didn't really matter, did it? He wouldn't be attending the welcome-home party that was sure to be thrown when her friends knew she was back. He would be on the train headed for Montana Territory, and no longer caring about what she did or who she did it with.

She looked up in time to see Ben toss his napkin in the middle of his plate and rise. "I'm just going out for a walk, Dessa, if that's all right with you."

She stood also. "You don't need my permission, but I think I'll just go back to my room and go to bed."

He nodded and threaded his way carefully between the seated couples, taking great care to keep his boots off the women's billowing spotted and striped skirts.

She felt a sense of intense sorrow and loss when he left the table. He was as much out of place here as if he had stumbled into a church in only his underdrawers. Funny how easily she had fitted in out in Montana. She had to admit that she had hoped Ben would develop an instant attraction to the way of doing things here. But it had been a dim hope and one she really hadn't expected would come true.

After she went alone to her room, it was a long time before she fell asleep, despite her exhaustion. She kept thinking of what the next few days would bring. How would she sort out the affairs of her daddy's business when she knew nothing about it? Should she sell it or try to find someone to run it? What would she tell Andrew when he asked her once again to marry him? When would Ben come back to the hotel? Had he gone to seek the company of a fancy woman?

That last thought filled her with a longing for his embrace. She thought of the passion he had awakened in her and her body felt hot with desire. His breath against her throat, his lips at her breast, teeth finding her nipples even through the layers of her clothing.

Dessa moaned and pulled her knees up tightly against her chest. "Ben, oh, Ben."

A long shaft of golden light cut the darkness of the street. Ben headed for it, stomping hard on the wooden boardwalk to get rid of the unexpected anger that rode within him. Why was he so angry? And who was he angry with?

Drawing up to the batwing doors, he peered inside, pretending that he was just taking a look, when all along he knew he would go in. It would be a toss-up between a couple of beers or a hand or two of poker. Maybe both. Hell, who cared?

The place was pretty tame compared to the Busted Mule or even Rose's place. But in the far corner a card game was in progress, and so he carried his mug of beer over and stood to watch.

"Well, Doc, you in or what?" the dealer asked of a white-haired gentleman who wore a watch fob and a golden chain across his vested and quite large midsection.

"I'm thinking."

"Well, don't take the whole night to do it," said a young, rough-looking man sitting near Ben.

Ben glanced at the hand and saw three treys and two jacks.

"What's the bet?" Doc asked, his fingers playing over a stack of blue chips.

"Hunnerd. Bet or pass, old man," the young tough said.

Ben coughed and gulped at his beer, hoping the older man would just fold and walk away. He'd never beat a full house.

. Doc looked all around and laid down his cards. "Reckon I'm out."

Ben let out a breath and watched the next man.

He looked to be a farmer, with protruding ears and a sunburn across the bridge of his nose. He held his pants up with suspenders and there was a patch on the sleeve of his faded shirt. Ben shook his head at him, and the farmer studied his cards some more, looking back at Ben before laying them down.

"Me, too."

The young one shot Ben a dark look. "Step back from me when I'm playing cards, mister," he said, and raked in the pot.

Ben was in no mood to be messed with. He was about to lose the woman he loved to a way of life he purely didn't understand, and that was making him angry in a way he only vaguely remembered being angry. That was back in the war when he realized that every man in his patrol was dead but him. Then he hadn't been sure if the anger was because he was still alive or because they were all dead. And the hot fury had been so mixed up with grief that he wasn't sure he could tell the two apart.

Whatever the feeling was, he didn't like it, and so most of the time he worked it off with physical labor of some sort.

This time he couldn't.

The young tough half rose and said, "Hear what I said, mister? Move away—now."

Ben shoved the fellow back down in his chair. And he did it out of pure orneriness. And he didn't care. He was going to lose Dessa and someone had to pay.

It was just a little shove, nothing violent, Ben thought later. It sure did set the fellow off, though. He came up out of that chair like a bobcat fighting for his female, lighting all over Ben, who was easily twice his size. He latched on to Ben around the neck, locking both legs around his thighs.

"Well, hell." Ben plucked the man off, tossing him halfway across the room.

The tough rolled like a wooden barrel, fetching up against the bar while folks moved aside, holding their mugs high and out of the way.

"Sic him, you little fart," an old drunk at one of the tables shouted. "Don't you let that big old feller throw you around thataway."

Ben shrugged and turned his back on his opponent. That was the wrong thing to do, he realized shortly, for this time he was locked in a leg hug that did little damage, but made it impossible for him to walk away.

He thunked his opponent smartly on top of the head, just enough to get him to turn loose, and the fellow bit him right through his britches. Ben let out a howl and dragged his attacker off by the hair.

As fights go, it wasn't much of one. The little man never got enough of a distance from Ben for him to haul off and bust him one. It was more of a wrestling match than anything, with Ben afraid to get too rough for fear he'd kill the little son of a bitch. On the other hand, he was bitten, gouged, butted, kicked, and scratched before he finally picked the man up and toted him outside, where he threw him in the water trough next to the hitching post.

"Stay in there, or I'll drown you," he commanded, holding the sputtering fool by his shirt collar. "You hear me? Don't come out of there till I'm out of sight. I mean it, now. You wrap yourself around me one more time and I'll break your arm."

The old drunk had followed the action out to the

street and stood swaying around on the edge of the walk. He continued to egg the man in the horse trough on to finer deeds.

"Silly little bastid, if you'd a just listened to me, you'd a had him whupped. Now look at yah. Look like a blamed skinny wet chicken. Come out a there, I'll finish the job fer him." The drunk danced around awhile, rotating his doubled fists in the direction of the unfortunate man in the water trough.

Ben felt like throwing the old codger in, too, but he restrained himself. One battle a night was enough, and besides, he didn't feel angry anymore. All he felt was just plain tired.

He headed back toward the hotel, fingering his swollen lip gingerly. The man had brought blood with his teeth and fingernails. All things considered, he was quite a little scrapper, but he had learned the fallacy of that old adage, "The bigger they are, the harder they fall."

Ben couldn't help chuckling when he thought of how the fight must have looked to spectators. That little runt just coming back over and over, time after time being tossed clean across the room. And when you got right down to it, Ben was at fault. You didn't go standing behind a man in a poker game and giving away his hand to the other players. Anybody'd done that to him, he'd have cleaned his plow, and quick.

Come to think of it, Ben thought with another chuckle, that's what the poor little fool had tried to do. He just hadn't been quite big enough.

He tried to make very little noise letting himself into his hotel room, but the bed creaked and moaned when he lowered his tired body onto the mattress. After sleeping on a bedroll on the ground most of his life, Ben had trouble relaxing on something so soft, and so he tossed and turned and the bed chirped and squawked.

The noise awoke Dessa from a light sleep, and after listening awhile, she got up and went to the door between the two rooms. She twisted the knob and found Ben hadn't locked his side, so she slipped through and into his room.

Her heart pounded fiercely. It was a wonder Ben didn't hear the drumming as she padded in bare feet across the cool wooden floor. He turned over once again; the bed groaned.

In a sliver of moonlight she could barely see the huge lump he made.

Suddenly, without warning, he sat straight up in bed and let out a few grumbled curses. The movement startled Dessa and she screeched.

It awoke Ben, who'd been dreaming the fight over again, and he hollered, "What the hell?"

"Ben, it's me. Dessa. Are you ill?"

"Ill? No, of course not. You gave me a hell of a fright. What's the matter with you, woman? Sneaking up on me like that. If I'd a had a gun, I'd a shot you. Are you okay? Is something wrong?"

She was quiet for a moment, considering whether she should just leave. He made the decision for her by fumbling around on the bedside table, finding a sulfur match, and lighting the lamp.

"Ben, what happened to your face?"

He touched the swollen lip, feeling a little ashamed.

"Did you get in a fight?" She went to his side, sat on the edge of the mattress, and studied the injuries up close. "And your eye." She touched the raw skin with the tips of her fingers.

Ben licked at the cut on his lip and grimaced.

"Oh, Ben, what happened?"

He lifted his shoulders and didn't answer right away. How could he tell her what had happened? It sounded so blamed dumb.

"Nothing much. Just a little scuffle is all."

"Why, Ben Poole. I never thought I'd see you get in a fight."

"Just shows what you know about me, Dessa Fallon. I've had plenty of fights, I reckon."

"Oh, yeah. Just how many fights have you had?" She was teasing him now, and feeling very exposed, sitting on the edge of his bed in her nightdress, and him bared to the waist and only wearing his long johns.

Without thinking, she leaned closer and gently kissed the swollen lip. Ben closed his eyes and sighed. She kissed the corner of his puffy red eye.

"Oh, Ben. Please, Ben. I don't know if I can . . . I mean, how can we—"

She didn't get the rest said. He wrapped his arms around her, gathered her close, and laid his head in the hollow of her shoulder. He smelled of the soap he had bathed in, and his freshly washed hair tickled her chin.

"I knew this would happen. I just knew it would," he said, his breath hot against her throat. "I can't stay here, Dessa. I plain just can't. And you have to. I see that. Dammit, why did this happen? Why couldn't we have just gone on our separate ways? Say you'll come back to Montana with me. Now, Dessa. Now. Or just leave me be. Don't come near me like this, tempting me with every breath."

He pulled back, taking her by the shoulders so he could look into her eyes. She saw twin flames burning there from the lamplight, saw his suffering, too.

When she closed her eyelids, tears overflowed and ran down her cheeks.

"Don't cry. Don't do that, please." He spread one large hand over the back of her head and pulled her to his chest. "Don't cry, my love. I'll try. I'll stay with you awhile. Oh, God, I'll stay with you. I can't stand this. I feel like my insides are being yanked out."

She threw her arms around him. "Oh, Ben. Yes, stay. Do. At least for a while. You'll get to like it here, I know you will. And the house, Ben. You'll love the house. It's big and out of the city a ways. There are fields and horses and trees, almost like Montana. We won't have to live in the city. Oh, Ben, just think, the two of us there. Together. Oh, Ben."

She held on to him so tightly he could hardly breathe. He rocked her back and forth gently. He would do anything for her. Anything.

"I love you, I love you," he just kept repeating.

Maybe that by itself would be enough to sustain him in this strange land. Having her, holding her, watching her awaken beside him each morning. Perhaps that would make up for living in a place he despised even though he hadn't even laid eyes on it.

Chapter Fifteen

B en disliked Andrew Drewhart from the very moment Dessa introduced them. He would have been disappointed if he hadn't. As for how Andrew felt about him, Ben couldn't tell, nor did he much care. The man treated him with cool civility, when he acknowledged his presence at all. It wasn't dislike so much as total dismissal. Ben might as well not have existed. Andrew, after all, had Dessa, didn't he? That's how he treated her, anyway, like a possession.

It might have been best if Ben had let Dessa settle the problem and stayed out of it, but he was, after all, a man of the wilderness. Dessa's friends would expect him to act uncivilized, wouldn't they? He decided not to let them down.

"You will, of course, stay in town until this dreadful business is settled," Andrew said as he directed the loading of Dessa's luggage on the rack of a shining black carriage. It was a handsome vehicle appointed with brass fittings and striped in gold. Ben had seen nothing so fine. A coachman sat up top and two seats inside faced each other.

Drewhart had already hugged Dessa and patted her, telling her how dreadfully sorry everyone had been to hear of her parents' passing.

He talked that way, Ben decided, because he had

learned it somewhere. No one would use such words as *dreadful* every time he opened his mouth unless someone said they should. Ben helped the porter from the train stack the luggage and lifted one end of Dessa's trunk to place it on the rack of the carriage. How had she managed to come by so many possession during her short stay in Montana?

Andrew tapped his walking cane and watched with a sneer, clearly indicating his disdain at Ben for helping a servant. Dessa chattered on brightly to both men as if she hadn't a care in the world. Ben knew better. He sensed her nervousness at being with the two of them.

Andrew took her by the elbow and steered her into the carriage, then climbed in himself. Ben hopped up top with the driver. Dessa would have ample time alone with the man to explain to him just what was what, set him straight. Besides, Ben wanted to get a good view of this city, this place where the woman he loved had grown up.

The buildings were quite tall compared to those out West, and there was a lot of stone and brickwork. The air smelled of the nearby river and the stink of too many horses in the streets. The dwelling of which Andrew spoke—Ben wasn't sure who it belonged to—was located along a tree-lined street away from the business district but conveniently nearby. From the street, rows of steps led to rows of doorways, and he wondered how people were supposed to tell one from the other. He soon discovered the houses were numbered, which he thought mighty handy.

The carriage drew up in front of 212, and Ben leaped to the ground and opened the carriage door with a flourish. The scowl on Andrew's face cheered

Ben considerably. The man handed Dessa out and Ben caught her up in his arms, whirling her around and around until she squealed with delight.

"Welcome home, my lady," he said, then favored her with an impish grin and kissed her square on the mouth.

She wrapped her arms around his neck and kissed him back, right there in front of Andrew and the coachman and anyone else who happened to be looking.

"Did you tell him?" Ben growled in her ear. "Did you tell him you're mine?" He rubbed his nose on her neck and nibbled with his lips. "If you want, I'll pop him one, settle him down."

"Ben, behave yourself. This isn't Virginia City." She giggled, pushed out of his arms, and straightened her hat, which had been twisted askew by his antics.

He grabbed her hand and pulled her up the steps, ignoring the luggage the coachman had piled nearby. "Well, come on, show me around. I want to see where we'll be living."

"Ben, hush, please."

"What, Dessa?"

Andrew followed them to the door, looking peckish. "Dessa, I'm afraid I really don't understand what is going on."

"Didn't you tell him, dear?" Ben asked in a fussy voice he hoped matched Andrew's tone, though he had to admit he laid it on pretty heavy.

"Tell me what?" Andrew asked.

He had produced a key from his waistcoat pocket and unlocked the door before asking the question, and now he stood poised in the opening, peering out at both of them.

The bastard was good-looking. Ben had to give him that. But he was just too damn slick, a namby-pamby. And what in the hell was he doing with a key? Was this Dessa's place or Andrew's?

"Well?" Andrew asked, having gotten no reply from either Dessa or Ben.

"There will be plenty of time to talk later, Andy," Dessa said, patting his arm soothingly and stepping past him. She took a deep breath and let it out slowly.

She ignored Ben, who was now glaring at her, willing her to look at him. She hadn't told Andrew about the two of them, and it was obvious he wanted to know why.

Andrew said, "Clarice had the place aired out and brought in flowers after we got your first wire. I'm afraid they're not as fresh as they could be, considering you are a day later than you thought. Was there an accident? Were you ill?"

"No, nothing like that," she said, striding through the hallways and pulling off her gloves, which she had only donned for the last leg of the trip from Kearney.

Ben thought her demeanor somewhat changed, but he couldn't quite put a finger on what it was. He hoped she wouldn't become as prissy as Andrew after she'd been around him awhile. It was enough to make you puke, the way the man simpered.

"The trip was dreadful," she finally said, then turned and posed in the sunlight coming through the window.

Ben cringed and eyed Dessa. Dreadful? Now she was doing it.

"And I just couldn't continue without a bath and some sleep. Those trains throw everyone all together like cattle. And of course the day coaches are much worse than our first-class coach. But we all ate together at the stops."

Her voice faded as she stepped from the hallway through a large arch and into another room. Andrew followed her, occasionally throwing in a *dreadful* of his own. Ben wondered if he was just imagining the change in Dessa. Maybe it was something in the air. It was like she walked through the door of the train station onto the streets of Kansas City and became another person. Well, she didn't really become so much another person, as she reverted to the one who had first ridden into Virginia City beside him. Back before she learned of her parents' death and before she met Rose and Wiley and Maggie. Before she became a real down-to-earth, honest-to-God woman.

Or maybe, thought Ben, just maybe it had all been his imagination. A thing he wanted so badly he made it so. Her becoming a sweet, caring, and beautiful person he could love. The kind of girl who would save the life of someone at the risk of her own. Saving someone who wasn't even particularly likable and who wore ragged clothes and spoke with a foreign and quite uneducated brogue.

Dessa stuck her head through the doorway. "Ben, come on, come on in. I want to show you around the place."

"Oh, will you be staying?" Andrew asked, drawing up his mouth so that his styled mustache twitched.

Ben glared at Dessa once again, but she paid him no mind at all.

"Well, yes, he will," she said gaily. She looked Andrew right in the eye and grinned like she'd swallowed a sweet. "And we need to talk, Andrew."

She glanced at Ben.

He glowered and she smiled again. "But not here, and not now. I'm so tired, all I want is a hot bath and a nap. Come to dinner tonight, Andrew. Seven o'clock?"

Andrew glanced from Dessa to Ben and back to her. "When will you speak to Cluney?"

"Tomorrow is soon enough for business, I would think."

"And . . . and what are you intending to do about the business? You need someone with experience, someone at the helm who is an expert in financial matters as well as merchandising, Dessa dear, unless you want your father's beloved business to go right down the gutter."

"I said tomorrow, Andrew. Tonight is for something far more important."

"Important?" Andrew raised his fine brows.

"Yes, Andrew. Important to Ben and you and myself as well."

"More important than your father's business?"

She glanced at Ben again, and he saw a glimmer of the Dessa he had known back in Virginia City. She was there, in the flash of the green eyes and the toss of her noble head, but most of all in the warm smile she gave him. Then she turned to Andrew and answered his question.

"Yes, Andrew. More important than daddy's business."

Andrew was not happy when he left, warning Dessa that it was extremely improper for her to have this man—he gestured like he smelled something horrible—under her roof, she being a young single woman.

Dessa had only laughed. "Ah, Andrew, sometime

you must go out West, and get some of that proper nonsense blown off you."

Andrew chose not to pursue the matter, but went off grumbling.

Dessa turned from the slammed door and opened her arms. "Come here, my darling, you look as if you've been run over by a herd of those wild buffalo you told me about."

"That wasn't a buffalo, it was a citified weasel. Dear God, Dessa." Then he burst out laughing and went to her, hugging her tightly and lifting her off the floor. He swung her up and tucked one arm under her knees.

"I don't want to forget how to do this, just in case you need me to tote you somewhere again," he said with a laugh, and carried her up the stairs.

Dessa held on to him tightly. Could it be true that she could have all this and Ben, too? Could God really be that kind to her? And why not? After all, he had taken her parents and Mitchell from her, hadn't he? It was about time something good happened in her life again.

"Where's your room, my lady?" Ben asked at the top of the stairs.

"There, kind sir," she said, and pointed dramatically.

She worked the latch on the door and he stepped inside with her.

He stopped and gazed with awe at the draped and bedecked, floral rose and cream and green room. "Good Lord, Dessa."

The bed stood on a pedestal and was draped with yards and yards of fabric that fell in gathers from the canopy. A wardrobe in one corner was decorated with curlicues the like of which Ben had never seen in one piece of wood. Those same twists and turns were cut in the wood of a desk and two bedside tables. A screen stood across one corner of the large room, and painted on it were huge roses in deep pinks with rich green leaves, all so outsized that they were nearly grotesque.

Wallpaper matched the pattern on the screen, as did a rug that covered all but about a foot of wood floor around the perimeter. Ceiling-high windows were also draped to match the bed canopy.

"Do you like it?"

"Well . . . I . . . well, to tell you the truth, Dessa, it's a little . . . uh, a little . . ." He couldn't find a word and gave up.

"Plain old Victorian didn't suit me. It's very new, called Moorish, but I lightened up on the mixture of colors and all that cluttered look, like pillows and draped fabric all over the walls—"

She broke off the chatter, for she had seen the room as he must be seeing it, and was scandalized.

He still held her in his arms and he turned slowly, taking in the whole effect, as if that way he could soften the blow to his sanity.

"Oh, Ben," Dessa said. "I'm sorry. It's . . . it's terrible, isn't it? I never realized, but—"

"Don't be silly. It just takes some getting used to, that's all. Well, maybe a lot of getting used to." Just like everything else in this godforsaken place. He let the thought go, for he held what he wanted right there in his arms, and if this hideous room came with her, so be it.

With a whoop, he took several long strides, tossed her on the enormous bed, and jumped right up there with her.

And wouldn't Andrew, the smartass, think this was absolutely dreadful?

She laughed with delight and together they rolled around until they had thoroughly mussed the floral bedcover. They came to rest with Ben astraddle her, pillows propping her head. She gazed up into his face and pushed the touseled hair away from his eyes.

"You didn't like Andrew even a little bit, did you?" she teased.

"What's to like?" He kissed her wrist, then captured both and held them above her head with an easy grip, fiddling with the buttons of her dress with his other hand.

"He's been a very good friend. And he is truly a decent man."

"You mean he's not dreadful?"

"Ben, stop."

He gave up on the tiny buttons and slid his palm over one breast. "Stop what, my dear?"

"Talking like that."

"But it's the way Andrew talks, and the way you talked once. For a minute there, when we first walked in here, you took it up again."

"I did not." She closed her eyes and basked in his gentle caress.

He leaned close, whispered in her ear, "Did Andrew ever make you feel this way?"

Gasping, she nibbled at her lower lip and he leaned down to put his tongue there. Whatever answer she might have made was drowned in the kiss.

Clinging to this man who had created a new world for her, she soared to join the heights of his passion. A passion she'd had no idea existed until she met him. Would it survive here, where he was torn from his element? Lord above, she didn't know, but as he explored her fully clothed body with his hands and mouth, she prayed it would. For to discover such an ecstasy and then lose it would be tragic.

Ben fumbled with the hem of her skirt, pulled at the layers of petticoats, lay his warm hand finally and gently on her bare thigh. "Dessa, will you marry me?"

"Oh, yes, Ben." She wanted to scream that yes so loudly that people riding by outside would hear her declaration of love. A still, small warning tickled at her senses.

"Give it time, though, Ben. I want to marry you this very instant, but we have to be sure. We have to wait until we're sure you can live here. I know you've said you can, but suppose you absolutely hate it? Suppose you just can't bear it? Then what? I won't have you miserable for my sake."

"With you, how could I be miserable?" He said the words, but he took his hand away, smoothed back the layers of fabric, and moved to lay beside her, one arm behind his head. "I suppose you're right. We'll wait a day or two, but you know something, Dessa?"

"What, Ben," she asked lazily, feeling a deep contentment for the first time since her parents had died. Everything would be wonderful, given time.

"We're going to have to do something about all these horrible flowers. It might be best just to move to another room. I'm not sure much can be done about this."

Dessa laughed heartily, then thought of what she was doing, lying in bed with a man in the privacy of her own bedroom and having a conversation about the decor as if it were the most natural thing in the world.

"You can have a guest room, a very plain one," she said primly.

"That might be best," he said, a twinkle in his eye. "I wouldn't want to smudge your reputation, even if we aren't up to anything too scandalous."

Dessa couldn't help chuckling. She decided right then that her parents and Mitchell, too, would have liked Ben on sight. They would have gotten along famously. And they would all have known they could have trusted this man with their daughter, no matter what.

She grabbed his hand, enclosed it in both hers. "Ben, will we have a lot of children?"

"Mmm. Probably. I'm lusty, you know."

"Oh, you are? I hadn't noticed."

"And you, what about you? Are you lusty, my dear Dessa?"

She snuggled up against him. "With you I am."

"And when are we going to break this news to dreadful Andrew, this news that we are going to have lots of children?"

"He's been a good friend, Ben. Please don't talk about him that way. I thought tonight at dinner. Oh, my goodness, I wonder if there's anything in the house to cook?"

"Who's going to cook?" Ben asked innocently.

"Well, I am. I can cook."

"I thought rich people didn't do their own cooking."

"We weren't always rich. Well, we're not even really rich yet. Not like the Vanderbilts"

"Yet? Do you expect to be richer than this?" He flung a hand around, indicating the room he found so distasteful. "What exactly do you want, Dessa?"

She stiffened at the tone of his voice. "Well, don't make it sound like a sin to have money."

He sighed and sat up on the edge of the bed. "Well, I didn't mean to. But to always want more and more no matter what you have . . . well, Dessa, that's called greed."

"And how do you think this country got where it is? It wasn't led there by men who are content to sleep under a wagon all their lives." As soon as the words were out of her mouth, she wanted to take them back.

When Ben didn't reply, she crept across the bed and knelt behind him, laying her head against his rigid back. "I'm sorry. I didn't mean that. I just don't like you criticizing something you know so little about. My father worked hard all his life. His father started with nothing and together they built this business out of sweat and tears, and I won't have either of them reviled. But I didn't intend to be mean to you."

He let out a breath he'd been holding. "I'm sorry, too. Let's talk about cooking supper . . . I mean dinner. I'll help, but I hope you aren't going to pick any weeds to put on the plates. I have trouble figuring out what to do with that stuff."

"Weeds?" Dessa asked, at a loss to know what he was talking about.

"Back there in Kearney. I distinctly remember my plate having weed heads right on the food."

"Oh, Ben. Ben." Dessa slid around and hopped off the bed. "That wasn't a weed head. It was parsley."

"What are you supposed to do with it?"

"Lay it aside."

"But why put something on a plate that no one can eat?"

"Well, actually, you can eat parsley, but no one does."

He eyed her and made a face. "Oh, well, then. That makes perfect sense."

She grabbed his hand. "Come on, I can see you've got a lot to learn about the kitchen. That is if you're serious about helping me cook. Most men aren't interested."

"Well, I cook beans over a fire. I even learned to fry fatback out of defense. You've tasted Wiley's." He followed her down the stairs and let her lead him to the back of the main floor where the kitchen waited.

Andrew arrived promptly at seven o'clock with his sister Clarice. She was tall and thin, one of those pale blonds whose skin is the color of flour and looks as if it would go up in a pouf at the slightest breeze. It was soon obvious that Andrew had hopes that his sister would absolutely charm Ben until he wouldn't pay any attention to Dessa at all. Clarice fell to the task with a fervor that made Ben very uncomfortable. He had never been actively pursued and wasn't sure how to handle it. Dessa was either at a loss as to how to help him or was amused by his plight. He actually couldn't tell.

Following a leisurely meal, Dessa fetched a flat metal disk punched erratically with holes, opened the music box, and inserted it. She wound a crank and out came tinkly music similar to that of the cremona in the Golden Sun. Ben had never seen such a thing, and went to inspect it.

"Andrew, will you dance with me?" Dessa asked coquettishly, and watched Ben squirm when Clarice arched a fine brow in his direction.

He turned away from the fascinating music machine. "I don't dance, never did," he said too loudly and to no one in particular.

With a secret smile, Clarice took his hand. He gazed at the fragile and pale flesh. Blue veins lay just under the skin and he was afraid to handle her. She might shatter.

"Well, then," she said in her sophisticated back East accent, "I'll teach you. I'm very good at that."

She smelled of sweet powder, a heavy cloying odor that caused Ben to sneeze when she placed herself carefully within the circle of his arms. He did not want to do this, and he glared at Dessa as she and Andrew whirled gracefully in a wide circle around him and his partner.

"Relax, Ben," Clarice said. She held him at arm's length, her right hand on his left shoulder. "Put your hand on my waist," she said, and took his other hand in her left one. "Now, we'll just stand here a minute and sway with the music. No, no, don't look at your feet. Look at me. And sway. Like this."

He did that awhile, still trying to figure a way out of his predicament. He felt plumb silly. Maybe the music would end. Under his touch Clarice was as fragile as autumn leaves, dry and crackly, not warm and moist and sweet like Dessa. If he wanted to dance at all, which he didn't, it would be with Dessa, not this wisp of a woman who might break at any moment.

Without warning she began to move, dragging him with her.

"It's called a waltz, Ben," Dessa said as she and Andrew swooped past once again. "Get into the spirit. It'll be fun."

He thought of the drawn-out, boring meal, and how he kept waiting for Dessa to announce their plans to her old beau, and how she hadn't even come near the subject. They had spoken of the August cotillion and what the "gang" had been up to while Dessa was away.

Then they had talked about past galas given by someone named Annette and her sister Jeannie, who must have been famous for throwing outlandish parties. Still the subject didn't come around to Dessa and Ben. Now, here they were dancing—well, more or less—all over the parlor and still no sign she would break the news. Was he going to have to do it?

He stumbled and shuffled, and could not get the hang of the dance step. Clarice slipped agilely from him to demonstrate alone. How very elegant she looked, turning high on her toes, arms lifted gracefully, head thrown back like a long-necked white swan. Her filmy skirts floated out around her, lacy and cloudlike. Surprisingly Ben found the solo dance quite erotic, and when he glanced at Dessa, he saw that she and her partner had stopped and were watching with equal fascination.

The music ended and all three applauded. Clarice bowed self-consciously. "I guess I got carried away."

"You should have been a dancer," Dessa said. "In the ballet theater."

Clarice glanced quickly at her brother, then away.

"She wanted to be," Andrew said. "Father wouldn't let her. He said absolutely not. I think it broke her heart."

Two bright red spots bloomed on Clarice's pale cheeks.

"Well," said Ben. "Nothing can stop her dancing here in the parlor, can it?" He went to her, took her hand, and said, "Show me again, would you?"

Tears lay pooled in Clarice's eyes and she gave him

a grateful look before replacing his hands and going through the steps patiently once again. He followed along, trying to feel the music like he felt the beauty of a Montana sunrise or experienced the awe of a crisp winter morning so quiet he could hear the beat of his own heart and the silent fall of snowflakes in the pines.

And then, almost miraculously, his feet got the message, and he and his partner tried a wide whirl. Dessa had rewound the music box, and stood beside it watching Ben with a dreamlike smile on her face.

He moved like a graceful animal, once his inhibitions were shed, and she found herself longing to dance with him, but not at arm's length and proper like with Clarice. No, she wanted to nestle in the curve of his long body, place her thighs against his, press her feverish flesh to the tight, supple muscles across his stomach. What would it be like to dance naked together, bare breasts to bare chest? The thought flittered through her mind so quickly Dessa almost wasn't aware of it, certainly had no idea where it came from.

Perhaps it was past time for the two of them to marry. Thoughts such as she was having were certainly not proper, and couldn't be carried out between the two of them while they were unmarried. So why did she still feel such hesitance? Some vague feeling of unrest warned her the time wasn't quite right. There were things yet to be finished, but for the life of her she didn't know what. That admission reminded her that she had a dreadful task yet ahead of her, and she forgot the beauty of the dance. She had to tell Andrew that she loved Ben, not him, and that his long, patient wait had been in vain.

She wondered if Andrew hadn't guessed as much

by now. Even so, she hated to have to tell him. She would do it soon, in fact as soon as the music finished playing. Should she do it alone with him? Send Ben and Clarice into the library, or take Andrew there and leave them here? What a mess. She knew she should have had this out of the way earlier. Alone with Andrew in the carriage with Ben riding up top would have been ideal, but she hadn't the courage. Andrew had been so glad to see her, so full of talk about how he had missed her and his plans for a future. Perhaps she'd hoped that if she put it off, Andrew would guess what was going on and bring it up himself. But he hadn't. Instead he had blatantly brought Clarice along as a partner for Ben, as if Dessa and Ben's relationship were entirely platonic.

The music wound down and stopped.

For an instant or two Ben and Clarice continued to move. Then they slowly came to a halt. Ben now seemed at a loss as to what to do with his hands. He held them in position for a while, then took them away and wiped his palms self-consciously down the sides of his pants legs.

Clarice smiled sweetly at him, and he forgave her everything she'd had in mind when she came into this house. She couldn't have known how he and Dessa felt about each other, or she would never have agreed to distract him for her brother. Surely she was much too kind a woman for that. He was silently grateful to her for teaching him to move around the room and he couldn't wait to dance with Dessa. How sensual it would be to hold her close and move about in such an erotic fashion. Just thinking of it made him want her terribly.

He glanced across the room to catch her eye and

saw her take a breath that appeared to pain her. Then she laid her hand on Andrew's arm.

"Come on, we have to talk. I hope you two will excuse us for a little while."

With one hand tucked firmly under Andrew's elbow, she led him out of the parlor.

Chapter Sixteen

Andrew was intent on holding Dessa's hands in his when they sat side by side on a sofa near the fireplace in the library.

He lowered his lips to touch her flesh. "I've missed you so. I thought we'd never be alone. Clever of me to bring Clarice, wasn't it? I think they're getting along famously."

"Andrew . . . I have . . . uh, I have something to tell you."

He turned his eyes upward in a gesture she well remembered. It signaled that he thought she was going to say or do something he would find absurd.

Most of the time he was quite handsome, but he could always ruin it all with one of his ridiculous expressions. On the other hand, when Ben even glanced her way, she'd always get feeble in the brain and the knees. She had never expected such a thing to happen, except in her wildest romantic dreams. And who ever believed they would come true? She wished her mother had warned her.

"What is it, Dessa?" Andrew finally asked, when she just sat there staring into space and daydreaming.

She had almost forgotten what she was going to

say to him, and had to think a minute. "What? Oh, yes, Andrew . . . uh, I have something to tell you."

He laughed uncomfortably. "You already said that. What is it?"

His expression this time told her he had finally guessed, or perhaps admitted to himself, what he should have known all along but was just too stubborn to acknowledge.

"Ben and I . . . we—"

Andrew leaned forward and put his lips on hers, quickly, almost harshly. "Hush. No, I don't want to hear it. You're just grateful. Sshhh. He saved your life, helped you when you were vulnerable. I won't hear this, Dessa. I won't." His fingertips tapped at her cheeks, but he didn't quite take her face in his hands.

She batted her eyes and pulled away. "You must. Andrew, I'm so sorry. But I do love him."

"He's a lout. A nobody. What would your father think? Your poor dear mother?"

"Don't you dare do that, Andrew. Don't you do that. You know how much I loved them, how much they loved me. They'd want me to be happy."

He squeezed at her hands tightly so she couldn't pull further out of his grasp. His eyes took on a frantic, darting appearance. "My point, precisely, my dear. How in God's name do you think the likes of him can make you happy? He's a bumbling fool. What does he do for a living? I'll bet he can't even read or write. Whatever are you thinking of, my sweet?"

Andrew voicing the same doubts she'd felt herself upon meeting Ben sent chills up her spine. She shuddered and tears flowed from her eyes. Returning to her old life had quite confused her, made her unable to think clearly.

Andrew pulled a clean white handkerchief from his vest and patted the tears away. "Now, now. It's all right. You can't blame yourself. You were grieving and he took advantage of you, pure and simple. I'll just have a talk with him and set him straight."

Dessa came to her senses and pushed him away, tottered to her feet. "You'll do no such thing! This is my business, Andrew. Mine, do you hear? I'll not have you or Clarice meddling in my affairs. I loved my parents dearly, but they never wanted me to grow up and make any decisions, either. Now you want to take over where they left off."

"For obvious reasons, Dessa," Andrew said, his earlier tenderness gone. "You're about to make a terrible mistake that you'll pay for dearly."

"Well, then, I'll be the one to pay."

"Dear Dessa, sleep on this. Don't make your decision now. We have the meeting with Cluney in the morning. At least delay any rash promises you might make until after that. Speak to Cluney, listen to your father's will first."

Dessa glowered at him. "What do you know about daddy's will? I think you forget yourself, Andrew. And Clarice, too. And you tell her she can flit herself around Ben all she wants, he won't be interested." Dessa sniffled quite unbecomingly, whirled, and left Andrew standing there gaping at her.

In the other room Ben listened to the raised voices. A moment later he sensed Andrew in the doorway by the way Clarice cut her eyes in that direction.

"We'll be going now," Andrew said, his voice brittle.

Ben rose when Clarice did, turned in time to see Andrew's hateful expression directed right at him. Dessa had broken the news. Ben couldn't help giving Andrew a victorious smile, but felt icy feet treading along his backbone at the murderous glare he received in return. He'd best not turn his back on this one.

"Good night, Ben," Clarice murmured as Andrew draped her wrap around her shoulders and donned his own cape. Andrew fetched the black top hat from the hallway rack and hurried his sister out the door.

Dessa was nowhere to be seen when Ben turned. He went upstairs thoughtfully, slowing in front of her closed door. He wanted to tap on the elegant and shiny wooden panels, step inside, and hold her for a moment to say good night, but he didn't. If she wanted to speak to him, she would not have gone to her room in such a fashion. It must have been harder than either of them had imagined to tell Andrew they were in love.

He went on to his own room, making no noise on the carpet runner. After what seemed an eternity of trying to get comfortable on the thick feather bed, Ben crawled from the bed and stretched out on the floor. He'd slept on the ground most all of his life; learning to relax in one of those things would take some doing. Maybe it would be easier with Dessa lying beside him.

The meeting at the law firm of Cluney & Brown was scheduled for ten o'clock the following morning. When Dessa crawled from bed, the mantel clock had just chimed once and she was amazed to see it was only six-thirty. She hadn't slept well at all. If her brain wasn't dithering over what would be the best way to handle Daddy's business, it was echoing Andrew's words. One part of her wanted to be rid of the entire thing, wanted to flee back to Virginia City with Ben, and even on to California, if that's what he wanted. The sensible side, which she'd evidently left behind when she went to Montana, said keep the business, appoint Andrew to run it. In due time, marry him and settle down in a house out on the hill above the river. Have everything she had always wanted. Be his wife, the mother of his children.

But send Ben away? How could she forget that when Ben touched her, she caught fire with a passion she could barely control, or how his mouth devouring hers filled her with ecstasy. Together they had come so close to committing sins of the flesh. Though she hadn't yet let Ben know her in that way, how much longer would it be before she did? What a wicked and lustful woman she had become. Perhaps no better than the women who worked for Rose. She should either marry Ben this instant or send him away, but she couldn't seem to decide on either course.

She went to stand at the window, pulling the curtain aside to stare down into the street. Dawn chased at lingering shadows, tracing silver fingers along the walkway. A lone carriage moved over the cobblestones, the clip-clop of the horses' hooves fading into the distance. Leaves on the trees were tinged with autumn colors. Winter would soon arrive, roaring across the plains from the mountains of Montana, carrying in the wind vague reminders of that exquisite country. She missed it already. She missed Rose and Maggie, the little house she'd furnished so carefully, and Wiley's dry humor. And the glittering stars and the sky bigger than the whole world and bluer than any flower or lake or indigo dress. A horse between her legs, the wind in her face, Ben riding at her side. Placing wildflowers on Mother and Daddy's grave every Sunday after church. Lord, how she would miss it!

She let the curtain fall back in place, her mind a turmoil of indecision.

Dismissing the fact that she still wore her nightgown, she padded from her room and down the hall, stopping to tap softly on Ben's door before opening it. The room was dark, but her eyes were accustomed to the gloom, and she saw right away that he wasn't there. The bed hadn't been slept in, but a blanket lay in a pile on the floor. His boots and coat were nowhere.

Where in the world could he be?

A flaming sun lightened the sky, painting riffles of the wide Missouri River in splashes of pink and purple and gold. Ben drew in a deep breath, inhaling the unfamiliar odors. The town lay all around him, its streets and buildings, its people stifling him. There would be quiet sometimes, like now, but then something would bang and crash, someone would shout, dogs would bark. Noisy paddlewheelers and barges used the river as if it were a massive road, hauling all manner of goods. Some would eventually end up in the territories north to the Platte or Yellowstone all the way to the Great Salt Lake with their wares, and he wanted to swim out to one, climb aboard, and head in that direction with no more thought of Dessa Fallon and her precious Kansas City. Let her have Andrew and all the things she seemed unable to live without. That awful place with all the windows covered by thick draperies that cut out the sunlight, the very air he needed to live.

Ah, Dessa, dammit, how he loved her. He couldn't leave her here, and it seemed he couldn't get her to go with him, either.

With a sigh, he stuffed both hands deep in the pockets of his trousers and turned his back on the river. He would stay a while longer, see how things went. But he had made up his mind about one thing for certain. He could not live in this ugly world.

A familiar carriage waited in front of the house when Ben returned on foot some time later. He went up the walk and opened the door carefully. The muffled sound of voices came from the library. What he wanted was to walk past the door and up the stairs without being seen, but as he drew nearer, tidbits of the conversation from inside—his name and Dessa's being bandied about—reached him, and he drew up against the wall. He couldn't stop himself from eavesdropping on the two people inside, for he recognized both voices from the night before. Andrew and his sister Clarice were in there and they were discussing him and Dessa, which Ben decided was surely his business.

"I understand her attraction to him," Clarice said. "He is quite handsome in a rugged sort of way."

Andrew snorted. "*Rugged* is being kind. I tell you, Clary, I will not allow this to happen. Fallon Enterprises is easily worth half a million dollars, and within a few years, with the railroads cropping up everywhere, a smart man could double its value."

"And you want to be that smart man, Brother."

"Oh, I will be, one way or the other. She's teased me since she was old enough to know the effect of her feminine wiles. I've waited a long time for Dessa Fallon."

"For Fallon Enterprises, I'd say."

"All right, I admit it. What's wrong with that? All our family has left is its name. Father and our no-good older brother have managed to squander all the money Grandfather left us. And you don't seem able to attract a suitable husband. What will you do when they take the house and what little we have left, Clarice? Go begging on the street? Or perhaps you'll dance for a living?"

"That wasn't very kind, Andrew."

"The time for kindness is long past, Sister. You'll help me with this or you'll starve, just as I will. Neither of us is equipped to make our way in this world."

"But I don't want to hurt Dessa. I've always liked her, even though she was a bit of a snob. Have you noticed how she's changed, how different she is?"

"Believe me, that's temporary. Let her get her greedy little hands on her share of the old man's business, let her realize how much money is involved, and we'll see how quickly she'll revert to her old ways. She was raised never wanting for anything. How long do you think she would put up living with that worthless no-good? Right now, it's just something new and different to her. Let her live in a house with cracks in the walls and no glass in the windows, let her spend winter out on the plains or in those dreadful mountains with little to eat or wear, and you'll see how quickly she would change her mind. Well, I don't intend to let it go that far, and you will help me."

"But Andrew. Even is she goes with him, she will have all the money. They won't have to live that way."

"Not all by a long shot, Sister, dear. In fact, it may not be enough. He's a money grubber, plain and simple. He only wants her for her money. He has a thing or two to learn as well." Here both paused and Ben struggled to hold his anger in check. The nerve of the bastard. Admitting in one breath that he expected a share of Dessa's money, and in the next putting Ben down the road. It was all he could do to keep from leaping into the room and socking that foppish son of a bitch right in the mouth.

But then Andrew went on, and Ben listened.

"You don't suppose he's already bedded her, do you? Dear God, if he has, she's spoiled somewhat, isn't she?"

Clarice laughed softly, bitterly. "I'm sure you'll be able to overcome that little scruple, Brother, dear. You've never been too particular about your own bed partners."

At that moment Ben thought he heard something and glanced up toward the landing. Dessa was standing there, gazing down at him, her features a mask of dismay. He had been caught skulking about, and there was nothing for it but to make the best of a bad situation.

"Good morning, Dessa," he called, and strode toward the stairs as if he had just walked into the house. "Did you sleep well?"

When he reached her, she studied him closely. "What were you doing?"

"Dessa, we have to talk, and now. Please."

He took her arm, but she pulled away. "No. Answer my question. Why were you eavesdropping down there?"

He ignored the question. "There are some things you need to know, and now, before you go to your meeting. What are those two doing here anyway? What do they have to do with your meeting this morning?"

"Andrew worked for Daddy. I thought you knew that."

Ben shook his head slowly. "How would I know that? And so what does it mean? That he has a part in the business?"

"He will have a say. He will advise me after we speak to our lawyer. Ben, Andrew knows all the ins and outs of Daddy's business. Much more than I do. I need his suggestions, his assistance. What's wrong with you?"

"Don't trust Andrew, Dessa. He means to—"

"No, I won't listen to that. Andrew has always been trustworthy. I've known him practically all my life. I may not be in love with him and that may be upsetting to him, but it doesn't mean he'll cheat me. I'm not going to throw him out of the business."

"I'm telling you, Dessa, Andrew is not to be trusted. I heard him and Clarice talking. They plan to—"

Dessa shoved his hand off her arm. A bright spot flared on each cheek and her voice tightened. "Ben, don't meddle in something you know nothing about. When this business is finished, then we'll talk about our future. Until then, why don't you just stay out of it?"

Ben jerked backward as if she'd slapped him. An ache closed around his heart. This was the Dessa he'd feared would return, the one he'd caught glimpses of when she first arrived in Virginia City. He'd thought that spoiled little brat long gone when the real Dessa appeared. The one who was compassionate and kind and forgiving. The woman he'd fallen in love with. Where had she gone in a flicker of an instant?

Before he could recover his voice, she hurried down the stairs, her action dismissing him like a servant. He watched her greet Andrew and Clarice in the hallway, and waited in grim silence while the three of them went out the door. The echo of its closing thrummed in his head. She didn't even look back; her desertion made him sick to his stomach.

Almost unaware of his actions, Ben rushed to his room, packed his few belongings in the small satchel, and hurriedly checked to make sure he had his money and return train ticket. All this in an unconscious flurry of anger and grief.

Down the hall, he paused at Dessa's door, which stood ajar, and pushed it open gently with his fingertips. Her nightgown lay across the unmade bed, yesterday's clothing was heaped in a pile on the floor, and on the dresser was a box of powder with a candy-pink puff.

He took a deep breath of the essence of her, closed his eyes tightly for a moment, then backed away. Her abandonment left him empty and bereft, much as the loss of his family had done so many years before. He thought he might not be able to endure it.

Damn her, damn her to hell. How could she do this to him? Treat him in such an offhand manner and just walk away with orders that he be there when she returned so they could discuss their future. Well, she could forget that. This good-for-nothing territory bum would be long gone when Miss Dessa Fallon got back. And she could just deal with Andrew and Clarice and their schemes. They were all of a kind, anyway. All of a kind.

* * *

P. L. Cluney actually owned the law firm of Cluney & Brown, having buried his father's partner, DuBois Brown, three years previously. Old Mr. Brown died without heirs and so P.L. inherited the firm his father and his father's best friend had begun back in the old days. Before Missouri gained her terrible prewar reputation, before the river became the road to the frontier, and before there were companies like Fallon Enterprises, the firm might not have been worth much. But today, ah, today that was no longer the truth.

As a practicing attorney, P.L. didn't lower himself to appear in court to defend the scum periodically arrested for various and sundry common crimes. He'd learned where the real money in law was, and so he represented businessmen in their endeavors to become richer and richer. In doing so, some of the crumbs—well, a lot of the crumbs—fell or were coaxed his way. In Kansas City, P. L. Cluney was known as the rich man's attorney. If you wanted to earn money, and if you wanted to hide money, and if you wanted to keep money, you went to P.L.

He stood, now, and greeted Dessa Fallon with a wide smile. The outcome of today's meeting meant little to him. Either way he would profit. With difficulty, he retained the smile when he shook hands with Andrew Drewhart and greeted his ghostlike sister. The woman gave him the creeps. She looked as if she had risen from the dead, and when she moved across a room, her skinny body appeared to float as if her feet didn't touch the floor. No wonder she had never married.

P.L. turned with relief back to the beautiful Dessa Fallon. At one time he had entertained hopes of his own where this lovely creature was concerned, but she apparently couldn't bear so much as his touch, so he had given that up, content now to simply get his share of her father's wealth.

He took his time opening the thick file he kept on Fallon Enterprises, pursed his lips as he leafed casually through the papers. Let them wait. In this office he was king and all their money couldn't change that. He knew well and good what he looked for and where it was, but he enjoyed making Drewhart sweat. He hated the simpering idiot.

The girl might be beautiful, but she was dumb when it came to business. Thank God, her father had known that, too. It made P.L. nervous to do business with Andrew Drewhart. He would have to tread very carefully. The man was a snake, no question about it.

He cleared his throat, glanced casually at his audience, "There is the matter of the will to be gotten out of the way first. As your father made me executor, I've been able to transfer funds and meet payrolls with no problem, seeing as how you were unable to return posthaste."

He glanced from under his disapproving frown straight at Dessa, then returned his attention to the papers. "Ah, here it is." Once again P.L. cleared his throat, and he began to read.

Dessa ignored all the whereases, and heretofores, scarcely listening to the drone of the dreadful man's voice. Daddy had left Dessa the farm and the house in town, as expected. Her mind wandered. She would soon be rid of Cluney, as her first act as the new owner of Fallon's would be to hire another attorney for the business. He was a detestable man, constantly putting his hands on her when she was little more than a child. She had always wondered what he held over her father's head.

Her ears perked up at the mention of Andrew's name. ". . . in total charge until such time as my son Mitchell is located or proven deceased."

"Mitchell?" Dessa cried. "Daddy believed he was alive?" She clasped both hands over her mouth.

Cluney glared at her. "Foolishness. Utter and complete."

He continued to read, his expression telling her not to interrupt again. But she did when he read, "My daughter Dessa will receive a monthly stipend based on a percentage of the net profits of the company as set down—"

"Wait. What does that mean?" She asked.

P.L. leered at Andrew, who smiled and leaned back in his chair.

"It means, my dear, that your father knew you would have no interest in the business. If you'll let me continue, his intent, I believe, will become clear."

"But Andrew . . . surely he didn't mean Andrew to have the business?" Her voice failed her. *Mitchell alive? Andrew in charge of Fallons?*

"Not entirely, my dear. Here, listen: 'From her half of the business, my daughter Dessa will draw a monthly stipend, a percentage of the yearly net income as recorded by said executor. The remainder of her half will be invested in a trust fund which will go to her in the event she marries."

Dessa interrupted. "But you said you needed me to return to handle the business, to . . . to decide if we should sell. You said you had a buyer and I had to come back to take care of it. You said . . ." Dessa rose from her chair, sending P.L. a blazing stare.

"I'm afraid I don't quite understand. I said nothing

of the kind. I simply wired you the money you needed. Drewhart here said he would wire that you should come home for the reading of the will." Cluney sneaked a quick glance at Andrew. What had that scoundrel been up to behind his back? He hurried to smooth over the damage.

"Obviously, your father expected you and Mr. Drewhart to . . . uhm . . . to marry, and that is why the will is drawn up this way. Husband and wife share equally, isn't that so? And it is really a moot point whose name the business is in, is it not?

"And of course your father's belief that Mitchell would be found alive has proved unsubstantiated. Dreadful business." The attorney shook his head.

"That doesn't answer my question."

P.L. raised his thick brows. "I'm sorry, I didn't hear a question."

"Why did you continue to wire me saying it was imperative that I return?"

P.L. glanced at Drewhart, glanced back down at the open file, stared at the wall. This was no time to make an enemy of Drewhart when he was about to control Fallon Enterprises. By God, why didn't the man say something?

Dessa took two long steps to the desk and slammed her fist on it. "Sell the business. Now! I will have nothing to do with this . . . this male conspiracy. Sell it to whoever made the offer."

Andrew and P.L. glared at each other, both refusing to meet her accusation.

"There was no offer?"

Neither answered.

Dessa turned to Andrew. "You did this?"

Andrew licked his lips and caught at her arm. "Listen to me, Dessa. It was for your own good.

While you were playing around with God knows what kind of people—the scum of the earth live out West, everyone knows that—I was keeping things going. Half the time when your father and mother roamed all over the country I took care of the business.

"It was me who built it into what it is. You didn't think your father had enough sense to do that, did you? And then he went off on that idiotic search for Mitchell when he should have been tending to his business. Buying a godforsaken failure of a store in a town destined to die. I told him, warned him, but he wouldn't listen. You see where that got him."

What was he saying? Search for Mitchell? He acted glad Daddy and Mother had been burned up! Hate roiled up from deep in her stomach. How dare he?

Andrew ranted on: "They were crazy, both of them. And look what happened. I could have told them as much, but they wouldn't listen to me."

Dessa scarcely felt the grip of his fingers, barely understood the meaning of the words. "What about Mitchell? What are you talking about? Andrew, answer me."

"Not you, too? Dessa, Mitchell is dead. Someone just wanted to blackmail them, that's all. Trick them out of some money. Listen to me. You and I will run this business together. Together we will grow very rich. Come to your senses, girl. Cluney, tell her."

Dessa yanked her arm from Andrew's tight hold and whirled to face Cluney. "Don't you say one word to me, you thief. I'll see you and Andrew out of my father's business for good before I'm finished. If either of you takes one penny you're not entitled to, I'll see you in jail. You understand me? In jail.

"And Andrew, I want to know exactly what was said to my parents about Mitchell, and I want to know this instant."

"Dessa, it was a scheme. That's all," Andrew said, his voice quavering. "You're angry at the wrong people. You should be shouting at the woman who wrote the letter and convinced your parents to go to that godforsaken place. It got them killed, girl. Think. We're not your enemies."

Clarice, who had not said one word, as was proper for a lady caught up in men's affairs, rose and took Dessa's arm. "You're distraught, that's all," she said soothingly. "Andrew, let me take her home. We'll call a doctor. She's not been well since that dreadful train trip from Montana. She needs to rest. We'll get the doctor to give her a sedative."

Dessa stepped back. Clarice had come along for just this purpose, to control her if she got out of hand. Andrew had thought of everything, and his sister, whom she'd thought of as a friend, had become his willing accomplice.

Dessa pulled from the fragile hold Clarice had on her. "I am not distraught about anything but this clever little scheme the three of you have cooked up. I don't want you in my home, any of you. And I'm seeing another attorney as soon as I can. You haven't heard the end of this."

She left the office, stalked across the anteroom and out into the hallway, where she paused to lean against the wall and catch her breath. Anger swelled within her like a pot about to boil over. She had to get away from them. She had to think about what to do. She had to find Ben!

Chapter Seventeen

Ben walked all the way downtown to the Union Pacific train station. He figured he could have hailed a hansom cab, but he was so angry the inside of a cab wouldn't have contained him. He needed to gesture and swing his arms and eat up yards with his long legs. Twice he made a wrong turn and had to ask directions. Finding his way in the city was a bit more difficult than out in the wilderness. There one only had to know east from west, north from south, and sometimes only up from down. Here matters were much more complicated. There were unfamiliar street names and alleys that led nowhere and had to be backtracked.

But he finally reached the impressive stone and glass structure of the station. He hurried inside, where a clerk informed him that the train bound for Kearney with connections west was at that very moment standing on the track. If he hurried, he could make it.

Steam hissed around his legs as he leaped aboard the last passenger car. The train jerked, hooted, clanged, and hissed into motion. He remained on the rear platform, hanging on to his satchel with one hand and the railing with the other. Soon Kansas City disappeared into the distance, and he watched until the buildings were only an ugly growth on the horizon.

He turned away then and let out an explosion of breath that carried a world of pent-up anger and frustration. Much as he hated leaving Dessa, he must face the inevitable as he had been forced to do time and time again. It was nothing new to him to have all he loved snatched away. One day maybe he'd learn to keep a distance from such entanglements, if he lived long enough. As for Dessa, he had to let her go; she belonged in this place, he did not.

Inside the car, Ben found a seat and crammed his long lanky body into the space, fitting the satchel under his legs on the floor. He was going home. Like Dessa, he needed to be where he belonged.

Dessa paid off the coachman and raced up the steps to the house. She jabbed at the keyhole several times before hitting it and unlatching the heavy wooden door. Inside she called out to Ben before she even slammed the door. When he didn't reply, she ran to the bottom of the stairs, called again, then started up, hitching the bronze shot-silk skirts above her shoe tops.

The echo of her own voice in the otherwise silent rooms scared her, made her heart thump all the harder as she trod along the carpeted hallway. The door to Ben's room stood open. What she already feared, she denied as she pawed through the empty armoire. The few clothes he had brought along were gone. In the drawer she found nothing. He'd had a small black satchel. It was nowhere, though she searched every corner and even under the bed. By that time her stomach was roiling and the backs of her eyes were burning.

"No, Ben. Nooooo," she cried, and flung herself across the bed. There was not even the smell of him there, and she remembered seeing the blanket piled in the floor earlier that morning. It was now folded awkwardly at the foot of the bed. She grabbed it up, buried her face in the folds, and breathed in his fragrance, all that was left of him in the empty room.

What had she done? Where had he gone?

There was no sense in asking such foolish questions. She already knew the answers. She had been cruel and stupid and unfeeling, and he had gone back to Montana.

She wasted little time crying into the blanket. Everything that had happened to her this morning, the innocent betrayal by her own father, Andrew's scheming, the dishonesty of the attorney the family had trusted—none of it mattered. What mattered was Ben Poole. He was kind and gentle, a man who had been hurt terribly by life, a man who had offered his love without strings, a man she had mistreated out of her own selfish desires.

Her heart ached for him.

"Oh, Ben, please forgive me," she cried, and tossing away the blanket, she raced to her own bedroom.

There would be no time for the trunk. She hadn't even unpacked everything yet. She jerked up the lid, intent on dragging out only the bare essentials to pack in her valise. There was no telling how many trains a day left Kansas City for Kearney, and she had no idea what their schedule was.

Rifling through the dresses, her hands touched crackly paper and she pulled from the folded clothing the package she had never opened. The one Walter Moohn had presented to her in that other life that seemed some distant dream. She ripped away the twine and paper, letting it all fall around her to the floor. And left in her hand was a stack of pictures and letters. On top was a tintype of Mitchell taken before he rode off to war.

She recalled Andrew's words about Mitchell and a mysterious letter. Was this what had taken Mother and Daddy out West?

Tears filled her eyes and she sank to the floor, skirts spreading out around her like a fall of autumn leaves. She touched her beloved brother's image with trembling fingertips. Another tintype showed the entire family, her skinny with braids, Mitchell looking all grown up at sixteen with his hair slicked down, Mother and Daddy stiffly posed like adults would do when faced by the formidable black-draped photographer and his paraphernalia. On closer inspection she saw that Mitchell's arm was around her shoulders, his fingers holding on to her as they stood in front of their parents.

It was almost more than she could bear, considering all that had happened in the past few days. For a long while she hugged the two pictures to her breast, scarcely breathing in her great sorrow. And now she had lost Ben, too, and not even a picture to remind her.

But there was! There was a picture. They had it taken at thousand-mile tree when they started back East together. The photographer was to mail the stereograph to her here after he returned to New Jersey. When would it come? How long would it take? She couldn't remember him saying, but she was sure he had. When it came, would that be all she would finally have of her lost love? Just like her brother.

Dragging herself away from such thoughts, Dessa laid aside the pictures and fingered through the letters. Two from Mitchell that she and her parents had read hundreds of times, and a couple Daddy had written when he'd been away from home, and one in a strange hand. The envelope was addressed to her father at Fallon Enterprises, Kansas City, Missouri. Just that and nothing more. There was a return address of Bannack, Montana.

The letter Andrew had spoken of. It had to be.

Dessa squeezed her eyes shut for a moment, took a deep breath and slipped out the single sheet of paper. She had never seen this letter before, and she was almost afraid to read it. For a while her hands shook so hard she actually couldn't make out the tight letters printed there, but she braced both arms on her knees and concentrated on each word in turn.

Sir,

This letter will probly come as a grate shock to you, but I deem it important as you will as well.

Yore son Mitchell did not die in the war. I know where he is and he is in great trouble. danger, I mean to say.

I only rite this in the hopes you will come to him, bring him some money so we can run away before they kill him. If you will come by train to Virginia City, Mont. terr. soonest, I will be in touch with you about how you can fine yore son. I repeat, he needs you badly.

My name is Celia Cross and I love him. Best regards.

Dessa shook her head, wiped moisture from her eyes, and reread the letter. It still said the same thing. Mitchell was alive! Glory to God, Mitchell was not dead.

Celia Cross. Who was she? Dessa wondered why no one in Virginia City had said anything. Surely if they knew about Mitchell they would have told her. Had her parents spoken to this Cross woman? And if so, what had they learned? Had they perhaps found Mitchell?

No, that wasn't possible, for where would he have gone? He surely wouldn't have run away from her. What had happened? Oh, dear God, what had happened and where was Mitchell now?

She searched the sheet of paper for a date, found none. How long ago had this been? Certainly before her parents had made their hurried trip to Virginia City under the guise of business. Now she understood why they had gone, of course. If only they had told her. But perhaps they weren't entirely sure the Cross woman was telling the truth, and didn't want her to get her hopes up. In truth, she knew they didn't tell her because they still considered her a child, had even arranged for that stupid chaperone to travel with her out West.

It hurt her terribly to learn that Daddy didn't trust her to run the business and had left it in Andrew's care. But in all honesty, before she had gone west, before she had met Rose and Ben, perhaps she would have been content to marry Andrew and let him handle the affairs of Fallon Enterprises. That was changed now, though.

Frantically, Dessa gathered up the pictures and letters, climbed to her feet, and stuffed them in her valise along with a couple of dresses, some spare underclothing, an extra pair of shoes and gloves. She must hurry to the bank and cash a draft, for she had spent most of her money on the trip from Montana.

* * *

Dessa stared with disbelief at the bank teller. "What do you mean, the account has been closed? It is my account. Who could do a thing like that?"

"I'm sorry, Miss Fallon. It's something to do with probate."

"This can't be. That's my money and I want it now!"

"Ma'am, please. I'll call the manager."

"Yes, you do that. You do that this instant."

After being led to the dark and stuffy office of a fussy little man who said he was a vice president, Dessa refused to be seated. She chose instead to pace back and forth in front of the condescending man's huge desk. A plaque said HORACE GREEN-WALLER, VICE PRESIDENT.

Greenwaller had a high, ineffectual voice. "You should speak to Mr. Cluney. He is, or was, your father's attorney, and the executor of his estate. We here at the bank have nothing to do with the accounts. We can only open and close them under directions from our clientele. Surely you must understand that."

"That's drivel, pure drivel. I want my money now, or I'll see you before a judge," Dessa shouted.

"Please, madam, don't get hysterical. Would you like me to call someone?"

"I'd like you to give me my money, every cent of it. I'll never set foot in this bank again."

"I'm afraid that's impossible. There is no money."

"This is a bank, isn't it?"

"Well, yes, of course. But—"

"Then give me some of the money you have here."

Greenwaller pinched at his mouth with pink, soft fingers. It was plain to see he wasn't used to dealing with a demanding woman, most especially one who made absolutely no sense. But Dessa was past making sense. Andrew had done this to her, thinking to make her a prisoner until she gave in to his demands. She wondered what he really wanted, the business or her. It might be interesting to find out. Anger gave way to grim determination. If she couldn't get the money here, she knew where she could get it. Bargains were struck all the time in her world, and she had one to offer Andrew Drewhart, the self-righteous, uncouth swindler.

"Madame, are you all right?" Greenwaller asked.

"Oh, yes, sir. I am indeed all right. But you, sir, had best be looking for another job, because when I finish, that's what you'll be needing."

The round face flushed, but the man managed only a sputter in reply.

She whirled and left the office, her full skirts sweeping over a spittoon as she hurried from the bank.

The hansom cab took her to Andrew and Clarice's extravagant three-story home overlooking the river. She asked the driver to wait, and without bothering to knock, shoved open the door and barged in.

"Andrew . . . Clarice," she yelled at the top of her lungs.

Clarice rushed into the massive entryway, eyes wide and face pale. Before the two women could speak, Andrew emerged from another room.

"Dear Lord, Dessa. Did you learn such manners on the frontier?"

"Manners be damned, sir!"

"Dessa, my word, your father would turn in his grave."

"Don't mention my father, you cad. You're not fit

to utter his name, nor mine, for that matter. I want my money, every cent of it, and I want it now."

Andrew shrugged and smiled. "I have no idea what you're talking about, my dear. You need some money. Here, let me . . ." He paused and pulled a clip from his inside shirt pocket. "How much did you need? Enough to pay cab fare? Or buy a new dress? Here." He thrust a bill at her, smirking with self-satisfaction.

Dessa slapped the bill away. "I want the money that was in my account at the bank, and I want my first month's stipend." She snarled the last word, spitting it out as if he had a foul taste in her mouth, which indeed it had.

Andrew widened his own eyes in innocence. "I'm afraid until the will is probated, that isn't possible. Now, why don't you go into the parlor with Clarice and I'll bring you a brandy. It will quiet your nerves."

"I will not go into your parlor, I will not sit with your sister, I will not remain in this house one minute longer than I have to."

She fastened a thoughtful glare on Andrew and he gazed back at her, not giving an inch.

"Bring me a paper and pen," she snapped.

"What?" Andrew looked around as if she were talking to someone else.

"I'm going to sign over half the business to you. Free and clear, this very instant. No ties to that thief of a lawyer, no courtrooms or judges. Simple as that."

Andrew's jaw dropped, his eyes popped. Clarice uttered a tiny sound like a kitten mewling.

"Well?" Dessa demanded.

"You don't mean it. It won't be legal."

"Of course I do, and of course it will. I'll sell it to you for a dollar. That will be legal and binding. Technically it belongs to me, even though you and that scoundrel intended to pretty well bleed me dry before I get my hands on it. Am I not correct?"

"I don't know quite what to say."

"I'm sure you don't. Paper, pen." She snapped her fingers at him. "Move, Andrew, or so help me I'll fight you both. I'll go to New York and get a lawyer who'll make Cluney look like a hound pup, and you'll none of you have a cent. I swear I will, if I have to bankrupt Fallon Enterprises to do it."

She narrowed her eyes. "And think about this. If Mitchell is alive, I'll find him and then you'll get nothing. And even if he's not, I intend to marry Ben Poole as soon as possible. Either way, you've lost, you high-handed bastard. At least this way you'll have half, bought all legal and proper."

Andrew backed into the room from which he had just come, gazing at Dessa as if she'd gone quite daft. She waited a moment, then followed him, sensing Clarice padding along behind her making small simpering sounds down in her throat.

Dessa took the pen Andrew offered, dipped it in ink, and began to scrawl across the paper. When she was satisfied with the wording, she read it aloud.

Andrew was speechless. She was indeed selling him sole ownership of one half of the holdings of Fallon Enterprises free and clear, to revert to her only in the event of his death. And all for the sum total of her current account at the bank.

"Now," Dessa said in a softly menacing voice, "I'll sign this as soon as you reinstate my account at the bank. Oh, and by the way, we will drop by our friend Cluney's office and break the news to him. I'll want all the legal papers he's holding. All of them. I will be having an attorney of my own look things over and draw up further papers that will make this business deal airtight. I may only draw a stipend from the half that's left, but neither you nor that bastard will get your hands on any portion of it. I promise you, if you don't do this I'll fight you both until every dime is gone."

"Dessa," Andrew sputtered.

"Shut up, Andrew. Just shut up, and get your coat. You're coming with me. We'll just take this along and when everything is settled, I'll put my signature on it. I'm sure someone at the bank will witness it for us."

"What are you going to do, Dessa?" Andrew asked as they went out the door together, leaving a white-faced Clarice standing in the three-story entryway under a glittering chandelier.

"I've already told you," she said, and pushed away his hand when he tried to assist her into the cab.

He got in beside her, sighing deeply. "I mean after we do this."

"I'm going to Montana, Andrew. I'm going home to Montana."

Ben arrived at Devil's Gate exhausted. He'd slept very little, having spent even the dark of each night worrying about Dessa. If anything happened to her, he would feel responsible. He should never have left her in the clutches of that spineless Drewhart. Over and over he dozed off only to awaken with a start thinking he'd heard her call his name. He dreamed once of that night he'd heard that small, frantic voice calling out in desperation and rushed out into the darkness to find her near death but still fighting to survive. He awoke covered with sweat, despite the cold drafty air in the coach.

On the morning of the second day of his journey

there'd been a prairie fire. It was as if the entire world were ablaze, from horizon to horizon. Soon smoke grew so thick no one could see or breathe. Far into the night passengers choked and gagged, finding little relief in the masks they fashioned for their faces. Even after the train passed through the worst of the smoke, the smell permeated every car. It had soaked into all their clothes until every movement wafted the odor up their nostrils once again.

Children cried incessantly. A pregnant woman at the front of the coach vomited over and over until a sour stench overpowered even the smoke. Her husband finally took her from the train at a stop where there was a doctor. Blessedly the conductor brought in buckets of water to wash away the vomit. Passengers rode with the windows open during the afternoon, but as they neared the mountains, the air grew too cold for that. Once again they were closed up in the overcrowded coaches, breathing each other's air and body odor.

As if that weren't enough, when Ben finally disembarked at Devil's Gate to inhale fresh air for the first time in days, he learned that the stage had been attacked by Indians and they were waiting for another to replace it before they could begin the trip to Virginia City. It might be another day and night, the clerk told him with a there's-nothing-I-can-do shrug.

Ben decided not to stay in a hotel, but instead walked over to the livery and asked if there was a horse he could rent.

"I ain't had a horse to let in a month of Sundays," the man reported. One bony old sorrel gazed despondently at Ben from its stall.

"What's that?"

"You may call that a horse, I call it glue," the man

said with a snort. " 'Tain't mine, in the first place; in the second place, it'd drop dead atween yore legs afore you was five mile out a town. Best you just bed down and wait for the stage.

"If you want, you can lay in the hay back yonder. Jest promise me you won't steal old Eb."

Despite all that had happened, Ben couldn't help giving the fellow a wry smile. "I've done a lot of things in my life, but I ain't never stole as sorry a horse as that."

The old man chuckled. "You'll be staying, then?"

"I appreciate the offer. I've got money, I can pay. I just don't take to hotel beds real well."

"Well, I can understand that, I surely can," the old man said, and took the coins Ben held out. "Stay till the stage comes. You can bathe in the horse trough, old Eb won't care one whit."

Ben thanked the man, tossed his valise in the hay, and dropped down next to it. He would wait till dark to take the old man up on the bath. Wouldn't do to get caught out on the street in the altogether by any of the gentler gender.

He must have fallen asleep, for he dreamed that Dessa lay in his arms, and he turned his face into clouds of her dark, sweet hair.

She touched him with her soft fingers. "I love you, Ben Poole."

"I love you, Dessa," he whispered, then moved his mouth down the side of her neck, lips coming to rest in the hollow of her throat.

Her bosom heaved and he nuzzled at the cleft between her breasts.

Miraculously, she was naked in his arms. The warm, moist flesh tasted sweet as honey to his tongue. He lapped at the flavor, kissing an erect nipple.

She cried out, thrust the breast into his mouth, and arched against him.

Hands cupping her buttocks, he pulled her to his rising manhood, and moaned in ecstasy. Moving to the other breast, he rose to straddle her, and she opened herself to him.

Smooth as silk, he slid inside her surging heat and clung to her. She was his very life, she fed his soul. Together they were complete; apart from her he was nothing but a man content only to survive.

"I will never leave you," he cried out as he reached the pinnacle and tumbled over.

The dream turned nightmarish and she began to scream, begging him to help her. But he had gone on without her, and when he turned to take her hand, to save her, she was gone.

"Dessa, no." He sobbed, and stumbled. He would surely fall over the edge of eternity. Alone forever.

With a shout he bolted upright, cried out, and woke himself. It was the black of night and he was alone. Despite the chill, sweat soaked his back and under his arms. A horse snorted softly. Breath coming in short gasps, he smelled hay and manure and leather, and remembered where he was. Tickling at his nostrils was the burnt smoky smell from the prairie fire he'd ridden through. It was in his clothes and his hair and his skin.

Making love to Dessa in the dream had been so real he felt dizzy with it, even though he was fully awake. It was as if she had reached out to him from far away, and given herself to him so he'd know how much she loved him. So he would realize that he loved her. He could still feel her lush bare limbs wrapped around him, her warm sweetness when he buried himself deep inside her. How stupid of him to think he could deny love, the most precious of gifts a man and woman can give each other. He had to go back to her. Life takes so much from a man, he would be wise not to throw away what few chances it offers for happiness.

Trouble was, he didn't have enough money for a return ticket on the train. Time was when Ben Poole wouldn't have worried much, he would simply have taken what he needed. That's what the war had done to him. Made him a thief and a sorry excuse for a man. A killer, even. There had to be another way. To do such a thing now would be to betray the woman he loved, and that wouldn't do at all. He would find another way to get back to Kansas City.

He sniffed his smoky odor and decided to use that horse trough first. Come daylight he would tackle his other problems. No doubt there's be a poker game in town, and he'd been known to win some hefty pots. Had lost some, too, he thought wryly, but let that go. He had very little left to lose.

The air was so cold he could see his breath when he stepped from the livery barn into the moonlit night. Looking quickly around to make sure no one was about, he slipped off his dirty clothes, carefully hung the clean spare pants and shirt over the hitching post, and stepped one foot into the trough.

"Holy cripes," he gasped when the icy water rose above his calf.

Gritting his teeth, he eased in the other leg and lowered himself very slowly into the wooden trough. It was all he could do to keep from shouting from the cold. He made do with a quick rub. Seeing as how he had no soap, it was certainly not a proper bath, but it would have to do. All the same, he rinsed some of the smell off, washed at his hair as best he could, then climbed out.

He hissed through his teeth and danced about on the boardwalk to warm up, thinking how funny it would be if someone glanced out a window about now and saw a naked man doing a jig in the moonlight. Probably just think he was drunk and go on back to sleep. And he *was* drunk. Totally drunk with the need to be with Dessa, drunk with the realization that he was not complete without her, no matter where he was.

Dessa boarded the Union Pacific train that left Kansas City the next morning after Ben's departure. She would be just a day behind him all the way across the prairie, if indeed he had headed back to Montana. Once they passed through a wide bare gorge where a fire had burned itself out. During most of the second day they traveled through the ugliness of that sorrowful, blackened plain.

On the morning of the third day it began to snow, the flakes blown by a stiff wind that made the snow look as if it were falling sideways instead of to the ground. But on the ground is indeed where the snow landed. As the train pushed its way west, drifts piled up that threatened to block their forward passage. The storm let up by the time the mountains came in sight, the great blue/purple peaks stabbing through low-hanging gray clouds that lay like puffy skirts around their feet.

Occasionally Dessa would cry softly, staring out the window at the beauty of it all. Montana waited to cradle her and she wanted to throw open the window and shout, "I'm coming, Ben. I'm coming home." And silently she offered a prayer of hope. *Let it be true, let Mitchell be alive like the letter said. Oh, please, God, let me find him.*

Then at long last, when she thought she couldn't endure another minute, the conductor came through the car with his announcement. "Devil's Gate. Next stop. Devil's Gate."

Dessa let the conductor hand her off the steps down onto the platform of the station. Since she had only brought a small valise, she had carried it aboard, and now the conductor placed it beside her and tipped his hat.

"Hope you enjoyed your trip, ma'am," he said, and walked away, leaving her there with a scattering of other passengers on their way somewhere besides where the train was headed.

For just a moment or two she felt terribly afraid. Suppose Ben stayed on the train, went right on to California? Then what would she do? Whether she located Mitchell or not, she needed Ben, loved him, wanted him at her side.

Oh, dear God, suppose she never saw him again.

Chapter Eighteen

Ben blinked as he emerged from the darkness of the Devil's Hole Saloon. Clutched in his fist buried deep in one pocket was a roll of bills, enough to buy a ticket back to Kansas City, and he hadn't stolen it. Well, he hadn't exactly stolen it. The two yahoos he'd gotten into a game with weren't the best poker players he's ever seen; actually, it had been sort of like taking candy from a baby. Still, anyone who sits in on five-card stud ought to know the risks.

He blinked again to accustom himself to the brilliant sunlight and started up the boardwalk toward the train station. He wasn't paying much attention to people on the street; his mind was already on what he would say to Dessa when he arrived on her doorstep in Kansas City. So when he bumped elbows with a lady, he automatically tipped his hat and said, "Sorry, ma'am."

The lady stopped, called his name.

He took another look, recognized the voice in the same instant as he beheld her face, and grabbed Dessa around the waist, shouting at the top of his lungs and whirling her around and around so her feet flew through the air.

"My goodness, Ben. Oh, Ben." Her valise went

sailing and she wrapped both arms around his neck, laughing as they twirled faster and faster.

After a few dizzying seconds he staggered backward against the wall of the mercantile and buried his face in her neck. He held on to her tightly, not sure whether he should laugh or cry.

He had her; he wouldn't let go. Never. Never. Ben Poole, who thought he had shed his last tears over his family's graves when he was fourteen, felt warm moisture slip from beneath his tightly closed lashes. He kept his nose against her shoulder and inhaled her scent. How could he have ever walked away from her?

"Ben, you're squeezing me," Dessa said gaily. "Oh, darling, I was so afraid you'd gone on to California. What are you doing here?"

He cleared his throat, but couldn't let her go, couldn't take his lips from her neck, her cheek, her mouth. She had called him darling.

Further, she let him kiss her, long and deeply, right there on the street in Devil's Gate, with one and all looking on.

That afternoon they boarded the stage for Virginia City, a long and arduous journey neither would much suffer from. They were happy to be alive and in love and together, no matter the conditions.

It rained much of the final day of their trip, so that they arrived in Virginia City as they had left, wading ankle deep in mud from the coach to the boardwalk. Neither had bothered to wire ahead, and the cold rain had driven everyone off the streets. It was a lonely, unheralded welcome.

"I don't know about you, but I'm ready for a bath and some sleep," she told him while they stood there, shoulders hunched against the icy pellets of rain.

He looked around, shrugged. "Where?"

They both grinned and laughed. Where else?

Small valises in hand, they made their way toward the Golden Sun, dashing along and dodging sheets of water running from store roofs. They arrived inside the quiet hurdy-gurdy house soaked to the skin and looking and feeling like a couple of drowned rats.

Grisham scurried from behind the bar. "Sorry, we're not open yet."

Ben took off his hat and whopped it against his equally sopping pants leg. "It's us, Grisham. Dessa and Ben. Don't you recognize us?"

The lanky Englishman raised his thick black brows and peered at the drenched couple. "Why, so it is. So it is. Well, Miss Rose will be glad to see you. But she's out at her place today. Weather's been so bad we've had little business. If it hasn't been snowing, it's been raining, so she took some time off to rest. Truth be known, I believe she's trying to make up her mind about selling the place. Needs the quiet."

Grisham grabbed his apron up in both hands and wrung it in his hands. "We didn't expect you back so soon. But I'm sure it'd be fine with Miss Rose if you went on up to her rooms."

From up above on the landing came a shriek. "Ben. Oh, Ben, is that you?" Down the stairs flew Maggie, long hair waving behind her like a fluttering flag, and a thin robe opened wide and trailing along. Her breasts bounced curvaceously above a bright red corset when she threw herself into Ben's arms.

"I'm all wet, Maggie," he warned too late, then gave up and hugged her close.

"Does Rose know you're here? And Dessa, you did bring her back with you."

Dessa gazed a question at Ben. Bring her back?

"Well, not exactly, it's more like she brought me back. But it doesn't matter. How is Rose, how is everyone? Grisham said something about selling the Sun? Is it true?"

Maggie shrugged and stepped back. "You're all wet. Come on upstairs, the both of you. We'll get some hot water so you can get cleaned up. What a trip that must be, up from Devil's Gate."

"It's a real bruiser. 'Course you ladies have a bit more padding, but I'll swear I feel like my bones have poked right through my rear end by now. I'd rather ride a horse across the whole country than that coach five miles, I swear I would."

Maggie chuckled and grabbed Ben's arm, swinging him around so she could look. She rubbed a hand over his butt. "Nope, no bones there. If you'd eat more, you wouldn't be so lank."

Dessa felt herself flushing at the sight of Maggie touching Ben so freely and so personally.

"Well, Maggie girl," he said, "I'd sure appreciate that bath and I know Dessa would, too."

"Come on up, then." Maggie stopped at the bottom step and glanced back over her shoulder at Ben and Dessa. "You going together or separate?" she asked with a wink.

Ben glanced down at Dessa, grinned at her flustered look, and winked back at Maggie. "Well, now, you'll have to ask Dessa about that."

"Ben," Dessa scolded. "Shame on you." Even as she spoke the words, she found herself wishing she had the temerity to throw caution to the wind. But she didn't. She had been brought up properly and decent girls didn't do such things. They only wished they could.

"Dessa can go first, then you can warm up her water for me," Ben said.

"Thank you so much, kind sir." Dessa executed a mock bow and headed up the stairs.

"I'll stay down here and see if I can talk Grisham into a cold one while I wait. Come on back down, Maggie, when you get Dessa settled. We can talk."

"Yes, okay, Ben, I will. I have a surprise."

Dessa followed Maggie thoughtfully up the stairs. She had never completely understood the relationship between this woman and Ben, or between Ben and Rose, for that matter. The entire situation puzzled her greatly. She wanted to know more about it.

During the long stage ride, she and Ben had discussed her financial problems with Andrew and how she had handled it. Ben appeared to have quite a head for business, making several suggestions for future investments in the territories that made good sense to her. She would definitely look into some of them. Ben had applauded her stance against the crooked Cluney and subsequent victory, though he did suggest immediately hiring another attorney to set matters straight.

She was pleased to learn that Ben had a natural affinity for bookkeeping and could keep numbers straight in his head without even so much as a piece of paper to jot notes on. That ability was something for her to consider. She had laughingly joked about hiring him to handle that part of the business, but on reflection she thought seriously that it wasn't such a bad idea. Not hiring him, exactly, but perhaps making him a partner. He had no money to put into the venture, but there would be enough money even after the sale of half the business to Andrew and Clarice. By law, Fallon Enterprises belonged to her and Mitchell, if he was still alive and she could locate him. Given a decent attorney, she should have no trouble getting things straightened out.

Then what she would need to run the business properly was someone with Ben's phenomenal ability with figures, since she had absolutely none in that area. Someone she could trust totally and completely. There was no doubt in her mind that Ben Poole was that man.

She had asked him where he learned to manage figures like he did. He just shrugged. "I guess I always knew it. I thought everyone did." He'd laughed heartily then. "It's like seeing colors and speaking the language. You just suppose if you can do a thing, then everyone else can, too. Especially if you always knew how to do it.

"I'm always doing Rose's books—she's such an absolute mess with numbers."

"That should have made you wonder. If Rose couldn't do it, there might be a few more people who couldn't," Dessa teased.

Ben looked at her blankly for a moment, then realized what she was saying and grinned.

Relaxing in the tub of exquisitely hot water, Dessa smiled at the memory. Some of the time Ben had such a wonderfully open expression, almost as if he were saying, *Here I am, surprise me, make me laugh.* Yet within the depths of his blue eyes dwelled a frosty barrier that he could throw up without warning, daring anyone to break through. She wondered what lay hidden there, and vowed to find out before much longer. There were definitely some questions that needed answering before they married. His relationship with Sarah Woodridge and the twins was a big one; Maggie and Virgie as well. She might share Ben with Rose, who was more like a mother to him, but she had no intention of sharing him with a widow or a couple of whores. Maggie said they were like brother and sister, but how did Ben feel? And what about Virgie?

But before any of that—before anything else, in fact—she had to try to find Celia Cross. If her brother Mitchell was still alive, then she would find him, no matter what it took.

On the trip back Ben had told her he would help search for Mitchell, but warned her not to have too much hope. He thought the entire thing sounded like an attempt to extort money out of her folks, and if she got involved it would amount to the same thing.

"Just promise me one thing," Ben had asked. "Promise me you won't go off on any wild goose chases. That if you hear anything, you'll come to me first, or even Walter Moohn. There are outlaws hiding out all over these hills. Some even worse than the two you encountered on your first trip out here."

Dessa shuddered, remembering Coody and his sidekick. She'd almost managed to forget the incident, in view of everything else that had happened in the ensuing weeks since. Thinking back on that nightmare, she had been glad to promise Ben she wouldn't go off on her own.

If anyone would know where this Celia Cross lived, Rose Langue would, and Dessa intended to bring it up as soon as possible.

The hot bath relaxed her so much she had almost dozed off, when Maggie tapped on the door. "We've brought water to heat the bath for Ben. Are you finished yet?"

She crawled from the tub and toweled down. "Just a second," she called, and slipped into the robe Maggie had laid out.

Despite her protests that she could get a room at the hotel, Maggie bundled her into Rose's bed and put up a screen around the tub so Ben could bathe in privacy. "That's nonsense. Rose won't be back before Friday. She would be pleased that you used her bed.

"I happen to know that your little house is waiting for you. She just shut it up like it was, said she was sure you'd be back soon. But it'll be cold over there today. You'll be needing to get yourself a stove. Old Mister Winter's tapping on the door, and you ain't seen nothing till you've seen him act up around these parts."

As if reminded of the cold damp weather, Maggie slipped a couple of sticks of wood onto the bed of coals in the stove and flipped the damper open. Soon a cozy, crackling fire warmed the room.

"I'll light a lamp, and then I'll just tell Ben he can come on in and take his bath. You need anything?"

Head already nestled into the pillow, Dessa stared with glazing eyes at Maggie. "No, I'm just fine," she murmured, and closed her eyes.

When Ben slipped into the room a few minutes later, he found Dessa asleep in Rose's big feather bed. He went to stand beside her for a few moments.

The hot bath had flushed her cheeks and left damp ringlets of dark hair around her face. He touched her tenderly, running the tips of his fingers over her cheek, down her throat, and stopping at the swell of her breasts. He was overcome with such a longing for her he could scarcely stand it. Not just a sexual urge like the kind that made a man grow hard and throbbing, but a deep-down desire to live with her, to lie beside her, to sit at a table and take a meal with her, to brush her hair and scrub her back and run through the woods with her. To see reflected in her green eyes the same undying desire for him.

Quietly he bent and touched his lips to her warm cheek. Her long eyelashes fluttered, brushed at his chin, and she sighed a breath of air that caressed him gently. Ever so carefully he kissed her lips, then left her there to sleep while he bathed in the warmed-over water steaming with her feminine scent.

No woman had ever attracted him in such a way. He found himself in awe of his own feelings for her. A girl not of a class he thought would ever be attracted to him, and certainly not that he would be attracted to. She had some city ways that needed toughening up a bit if she were to live in the territory, but he had no doubt that she could handle whatever came her way. Her facing down Andrew and that sister of his had impressed Ben.

Maybe Rose was right. He and Dessa could cut a swath across this great new land the likes of which none had seen. With the coming of the Union Pacific, other railroads would open up the rest of the West. It was already beginning up north, and if they were careful and paid attention, he and Dessa could be ready for the movement of the rails, investing in businesses all across the land even before anyone else could guess their value for the future.

Ben lowered himself till the water lapped on his ears, and chortled. Who would have thought it? Who would have thought Ben Poole would ever care for anything but a Winchester and a blanket to throw on the ground?

He only saw one obstacle in their path right now, and that was Dessa's search for her brother. He'd have to try to find that Celia Cross and put the fear of the Lord in her. He wouldn't have the woman, whoever she was, messing with Dessa's mind, for he could see how much she loved and missed her brother. He decided to put a stop to this nonsense straightaway, so he and Dessa could get on with their lives.

Dessa awoke sometime in the night. From somewhere she heard a light snoring. Startled, she sat upright and self-consciously crossed her arms over both breasts. The noise was coming from the other side of the bed. She leaned over. It was so dark in the room, she just could make out someone lying on the floor all covered with quilts. It took only a moment to realize that Ben Poole was asleep next to her bed.

"Oh, Ben," she whispered. "Dear Ben."

She lay back and let her hand trail off the bed so that it rested lightly on the lump that she took to be his shoulder. When she awoke the next morning, he was gone, the quilts folded neatly at her feet. She wondered if perhaps she had dreamed the whole thing.

Downstairs she learned that Ben had gone out on a freight run with Wiley. She was disappointed, having thought he wouldn't go back to work for the Bannon Freight Company. Certainly not the very next day after they returned, even before she could run down Celia Cross. She would need Ben.

"He said the old man had his ox in the ditch, and that you'd understand," Maggie reported.

Though disappointed, she did understand. It was Ben's habit to help where he was needed. She wouldn't have him any other way. She telegraphed that message to Maggie with a warm smile. "Well, I'm going to get my house opened back up. I'm sure it could stand a good airing. Looks like the rain has moved out for a while."

"Uhmm," Maggie said. "But it's a mite chilly out there today. Winter is definitely in the wind."

"Looks absolutely perfect to me," Dessa said. She started out the door, then turned back. "Maggie, do you know a Celia Cross?"

Maggie knitted her brows, then shook her head no. "Rose might, though. She knows just about everyone."

"I might just ride out and talk to her, if you think she wouldn't mind."

"She'd be real happy to see you."

"Where does she live?" Dessa asked.

"Oh, just a mile or so out of town. It's a little cabin surrounded by flowers. Roses. They're her favorites. The whole backyard's full of roses. She has water hauled to them in the dry months. It's a sight. Folks say she loves those roses better than most mothers love their babies. But they just don't know Rose real well. Rose, she loves her friends, those she takes in, like Tressie Majors, who's now Tressie Bannon, and of course Ben. And now you."

Dessa looked up sharply. "Me?"

Maggie nodded. "She was so afraid you wouldn't come back, I caught her crying the day after you left."

"Rose? Crying?" Dessa had thought the woman tough, and unrelenting in that toughness.

"You should have seen her when Tressie went off

with that Reed Bannon. 'Course it's all right now, and once in a while she gets to see their babies. Just like she's their grandma or something." Maggie tucked her chin, then looked up brightly at Dessa. "And it'll be the same with me and Samuel. Oh, Dessa, we're getting married, and Samuel says we'll have lots of babies, and he's going to build me a house."

"Oh, Maggie, that's wonderful. When did all this happen?"

"While you and Ben were gone. Well, at least the part where we decided to get married. He used to come and dance with me, but he was so quiet, I never dreamed. And then one day he just dressed all up in his finest—we didn't even recognize him, me and Rose—and he came and asked for my hand.

"Oh, Dessa, do you think it's all right? A woman like me marrying and having a family? I'm so happy."

The girl rushed to Dessa, threw her arms around her neck.

"Sweetheart, I think it's wonderful if you love him, if he loves you," Dessa said with a laugh.

"Oh, I do, we do, he does." She broke out laughing, and whirled around and around.

Dessa got caught up in the girl's gaiety, and soon they were both chattering away about weddings and men and having babies.

"I don't go in the cribs anymore, you know," Maggie finally told her seriously. "It wouldn't be right."

Dessa kissed the girl on the cheek. "I wish you and Samuel the very best. You must stay in touch with Ben and me. Where will you live?"

"Samuel has a farm in Nebraska. He got the land

from his older brother, who homesteaded it and then died."

Dessa nodded her head. A great weight had lifted from her shoulders. It was really true, then, that Maggie and Ben had a platonic relationship. And she was very happy that the woman had found love before it was too late for her to change her life.

After Maggie went upstairs, Dessa decided not to ride out to Rose's place, but to wait till the Golden Sun's owner came in Friday. She had plenty to do getting her own home livable in the meantime.

Ben didn't return until the next day, riding in with Wiley and hopping off the wagon in front of Dessa's. He swung the door open without knocking and stood in silence watching her sweep the floor. A frown of concentration wrinkled the skin between her lovely eyes and she had sucked her lower lip into her mouth.

She didn't sense him in the room, so intently was she working at the task. As she turned so that her back was to him, he strode across the floor, grabbed her around the waist, and lifted her so he could nuzzle the skin at the back of her neck.

"Whoop . . . Ben," she hollered, and turned to throw her arms around his neck. "Lord, you scared me."

"Didn't mean to." He grinned down at her, and pushed a lock of hair from her face. Dear God, how he loved her. "Ah, Dessa. Come away with me. Be my love. Ride with me into the sunset, or some such nonsense. I love you, girl, what are we waiting for? Let's get married."

The outburst overwhelmed her, and she was temporarily speechless. Then she leaned back to get a good look at him. "Well, of course you're right, Ben.

We should just ride off into the sunset. Only, on what? You don't have a horse, and neither do I. We could steal Rose's blacks, perhaps. Neither of us has more than a stitch or two of clothes, we have no place to live but here, and you can see with the two of us in the room, elbows bump walls. But yes, Ben, let's throw caution to the wind and get married."

He squinted at her. "You're making fun of me."

She laughed, tousled his hair until he joined her. "Not making fun of you, Ben, just being practical. First things first." She grew very serious then. "And first thing with me, I think you know, is to find this Celia Cross and see if my brother really is still alive. I thought you understood how I feel about that."

"Wiley and I run across a fella telling about plans under way to build a railroad up north of here. It may be way in the future, but if we could get up there now, buy up some of those businesses that are struggling to stay alive, folks that would welcome cold hard cash, we'd be sitting pretty. Hell, we could start out feeding the crews that lay the rails and go from there."

"I know you're right, Ben. And I agree, but not until I find Mitchell. Then will be plenty of time for us. I promise. Just this one thing. You must understand, Ben. I love Mitchell, ever since he didn't come back from the war I've had this feeling about him, this sense of a connection. If it weren't for that, I would have died that night you found me. It was Mitchell, or my memory of him, that kept me going, kept me alive. Have you never loved someone that much, Ben?"

"Yes, I have. And I love you that much, too," Ben replied. "So let's get to looking for this Cross woman. Sooner she's found, sooner we can get on with it."

Dessa planted noisy kisses all over his face, hanging on to him so that he had to bend down. Both ended up laughing hilariously and he finally lifted her off the floor and straightened.

Arms firmly around her, he drew her close, their bodies welding together.

She looked up into his eyes, saw they had turned deep and dark as pools in a forest. A faint joyful purling, primitive in its rhythm, captured her, and she wanted only to have him deep inside her, probing, searching for her very soul. His presence became everything; there was nothing else. She let herself go, became his, became part of him.

He bent forward until his features were a blur. "Oh, God, Dessa, I need you," he said into her mouth.

He was fire, he was sweet, cool nourishment, and she drank, tasting the essence of this man. His desire rose against her, fierce and throbbing, and she shifted so that through her clothes she could feel that live, wonderful part of him pulsating at the heart of her own ravenous need. If he asked, she would give him what he wanted, what he must have, right here, this very minute.

"Dance with me," he said in a husky whisper. "Like this, up close." Then he began to sway, holding her so close she sensed every tenuous motion. A dizzying sensation of desire swelled within her and she moaned softly. He continued to move, breathing heavily against her neck, making tiny sounds down deep in his throat.

Arms wrapped tightly around his neck, she tasted of his flesh, whispered, "Love me, love me, love me."

"Oh, yes. Yes. Always and forever. Listen, my love. Hear the music?" He swept her around the room then in a graceful waltz, their bodies moving as one to the imaginary strains.

She heard the music, a melody from Leibstraume that welled as if from the most beautiful place imaginable.

His hot breath came in short puffs, stirring her hair. He groaned. "Oh, God, Dessa. I thank Clarice for one thing."

"Uhm, what is that?" she asked in a fuzzy voice, her tongue and lips thick with desire.

"She taught me how to dance. And I see the attraction, I surely do." He chuckled gruffly and lifted her feet off the floor, whirled her once, twice, three times, then let her go. Set her back from him.

"Whoo, that's enough of that!"

She felt dizzy, disoriented, and staggered a couple of steps before righting herself. What would going to bed with this man be like when the simple act of dancing or holding each other could be so passionate, so physically disturbing?

"'I love you, girl, but stay where you are. I'm warning you." He turned quickly away, shoulders rising and falling as he took deep breaths and collected himself.

"And I love you, too, Ben. Oh, indeed I do."

Ben laughed self-consciously and turned back to her.

How wonderful that laughter was. Dessa thought he didn't enjoy life enough, and wished she could do something about that.

They parted reluctantly, the issue of her brother unsettled. She remained stubborn about finding him before they got on with their own lives, and he vowed to hold himself in check, not forcing his hungry needs on her before they were married.

Dessa stood in the doorway, waving good-bye, and realized it was Friday. It was time for her to visit with Rose at the Golden Sun and asked her about Celia Cross.

Some time later she backed from her door, closing it and securing the hasp. As she turned, she spotted a familiar figure on horseback and froze in horror. He wasn't looking in her direction, and for that she was thankful. For Coody, the vicious outlaw who had dragged her off the stagecoach some two months ago, was riding bold as brass right down the middle of the street.

"Just as if he were an ordinary person," Dessa muttered under her breath. Her heart thumped hard against her ribcage. Suppose he turned around, saw her? What would he do? What should she do?

She remained motionless in the doorway until he passed on by, then ran across the street. Something behind her attracted Coody's attention, the barking of a dog or someone shouting, and he swung around to look directly at her. She had no time to turn away. In that terrifying moment when their eyes met and locked, she knew he recognized her. She also saw that he wouldn't let it go at that. He hunkered in the saddle and spurred the horse back in her direction.

Crying out, she scrambled up on the boardwalk and raced for the alley along one side of the Golden Sun. Dusk had fallen and the narrow opening lay in deep shadows. A side door that led into the back room where Grisham kept the whiskey stored might be unlocked, and if it was, she could sneak through there before Coody spotted her.

She hit the door with the flat of both hands and it popped open. With a heavy sigh, she slid inside and leaned against the wall until her breathing slowed and the fear that had boiled into her throat became a settled monster throbbing in her chest.

Then she ran through the storage room, intending on going into the saloon, where she would be safe. She ran right into Maggie, who had just stepped behind the bar.

"Dessa, whatever is wrong? You look awful."

"Hide me, Maggie. Hide me. It's him. I saw him. Right outside. He'll kill me. Hide me." Dessa panted and gasped out the words, squeezing Maggie's upper arm painfully.

"Who, Dessa? Where?" The girl waited, blocking their escape up the stairs and out of sight just long enough for Coody to burst through the saloon doors astride his sorrel horse. Patrons scattered in all directions, hugging walls and hitting the floor behind upturned tables.

Maggie grabbed Dessa's arm and together they bolted for the stairway. It was too late. Dessa barely saw the reaction of the early evening patrons before Coody drew his pistol and started firing. She thought she saw Ben at the bar, and Rose behind it, down on the other end, but it was all a reddish blur in the half-light.

Women screamed, men shouted, shots rang out, and Maggie went down, her grip still tight on Dessa's arm, so that Dessa, too, was pulled down to sprawl on the staircase.

Ben scarcely had time to realize what was happening, and he watched with disbelief. His Winchester stood against the bar because he'd been on his way back from the short freight run with Wiley Moss. The rifle was loaded and he snatched it up, threw himself over and behind the bar to draw a bead on the man riding the terrified horse.

Sweat popped out on his forehead. He heard the screams of a thousand men dying on the battlefield, listened with disbelief to the echo of his vow that he would never put a bullet in another human being. He wiped sweat from his eyes with one arm, remembered Clete Woodridge's dying eyes beseeching his own murderer to take care of his wife and children. And he couldn't pull the trigger, he couldn't kill Coody.

Then the outlaw was gone, riding out the door and off the boardwalk, spurring his bucking horse, firing into the air as he rode hell-bent for leather out of Virginia City.

Ben lowered the rifle slowly, again wiped sweat from his eyes with his shirtsleeves, and gazed around the room. Upturned tables shielded men who had only recently been peacefully sipping beer or talking to their favorite dancing partner. A couple of girls peered wild-eyed from behind the staircase.

Then someone started screaming, and the screams grew in intensity until they split the air and set his nerves on end.

He located the screams beyond the solid railing of the stairs. He vaulted over the bar and then saw that it was Dessa screaming. She was holding Maggie in her arms and both were covered with blood. They might have been bathing in it. And Dessa just kept right on screaming and rocking the limp body back and forth.

For the longest moment in his life, Ben couldn't move. Then he leaped up the stairs and knelt with his arms wrapped around the women he loved, one alive, the other dead.

Chapter Nineteen

Ben's thoughts, his very existence clouded as he roughly embraced the two women. A blackness washed over him, driving all sanity into the farthest and darkest corners of his consciousness. Rose knelt beside him, but he was barely aware of her. He could only stare into the dead face of dear, sweet Maggie, who had literally dragged him back from the depths of despair when he was no more than a child. He couldn't speak or cry out; he thought he could not draw a breath. He prayed his own heart would just stop beating and solve everything. He'd had Maggie's killer in his sights and couldn't pull the trigger.

Rose lay her hand on his arm. Dessa stopped screaming and began to cry in jerking sobs, her face buried in his shoulder. She repeated Maggie's name over and over and over like a litany that might somehow restore life. When Ben didn't respond to her touch, Rose lay her hand on Dessa's head and just sat there on the step, staring sightlessly.

Dear Maggie was dead, and Rose's tough exterior fell away as if someone were chopping at her with an ax. But she had to minister to the living, these two young people whom she loved with all her heart and soul.

From deep in Ben's throat there rose a roar of agony that turned every head in the room. He lay Maggie gently down, pulled away from Dessa, and rose from where he knelt, still making the awful noise that those in the saloon that night would speak of in awe for years afterward. He staggered to the bar, retrieved the Winchester from where he'd thrown it, and burst out the door. His wounded cry could be heard echoing into the distance long after the doors stopped swinging. Still no one in the Golden Sun moved. It was as if they'd been stricken mute and turned to stone.

Dessa's trembling query broke the silence. "Rose?"

"I don't know, child, I just don't know."

"Where is he going?"

"To kill that monster, I would think. And if and when he does that, he might as well shoot himself, too."

"What do you mean?"

"I mean if Ben Poole causes one more death, he will not be able to live with it. I saw him the last time. If you love him and you think you can stop him, child, please go after him. If you don't, we'll all lose him forever."

"That awful man deserves to die, Rose. He killed Maggie. He came after me and he killed Maggie. Oh, Rose, my God," she wailed. "I . . . I came . . . I came in here. She was helping me get away. Oh, Rose."

"Sshh, sweetheart. You mustn't blame yourself. It was him that caused it all, from beginning to end. That brutish Coody Land. And yes, he does deserve to die, but Ben doesn't deserve to be the one who kills him. Let someone else blow the son of a bitch away. Let it not be Ben. Pray it's not Ben. I'm going to fetch Walter Moohn. If you love that man, go after him, right now. Take one of my horses. Quick, go!"

Rose lifted her skirts from the gore and ran down the stairs, her own blood running as cold as the snowmelt off the mountains. Shock would not yet allow her to cry for the death of sweet, sweet Maggie, who had been like a daughter to her for so many years. Later, much later she could wail and tear her hair. Now she had to do what she always did: take care of things. It was her purpose in this life. There was Samuel to notify. He had gone back to Nebraska to make ready for his new wife . . . Maggie, his new wife. Rose's breath caught in a huge sob.

Don't think. Just keep moving. Keep moving. Outside the batwing doors she stumbled into the arms of a pale-faced Walter Moohn.

"Holy thunderation, Rose. What happened in there?" the sheriff asked, holding the trembling woman close to his chest.

Behind them Dessa ran onto the boardwalk, eyes wildly searching up and down the street.

"Where did Ben go? Did you see him? Which way did he go?"

"Rode that way," Moohn said, and pointed in the direction opposite from the livery. "I hollered, but he didn't pay me no mind. Now will someone tell me what went on over here? All the uproar sounded like war had done broke out."

Rose pulled him inside and glanced once over her shoulder in the direction Dessa had gone. Down toward the livery and a mount.

"Oh, dear God, let them both come back safe," she said aloud, then turned to the matter at hand. The poor, bloody dead woman sprawled on the stairs. Most of the rest of the girls were nearly hysterical. Everyone loved Maggie. What would they all do without her pixie face, her cheerful laughter, her caring heart?

Blinded by tears, Dessa fingered a bit into Baron's mouth, slipped the bridle up and over his ears, and crawled on his back. No time for a saddle. Ben had taken Beauty, the faster of the two blacks, and she might never catch him, but she had to try. She had led the evil Coody Land into that saloon, no matter how Rose might rationalize it, and she would not allow Ben Poole to kill because of her.

He would never forgive himself. He would never smile again and those blue eyes would frost over forever.

Dessa hunkered low against the gelding's neck and urged him on, past the sheriff's office and beyond the straggle of empty miner's shacks on the outskirts of town, up the slope past Boot Hill and into the face of the rising full moon. The horse's hooves hammered along the trail. She prayed the two men had not cut cross-country, for she might never find them. But she had to try. Dear Lord, she had to try. The huge golden moon swelled into the darkened sky to light the way. The trail grew more treacherous and she was forced to slow down or she would tumble head over heels into the ravine far below.

The gelding blew and snorted as he trotted, sweat lathered his hide, stiff hairs chafed her skin through the thin cotton pantaloons. She thought she heard the soft whinny of another horse and drew up to listen. In the ebony stillness rocks clattered from somewhere high above and off to her left, and she craned her neck, staring in that direction. Another scattering of loose gravel, and then all was quiet. Shadows probed the night, hung around her like hungry ghosts waiting to pounce.

Someone or something was up there, hiding and watching. But who? Land or Ben? And if only one of them, where was the other? The distant whinny came again from up ahead, and as she urged Baron forward, she heard the chatter of rushing water and spotted a vague trail heading downward off to the right.

The gelding whickered and an answer came back from the shadows where patches of moonlight played tag. She reined him down the trail, riding slowly, ears tingling with an overpowering silence. If Land lay in wait, she was lost. But if it was Ben . . . oh, please let it be Ben.

She and her mount broke through the canopy of thick foliage into a small clearing along the bank of a roiling creek that shone silver in the moonlight. And standing there, head thrown back and arms spread, was Ben Poole, golden hair glowing like foxfire.

Dessa slid off Baron's back and left him rubbing noses with Beauty. She didn't know what to say or do. A relief grew within her, so exquisite, so overpowering that all she could do was reach out to him, feel his aliveness and soothe his soul. Gently she lay one hand on his back. Under her fingers muscles quivered and twitched; otherwise he didn't move or say anything. His flesh burned. She could feel the heat emanating through the sweat soaked shirt.

"Ben?" she crooned, and reached to entwine the fingers of her other hand into his upraised one.

He sucked in a deep, jagged breath.

"Oh, Ben," she said, and moved around him, tucking herself up against the statue of stone he appeared to be.

"She's dead," he whispered in a voice dry as husks.

"I'm sorry." She breathed the words against his chest as if in doing so she could bring him back to life. How much had he loved Maggie, to grieve like this? She ached with an envy that came and went. She loved Ben that much and more; she had to help him.

Without warning, he wrapped both arms around her, cradling the back of her head with one large hand and burying his face in the curve of her shoulder. "Oh, God, oh, God. Why didn't I kill him?"

He stood hunched over her, swaying, and she feared she would collapse under the weight of his sorrow.

Finally, after what seemed an eternity, he stirred and kissed her ear, her neck, her throat.

Her pent-up grief exploded in a moan and she turned to meet his searching lips with her own.

"Hold me, love me," she cried, as if somehow she could steal him away from the spirit of sorrow. At last she understood his love for Maggie, for she saw in him the same agony she had experienced when they told her Mitchell was dead.

"Oh, Ben, my love. I know. I do know."

He clung to her, seeking her love, her warmth, her compassion. She was alive and sweet and caring. Her breasts rose and fell and he lowered his head to their lushness.

"I love you, Dessa. Don't leave me, I love you." Fingers fumbling along the swell of her flesh, he unhooked the fabric of her dress, then tore at the shift, his need a pulsing, living thing. Mouth at her bared breast, he groaned and cried out, like a baby starving for nourishment.

The wild wet caress of his tongue and teeth and lips ignited the smoldering desire she had so carefully kept under control, fanned the coals so they burst to life and roared within her. She arched her back, gave him first one breast, then the other.

He fed there, the sweetness of his kisses mixing with the heat of his tears on her flesh. The ecstasy of giving him sustenance, his taking it with such frenzy, awoke in her a fever of lust. She vibrated with it, blind to everything but her passion.

If she could have crawled inside him, felt his heart flutter, touched the trail of his thoughts, she would have. He caught her up in his arms and went to his knees in the crackle of last year's leaves and drying grasses. Long legs astraddle her, he loosened the opening of her skirt, tugged it free of her hips along with the slips and underthings.

In the cold air, goose bumps rippled across her stomach and she was overcome with an intense desire to touch his bare skin, to see it and feel it and kiss it. She reached a trembling hand to the waist of his jeans and when she touched him, he sucked in his breath. He put his hand over hers and slid it downward until she cupped the throbbing center of his desire.

Until that moment their lovemaking had been a frantic denial of death, a human celebration that, despite what had happened, they were still alive. Now Dessa felt him calm down, rein in his passion so that they paused on the brink of desire. From the moment he had begun this primitive ritual, she had gone along with him, moved with him, and grown heavy with a deep need to complete the act no matter the consequences.

Now he let her decide. He held her hand on his manhood an instant longer, then took away his own and gazed down at her, the blue of his eyes glittering like ice in the moonlight.

Slowly, never taking her eyes from his, she began to unfasten the buttons down the front of his pants.

Ben rocked backward and tilted his head until he was looking up into the moonglow of the sky. The cool caress of her hands as she pulled the jeans down over his hips soothed the heated agony in his soul. His desire became a palpable thing, something he could actually touch with the fingers of his mind.

Maggie was dead and it seemed no disrespect to her memory to take this woman, whom he loved with all his being, for his own true spiritual mate.

Her hands cupped his buttocks and he leaned forward, settling into the dark nest between her legs. Probing there, searching for the sweet well.

In a pool of golden light he saw she had her eyes closed, as if frightened, her arms thrown above her head in submission.

"Dessa?"

"Oh, Ben. Yes, please, now." She lifted her hips so that he was pressed tightly against her.

A wild, wonderful feeling came over him, as if moonlight had turned to warm liquid gold to spread over them, encasing their bodies forever in a statue of love. He entered her with a deep-throated moan. She answered in kind, cried out sharply once, twice, when he broke her maidenhead. Then they were together moving as one. Flowing beyond the singing water, above the softly swaying trees, riding beams of moonlight into the purple darkness of space. Shards of stars crackled around them, like ice, like fire, like the promise of eternity. They moved on. Together. Forever.

He thought he might have lain there always, had she not turned so that he no longer felt her body coiled against his.

"Dessa?"

"Yes, Ben. Oh, yes."

"Did I hurt you?"

"No . . . well, only for an instant, but then it was fine. Very, very fine."

He turned, propped himself on an elbow. She lay on her back, her skirt kicked off into a pile at her feet. Cold air danced all around them, laden with a rising mist from the water. He reached a tentative finger and touched the erect bud of her breast.

"Cold," she said, and lay her palm alongside his face.

He closed his eyes. "Don't be sorry. I'm not."

"Sorry? I'm not sorry. Why would I be?"

"Well, like maybe it was disrespectful, with Maggie dying and all, that we finally . . . well, made love."

"It was love. It was that. Yours. Hers. Mine. Ours."

Ben gazed fondly at her. "Yes, it was. It is. I remember the feeling. . . . It's like in the war. Bodies lying everywhere, men you loved, fought with, should have died with. Death brings it on, a feeling hard to describe. You feel guilty you're alive and they're dead, but you can't help but thank God for letting you live. And you feel suddenly more alive than ever before."

She breathed softly for a while, said nothing.

He went on, his voice so muffled she could barely hear it above the rushing water. "I thank God you're alive. What if he had killed you, too? When I saw all that blood, I thought he had." His voice choked, and he closed his eyes momentarily.

She experienced a quiver of . . . regret, pleasure, relief? She wasn't sure. Ben was right, there was no describing it.

Beyond his shoulder hung the depths of the night sky. How good it was to be lying here in his arms. How exquisite to feel his body against hers. A deep swell of contentment filled her.

"Do you think she . . . Maggie . . . would mind?" he asked, his voice breaking once again and tears gleaming.

"Did you love her truly?"

He nodded. "She was my anchor, she was my sister. She saved my life, and I don't know what I'll do without her."

"Your sweet sister," Dessa whispered. She rubbed a thumb over her full lower lip. "I know . . . like Mitchell."

He nibbled at her thumb. "I wanted to kill him for what he did to her . . . to you. I came out here to do that, but in the end I watched him ride away from me and didn't take my shot. I could have put a bullet right between his shoulder blades and I didn't."

"Oh, thank God you didn't, Ben. Maggie wouldn't have wanted you to do that."

"What, shoot the man who killed her?" His voice was disdainful, unbelieving.

"No, ruin your life for her. If it had been me, Ben, me he killed, I know I would never want you to ruin your life to avenge my death. Rose said . . . she said that you . . . that you . . . once, you told me you had killed someone. Once, a long time ago when we were still trying to find reasons we shouldn't fall in love. And tonight when Rose sent me after you, she said that if you killed again, I would lose you forever. We would all lose you forever."

"Maybe so. I don't know. It's a weakness in me, I guess. I saw so much killing when I was so young. My mother, my sisters, slaughtered and raped before my eyes when I was only thirteen. Men blown to bloody bits all around me during the war when I wasn't much older. I made a vow—I pledged never to kill again. Never to have anything to do with death.

"And then I . . . there was a robbery in town." He paused, shuddered.

She put her arms around him. Head resting in the crook of his shoulder, she listened in silence, grateful that at last he would tell her.

"The bank. I was in town, walking down from the freight station carrying my rifle, when three of 'em busted out the doors shooting at anything that moved. They killed Mrs. Drew and her young'un, just shot them down in the middle of the street.

"I fell to my belly, rolled behind a horse trough, and when one of 'em started to mount and ride away, I came up shooting." Ben gulped audibly, rubbed harshly at her skin with his thumb.

"I didn't see Clete. He ran out from around the other side of the livery. One of my bullets caught him in the chest, must've got his heart. But he . . . but he lived long enough to look into my eyes. I swear, Dessa, he never knew it was me who shot him, but I've always been afraid he did. Oh, God, suppose he knew."

"Oh, Ben, no. How could he? For that matter, how could you? Bullets flying everywhere. Where was the sheriff, other men in town? All of you shooting, I'd bet. Why, even one of the outlaws could have shot him.

"Ben, is that why you and Sarah Woodridge . . . Was Clete her husband?"

He nodded. "Last thing he said to me was, 'See to my wife and babies. Promise you'll see to them.'"

"And so you promised."

He nodded. "I didn't want to talk about this now, after we've been together. Ah, Lord, Dessa. You are a wonder. I've never felt such a thing as we had tonight."

She smiled. "Neither have I, Ben, neither have I."

He shivered and hugged her up close. "It's freezing out here. Let's get back."

They dressed quickly, self-conscious in a way that surprised Ben. They had, after all, been together as man and wife. He hoped soon to make that a reality.

It was deep in the night when Dessa and Ben quietly led their mounts into the livery and darted through the darkest shadows of a sleeping Virginia City, sneaked into her small house, and fell exhausted into bed.

They didn't learn until the next day that Walter Moohn and a quickly organized posse had left at sunup to track the outlaw Coody Land. They had followed his trail into the foothills of Alder Gulch where, as time and time before, they lost it on the hardscrabble rocks.

They sat in the Golden Sun early the next evening, Rose and Walter Moohn, Ben and Dessa, trying to make sense out of the horrible killing. Maggie's funeral, held that afternoon at Boot Hill, had brought out many of the men in town. Men, that is, who weren't married.

Rose laughed bitterly. "The rest would have come, too, if they dared. Maggie had a way of making any man feel like he was the best there was. But they daren't be seen at the funeral of a whore. Ah, my poor, poor Maggie. And poor Samuel. I shudder to think what he'll do when he gets my wire."

Moohn squeezed Rose's hand and didn't say anything until the mood passed. Then he said, changing the subject, "Yank and his gang are hid out in Alder Gulch. Ain't no posse gonna ride in there to get bushwhacked. There just ain't enough law in Montana Territory to face down such a gang of cutthroats and owlhoots."

"What's wrong with the army?" Ben asked, sipping at his cold beer and holding tightly to Dessa's hand under the table.

"They're too busy protecting the railroads and riding herd on Sitting Bull to worry too much about outlaws yahooing a town like Virginia City. We could catch Land out and away from Yank's bunch, we'd take care of him."

"We?" Dessa asked.

"I'll deputize some townfolk. It's all we've got," Moohn said.

"What would you do to him?" Dessa said in a small voice.

"Same thing we done to Joseph Slade. He wouldn't leave the town alone. Got to where ever damn Saturday night he'd ride his horse right into the Busted Mule or Sadie's—Rose wasn't here then—and just shoot up everthing. Killed a few folks, too. We just got plumb fed up with it. Finally run him down one evening, hung the son of a bitch from a corral post. His wife pounding her poor old bony chest and pleading for his life. But when you've had enough, why, then you've just had enough.

"There weren't any sympathy left, not even for his pitiful wife."

Rose nodded. "Well, as far as I'm concerned, the time has come I've had enough of that Coody Land, so I hope you're set to stretch his neck the very next time he comes yahooing this town."

"You know I ain't never been a gunhand. Folks just grabbed me up to serve as lawman 'cause I was handy. Hell, they ain't no law in the territories but what we can make ourselves. Best we can do is wait for that bunch to try something, and this time we'll be ready. We'll either hang 'em or shoot 'em down, and there won't be anyone crying over it either.

"Sometimes, Rose, I wish I was anything but sheriff. It just don't suit me too much. I reckon I just never took to the job."

She covered his hands with her own and didn't say anything.

Ben remained content to listen to the conversation. He had done his best to put away his sorrow over Maggie's death. It was time he and Dessa made some plans. There was nothing for it but to find Celia Cross and learn just what she knew about Mitchell Fallon. Because until they did, Dessa wouldn't even consider talking about their own future. And then, of course, there was the one chore he'd put off too long. There was Sarah to deal with, and he had to face the fact that she loved him. It would hurt her some, but he knew now that it had to be.

Not being one to let things lie too long, Molly Blair picked later that very evening to launch yet another attack with her hoe-, shovel-, and broom-wielding army. On Saturday the saloons and the hurdy-gurdy house were crammed to overflowing. The unholy brigade hit the Busted Mule first, for gamblers seemed to gather at an earlier hour than did those who wanted the company of a fair young woman.

By the time the ladies reached the Golden Sun, word had spread around town that the preacher's wife was on the rampage. Rose was in a fury. How dare that bunch do such a thing, with poor Maggie not cold in the ground? The least they could have done was have a little decency and give everyone time to mourn.

So it was with fire in her eye that the owner of the Golden Sun marched out on the boardwalk to face down her detractors. And she carried the shotgun Grisham kept tucked behind the bar. The one he never got a chance to use on Coody Land.

Before Molly Blair could open her mouth, Rose hugged the stock into her shoulder, aimed the twelve-gauge over the heads of the crowd, and pulled the trigger. The kick knocked her backward into the wall of the saloon. She sprung forward, set her feet wide apart, jacked another round in, and raised the weapon again.

The stampeding herd of women halted fast and milled about like confused cattle, looking to Molly to make the next move.

Rose never took the gun from her shoulder. "That's all the warning you're getting, you church-house mice. I'm going to count to three and if you ain't showing me the tails of your skirts by then, I'm gonna blast a hole right in the middle of the bunch of you. Who catches buckshot catches buckshot, and that's all there is to it."

About that time, fresh from the altercation at the

Busted Mule, which had taken a while to settle after the women left, Sheriff Walter Moohn came striding along the boardwalk, spurs jingling and bootheels thunking hard like he meant business.

The tone of his voice proved he did. "Now, hold it just a minute. I've had me about enough of law-breaking for a while. You ladies git on back home where you belong, and Rose, you put that hogleg down before you do something you'll regret."

"I won't regret filling any one of these old heifers with buckshot, Walter Moohn. And I'll thank you kindly to just butt out."

Moohn drew up and gaped at Rose. "Butt out? Rose, I'm the dang-blamed sheriff."

"Lot of good that does me. I'm gonna pick me out one and shoot." She swung the barrel around, drawing bead on first one, then another of the frightened women who looked like they wanted to run but were waiting for Molly to give the word.

Moohn dove for Rose, knocking the business end of the shotgun skyward just as it went off. Rose staggered into a post in front of the Golden Sun.

Moohn drew out his own gun, a long-barreled Colt .45 that he'd once bragged he used to take a potshot at Jessie James. No one knew if that was the truth. Moohn himself wasn't sure anymore, he'd told the story so many times.

"Now, ladies. I'm not the kind of man to lose my temper with the fair sex—"

An audible sigh went up from the church ladies at the mention of such a word as sex, in any connotation.

"But I've just about had my fill of all of you. Now, Miss Rose, you can't go shooting people just 'cause they're gathered in a public street. And Mrs. Blair, you can't take it upon yourself to close down a place of business just 'cause you don't approve of what goes on behind the doors.

"So I'm giving you all fair warning. I've had you all in jail oncet, and I ain't agin putting you all there again. Now, disperse, the lot of you, or I'll start rounding you up. And this time no husband is going to appear to drag you off home. You'll stay till I say you can leave."

He held the Colt down along his thigh and glared hard at everyone. Then in booming voice that caused horses down the street to whinny in fright, he shouted, "Move it, now!" He turned and tipped his hat to a wide-eyed Rose. "And you'll excuse me, Miss Rose, but that means you, too. Inside, now."

Nearly an hour later, Walter Moohn strolled down a peaceful Saturday night street in his town of Virginia City, turned sharply to his left at the batwing doors of the Golden Sun, and went inside. He ordered a beer at the bar and carried it to the table at which Rose Langue sat scowling and nursing her own mug of brew.

He got himself situated, being careful that he didn't jar the table, then looked squarely at the beautiful saloon owner and said, "I want you to marry me, soon as we can arrange it, and come away with me out West."

A tight-lipped, angry Rose stared hotly at her suitor. "Not in a million years, Walter Moohn. Not in a million years. Now get your butt out of my saloon, and don't you come back."

She took a deep breath and rose, expanding her awesome breasts to their fullest. "And I don't want you to look at me or speak to me. I want you to even cross the street when you see me coming."

"Aw, Rose, don't get all ornery on me. I was doing my job."

"Your job? I've never been so humiliated in my life. Manhandling me like I'm a common whore.

"I'm leaving this town, all right, but not with you. I'm going somewhere where folks appreciate a place where they can relax and have a good time. This is a decent place, and I don't have to put up with the likes of that oh-so-snooty, sermon-spouting Molly Blair. Just who does she think she is? And dear Maggie not even cold in the ground."

Rose began to cry then, and whirled away, hoping Moohn wouldn't see the tears. She'd not have him thinking her weakening in her resolve.

Walter felt bad about the entire episode, but he couldn't think how he could have handled it any other way. He'd kept everyone from getting hurt, hadn't he? And that was what he was there for. He stood in the middle of the floor and watched Rose climb the stairs to her private rooms. Then, when she was gone, the door upstairs slammed firmly behind her, he crammed his grimy hat down tight on his head and stalked out of the Golden Sun.

Maybe she'd be in a better mood the next day and he could try again. He had no intention of giving up his attempt to marry Rose Langue. She was the most beautiful woman he'd ever seen, and while he had no notion what she might accidentally see in him, she had taken a liking to him and let him know it. He wasn't a man to give up easily.

Second on his agenda that night was a surprise for the next owlhoot who rode into his town, and he headed down toward the livery, where a few trusted men waited. There was no sense in putting this off.

Chapter Twenty

The issue of his debt to Sarah Woodridge rested heavily on Ben's shoulders, and so he rode out Sunday morning while Dessa attended church. She wanted to pray for Maggie, she said, and he nodded. He would pray on the creek bank or out beneath the tall pines. Besides, it was time he straightened out this problem with Sarah. It had already gone on too long.

The nearer he came to the Woodridge place, the slower he rode. Oh, how he dreaded facing her. She loved him, he knew, and he cared for her and her boys, but it wasn't the same as love. Not the same as the way he felt about Dessa. Guilt was not a proper companion for two people starting a new life.

The Woodridge home was almighty quiet when he rode into the yard. It was a blustery day, and he knew she hadn't set foot in church since Clete died, so she and the boys must be inside. Where would she go?

The twins heard his steps on the porch. Shouting madly, they burst out the doorway and hurled themselves around his legs. He hobbled stiffly inside, dragging the laughing boys along.

Sarah stood in the center of the room, a hump-backed wooden trunk open beside her. She held something in her hand that could have been a bedsheet or a tablecloth, he couldn't tell.

"Ben," she said, and her eyes filled with tears. "Oh, I'm so glad you came. Where have you been so long?"

Clearly she knew, for everyone in town was aware that Ben Poole had accompanied Dessa Fallon to Kansas City. She would be no exception, despite the remote locale of her farm.

He dragged the two youngsters along with him as he crossed the room and planted a kiss on her forehead. She leaned up against him for a moment, then pulled away.

"What're you doing?" he asked, and hefted the squirming boys, one on each arm. They giggled and pulled at his hat. "Look out there, tadpoles, you'll rip my best hat in two if you aren't careful."

Sarah offered a weak smile. "Packing. I'm packing up."

"I can see that, but what for?"

She dropped the cloth. "Let me get you some coffee. Boys, git on in the other room and finish your jobs. Mama wants to talk to Ben. Git, now, go on."

The boys obeyed when Ben fanned playfully at their backsides with his hat.

Sarah waited until she had poured coffee and they were both seated at the table. She ran a finger around the rim of her cup, then raised her eyes to him. "I'm leaving, going back to Philadelphia. It's Clete's folks. They want to see the kids, want to watch them grow up. Say they've lost their son, it's only fair they have a replacement. I . . . oh, Ben, I . . ." Tears flowed freely down her cheeks.

He gazed down at the table. "Sarah, I'm so sorry. God, I'm sorry. For . . . for everything." He gestured wide, taking in the room, the whole outside, the world.

She nodded. "You can't go on being sorry all your life, though. It ain't fair. Not to you nor me nor . . . nor Clete. It happened. It just happened, and Lord knows we've all paid dearly. It's enough." She waited a moment, picking at a thread in her apron. "You love her, don't you?"

He nodded his head.

"She's real pretty, a sweet little thing, from what I could see. Oh, Ben, I wish you well. I truly do. And I thank you for what you've done for us, me and the boys. The other, well, it just couldn't be helped, and you hadn't ought to go on blaming yourself anymore."

The were both quiet for a long while, listening to the boys bickering softly in the other room.

He cleared his throat. "When will you leave?"

"Midweek. They sent me money to ship our things. I'll be hiring a freighter to take them down to the train station in Devil's Gate."

"Bannon's a fine line," Ben chided, trying to lighten the mood of the moment. There were other freighters in town, and he wasn't even sure he'd be making any more runs with Wiley Moss. It depended on what he and Dessa decided to do.

As if reading his mind, Sarah asked, "Will you marry soon?"

"I think so, as soon as a few things are settled."

"Well, Ben, don't wait too long. Time can sometimes be short, and we need to go on with things fast as we can."

"Yeah, well, we will."

"Tell her I said . . . tell her I said she's getting the best man in Virginia City and she'd better treat him right."

Ben rose as Sarah did and gave her a brief hug. "You take care of those boys, and yourself, too."

"Oh, I will. Now, go on, git out of here. I've got work to do."

Ben didn't look back as he left Woodridge farm behind, but kept his eyes on the trail ahead.

It seemed as if the small town of Virginia City was doomed, for soon after Sunday midnight, Coody Land and his sidekick paid another visit.

Ben was asleep in the hay of the livery. He was trying to work himself up to sleeping in a bed by stretching out in the loose hay. He figured he was coming ever closer to being comfortable on a civilized mattress. Dessa and he had said goodnight hours before after an evening of discussing her riding off into Alder Gulch on her own to try to find her brother. It had been a bitter argument, but they had parted warmly. Ben figured it wouldn't be much longer before he'd have to tie her to the bed to keep her from heading out on her own.

Satisfied he had convinced her sufficiently to keep her from running off that very night, he was sleeping deeply when the gunfire erupted. It sounded like a war breaking out. He hopped into his britches on one foot, then the other in the middle of the barn before he realized where he was or what he was doing.

As he raced out into the street, he heard breaking glass, the pounding of hooves, and the staccato sound of more rapid gunshots. Two men on horseback came right at him, firing randomly. He scurried for cover inside the livery. Damn! Why hadn't he grabbed his Winchester? It lay back there in the darkness beside his bed of hay. Before he could hunt for the rifle, a bevy of mounted men thundered by, hot on the heels of the vanishing outlaws.

Ben ran out again. What the hell was going on?

Sheriff Moohn slowed his prancing Appaloosa and shouted at him. "Mount up, we're gonna get those sons a bitches this time if we have to chase 'em clear to California."

Ben was dumbstruck. The sheriff had been ready and waiting. What was wrong with that fool Land? What was he after, or who? After shooting Maggie, he'd gotten away free and clear, only to turn around and come back now. Ben wasted no more time. He was going with the posse, for he couldn't wait here while they avenged dear Maggie's death. He had to have a hand in it, even if he didn't pull the trigger on the man. He might have a cowardly weakness for outright killing, but he had no aversion to assisting in carrying out justice.

Lamps were lit in windows all over town as the men rode out. Ben followed along on Rose's black gelding, his Winchester in its scabbard at his knee.

The posse galloped past Dessa's. Scared awake by the earlier noise, she peered out through her window holding a lamp high in one hand. Ben spotted her pale, wide-eyed face in a blur, not sure if she saw him. He didn't wave or slow. Just like Moohn and the rest of the town, he'd had enough of Coody Land. If they caught the outlaws this night, Ben knew he would do what had to be done, along with the others. It was distasteful, this vigilante business, but there was nothing else for it. Men would break the law, and until some kind of law enforcement agencies were formed, ordinary men like Moohn had to pin on a badge and hope to keep some semblance of peace.

Land had tried to kill Dessa and, worse, would have if she hadn't escaped; he had succeeded in killing poor old J.T. and Artie and then dear Maggie. It was time he paid for his crimes. Justice would be meted out in the only way Walter Moohn and every man-jack in that posse knew. Ben wanted to be there for it. He wanted to make up for not shooting that coward Land in the back when he had the chance.

A combination of luck and the sly planning of Sheriff Moohn brought about the capture of Coody Land and his young sidekick. Justice would at last come down on the two men who had brutally murdered the stage driver and his guard, then dragged Dessa off the stagecoach and sent her wandering into the arms of the man she now loved.

Land and the younger outlaw, known only as the kid, obviously assured they had gotten away clean, lay in a stand of pine not ten miles from town sharing a jug of whiskey they'd stolen from the Busted Mule.

"Nothin' like a good hurrah to get yore blood to the boiling point," the kid remarked to Land as he gulped more fiery liquid down his throat.

"Danged idjit. I wanted the gal. What'd you have to go and start shootin' for?"

"Sheiit, fool. How'd you think you would find her?"

Land slobbered all around the neck of the bottle drunkenly, finally managed to upend it and pour whiskey into his mouth. Wetly, he mumbled, "Take her to that sumbitch Yank, show him whose boss. Ignerant jackass. He don't quit shoving this ole boy around, I'm a gonna shoot him and be done with it."

The kid snickered. "You and what army? Lucky

you didn't find the gal. Touch a man's sister, he'll do worse than just shoot you."

Riding at the head of the posse, Moohn spotted a saddled mount and called the boys to a halt, signaling silence. He slid to the ground and took up the dangling reins of a pair of meandering horses. Tying them to the nearest tree, he made a motion to the others to dismount.

It then became a simple matter of following the noise of the drunken argument, surrounding the men, and drawing their guns. There wasn't even a fight.

"Hang 'em right here," one of the posse members said, and holstered his pistol. "I got a rope. Alls we need is another'n."

"We'll have none a that," Moohn cautioned. "We'll take 'em back to town and hang 'em proper. That's what we got Hanging Gulch for. We'll let the whole town watch, then we can bury 'em right handily in Boot Hill. It'll be the end to another of our problems.

"Come on, Ben. Help me tie these ornery cusses to their horses. Blamed fools. Makes a feller wonder why they're either one still alive, stupid as they are."

"Hey, don't call me stupid," Land shouted, and passed out flat on his face in the pine needles.

The posse rode back into town as dawn silvered the eastern sky, Land and the kid draped belly down over their saddles, ropes securing their feet to their wrists.

They hung the two outlaws bright and early that same morning. There was no question they were guilty—everyone in the Golden Sun had seen Land gun down Maggie. It was justice, pure and simple.

Dessa went to the hanging, as did everyone else in town, but she turned away at the last moment, when the two horses were slapped into bolting from beneath their riders. She would never forget the sounds of that violent event, though, the thick, guttural babbling, the cut-off moans, the creaking as the bodies twisted back and forth beneath the heavy limb of the hanging tree . . . the joyful shout that went up from the crowd, a baby crying in the stunned silence that followed.

"There, Maggie, there," she murmured, and tears flowed once more.

Ben took her arm and walked her away. Behind them she could hear the sharp chinking sound of shovels as two men finished digging the graves. She raised her eyes to look at the intense blue of the Montana sky. Far off to the northwest a bank of dark clouds gathered, boiling higher and higher as she watched. A gust of wind caught the hem of her skirts and in it she felt the kiss of approaching winter. It had already arrived in high country. Every morning the pristine peaks gleamed with new-fallen snow. Soon it would move down the mountains. She had only heard of the brutality of winter here in Montana Territory. A shiver of anticipation ran through her. Her and Ben in front of a fire, wrapped in quilts and each other's arms. But there was one bit of unfinished business to attend to before she dared let herself dream of such a wonder as that.

"I have to find Celia Cross, Ben. I have to find her now," she said, and her tone brooked no further nonsense. She had waited as long as she could.

Ben knew he would have to give in and go with her, or she would go alone. No matter how closely he watched her, one day she would ride out in search of her brother.

"Have you asked Rose?"

"She doesn't know a Celia Cross. She said that she probably belongs to one of the outlaws living out at Alder Gulch. That's where Mitchell is, Ben. I just know it. Otherwise, someone in town would know him or remember seeing him."

"You think he's an outlaw?" Ben hurried her along the steep incline back to town. A cold wind whipped at his back like dread.

"A lot of men who survive war end up on the wrong side of the law, for one reason or another. He's in danger, Ben. We've got to find him."

"I'll ask around. Might be someone coming through and stopping at the Mule or at Rose's will know something about him. Then we'll see."

"I don't want to wait."

They were at her door now, and looking up, Ben saw Wiley Moss striding toward them, a purposeful glint in his eyes. "Uh-oh, looks as if I'm going to have to go to work."

"Oh, Ben."

"Promise me you won't do anything till I get back, Dessa. I'll go with you, but you have to wait. You could get yourself killed going out there alone."

"Mitchell wouldn't let anything happen to me."

"You don't know that he's out there. Please, don't be foolish. Promise me. This could just be a trick. Why hasn't the woman gotten in touch with you since your parents' death? I think she was trying to trick them into giving her some money, then she was just going to disappear."

Dessa secretly thought Ben might be right, but she hoped fervently that he wasn't. She couldn't bear to think it was all a lie, not after getting up her hopes.

Ben leaned down to kiss her, and Wiley averted his gaze, looking embarrassed.

"I just know he's alive, Ben," Dessa whispered, and opened the door.

He touched her cheek. "Okay, we'll find him together."

"When will you be back?"

Ben glanced at Wiley. "Three Forks," the old driver said.

"Late tomorrow," Ben told her.

She nodded, then grabbed Ben around the neck and held on tightly. "Be careful," she said into his ear.

He shivered from the heat of her breath and hugged her close. "I love you."

She let him go and backed into the open doorway. She wouldn't say she loved him in front of Wiley, but she let her eyes tell him so before closing the door.

Rose came to visit the next day and the two women had dinner together at the Montana House, a welcome, down-to-earth change from the civilized cuisine of the Continental. Rose spoke of when Maggie had first come to the Golden Sun, reminiscing in a soft, faraway voice. Then she grew silent and Dessa didn't know what to say, so they finished their meal without speaking.

"Walter asked me to marry him," Rose blurted over dessert.

"Oh, Rose. That's wonderful."

"Would be if he hadn't gone about it in such an all-fired typical manlike way."

Dessa couldn't stop a laugh. "Well, Rose, what did you expect? He is a man, after all."

Rose joined her merriment. "I guess you're right there."

"Are you going to?"

Rose picked at her apple pie with the tines of her fork. "I think so, but I'm not going to tell him for a while. Let him stew in his own juices, the old fart."

"Rose, shame on you."

"What about you and Ben?"

Dessa leaned back and gazed past Rose into the distance. "I love him."

"Well, of course you do, having good sense and all. He's the finest man a woman could want."

"Rose, you always were biased where Ben was concerned."

Rose sipped at her tea. "What will you do?"

"Do?" Dessa widened her eyes.

"You and Ben. What do you plan to do after you marry?"

"Oh, that. Well, first we have to see a good lawyer and get my father's will straightened out. That's a long story. Then Ben wants to go up north, says they're going to be building new railroads up there. We can invest in businesses, build up my father's holdings. Did you know Ben is brilliant with figures? I couldn't cipher my way out of a paper sack, and he just thinks it all out in his head, without even using a pencil or paper."

Rose laughed heartily. "Many's the time he's got me out of a bind that way. I run a mean hurdy-gurdy house, manage my girls, and charm the pants right off our customers, but when it comes to figuring, I'm useless. Ben has taken care of it for me for years. Before that, I like to went broke. You could do worse than have him as a full partner in Fallon Enterprises."

Rose hesitated and pinned Dessa with a flat stare.

"What does he think about you having all that money? Some men are funny in that respect."

"It doesn't seem to bother him. He says he really doesn't care if he has money, but if I'm set on keeping mine and earning more, he'll be happy to help me do so. What's important, Ben says, is what we are to each other. Having someone to love who loves you back." Dessa smiled. "I guess it is that simple, when you think about it. And the Lord knows I do love him."

Rose nodded and studied Dessa fondly. This child would be good for Ben. She had done a lot of growing up, and she cared about things most women didn't take the time for. Rose wondered idly if they had laid together yet. She would guess they had, the way they looked at each other, touched each other, exchanged secret smiles when they thought no one was looking.

Dessa took up her knife and began drawing lines on the tablecloth. After a while, she looked up. "Rose, do you think I should forget about Celia Cross? About my brother?"

"Lands, child. How would I know? If it's going to pester you to leave it be, then you'd best look further into it. I wish I could help you there, but I just can't recall knowing a woman by that name at all. Surely if she's from these parts, I'd a heard of her. Who else have you asked?"

"Ben asked around, he said. I'm not sure where. He told me to wait until he comes back and then we'll ride out to Alder Gulch and see if we can find Mitchell."

"Oh, my dear goodness, child. Don't the two of you go riding out into that outlaw country. All you'll do is get yourselves shot, or worse. Have you talked to Walter?"

"Ben did. He doesn't know anything, either. I don't know what to do next, Rose. I can't just let it be."

The two women left the restaurant together, but parted outside.

"Promise me you won't do anything crazy, you and Ben," Rose admonished. "Talk to Walter. Maybe he'll get up a posse and go with you."

Dessa nodded, but she knew the futility of such a plan. Walter Moohn had no intention of riding into Alder Gulch, even if he could get some men to go with him. It was a foolhardy thing to do, and he had told Ben as much. If she and Ben did this thing, they would be completely on their own.

The woman showed up late that afternoon, when Dessa was actually watching for Ben and Wiley to return from their run to Three Forks.

Dessa had just lifted the curtain to study the street, then dropped it for at least the tenth time when she heard a light tapping on the back window. She was startled to see the dark, round face of an Indian woman peering in at her between cupped palms.

Quickly she crossed the room and raised the window.

"You must come with me," the woman said, her tongue and lips forming the words as if they were a foreign language.

She was dressed in buckskin that was quite soiled, but her shiny black braids were interlaced with crisp red ribbons and her mahogany skin was clean. During her quick study of the visitor, Dessa remained mute.

"Hurry. I have brought horses." The woman gestured, and Dessa saw two spotted ponies with blankets where the saddles should be, reins hanging down on the ground.

"Are you Celia Cross?" she asked, but knew without waiting for the reply that she was.

How could she not go with this woman, despite what Ben had said? She could lead her to Mitchell. Still, fear formed a lump in her chest. Suppose it was a trick?

When the woman only watched her closely, she said, "I don't know. Please, where is my brother? How is he? How do I know you come from him?"

"Mitchell," the woman said. "He is my man and they will soon kill him. I cannot make him leave. He says that if that is to be, it will be, he will not run.

"But at night I hear them plotting, and each evening more of them sit on the opposite side of the fire, leaving Mitchell more and more alone. And it is as if he does not see, or perhaps he does not want to see.

"Please, you are his sister. He wishes to see you, and will not leave until he does. Come now."

Dessa's mouth went as dry as tinder. She thought of Mitchell, riding off to war, waving his hat above his head, back and forth, back and forth, until he rode out of sight shouting at the top of his lungs. How excited he was to be going off to fight for his country. And how she had cried for hours, for days. And she remembered all the years she'd thought him dead but sensed his spirit within her.

Seeing her hesitation, the Indian woman reached inside the bodice of her dress and pulled out a small deerskin bag. She shook two rings out in the flat palm of her hand.

Dessa gasped and took them. The smaller one,

hers, with the Fallon markings surrounded by diamond chips, the larger one matching it.

Tears formed in her eyes. She had to go. No one but Mitchell could have sent these rings, could have known what they would mean to her. It must be true, then, that he was an outlaw, connected to that dreadful Coody Land, else how had he come by her very own ring that Land had jerked from her finger, the ring that matched his?

"He watched you at the ceremony for the dead."

Dessa wiped her eyes and clutched both rings tightly. "The funeral for our parents? Oh, yes. I saw him. That was him. Oh, I knew. Oh, yes, yes. Oh, Mitchell. How is he? Is he well? What does he look like? Does he still wink and scratch at his ear when he teases? Oh, please, tell me."

Celia Cross nodded her head solemnly. "Come and you will see. Come before your man returns. There is great danger. Hurry, now." The Indian woman gave her the bag and Dessa dropped Mitchell's ring inside. The other she slipped on her finger.

She hesitated no longer. "Wait, wait right there. I'm coming."

Snatching at a wrap hanging on its hook, she pulled the door closed hurriedly without latching it and ran around the side of the house. Celia was astride her horse, holding out the reins of the other.

"White women do not ride with legs spread. Can you do so?"

Dessa nodded, and mounted the small Indian pony, clenching her knees tightly because there were no stirrups. She turned the horse to follow Celia Cross. They rode out across the hills, not keeping to the road, and at the rise, Dessa glanced once over her shoulder at the small town nested below. It looked very tiny.

Ben didn't bother to ask Wiley to slow at Dessa's; he simply hit the ground running, the Winchester gripped in one hand. He raced to her door and banged on it carelessly. It inched open under his fist.

He stuck his head in. "Dessa, honey. I'm back."

No reply. He called out again, then stepped inside. The small woodstove was crackling merrily, warding off the chill of the late fall day, but the back window stood wide open.

Ben muttered and went to close the thing. As he reached up for the sash, he saw two figures riding over the crest of the hill west of town. They were gone before he had time to study them much, but he could have sworn two women rode those spotted ponies, one an Indian.

Without thinking, he shouted Dessa's name, but the riders had passed out of sight beyond the ridge.

"Oh, dammit, Dessa." He knew immediately what had happened and he was furious. He'd told her not to go alone, and as soon as his back was turned, off she went.

Well, they weren't riding hell bent for leather. He'd catch them. He raced to the livery, saddled Beauty, and rose around the back of Dessa's house and up the hill, the horse's pounding hooves kicking up mud. He was glad of the recent rains. There would be no trouble tracking the women if they got out of his sight. He halted his mount at the crest of the hill and gazed off into the distance for a moment. Ahead lay Alder Gulch, far off past what he could see. And below, threading their way through scrub and outcroppings of sandstone, were the women on the two spotted ponies.

Ben touched the scabbard that held his Winchester, then with grim determination dug in his heels. "Git. Git up," he said, and his voice sounded like sand gritting under bootheels.

The sun had set when the two women headed up the draw into Alder Gulch. Gold miners were gone now, the creek banks deserted. No rockers or pans, no bearded men squatting to grab at what color they could find. Prospectors had moved on to Wyoming, where the fever had caught new fire, giving this place back to nature. Here and there lay remnants of a deserted camp, a tin cup and plate, a broken-handled pick, a cross pounded into the earth marking the grave of someone who hadn't made it to the next strike.

Celia Cross hadn't spoken since leaving Virginia City. It was as if she had exhausted her entire knowledge of the white man's language persuading Dessa to make the journey. Dessa gave up asking questions when she heard no answers.

Several times they had stopped for water, letting the ponies wade out into the cold, clear creek to fill their own bellies, while they cupped up handfuls for themselves. Dessa thought of Ben, wondered what he would do when he returned to find her gone. He would be angry, perhaps even frightened. She should have left him a note or told someone, but there had been no time. She had been so afraid the Cross woman would grow impatient and ride away, and then she would never find Mitchell.

Then she thought of her brother. She had always been so proud when folks remarked how alike they were. How her dark hair and his curled just so away from the face. How their matching eyes would flame at precisely the same instant they got into some mischief. But Mitchell had always been smarter than her, braver, kinder. She couldn't picture him as an outlaw, no matter what the war had done to him. It just wasn't possible.

Her buttocks and thighs ached with the long ride, but still the Cross woman rode on, into the lengthening shadows. It was dark when they rounded yet one more outcropping on their steep climb up the mountain's face and spotted the campfires in a box canyon.

Celia Cross reined in her pony. "They have seen us. They know we are coming."

The words startled Dessa, for she had thought the woman would not speak again. "How can you tell?"

"Lookouts." She pointed high to either side of the trail.

"It's so dark, I don't see anything."

"They hear. They know."

"What will they do?"

"Nothing yet. I am Yank's woman, you are his sister. He still has his power. But I fear not for long. Come, we must go to him. He has waited so long."

"So have I," Dessa said. "Oh, Lord, so have I." Mitchell . . . Yank? Could it be?

As darkness slithered over the land, Ben began to curse softly. He couldn't track them at night, not until the moon came up, and it would be late this night, for the moon was on the wane. There was no doubt in his mind that they were headed for Alder Gulch, but that was a big place, and the outlaw camp wouldn't be easily found or easily approached.

He would get shot if he was spotted, and that would do Dessa no good at all. Of course, if her brother was really there, perhaps he could bluff his way in. Surely even an outlaw wouldn't want to kill the man his sister was going to marry, if Dessa had a chance to tell him.

At last, defeated by the dense night, Ben reined up and made camp. He'd had no time to pack food, but the bedroll was tied on his saddle, so he would have a place to lay his head and something to protect him from the cold that had descended quickly with the setting of the sun.

He fell asleep instantly, and didn't awaken until the moon crept past the mountain peaks to bathe him in its frigid light. Then he rose, repacked his horse, mounted up, and rode on. He didn't let himself think much about what might happen when he showed up in the heavily armed camp of these outlaws. He just kept thinking of Dessa, and how she turned her pretty head to study him when she was perplexed by his actions. And how it had felt to make love to her after Maggie was killed. That night he had experienced the pure sweet glory of life, and saw how it had to continue despite the agony of loss.

"Dessa," he whispered. He rode with his head bent down alongside the neck of the horse in order to follow the prints of the unshod ponies. "Dessa, my love. Don't go on without me. I'm coming."

The earlier brisk wind had calmed, and there was no answer in the hushed, moonlit night.

Chapter Twenty-one

The camp was enormous, big as some of the settlements Dessa had seen along the railroad. Tents and primitive lean-tos were thrown up around a central gathering place. There a large campfire burned, and smaller fires flickered in front of some of the dwellings. In the flickering light, Dessa could make out men squatted around the fire, scattered groups of women and children, an occasional solitary figure off to himself. She could smell horses, knew by the sounds they made that they were kept nearby. The aroma of meat hung in the smoky air. The camp was very well hidden and would never be spotted by accident. Other than the posted lookouts, everyone seemed relaxed and unafraid. It was obvious they were quite sure no one would find them.

Guards such as those who had watched the two of them approach probably ringed the camp. There might even be no trail in except the way she and Celia had come, unless one were a mountain goat. Surely the outlaws had left themselves an escape route should they be surprised by a posse.

These observations came to a halt as she followed Celia's lead and dismounted. She looked all around, tried to spot Mitchell. Being so close to him gave her goose bumps, and she felt skittish, nervous, expectant, anxious. The moods came and went, nearly overpowering her in a turmoil of emotion.

"Where is he? Take me to him now," she finally demanded of the Indian woman.

Celia hailed a young boy who was running about with several other children, and he came to take the horses, staring at the ground after flicking a quick glance at Dessa.

"There are a lot of families up here," she said.

Celia didn't reply, but skirted the campfire. Everyone appeared to deliberately ignore their arrival, and Celia spoke to no one. She hurried on her way. Dessa had to run to keep up, and they approached a dirty white tent tucked back in the trees. It was obviously the largest and best of the dwellings. No others were nearby, though across the way were a variety of living quarters thrown up side by side. It would seem that her brother had drawn an invisible barrier around himself. A lamp burned inside the tent, and she could make out the shadow of a man.

Her heart pounded in her throat as Celia pulled the closed flap away and motioned her inside. The Indian woman did not enter with her, and when the flap closed at her back, Dessa finally let her gaze land on the face of the man standing before her.

Her brother's familiar high, wide cheekbones were stretched taut, eyes like nubs of glass reflected the lamplight, a scar through one eyebrow and up across his forehead led to a streak of white that spilled into locks of thick dark hair. The man at her parents' funeral! She had known all along, hadn't she? Deep down inside in that place that kept her brother's spirit alive, she had known it was him, and had been afraid to think it or speak of it.

He studied her intently before the somber expression fell away to be replaced by delight. "Dessa? My God, it is you. Oh, sweetheart. What a beautiful woman you've become." He spread his arms.

She cried out, unable even to utter his name as she flew into his waiting embrace. He held his long, lank body rigid, skin and muscle stretched like rawhide over bone, but he hugged her so tightly she could scarcely breathe. He smelled of whiskey and tobacco and leather and of being out in the cold too long.

"Dear God, little one. I thought I'd never see you again."

The voice was Mitchell's, but with a bitter edge to it that even being with her didn't soften.

She began to cry, burying her nose in his shirt and sobbing as if her heart were breaking.

"Here, now. No sense in that. Don't cry, Dessie, my little Dessie."

But she couldn't stop. She cried for all the years she'd thought him dead. She cried that mother and father would never know this joy. She cried for what the war had done to him.

He patted her back awkwardly, but he didn't release her. Instead he patiently held her while she cried it out. There in the middle of an outlaw stronghold where he ruled over the roughest bunch of men to ever gather in one place, Mitchell Fallon, alias the feared outlaw Yank, held his baby sister in his arms with a loving tenderness no one who knew him could ever imagine. Most, even seeing his kindness with their own eyes, would later deny it. It was what he himself would demand of them.

After a long while, when she could cry no more, they sat on the canvas floor among tanned hides and stacks of wooden crates marked U.S. ARMY, and talked.

She brought him up to date on what had happened since their parents' death because that's what he insisted on; she had wanted only to talk about him.

Naturally, the matter of lawyer Cluney and Andrew's betrayal came up.

In telling him, she stopped in midsentence, eyes glowing. "Mitchell, you're alive. You can—"

He couldn't help laughing, interrupting her.

She joined him for a moment, then grew serious. "I mean, Daddy wanted you to have everything if you were alive. And now you are and so we can . . . oh, Mitchell, I gave that terrible Andrew half of our . . . of your inheritance. If only I'd known for sure. But he wouldn't even let me have any money. I had to do something. Now you can write to Cluney and tell him you're very much alive and intend to claim your inheritance. I won't have to go through all that trouble of getting a lawyer and straightening out the mess.

"Oh, how could Daddy have mistrusted me so much? I loved him so, and then to find out he didn't even believe I could handle things. To let that horrid Andrew and P. L. Cluney have control."

Mitchell patted her awkwardly. "He'd be proud if he could see you now. I know I am. You've taken care of things very well. I see no reason for me to step in. I don't want Dad's money or his businesses. What would I do with them if I had them? I can't show my face in proper society, and I'll never be able to. Not in this country. Perhaps, though, I could do something . . . later to straighten it out . . . from a distance."

He studied the view through the open flap of the tent, not ready yet to reveal his plans. There was no point, for the chances he could pull off such a thing with his hide intact were not very good. No sense in getting her hopes up.

God, it was so good to see her this way, if only for a little while. The memory of this day would have to last him a lifetime, and he embraced her every word and expression.

"Ben says the railroads will go in soon up here," she said.

"Ben?" he asked, rubbing at the hair over one ear. "And just who is this Ben?" Such banter seemed strange to Mitchell, having lived the life of the outlaw Yank for so long.

She tucked her head, feeling a bit shy talking about Ben Poole. It was hard to tell this man, whom she loved but no longer knew, about a personal part of her life that was still very new to her.

"He lives in Virginia City, and works for a freighting company, but he's so kind and gentle, and smart, too. He has one of those minds that latches on to figures and turns them inside out. It's amazing. He says we can go up north and put in some more stores, even thinks hotels might be a good idea. That is, he says, if that's what I want."

Mitchell listened intently, watching his sister's expressions with an unfamiliar longing. This was what he had sacrificed for his beliefs, this feeling of family and belonging, of sharing and love. Would he ever recapture that in his lifetime? He doubted it. The path he had chosen was a demanding and harsh one, and he feared he could never turn from it, would not be allowed to do so. Someone would always be just around the bend, waiting to remind him that he was an outlaw, a man wanted by every gunslinger and lawman in the territories. Even the Army would like to get their hands on the notorious Yank.

When Dessa finished telling him about Ben, he scratched at the hair above his ear and winked. "So my little one has found her a man to love? How is it with you and him?"

She felt for an instant as if she were twelve years old again and he was teasing her about an admirer in the schoolyard. "You don't change, do you?"

"What?"

"That," she said, and reached over to tickle at the hair above his ear. "You always did that when you were teasing me. That's how I knew when you weren't serious. And you still do it."

Mitchell's eyes glowed and he laughed deep in his throat, as if he weren't quite used to the experience. "I guess I did. And you didn't forget."

"I didn't forget anything."

"Remember where we hid our treasure?"

Dessa furrowed her brow, thinking back through the years.

"The old—"

She held up a hand. "Don't tell me. I'll remember. Just a minute. I know, I know. In that old barn Daddy left standing when he tore down the cabin to build the new house."

Mitchell nodded.

"Under the feed trough. We pulled the boards loose and put them in there."

"I wonder if all those things are still there. The marbles and that round stone you found, the pink chert arrowhead we fought over. What are you going to do with the place, now that they're gone?" Mitchell asked.

Dessa covered her mouth with both hands. "Oh, heavens. I don't know. I guess I hadn't thought about it. With all the other things that have happened. That bastard Cluney trying to cheat me and Andrew helping him."

"Why, Sister. How you talk. Who taught you words like that? My sweet little girl, who talks with the mouth of a loose woman."

"I do not!"

"Did he teach you that, this Ben Poole?"

"No. Ben is the sweetest, kindest, gentlest man in he world. Oh, I don't know what I'll do with the place in town, sell it, I guess. But I think I'll keep the farm, Mitchell. So many memories. When I think of all of us together, it's always there where we were so happy, where we grew up and learned to embrace life. Oh, Mitchell."

He saw the pain in her eyes for all that was lost, and practiced his laugh to turn her thoughts in another direction. "As you always did, you make me happy, Dessie."

"Oh, Mitchell. Why didn't you come back? We missed you so. It was so hard in Missouri, even after the war."

His eyes grew hard as flint. "You seem to have made it very well without me. The money just kept coming. Dad had a knack for making money, as I recall. I'm sure he profited well during the war."

Dessa snapped her head around to gaze at him. "Why, Mitchell."

He unfolded his long legs and rose, turning his back on her. "Don't tell me about hardship, Dessa. You had our parents, money, friends, all the clothes you needed, food enough. And nobody ever tried to take any of it away from you, even in the hardest times during the war and after."

She waited a long time before she answered the harsh words. Then she said, very softly, "They took you away from us, Mitchell. They took you and we never got over it, never."

He felt as if he had been struck in the heart with a lance. The forlorn words from his sister found their way into his soul as no others could have, and the pain grew until he feared he might burst out crying. After a few deep breaths he regained a bit of control, but still couldn't turn to face her once again.

She watched the rise and fall of his shoulders as he breathed, and wanted to reach out and touch him. After a while she did, and he shuddered, turned, and took her into his arms, burying his face in her hair.

Ben spotted the lookout, who made the mistake of rising for a brief instant, so that he made a silhouette against the moonlit sky. Ben had dismounted and left the black tied in a dense copse of trees half a mile or so back down the trail. In the war he had learned patience and fortitude when it came to sneaking up on the enemy or staying out of sight. He now had to do both, and he took his time. Getting caught would do Dessa no good at all. One misstep, the cracking of a twig or the rattle of rocks, would betray him. He wasn't sure he could explain why he didn't ride into the place and trust Dessa's mysterious brother to save his bacon. Something didn't feel right to him. The entire situation was unknown, and Ben thought it best if he just snuck in for a look first.

By dawn he had worked his way near enough to the camp to smell smoke of the campfire and tobacco, the waste of humans and animals, to hear the cry of a baby, the snore of someone sleeping, the muted enjoyment of a man and woman making love.

As the sun lightened the mountainside, he had his first glimpse of the hideaway. People lived here, not monsters. Whatever they did, most of them did it out of necessity, in order to survive. They might kill him for that reason, too, and without any hesitation, if he wasn't very careful.

He watched the place come to life. A fat Mexican woman stirred up the central fire and began to pat out cornmeal between her palms, lying the flat cakes on a rock in the coals. A gray-haired white woman approached with a coffeepot and shoved it into the glowing embers. The two spoke softly for a few moments, then the older woman went back to the lean-to built from tree limbs and woven grasses. A couple of boys—one looked Indian—chased each other across the clearing, laughing.

It was hard to realize that this wasn't a town, just like any other town in the territory, but was instead the lair of one of the most hunted outlaws since the end of the war. Ben felt a tremor of excitement. He might soon come face-to-face with the notorious Yank, who had a bounty of $1,000 in gold on his head.

A woman came from the dirty white tent across the way, stooping at first, so that he couldn't see her face. But he recognized Dessa just the same, and it was all he could do to keep from shouting at her. Another woman, an Indian, followed her out, and together they walked around to the back and disappeared into the woods. While Ben was trying to decide if he should work his way along the periphery and try to catch up with the women, a tall, lean man stepped out and stretched his arms above his head.

"My God," Ben whispered, for he knew immediately who the man was. There was no mistaking the resemblance. This was Dessa's brother, no doubt about it. Same hair, same bone structure, and take away what harsh living had done, there was the same look about the eyes and mouth. From that white stripe in his hair there was no doubt, either, that this was Yank. It was described on every wanted poster in the territory.

Ben moved closer, and contemplated simply standing up and approaching the man to introduce himself. He halted when a rough-looking fellow meandered into his field of vision and began to talk to Yank.

"Make up your mind about the bank?"

Yank shook his head.

"Some of the boys ain't gonna wait no longer. Hell, it's ripe for hitting. What's wrong with you? Going soft in your old age?"

With mouth agape, Ben listened to the men actually discussing a bank robbery.

Yank finally spoke, a cutting edge to his deep voice. "We go when I say, we do what I say. I hear any more of this, you and your damned friends'll find yourselves at the bottom of the gorge. I'd been handling things a long time when you come here, and I'll be here when you're long gone."

"Maybe that's the problem. You been around too danged long for our taste."

Yank grabbed the man by the front of his shirt and lifted him up right into his own face. "Anytime, Grady. Anytime you please." He tossed the man backward as easily as if he weighed nothing.

Grady landed on his butt. He scrambled to his feet, and for an instant Ben expected him to tackle Yank, but instead he glared daggers at his leader, then walked away grumbling. He passed near Ben, so Ben heard the tail end of a threat ". . . might be sooner'n you expect, Yank."

Sounded like there was trouble in outlaw land. So the warning from the Cross woman that Dessa's brother could be in danger hadn't been off target. But Ben couldn't be overly concerned about that. He was too worried about learning that Dessa and the outlaw Yank were brother and sister. He wasn't sure just what that might mean to their plans. She loved the brother she had lost, loved him dearly. Suppose she wanted to stay with him?

Immediately Ben dismissed that thought. Dessa would never do such a thing, he was just being foolish. His immediate concern had to be letting her know he was here, and the both of them getting the hell out with their hides in one piece.

Dessa watched her feet as she climbed up the rough incline behind Celia. What a way to live, especially for a woman, and more so if she had children. How did they do it, these women who loved men like her brother?

Off to one side she glimpsed deliberate movement and was astonished to see Ben peering from the woods and signaling to her. She cut her eyes toward Celia, who walked on around a curve in the path. Then she shooed Ben away with both hands. He shook his head and beckoned again.

Resigned, Dessa ran to him. "What are you doing here?"

"What are you doing here? I warned you not to come out here alone."

"My brother is here. Oh, Ben, Mitchell's alive and he's here. How could you expect me not to come?"

The expression of joy on her features was enough to make him forget his anger. "I just wanted to come with you, to keep you safe."

Dessa glanced nervously up the trail. "Well, you're here. Come on with me. We might as well tell Mitchell. I've told him all about you anyway."

He grabbed her arm, holding her back. "Did you know who he is?"

"What do you mean? Of course I know my own brother."

"No, I mean, did you know he's the outlaw Yank? The one the law's been chasing since the end of the war."

Dessa studied Ben hard. "No," she said firmly. "That's not true." She knew Ben was right, but couldn't help denying it aloud. No one need know, not even Ben. Perhaps saying it wasn't so would make it not so.

"Well, then, what do you suppose he's doing up here with all these thieves and cutthroats?"

"Hiding, that's all. He's in trouble and he's hiding."

"Oh, Dessa, think. He's in trouble, all right, not only with the law but with these men. They're fixing to mutiny. It wouldn't take much to set them all on him, and if they do that, they won't hesitate to get rid of you . . . me, too, for that matter. We've got to leave, now."

They both turned at the sound of footsteps shuffling through leaves up ahead.

It was Celia, coming back to see what was going on. "Dessa, where are you?"

Ben pulled at her arm. "Come on, come with me now!"

"I won't, I won't." She jerked away and called out, "I'm coming, I'm here." She threw him one last dark look. "I won't leave my brother now that I've found him. Go on if you want. I'm staying."

Ben considered his options for only a moment. He could either cold cock her and drag her out of here or stay with her. He would not leave without her. As Dessa ran toward the sound of Celia's voice, he trotted along behind.

Ben's arrival in camp created quite an uproar. Upon learning that a man from the outside had actually penetrated the security of the camp, Grady, who was already at odds with Mitchell, had called his followers together. He made no bones about his displeasure, and spoke so all could hear.

"He's old and soft, I tell ya. Living in the past when we could hit a stagecoach once a week and make out. Well, them days is gone. We either take what we want in some of these backwater towns or we figger a way to get on the trains.

"Them sons a bitches what ride them trains got more'n God, and they can share some of it."

A few nodded and cried out their agreement.

A red-haired, sunburned man shouted at the grumbling cluster of men around Grady. "Don't be fools. They could shoot ever man-jack of us, pick us off from them cars 'fore we could even get on board. I'm with Yank. He's done us good all these years."

Someone else spoke up. "Yeah, look what hurrahing Virginia City got Coody. Got him and the kid hung, that's what."

"Coody was a jackass, never had enough sense to

come in out of the rain," Grady said. "He didn't have brains to pour piss out of a boot. But if we keep doing it Yank's way, we'll all starve. Women and kids and all. Winter's a comin'. What we supposed to do?

"And what I'd like to know is how'd this yahoo sneak up on us? First Yank's woman goes out and brings in an outsider, then this here other'n shows up. Next it'll be the posse, watch and see if it ain't."

During the squabble between the two sides, Yank remained aloof, his green eyes following the action with a bright glitter.

Dessa and Ben tried to remain in the background. She was feeling more and more uneasy about being there, even with Mitchell so close by. He had urged Ben to leave his Winchester inside the tent after Dessa introduced the two, claiming it might stir up even more trouble if Ben were armed.

Celia urged Dessa to talk to Yank. "I've been trying to get him to leave this place," the Indian woman said. "I'm afraid he'll stay until they kill him. His time has come and gone. Most of the men who came here with him are gone on, either dead or rode back to their homes to take up their lives once again. Perhaps he will do that, if you persuade him."

Dessa was amazed at the woman's vocabulary, and wondered what tribe she was from. Not that it mattered, but she had always thought of Indians as naked wild savages who grunted and scalped people. She had no idea they wore clothing and spoke English so well. The woman's suggestion seemed a reasonable one, so when things had quieted down a bit and everyone had gone off to eat their noon meal, Dessa approached her brother.

Mitchell sat on the floor of the tent, cleaning a long-barreled rifle. Despite a cold wet wind that had blown up by midmorning, Ben refused to come in, but remained squatted outside the door, on watch.

"I've been wondering, Mitchell, if you wouldn't like to go back to the home place, take care of it. I would like that better than renting it to strangers. Ben and I want to stay in Montana, or go on farther west."

"Can't do that," Mitchell said, and pulled a wad of cotton cloth attached to a string from the gun barrel.

"I don't understand."

"I'd be arrested before I could unsaddle my horse."

"What for? What have you done that's so terrible?"

He dropped the weight into the barrel once again, then glanced up at her. "Broke the law. I broke a lot of laws for a lot of years, and they'd like to string me up if they could just lay hands on me."

She swallowed over a hard knot in her throat. "Did you ever kill anybody?"

He continued to gaze at her, then busied himself once again with the cleaning chore. "Men in war kill people. That's the idea."

"I didn't mean then. I meant after."

Mitchell chuckled harshly. "What the hell difference does it make? Killing is killing, any way you look at it. They taught me how. What made 'em think I could just stop when they said it was over?"

"Oh, Mitchell." Tears filled her eyes. She thought of what killing had done to Ben. She couldn't bear the thought that her brother was a killer. And it was different, the war. Ben had said so, and she believed him.

"Well, what will you do now?" she asked when he didn't say any more.

He shrugged, and began to shove long gleaming brass cartridges into the breech of the rifle. The oily *snick, snick* as the ammunition slipped into place sent shivers running down her spine. Unconsciously she counted them. Sixteen. He could kill sixteen men with that horrid gun without ever reloading!

Frustration made her angry. "Mitchell, they'll kill you. I heard them talking. They're just a breath away from declaring war on you. And if they're as terrible as that awful Coody Land was, they won't care what they do."

Mitchell lay the Army-issue Henry rifle close by and drew his legs up, wrapping his long arms around them. "When he brought that ring in here, I almost killed him," he said, the bitter flavor back in his voice. "I thought he'd hurt you. I couldn't believe my eyes, couldn't figure out what in the world you were doing here. I knew it couldn't be by chance. Something had brought you here."

"As it turned out, it was you who brought me here."

He nodded solemnly. "I know, I found out. Celia admitted she wrote to them about me. That's when I first realized that she really loved me, that she didn't just latch on to me like the others, for the thrill of it. So I sent her to town. She found out about the fire and your arrival and the funeral." He smiled remotely. "I wanted to come right up to you, stand beside you out there in Boot Hill at their grave, but that damn sheriff was always right there, hanging on to you. I was afraid he'd guess who I was. Aw, hell, I was just too jumpy to be around the law at all. He probably wouldn't have known me, I had kept my hat on. I don't reckon there's a likeness anywhere, not even on the wanted posters, except for telling about this blamed stripe."

Celia entered, eyes wide. Right behind her, Ben

stuck his head in the doorway. "Better git out here, trouble's a-coming."

Yank came to his feet, the gun in one fist like a growth that belonged there. "Fetch Poole's Winchester," he told Dessa curtly, and stepped outside.

Celia threw Dessa a frightened look and followed her man, leaving Dessa to get Ben's rifle.

Muted shouts and the drum of hoofbeats heralded the arrival of a frantic rider. He slid from his horse, panted out his message. "Posse's a-coming. Passed the word from down the line. Said ten, maybe fifteen men. Got a Indian tracker with 'em. Trackin' someone."

Grady roared and with one hand pointed his rifle in the direction of Yank, Ben, Celia, and Dessa. "You led 'em in. His woman led 'em here. What'd I tell you? What'd I say?"

He whirled around, facing the men. "Time we settled this. Who's ever with me, say so now. Rest of ya, look out 'cause we're gonna take care of the enemy in here first, afore them sons a bitches ride in."

Chapter Twenty-two

A shot rang out, fired from within the ranks of the traitors, and Grady spun around with a yell. Momentarily, the two factions ignored Yank to fire at each other.

Dessa broke into a run back toward the tent, shouting for her brother, then for Ben.

Ben grabbed her, rolled them both behind a fallen tree nearby. Celia followed. Mitchell stood out in the open, rifle to his shoulder, pulling off several shots from the powerful gun.

"Mitchell, for God's sake," Ben shouted. "Let's get the women out of here."

A bullet whined, chipping wood from the huge log behind which they hid.

"Yank, you bastard, I'll get you," Grady cried.

Whirling, Mitchell fired again in the direction of the shout.

He hustled to join the others. "Celia, take 'em to the cave. I got horses waiting on the other side, enough for the three of you. Git on 'em and ride, and don't look back."

Both Celia and Dessa cried out at once.

"I'm not leaving without you," Celia said firmly.

"Nor I," Dessa declared, watching Ben through slitted eyes.

"You have to understand," Yank said. "It's the war. It never ends. Always someone coming after you. I don't reckon the killing will ever stop."

Dessa grabbed his arm, tugged at him. Fear roiled deep in the pit of her stomach. "You can stop it, Mitchell. Just say *enough*. Come with us. Now!"

Mitchell snorted. "Run away? Put down this gun and walk off? I don't know that I can. It always follows me."

Ben dragged Dessa away from the hold she had on her brother's arm. When he spoke, it was to Mitchell. "We've got to get the women out of here. Fight your damn war some other time. I won't get Dessa killed."

The battle that had raged in the center of the camp escalated as the posse rode in and joined it. For a while it appeared that everyone was shooting at everyone. Ben spotted the sheriff, saw an outlaw's rifle pointed at him, and without hesitation raised the Winchester to his shoulder, took aim, and brought down the man before he could shoot Walter Moohn.

Quickly he swiveled toward the woman, ducking his head. No time to think. No time. "You two go on, now, get started. I'll stay with Mitchell. We'll cover you and follow. Now, git, or I'll drag you both off and leave Mitchell to see to himself."

"I'm not—" Dessa began, but Ben pulled her to him.

"Go with her. I swear to you, if you don't, I'm taking you out of here. You know I can do it. Dessa, I love you. I won't see you hurt." He kissed her hard, then pushed her away. "Nor your brother. I'll stay with him."

Mitchell grabbed Celia's arm as bullets whined over their heads. "Take her to safety, and yourself, too. I'll be right there, I promise I will. Now go, dammit."

"You'll come?" Celia pleaded.

Hand over her mouth to capture the kiss Ben had given her, Dessa watched her brother's brisk nod. Debris spat up around them in the hail of bullets.

"If you two don't get out of here, they'll kill us all," Mitchell shouted, and vaulted over the fallen log to take cover behind a tree. He raised the Henry and laid down a barrage of bullets. Ben joined in with the Winchester.

Celia dragged Dessa to her feet and, hunkered low to the ground, the two women clambered into the woods, leaving behind the sounds of battle.

Tears flowed freely down Dessa's cheeks and she sobbed so hard she could hardly stay on her feet. *Ben. Oh, Ben. And Mitchell. God protect them, don't let them die.* She couldn't bear to lose them.

Celia led her down the steep embankment, both women slipping and sliding, scarcely able to keep their feet under them. Beneath a bluff overhang she shoved Dessa into a dark cavelike opening.

Battle sounds echoed in the distance, and they stopped to get their breath. No one appeared to have followed.

"Everyone knows about this. It's our escape in case we were ambushed . . . if anyone ever found their way up here and the men couldn't stop them. So we'll have to hurry. Some of the others will surely decide to run away, too."

"All the women and children. What will they do?" Dessa asked between gasps.

Celia was awfully quiet for a moment. "Who knows? Some will die, I suppose, others will live. They knew that before they came here."

"But not the little ones. They didn't know. How could he do this? How could he?"

"He did nothing; they did. Come on," Celia urged. "Time to get moving. Follow me. Keep low, it is very close and we will have to crawl."

As they moved deeper into the cave, absolute darkness closed around them, so black they could only sense each other's presence by the sound of their breathing. Then they were crawling, feeling along the smoothly worn rock floor, shoulders rubbing the sides.

After what seemed like an eternity, a time in which all sounds of battle faded, a light appeared ahead, only a pinpoint, toward which they crawled for what seemed forever. Time held no meaning, nor did the terror that spurred them both. It was as if they had escaped into another world.

At last they reached the opening and Celia scrabbled out and to her feet, turning back to help Dessa.

"Will they come? Do you think they're okay?" Dessa asked.

"They will come," Celia said. "I'll find the ponies."

Shivering and hugging herself against the lash of a cold, wet wind, Dessa waited miserably until Celia appeared with three saddled horses.

"He went out last night. This is what he must have been doing," the Indian woman said.

"Only three?"

"Your man had not made his presence known."

Or her brother had no intention of getting out alive. Dessa pushed away the awful prediction and nodded, turned to stare at the black yawning hole from which they had emerged.

"He knew what would happen. We are to escape. It was his plan, you see." Celia sounded proud of her man, aloof from Dessa's concerns. "It will be all right, you will see."

Dessa shuddered violently with the cold. Dampness dripped from her hair, the air wet as rain. The Indian woman led the horses to the lee side of a huge boulder and signaled Dessa to follow. There they hunkered and waited, unable to do anything else but hope and pray.

It was a long, frightening time before they heard the clatter of rocks coming from within the mountain. Ben emerged from the opening first and Dessa launched herself into his arms.

"Where's Mitchell?"

"Coming," Ben said, and held her close. The heat of his exertion warmed her shivering cold body.

Then Mitchell emerged through the opening.

Celia welcomed him in much the same way Dessa had welcomed Ben. All four huddled close.

Mitchell spoke with chattering teeth. "The sheriff and his men won out. We guessed it best to take off before he saw this damned white streak in my hair and put me in with the rest. Let's mount up and put some miles behind us before anyone misses us."

On the far side of the rocks, the horses waited, haunches turned to the wind. "Sorry there's not one for you, Poole," Mitchell said. "You and Dessa will have to double up. I didn't know you were coming."

"That's where you went last night," Celia said.

Mitchell nodded. "We'd better quit jawing and mount up. One or two of them gets away from the posse, they'll figure out pretty quick where we went, or hell, they're liable to tell the sheriff just for spite. Grady and his bunch would like to see me strung up. Some are apt to be on their way already."

"What about the women and their children?"

Dessa asked, reaching a hand up to let Ben pull her on the horse behind him.

"Sheriff had them all corralled in the big tent. Hollering and screeching, but I don't think any were harmed too bad. Some of the men didn't fare so well, though. Someone saw fit to shoot that bastard Grady." Mounted on an Appaloosa, Mitchell took off at a gallop, leaving the others to follow along.

At the mouth of the canyon, where the trail forked back toward town to the southeast or northwest into the mountains, he reined up.

"I don't know about you two, but me and Celia are going north, maybe all the way to Canada."

Dessa's heart skipped, then thundered in her ears. "But we just found you."

Mitchell rode close and reached out a hand to her. "I know, and I'm sorry, but I can't stay here. Everyone in the territories and back in the States would like to collect the bounty on my head. Some'd prefer to carry in this striped scalp. I'm tired of running, of looking back. I want some peace." He gazed with tenderness toward the Indian woman, watching and waiting patiently. "We want some peace."

"I can't let you go," Dessa sobbed, and clutched at his arm. "We'll go with you. Ben and I. We will, won't we, Ben?"

Ben watched in silence, his eyes like deep pools.

"And always be on the run?" Mitchell replied. "No. You stay. You and Ben help settle this territory. Use our father's money the best way you can. I'll see to that matter we spoke of. You'll hear from me.

"I've always been with you, little sister, and I always will be. Dear, sweet Dessie, go with Ben. Maybe we'll see each other sometime."

She shook her head back and forth. "No, oh, Mitchell, don't leave me again. I love you."

"Take her away, Poole, and you be good to her or I'll come back and find you."

Ben nodded grimly and shoved his heels in the horse's flanks. Dessa leaned her face against his back and clutched him around the waist, crying out her brother's name over and over. The heat of her tears soaked his shirt as he rode away without looking back.

Tired, wet, and cold, the couple rode into Virginia City, but didn't stop at Dessa's place or at the sheriff's office. They went directly to the Golden Sun Saloon.

Ben lifted his right leg over the saddle horn and jumped to the ground, then held up his arms to catch Dessa as she slid off.

"Go inside. Tell Rose and the rest what happened. If there are any men in there who can ride, send them out. Tell them to meet me down at the livery. I'll go round up some more men."

"Oh, no, Ben. What are you going to do?"

"Go help Moohn and his posse bring those outlaws in."

She clutched at his shirt front. "I won't let you go. What's the use? You said it was over. No, Ben, don't."

To watch him ride away was beyond anything she could imagine. All she wanted was for him to hold her close. Saying good-bye to Mitchell had been nearly more than she could bear. All she could think of was hanging on to this man she loved. Suppose he was killed out there. Then what would happen? What would she do? She couldn't lose him, too. It was irrational, she knew, but she couldn't help herself.

"It's all over, Dessa," he said softly. "Nothing will happen to me. Now you go on inside. Surely you understand that I have to do this, I have to see it through. For you, for Maggie, and for myself." Gently he pried her fingers loose and held both her hands in his, staring into her tearful eyes.

She nodded miserably. Of course she understood.

"Then hurry, do what I said. There's no time to waste."

She lifted her skirts, stumbled up onto the boardwalk and through the swinging doors, right into the arms of Rose Langue.

"What is it, child? What is it?"

As quickly as she could, Dessa related what was going on out at Alder Gulch. She left her brother out of the story completely. The moment she finished, Rose hurried to the bar. She pounded with a thick beer mug until she had everyone's attention.

"Walter Moohn needs help out at Alder Gulch. Every man-jack of you that can ride and shoot, get your tails out there, pronto. Ben Poole is waiting at the livery. Go, now," she shouted, and over half the seated men bolted to their feet and ran out the door. Those remaining either couldn't shoot, couldn't ride, or both, for most would rather face the guns of outlaws than the wrath of Rose Langue.

Dessa collapsed in a chair at a table where Virgie and one of the girls sat nursing mugs of tea. Rose joined them and signaled Grisham, who brought over two more mugs of the steaming dark liquid.

"Now, child, tell us the rest. Did you find your brother? How did you escape that godawful nest of thieves? Wiley Moss saw Ben light out, and it didn't take long for the sheriff to figure out what was going on, with you missing, too."

Dessa told Rose about finding Mitchell only to lose him again, but she didn't reveal that he was the hunted outlaw Yank. She would never tell that to a living soul as long as she lived. She hoped that when this was all over, everyone could be made to believe Yank was dead, shot in the battle with the sheriff and his men. It was time Mitchell had a little peace, and Celia, too. She prayed they were safe, and that reminded her of the danger Ben would be riding into, so she added a prayer for him, too.

Even riding hard as they dared, it took Ben and his makeshift posse some time to reach the place where the night before he had tied Baron in order to sneak up on the outlaws' fort. He reined up and let the clatter of their arrival die away. In the silence, they should have been able to hear gunfire if the battle had broken out again. It had been all but over when he and Mitchell had left—the man would have it no other way—but something could have happened to turn the tide, and he hadn't wanted to chance such a thing.

Baron raised his head from nibbling at a patch of grass and whickered at their arrival, but that was the only sound they heard in the somber air that spat flecks of wet snow into their upraised faces. Ash-gray clouds hid the mountain peaks and darkened the afternoon sky. In the thick air hung the smell of gunpowder and campfire smoke.

Good God, suppose they were all dead.

"Come on, men," Ben shouted. "This ain't no time to be shy. Let's get up there."

Throwing caution to the wind, he headed the sorrel Yank had supplied up the narrow winding trail, trusting the dozen or so men who had come with him to follow. Before they had gone more than a few hundred feet, they heard the thud of hoofbeats, the low grumble of voices, a nervous ripple of laughter.

Ben raised a hand. "Hold up, there. Sheriff ... Sheriff Moohn, that you?" He waited, wondering what he would do if he was leading the men into the face of the outlaws. But he didn't think so. He figured if any of the outlaws had survived the battle, they would ride out hell-bent for leather. This had to be the sheriff and his men.

A horse and rider came in sight from around a sharp bend in the trail. "Who the hell is that? Say, or I'll shoot!"

"It's me, Ben Poole. Same to you up yonder. Identify yourself."

"It's Wiley Moss. The sheriff took a bullet, but he's okay. We got the sonsabitches, Poole. You hear me, we got 'em, ever one."

Almost everyone, Ben thought with a small grin.

The undaunted Wiley kept up his chatter as the two bands of men joined forces to herd the captured outlaws toward Virginia City. "It's gonna take a while to sort things out, and we'll have some burying to do. They's sure a bunch of caterwauling females and young'uns to deal with come morning, but they're okay.

"We thought it best to git this bunch in to the jail and the sheriff to the doc first off."

Ben nodded and rode along beside his friend, his mind back at the Golden Sun Saloon with Dessa.

Dusk had a firm grip on the land by the time the weary riders plodded back into Virginia. Ben led the black gelding, and left him and Yank's sorrel at the livery. Wearily he trudged to the Golden Sun and joined the merrymakers. The saloon's walls were bulging and Grisham, Rose, and two of the girls busily drew beer for everyone.

"On the house," Rose shouted to a tumultuous uproar.

The men were high-strung and boisterous, talking too loud, laughing too hard, drinking too much. Ben had seen it before, this emotional outburst after a victory. All he wanted was to go somewhere quiet and be with Dessa, hold her close, celebrate their survival. One look at her told him she felt the same, and he drew her through the celebrating crowd to a table in the far corner of the saloon.

Moohn lay upstairs, where the doctor was busy cleaning his wound. The bullet had passed through the fleshy part of his shoulder, and it wasn't long before the sheriff staggered downstairs, a white bandage wrapped around his arm where the shirtsleeve had been ripped away.

"Walter Moohn, you ought to be in bed," Rose scolded, and wiped her hands to go to him. Together they settled at a table.

Dessa and Ben sat close together, tentatively touching as if to convince themselves they were both alive and unhurt.

"Will you marry me now, Dessa?"

She cupped his cheek in her palm. She already missed Mitchell, but just knowing he was alive made the ache in her heart less painful. Besides, there was this wonderful man, holding her, loving her.

She looked deep into his clear blue eyes. "Oh, yes, Ben. Now, this minute, if you say so. I was so afraid for you."

"It's okay. Everything's okay now. It's as if all this made me into a different man."

She laughed and leaned against him. "Not too different, I hope. I kind of like you the way you were, if you know what I mean." She lay a hand high on his thigh suggestively.

"Dessa, shame on you," he said. "Oh, God, it feels good to be with you like this and know it's forever. Just think of what we're going to do together. It's all out there waiting for us, and I can't wait to get started." At last he truly belonged to someone who loved him. He could put all the memories to rest, once and for all.

"Do you suppose we could get married now, this very minute?" she asked. "The way I'm feeling, I don't want to sleep alone tonight."

He held her back a ways so he could study her lovely face framed by long strands of flyaway hair. Then he laughed and hugged her up close. "Let's just go find the preacher."

Together they rose and slipped quietly through the swinging doors, leaving the victory celebration behind. The big Montana sky deepened to velvet and was sprayed with the glitter of millions of stars. Clouds that earlier had dropped snow glowed like gunmetal on the horizon to the southeast and there was a bite in the air.

Ben gazed down into her eyes, his own gleaming with love.

"Want me to carry you?" he whispered.

She remembered the night he had come to her out of the dark, his strong arms sweeping her up as she collapsed, and she smiled.

"Yes, that would be wonderful."

He laughed, swung her easily off her feet, and carried her down the center of the deserted street toward the church.